A Twist of Fate

Karen Michelle Nutt

A Twist of Fate

Presented by *Karen Michelle Nutt*
Copyright 2013 Karen Michelle Nutt
Cover Art Copyright 2013 Karen Michelle Nutt

Praises for *A Twist of Fate*

A Twist of Fate was a **P.E.A.R.L** Finalist for Best Time Travel   2008.

"I particularly think it is a stroke of genius placing a Scottish pirate in the American south. Ms. Nutt has written a gem of a tale."
  ~Bonnie-Lass, Reviewer for Coffee Time Romance

"A superbly written romantic love tale."
  Amy J. Ramsey, "Ramsey's Reviews"

"All I can say is WOW! The story flowed remarkably well and the characters were very lovable.
  ~Breia Brickey, at PNR Paranormal Reviews

"Ms. Nutt brings magic to the pages of her story, keeping your attention
  with spellbinding mystery."
  ~Reviewer: Tabitha, Ghost Writers Reviews

To Cathy and Briana because they enjoyed this adventure the most.

To my biggest fans: Kendra, Katrina and Vincent, and to my family.

"The real journey is the souls."
~W.B. Yeats~

CHAPTER ONE

The Present
Blue Run Plantation, South Carolina

Songs from Aerosmith blared from the roller coaster ride drowning out the screams as the people in the cars sped around the track. The aroma of the sweet, sugary smell of cotton candy and buttered popcorn filled the night air. Paper wrappers, cups and cheap stuffed animals littered the fairgrounds. Families, couples—young and old laughed and joked as they tried their hands at the carnival games while stuffing their faces with hot dogs, hamburgers, or big turkey legs.

The muggy air promised rain later tonight, but no one seemed anxious to leave the festivities. Arianna plopped down on the bench and smiled. She had helped the historical society plan the event and all proceeds from the carnival's productive night would go toward the restoration of Blue Run Plantation.

Her eyes wandered toward the mansion silhouetted against the darkening sky of blue, orange and gold. In the colonial era, the river served as a highway for the Low Country plantations and the families used the tides to travel. She could only imagine how majestic Blue Run would have stood facing the Ashley River.

"Arianna!"

She turned and waved as she caught sight of Megan hurrying toward her. Her long brown ponytail swung behind her with purpose, making Arianna suspicious. "What does the spitfire want me to do now?" she whispered under her breath.

Megan pulled Arianna to her feet. "Everyone's been talking about Madam Carlotta."

"Who?"

"The gypsy fortuneteller. People claim she has been freakishly accurate. We have to check this out."

"And why would I care?" Arianna dragged her feet.

"We're going to have our fortunes told. I want to know if Gregory plans on proposing to me on my birthday."

Megan and Gregory had been a couple since their first year of college and the way he's been scraping and saving, Arianna could give the prediction herself. Gregory would propose no doubt about it. "Megan, I don't—"

"And you're going to find out who your one and only is."

Arianna drew in a frustrated sigh. "Not everyone is destined to find his or her soul mate." At twenty-six, Arianna had become a successful music teacher at USC School of Music. With heavy schedules, concerts, and her time with the historical society, dating became a distant memory.

Megan stopped in her tracks and spun her around. "You don't give a guy a chance. Look at you." She swung her hand up from Arianna's head to her toes. "Talented, tall, slender, blonde with cornflower blue eyes—men should be lining up to snatch you up, but you snub your nose."

"Do not." She lifted her chin.

Megan laughed. "Sure you don't. You spend all your free time researching for the Historical Society and with the new items they uncovered you've been busier than ever. And I'll have you know, I've seen you stare at the portrait."

"What portrait?"

"Oh, don't act all innocent. The portrait of the dark, handsome, brooding man related to the Buchanans of *Blue Run*. If you ask me, the family buried the portrait for a reason. He was probably an embarrassment to their refined upstanding position in society. I don't need to do research. The man's arrogant stance reeks of danger and my guess is he paid for it with his life."

"It appears I'm not the only one obsessed with the portrait."

"Only because I was curious as to why you've become a hermit. If you want someone dangerous, at least make sure he's alive. Now stop stalling and let's find out if Carlotta knows where your dark and dangerous guy is hiding."

"Very funny." Arianna shook her head. "Where are we going anyway?"

"To the mansion. Don't you find it perfect?"

"No, I don't find it perfect. The mansion isn't safe for people to run in and out of; it's still being restored. How did this gypsy woman obtain permission?"

"Oh lighten up, Arianna. Someone from the Historical Society must have given her the keys. Besides, she's drawing in loads of money. Isn't that the plan?"

"Sure, but—" Thunder rumbled cutting off Arianna's words and she gave up arguing. "We're in for a storm tonight." Arianna looked up at the sky as a flash of light sizzled across the heavens.

"All the more reason to hurry. My hair will frizz worse than it has already."

Torches lined the walk like breadcrumbs, leading them to their destination. Arianna stopped and placed her hands on her hips. She frowned at the big purple sign over the entrance of the mansion that spelled out FORTUNES, in bold black letters. "She's defacing private property."

Megan yanked her arm. "Sue her later, but first our fortunes."

They stepped into the front foyer of darkness. A battery operated globe stood on the floor giving the illusion of the heavens opening up to them. A foldable card table stood in the center of the foyer with a large crystal ball on display. Inside the glass an eerie glowing mist swirled around in milky silence. The fortuneteller wore a colorful scarf like a headband to keep her dark curly hair away from her face. She adorned herself with gold jewelry, hoops in her ears, chains around her neck and bands around her wrists. The whole ensemble gave the appearance that she could be a descendant from gypsies.

Carlotta beckoned her forward, her bracelets tinkling like tiny bells. "One at a time, please." Her voice was rich and flavored with a fake Romanian accent. "Let Carlotta tell you what you want to know."

Megan gave Arianna a slight push. "I'll wait outside."

Arianna rolled her eyes at her friend, but she approached the table and sat down.

"For the cost of my eyesight into the future, there is a small donation of twenty dollars." She held out her hand and waited.

"Twenty …" she huffed. "Fine." She reminded herself this was for a good cause. She pulled out a crisp bill from her purse and paid the hefty price.

Carlotta stuffed the money into a skull-adorned black box. "Now, we shall see what the cards hold for you. She shuffled the tarot cards before she turned them over revealing first the Death card, then the World card and then the Lovers card. "This cannot be right."

"What?"

Carlotta chuckled nervously. "Sometimes the cards are not clear." She scooped them up and put them back in a pile. "Let me see your palm."

Arianna leaned forward and held out her hand.

The fortuneteller's brows furrowed as she concentrated, a look of fear passing over her features before she concealed her anxiety.

A primitive warning sounded in Arianna's mind. She suddenly didn't want her fortune read. She tried to pull her hand away, but Carlotta wouldn't release her.

"You have an interesting palm." Carlotta pointed to the line that ran the course of her hand. "This is your life line. You will live a long life."

"What's the shorter one next to it mean?"

Carlotta didn't answer. Her eyes rolled back in her head and her whole body jerked as if she was being controlled by another force. She flung to one side then the other before she sat up ramrod straight.

Blood slid through Arianna's veins like cold needles and she tried to break free, but Carlotta's grip was like a vice. As if this wasn't freaky enough, the woman began to hum.

Arianna froze and her eyes widened in surprise as she recognized the melody. It was an old Scottish tune, she'd been haunted by as long as she could remember. The melody lingered in her subconscious surfacing at odd moments like an annoying tick. Her parents swore they never taught her the song and no one knew where she'd picked up the tune.

How did this fake fortuneteller know it? Arianna again yanked her arm and this time pulled free. She rubbed her bruised hand, staring at the woman with suspicion.

Carlotta blinked rapidly before she focused her gaze on Arianna. "I am sorry. Did I hurt you?"

"I'm fine," Arianna answered, surprised that her voice sounded calm. "But I think I'll skip the fortunetelling, if you don't mind?" She didn't wait for Carlotta to say anything, but stood and hurried toward the exit.

"Arianna," Carlotta called.

She halted and whirled around. "How did you know my name?"

"Does it matter?"

She arched her brow. "Yes, I believe it does. Is this some kind of hoax?"

"You don't belong here." Carlotta dropped her fake accent.

"Excuse me?"

"There are souls out there… wandering… lost, but time always has a way of sorting out the mistakes. You belong to Blue Run. Your destiny intertwines with his."

"What are you talking about?"

Carlotta walked around the table to face Arianna. "You must listen, for you don't have much time. You will think you have met your end, but it won't be over. You'll return to where you belong, and another woman will take your place of doom."

"Is this all a part of your theatrical presentation because if it is, I don't like it?"

"In this other era, you will meet a very strong man with the blackest of hair."

"Did you hear me?"

"His eyes will be green, clear and sharp like a cat," Carlotta continued. "He is called …" She chewed on her lower lip, but then her eyes lit up. "The Scotsman. He is called the Scotsman. Trust him, for he will protect you. He may feel mistrust for you because of the other woman's black heart, but in time, he will see you for who you really are. He's your soul mate. It will be his child you carry."

Terror had kept Arianna frozen in her spot, enduring Carlotta's eerie premonition, but now the woman had finished and Arianna took a step back. "You're crazy." She pointed her finger at her.

Thunder rolled shaking the rafters. Dust and debris fell around Arianna and she held up her hands to protect her head. Coughing, she turned and ran for the door, but a sharp pain to the back of her skull brought her to her knees.

"Watch out!" Carlotta warned.

Arianna looked over her shoulder. Her eyes widened in horror as she watched the wood beam hurdling toward her.

*****

Carlotta finished what she set out to do here and packed her belongings. A crowd had gathered in the cramped foyer as the young paramedic frantically worked on Arianna, but in the end, he turned toward her friend, Megan and shook his head.

"Oh my God. I can't believe it. She can't be gone. She can't."

Carlotta heard Megan's heartfelt cry and stepped forward, placing a hand on the young woman's shoulder. "She's not dead," Carlotta told her.

Megan sniffed and wiped away the stream of tears running down her cheek. She turned toward the paramedic as he pulled a sheet over Arianna's face.

"Listen to me," Carlotta insisted and Megan looked back at her again. "Listen to your heart. Arianna didn't die here tonight. She went back to where she belonged, back in time."

"What are you talking about?"

"Don't take my word. The proof is on her finger. Your friend wasn't married, am I correct?"

Megan nodded, her brows furrowing. "I don't understand what her being married or not has to do with it."

"Check the woman's finger for the proof of what I tell you. Trust me, Megan," Carlotta insisted.

"How do you know my name? Who are you?"

"Who I am is not your concern. I only tell you what I know because Arianna would have wished you to know she is safe."

Megan held the fortuneteller's gaze for a moment longer before she knelt down. She reached beneath the sheet for her friend's hand, surprised of how warm her flesh still felt. She stared at the huge sapphire wedding ring set in gold. "This isn't hers." Her voice was thick and unsteady. She whipped back the sheet and stared at the woman who had lost her life. "Oh my God!" She covered her mouth with her hand. The woman's haircut was slightly different without the streaks of pale-blonde. Her lashes were void of mascara, and she didn't have a sprinkle of freckles across her nose. "This isn't Arianna," she said aloud knowing how ridiculous she sounded. How could this be? She looked up wanting answers but Carlotta had already vanished.

CHAPTER TWO

Blue Run Plantation,
South Carolina, 1814

Keldon looked up from his desk as Leighton threw opened the study doors, his gray hair windblown, his face wrinkled with worry. "Ye better come quick, Keldon."

"What seems to be the urgency?"

"It be Annabelle," Leighton answered. "Horse must have thrown her. She's out cold and her mount is grazin' in the garden."

Keldon showed a brief moment of concern, before his features turned cold. "What mischief is she aboot now?"

"Looks like, she may really be hurt. I left Samuel with her."

Keldon was reluctant to leave his long neglected paperwork for one of Annabelle's theatrical ploys. He sighed with indecision as he rubbed his chin. Leighton was probably more skeptical of Annabelle than he was. He'd better check on her. "Come on then." He rose from his seat and grabbed his hat. "Show me where she is."

They led the horses down toward the water's edge where Samuel waited.

"She ain't moved none," Samuel informed Keldon, as he took the reins from him.

In slumber, Annabelle looked like a beautiful angel, but Keldon knew her true demeanor. "Deceitful and selfish witch," he mumbled, reminding himself of her worth. She'd faked a fall before and he'd be damned if he'd let her play the game again.

He knelt down next to her, moving her head from side to side. She didn't respond in any way. She was obviously taking the ruse to the fullest.

He stood and strode over to the small pond and filled his hat with the cool water, before returning. Without hesitation or delicacy, he threw the water in her face. She immediately sat up. Her eyes popped open with her gaze wild and confused as she sputtered like a drowning rat.

Keldon bit back a chuckle, thinking he gave the witch exactly what she deserved.

"What happened?" Arianna gasped. Through the strands of her dripping hair, she stared at the three men who were in turn eyeing her just as intently. She flipped the wet strands back, clearing her vision. She didn't know these men, did she? She wasn't sure. Her head was spinning, making her feel as if she wanted to throw up. She blinked and focused again, trying to discern if she should fear for her life.

The man farthest from her had skin the color of strong dark coffee and his course black hair was pepper-gray at the temples. He wore tan pants and a cream-colored linen shirt. Her eyes lingered on his feet and frowned. He wasn't wearing shoes.

The man standing next to him was attractive in a weathered kind of way. His hair was long, light colored mixed with gray strands. He wore dark pants, which tapered at the knees and were tucked into his boots.

Her gaze slid to the man standing over her like a redwood tree. He had rolled up his white shirtsleeves exposing tanned forearms and he wore dark formfitting pants tucked into knee length boots. Against the glare of the sun, she took in his dark hair, which framed his rugged attributes. A shadow of a beard darkened his defined jaw line and a scowl penetrated his features. Her breath caught in her throat and her heart pounded against her ribcage at the way the man stared at her. Just her luck, gorgeous, but lacking in the personality department. She tried to stand and winced, sitting back down again. "Who are you, and where am I?" Her voice croaked as she fought her way through the cobwebs of a nightmare-filled sleep. She tried to remember what had happened to her, but failed to recall anything before she woke up. "Why am I soaked?"

Like his expression, Mr. Personality's deep voice held no warmth. She managed to meet his gaze and found herself lost in his alarmingly green eyes.

"What is this aboot, Annabelle?"

She detected a slight lilt to his speech; about sounded more like *a boot*. He seemed irritated with her, but she didn't know why. Did she know him? He spoke to her as if he did. What did he call her? "Annabelle," she said testing it, but it didn't roll off her tongue the way it should. Annabelle simply couldn't be her name, but for the life of her, she couldn't think of what it was. "Wait, wait." She did know. She was Ari... yes, her name was Arianna. Arianna what? What was her last name? Her head pounded in time with her pulse and panic struck her. "Oh God, I'm having an aneurysm."

"Weel?" Mr. Personality questioned with no compassion for her dilemma. "What game is this Annabelle?"

"Game?" The man was obviously thick in the head. "I'm not playing a game." She closed her eyes and rubbed her temples. "And why are you calling me Annabelle? My name is Arianna."

Keldon exchanged a troubled glance with Leighton. Maybe Annabelle wasn't acting. He knelt down beside her again. She opened her eyes, flinching as he ran his hand down the back of her head. His fingers glided over raised skin at the base of her skull. Her luminous blue eyes stared up at him with a gentle gaze he didn't recognize. He blinked and shook his head at the absurdity of his revelation, "Ye'll be fine." Keldon moved from her, only long enough to speak to Leighton. "Bring Doc Hathaway back to the house. He's out at the Draytons."

"Aye." Leighton nodded and went on his way.

Keldon turned his attention back to Arianna. "Are ye able to stand?

Arianna paid attention, hoping Mr. Personality would say something she'd recognize, but he only blurted out names that meant nothing to her. Like the older guy Mr. Personality sent away, he had an accent that was similar. They pronounced some of the words with long *e's* like in well, sounding more like *weel* and other words with the rolling *r's* and soft dropped g's. They were Scottish, she thought. "Scottish," she said aloud. That one word seemed important. She was on the verge of remembering why, when Mr. Personality interrupted her thoughts yet again.

"Annabelle, do ye need help gettin' to yer feet?"

Arianna wasn't sure. Furthermore, she wasn't sure she wanted to go anywhere with this man. She didn't like his attitude. Maybe she didn't know him and yet... his eyes, clear and green with a slight tilt at the outer corner reminded her of a cat. A memory flashed. Someone warned her about a dark-haired man with green eyes.

"Annabelle?"

The concern in his voice drew her attention.

"Ye look as white as a ghost. Are ye goin' to swoon?"

Arianna remembered something else. Trust the... Her gaze locked onto his. "Are you the Scotsman?"

Her announcement must have caught him off guard for he froze as if a chill settled over him, but then his eyes narrowed blazing with mistrust.

"You're angry with me. Why?"

Mr. Personality didn't answer, but held out his hand. "Come on, Annabelle."

Not knowing what else to do, she reached for him. She held on tight, but once on her feet, the world around her spun on its axis. She closed her eyes, hoping the spinning would stop. It didn't. Her legs wobbled like Jell-O and the earth came hurdling at her, but Keldon saved her from falling, pulling her into his arms.

Her eyes fluttered open. Her hand came up to rest on his rugged cheek. "Trust, the Scotsman," she whispered, before she succumbed to the darkness.

CHAPTER THREE

Arianna choked as she inhaled, tears burning her eyes. What in the world did they stick up her nose?

"Doc Hathaway is going to take a look at ye," Keldon told her.

She blinked and stared at the portly man with the bulbous nose.

Doc Hathaway sat down on the edge of the bed. He looked over his shoulder at Keldon who hovered over him. "Why don't you wait downstairs?"

"I should—"

"It would be for the best," Doc Hathaway insisted.

"Fine." He marched out of the room shutting the door behind him.

"Who is that man?" Arianna asked. "Do you know him?"

Doc Hathaway opened his mouth and closed it again. "Mrs. Buchanan, he's your husband."

"My what?" Arianna shook her head and regretted the effort. Her head felt like it would explode. She stared at the doctor. Any minute now, he'd laugh and say he was only joking, but he didn't even crack a smile. "I couldn't possibly be married. I would remember something so important."

Doc Hathaway cleared his throat. "How much do you remember?"

She wrinkled her forehead. "I'm Arianna Ward." Her gaze locked onto the doctor as she grabbed his arm. "I'm Arianna Ward! See, I couldn't be Mrs. Buchanan."

"Your husband—"

She released her hold on him. "Please don't call him that."

The doctor nodded. "Keldon told me you hit your head?"

She lifted her hand and touched the tender area at the back of her skull. "So it seems."

"I've been your doctor for a long time and you know I've never revealed your secret."

"My secret?" Her gaze riveted to his again.

The doctor fidgeted looking uncomfortable under her gaze. What secret did she have and why would she tell the doctor and not her husband? *Assuming she had a husband.*

"We'll discuss that at a future date. Let us concentrate on now. You can trust me when I say your name is Annabelle Buchanan and the man who went downstairs to wait for me is indeed your husband, Keldon Buchanan."

Arianna shook her head in denial, but she could think of no reason why this man would lie to her? She leveled her gaze on him. "You swear, you're telling me the truth?"

"Yes."

She sighed, her shoulders sagging. "Fine."

"Fine?"

"For now, I'll have to accept your word."

"But you still don't believe me."

"I have no idea what to believe. Why don't you enlighten me? Tell me about my life, Dr. Hathaway."

*****

Keldon wanted to question Annabelle about why she called him the Scotsman. Unfortunately she didn't wake up until Doc Hathaway used the smelling salts. He'd wished he'd thought to use them.

Leighton stood as Keldon entered the study.

"Did Samuel tell ye?" Keldon asked.

"I ken what happen after I left," Leighton voiced. "Do ye think she knows then?"

Keldon ran his hand through his hair. "I doonae know. She dinnae sound like she was sure. She spoke as if she was testin' the sound of it."

"I'd say she's toyin' with ye. Ye better watch yer back. She may strike without warnin'. We doonae know where she was headin' before we found her. I doonae trust her one lick."

Keldon paced, going over every detail in his head. He'd been careful. He'd sneak out long after Annabelle retired for the night. She couldn't have found his disguise since he hid it on the Schooner.

He didn't need this right now, not with the run already scheduled. Had Annabelle been heading out to warn someone? He stopped pacing and looked at Leighton. "We better lie low for the time bein'. Tell the others, we'll meet at the end of the week. Hopefully by then, I will know more aboot our situation."

"Aye. I'll spread the word." Leighton motioned to Keldon not to say more.

Understanding the warning, he turned to find Doc Hathaway had entered the room. "Your wife seems to have suffered a severe blow to the head. She will recover, but her memory is a little hazy."

"What do ye mean by hazy?"

Doc Hathaway shook his head. Come take a seat and we'll discuss the situation."

Keldon harrumphed, already coming to the conclusion he wouldn't like what the doctor told him.

Leighton poured a dram for everyone while Keldon waited for the doctor to give his prognosis.

"Annabelle is disoriented and may be for some time."

"Is she addled?" Leighton tapped his head to emphasize as he handed the doctor his drink.

The doctor shook his head. "No. No, nothing so severe, but she does seem a little confused."

"Confused?" Keldon questioned wanting the doctor to get to the point.

"She doesn't remember anything prior to when you found her." The doctor waited for his information to sink in. "It doesn't mean she won't regain some of her memory back."

"She doesnae remember a thing?" Keldon wasn't convinced.

"I questioned her, thoroughly. She didn't even know her name. She kept insisting her name was Arianna Ward. I'm sorry to say she has no recollection of being married, either."

"Nay?" Keldon's brow lifted slightly. He'd never heard of such a thing. He wondered if Annabelle was trying to trick them in some way, but for the life of him, he couldn't see the reason for it.

"You'll need to be patient with her. Surround her with familiar items and activities she enjoyed in the past. Sometimes this helps the memory to return."

"Ye've seen the condition before then?"

"Yes." He inhaled deeply. "Unfortunately not all recover their memory. I'd say Annabelle's memory loss is most severe. I wouldn't hope for much." Doc Hathaway finished his drink. "If you don't mind me saying so, maybe it would be for the best. Annabelle is…"

"Is what exactly?" Keldon's eyes narrowed.

"She's different. I can't put my finger on it, but… she's gentler."

"Gentler." Keldon couldn't believe his ears.

The doctor cleared his throat. "Listen to me babble. It's late." He stood. "My wife will be worried if I don't head home soon."

"Hmm. I'll walk ye out."

*****

Keldon stayed up late going over in his mind what possible motive his wife would have to masquerade as someone who'd lost her memory. "What are ye up to?" he murmured under his breath as he poured another drink.

His marriage to Annabelle had been a farce from the beginning, but he'd been too love struck to see the truth of her nature.

An arranged marriage, he accepted the engagement with reluctance until he met her. She wore her shimmering pale blonde hair unbound and curled, looking like a fairy princess and when her gaze touched him, he'd been lost within the depths of her blue eyes, sinking beneath the surface and not caring. He would have done anything for her and he tried, but their marriage became a nightmare he couldn't escape. He failed somehow. Annabelle loathed him in every way—his touch sickened her and when she'd become pregnant, she cursed him daily as if he'd committed an insidious act upon her.

Annabelle never wanted the baby. However, he did. He would have asked for nothing more if she'd given him a child, but she had miscarried in her third month. God help him, he suspected she induced her labor. She almost died. By the time he found her, she'd hemorrhaged, losing so much blood, her skin grayed and she felt cold to the touch. By some miracle, Doc Hathaway saved her life.

As soon as Annabelle was well enough, she moved her belongings out of their room and across the hall. She threatened if he ever touched her again, she'd kill him. He thought she needed time to adjust from the shock of losing their child, but she proved how foolish he was. She despised him, and slowly her bitterness crept into his soul, until any love he felt for her died.

He proposed they end the marriage but Annabelle refused. She pleaded with him to give her a second chance and like a fool, he agreed. It wasn't long before he discovered her true reasons for wanting to save the marriage.

The day was burned into his memory…

"Ye lied. Ye want my name only to receive yer inheritance."

"You surprise me Keldon. I didn't think you were bright enough to figure it out."

"It's over."

Annabelle laughed. "It'll never be over, dear husband. If you ruin my reputation with a divorce, you have my word I'll drag you down with me."

"What can ye do?"

She walked over to him and ran her hand down his arm. "Don't tempt me, Keldon. It won't be pretty."

He often wondered if Annabelle's father knew of his daughter's cold, uncaring heart and placed the binding stipulations in his will. Did he also realize the husband would be miserable?

Keldon couldn't live the lie anymore. He wanted a wife who truly cared about him, a wife he could trust. Let Annabelle do her worst to ruin his reputation. He didn't care anymore. He had requested the divorce and waited for the papers to arrive to make it official.

Now with Annabelle's memory loss, he wasn't sure how he'd present the divorce papers to her. Maybe this was her ploy. Maybe she knew of his request for the divorce and her revenge would be to make him look like a heel for abandoning his wife in her time of need. Keldon drained his glass and slammed it down. "Damn her."

He headed upstairs, pausing in front of Annabelle's room. He couldn't resist poking his head in to see if she'd fallen asleep.

Still darkness greeted him with only the illumination from the full moon casting any light. Annabelle rested in the middle of the bed with her pale blonde hair haloed around her. She murmured in her sleep and rolled to her side.

Curious to know why she seemed restless, his steps took him closer. Her brows drew together and she mumbled something under her breath he couldn't make out. He leaned down in hopes of hearing what she said, but she sat up with a guttural cry of terror. He stumbled back swallowing his own bellow of alarm.

Annabelle hadn't seen him yet and she trembled as she hugged herself.

His heart constricted, making him wish he could slink away unnoticed. He took a step back, but she heard him. Her doe-like eyes, wide and scared, locked onto his. Her lower lip trembled, and he had the distinct feeling she might scream again.

"Annabelle, ye're safe," he soothed

"It's you," she let out a breathless whisper.

"Aye. Did ye have a bad dream?"

She nodded and a heart-retching sob escaped her lips.

A strange surge of affection assailed him making him question his sanity, but he couldn't help himself. Annabelle never cried. He approached her. "Do ye want to tell me aboot it?" He sat down on the bed beside her. She moved closer to him, resting her head on his chest. Keldon's first impulse was to push her away, but as her sobs continued, he put his arms around her, drawing her closer. "What happened?" he coaxed.

"I dreamt about a Ferris wheel, a fortuneteller and...this place. It was in ruins. I died here."

Did she think her life here so miserable, death called her? "What is a *ferret wheel*?"

"Ferris wheel," she corrected.

"*Fare...issss* wheel. What do ye speak of?"

She didn't answer.

"Annabelle?" He looked down at her and realized she'd fallen asleep or maybe she had never been awake at all. He eased her back down and covered her with the thin white sheet. He stared, troubled how her brows puckered as if the dream still haunted her. He gently caressed her cheek, but abruptly pulled his hand away as though her skin burned him. What was he doing? This woman didn't deserve any sympathy.

"You sees it, too?"

Keldon swung around. His face grew hot with humiliation, wishing Maeve hadn't witnessed his moment of weakness. He forgot that Annabelle's servant slept in the corner for the night.

The young black woman stood and walked out of the shadows to stand at the edge of the bed. She glanced at Annabelle before her dark brown eyes pinned him down.

"What am I suppose to be seein'?" Keldon asked.

"Dat dis here woman ain't Miss Annabelle. Dat devil woman be gone from us." Maeve crossed herself. Her eyes darted around the room as if she feared a demon would appear.

The night was warm, but Keldon shivered. He had to admit, he sensed a difference in his wife something he couldn't put his finger on. As for her becoming another person…impossible. "Maeve, ye have to realize Annabelle hit her head with such a force her memory escapes her for now."

Maeve shook her head. "I know better. Dis woman be Arianna likes she says. Dis here woman be kind in her heart. I see dis." Maeve held Keldon's gaze refusing to waiver from her conviction.

Keldon opened his mouth but shut it again. Uncertainty plagued his mind as he stared at his wife.

*****

Arianna awoke with a start. "I have to…" She paused trying to remember where she needed to be. Then fear hit her full force as she realized the nightmare of yesterday continued today. She took in her surroundings—a wood carved dresser and mirror against the wall with pretty bottles, silver brush, and comb. Her gaze touched the lovely lace curtains, framing the opened window, the large bed with an endless array of pillows. Nothing. Nothing, not one item looked even vaguely familiar.

Pulling back her covers, she stepped onto the cool hardwood floor and walked over to the window. She pulled back the curtain and looked down below. She spotted two of the men she had met yesterday, Leighton and Mr. Personality. The doctor claimed he was her husband. "I'm married," she said it, but she didn't believe the words. It didn't seem right, but again she couldn't remember a single thing about her life.

Keldon and Leighton conversed with another man. She looked in the distance and noticed a boat docked at the landing, indicating the man had just arrived. The newcomer stood five-foot nine, judging by how tall he stood next to Keldon, who she figured to be over six foot. After a few minutes, the three men walked toward the house and disappeared from her view.

She turned when she heard her bedroom door open. Maeve, the woman who had been so kind to her last night, came in with a tray of food and Arianna's stomach grumbled.

"I thought you might want a bite ter eat before you ventures downstairs."

"Thank you, Maeve. I would." The thought of going downstairs to face people she didn't remember had her nerves on end.

Maeve put the tray down at the edge of the bed and turned to eye her closely. "You don't sleep well?"

"No, I didn't. Everything seems so... I don't know."

"You need to sits yourself down and eat. A full stomach does wonders."

While Arianna ate her breakfast of warm cereal and fresh rolls with fruit preserves, she watched Maeve hurry about the room, picking up the discarded clothes from last night and piling them at the door. Maeve was a pretty woman with smooth dark skin. She looked to be about her age, but acted so much older as if she'd lived a lifetime already.

Maeve took out garments, which Arianna assumed she would be wearing for the day. She stared at the clothing convinced they weren't hers. What had happened to her jeans and t-shirts? She could see these items perfectly in her mind, yet she didn't see them in her armoire.

"Maeve?"

She turned to look at her.

"Where are my t-shirts and jeans?"

"I don't know these things. Whut be dis *t-shuts* and..."

"Jeans," Arianna finished for her. She owned a pair of Calvin Klein's. She did, didn't she? Her head throbbed and she rubbed her temples, hoping to ease some of the pressure.

"Does your head bothers you much? I kin gives you somethin'." Maeve moved around the bed and took her hands.

Arianna felt Maeve tremble as she turned her right hand over so she could see her palm. A flash of a memory tried to take hold, but slipped away before it took root.

Maeve took a deep breath and smiled. "You still with us."

Arianna looked at the dark skinned woman, wondering what the woman meant by her statement.

"Did you want de powder fer your head?"

"No, I'll be all right."

"Then let me gets you dressed."

"I can dress myself." She hurried to tell Maeve. "I'm not an invalid."

Maeve froze. Her eyes widening as her hand came to her chest. "Dress yourself? Lordy, I always help you gets dress. Well ... I did, dat is."

"You did?"

"I wuz bought fer dat service, Miss Arianna." Maeve went over to the bed and picked up the dress she'd laid out.

"Bought?"

"Yas'm, Miss Arianna." Maeve brought the dress around to the other side of the bed.

"You're a slave?"

Maeve nodded.

"That can't be right. Slavery's illegal." She seemed so confident this was true, but after the strange look Maeve gave her, she wasn't so sure after all. "Isn't it?" she questioned. "Hasn't slavery been abolished for over a century?"

"Miss Arianna, I don't know whut dat means. I jest know I be a slave as long as I kin remember and dat's a very long, long time."

*****

Arianna wandered around the house, taking in the surroundings and hoping something might trigger her memory.

The first room she entered had a large floral carpet, and striped wallpaper covering the walls. There were two blue overstuffed chairs stationed toward the back of the room and a plush covered round table in the center. Two framed pictures stood as witness to the display of cards scattered on top. She casually walked over to the table and lifted each frame to get a better look at the portraits they held. One was of Keldon. She hesitated, fingering the likeness of her husband. "I've seen this portrait." She frowned then not sure if that was true. "Maybe I just recognize Keldon's somber expression." She sighed in frustration. She picked up the other frame. The woman looked like her. She stared checking out every feature. She recognized the similarities: Light blonde hair, blue eyes, but a misty doubt clouded her mind. The woman in the portrait was a stranger.

She put the portrait down when she heard voices coming from the room next door. She moved to investigate, but as she reached the door, she hesitated. "This is my home," she reminded herself, but doubt made her feel like an intruder. "Don't be ridiculous. This is my house."

Before she lost her courage, she strode over into the hall and opened the twin doors simultaneously as she made her grand entrance.

The men's conversation came to an abrupt halt, each turning to stare at her. Their expressions gave her the opinion she'd committed some horrible crime.

Arianna felt the heat rise in her face before spreading down to her toes. Keldon's murderous glint didn't help either. He stalked toward her and she immediately backed out of the room, slamming the doors in his face.

*****

Keldon froze, stunned at his wife's display before he became furious. He ripped opened the doors once more thinking he would have to chase her down, but she stood there with her hand over her mouth and her blue eyes as wide as saucers.

"Sorry," she sputtered. "I didn't mean to—"

He grabbed her arm leading her away so the others couldn't hear them. "Have ye resorted to spyin' now?" he hissed.

"What are you talking about?" She tried to yank free, unsuccessfully. "I've been looking around, trying to discover something familiar. This is *my home*, is it not?"

Keldon relaxed, loosening his grip. Perhaps he over exaggerated, but he didn't trust her. "Go to the drawin' room and wait for me. As soon as I'm finished with my business, we'll tour the grounds together." He turned to go back into the room, but Arianna halted him with her question.

"Where's the drawing room?"

He turned, his eyes narrowing at her innocent expression. Did she deceive him? He pointed down the hall. "It is the last room on the left."

Arianna nodded and headed toward the door he indicated.

*****

Arianna knew he watched her with his cat-like eyes. He didn't trust her and she knew it wasn't her imagination. His every narrowed-eyed glance spoke the obvious.

Her hand on the doorknob, she looked back at him. She smiled sweetly and waved, knowing she'd irritate him with the gesture. She could almost hear his snort as he went back into the study.

She chuckled and opened the doors. She stepped into a world of elegance. "Wow!" Was the only way she could fully express herself. The gorgeous painted harpsichord displayed in front of the bay window caught her attention first. The beautiful scene of a man and a woman sitting among the flowers of red and gold adorned the piece. The sky displayed an unearthly blue and the grass came alive with different shades of yellowish greens.

Arianna couldn't resist; the instrument called to her. She sat down on the bench and ran her hand lightly over the exquisite piece, until her fingers rested on the keys. *Do I know how to play?* She asked herself. Somehow, she knew she must. She poised her hands and they took over. The sweet melody flowed freely, and the words popped into her mind as if bursting for release. Finally, she found something familiar. She sang from the heart, rejoicing over the new discovery.

*****

As the melody reached the men down the hall, once again, their conversation halted.

"Who's singing?" Vincent Aubrey asked.

Keldon and Leighton exchanged glances.

"I dinnae realize Annabelle would be entertainin'." Leighton raised a brow.

Keldon shrugged, for he hadn't expected company either.

The three left the study, curious over whom the mysterious vocalist was. Keldon became more anxious with every step. He recognized the melody as one he played often on his bagpipes. He hadn't heard the words to the song in a long time.

The men entered the room as Arianna finished the last stanza. She turned and looked at them. She grinned, laughter bubbling out of her. "I remembered something. Isn't it wonderful?"

Vincent looked to Keldon for an explanation. "What does she mean?"

"Annabelle had a little accident, yesterday. Her memory isnae as it should be." Keldon walked over to Arianna who was still grinning. The sweet melody she sang had unnerved him. How could she know that song? He himself had not heard the words since he was a small lad. His mother, God rest her soul, had taught it to him, a memory he treasured, and he knew he had never shared it with Annabelle. Furthermore, when did Annabelle learn how to play the harpsichord? And her enchanting voice… His wife croaked like a frog.

"Do I know anymore songs?" Arianna asked hopefully. "I must. I put my hands over the keys and…"

"Annabelle," Keldon tried to interrupt.

"…I played like I was born to do this."

"Annabelle."

She turned toward the harpsichord, her fingers flying over the keys as another melody took shape.

"Annabelle!"

Her hands slipped, pounding out a horrible sound. "What?" She glanced at him, annoyance evident in her voice.

"My dear," Keldon retorted in cold sarcasm. "Ye have never played before in yer life."

CHAPTER FOUR

Ye have never played before in yer life. Keldon's claim bothered Arianna. Maybe she took lessons and never told him. Maybe he didn't know her as well as he thought. "Stubborn, arrogant man," she mumbled. She wanted to experiment with the harpsichord to find out if she could play anything else.

"Ye cannae play." Keldon took her arm and led her out of the room.

"But …"

"Yer disturbin' our guests."

Arianna looked over her shoulder. Leighton frowned, but he never smiled as far as she knew, but the other man's mouth curved. She returned the gesture, which obviously perturbed her husband by the way he harrumphed and yanked on her arm again.

"I shouldnae be much longer. Do ye think ye can stay out of trouble until then?" He left her stranded in the hall.

She turned and opened a door to another room full of items she didn't recognize and shut the door without bothering to explore. *Trouble indeed. All I wanted to do was play the piano… No, harpsichord.* She corrected herself and frowned. "Piano," she said the word, testing it.

A grand piano made of solid spruce flashed in her mind, but the vision disappeared before she could grasp it. She shook her head. "Did I see a memory or am I losing my mind?" She had her hand on the doorknob to yet another room, but she heard voices down the hall and changed directions.

Company was exactly what she needed while she waited for her husband to find time to fit her into his busy schedule. She opened the door to find the room empty, but then she caught sight of a woman heading out a door, which led outside. She followed. The smell of spices and cooked meat tantalized her nostrils. "Ah, the kitchen is in a separate building from the house." Somewhere in the back of her mind stood a memory of why she knew this, but she pushed the thought aside. No more thinking about what she remembered and what she didn't remember. She wanted a friend.

She entered the kitchen with a smile. Two women prepared food, talking and laughing as they worked. The heavyset woman with dark almond skin and round cheeks had a deep rich voice. The other woman had skin the color of toffee. Her pretty face lit up when she smiled. "Oh Oni, he kicked again." She turned to the side, revealing her full belly.

"This here baby is goin' ter be strong."

The pregnant woman noticed Arianna and gasped. She lowered her eyes, the smile slipping from her face.

Oni turned. "Oh." Her gaze dropped to her feet also.

Arianna didn't want to ruin the mood. She wanted to join them. She cleared her throat. "Do you need any help?" She hoped to break the awkward silence.

Both women looked startled by the suggestion as they exchanged nervous glances.

"We's jest fine, Miss Annabelle," Oni said. "I wuz de one at fault. I wuz jest askin', Sophie how she wuz. We will stops talkin' and gets bizy."

If Arianna didn't know better, she'd think these women had committed a horrendous crime. What did she care if they talked to each other? She wanted to join in.

She decided to try again. "I should be the one apologizing. I didn't mean to interrupt. You see I'm bored out of my mind. I need to do something, anything. Only, I don't remember what it is I do around here."

Before the bewildered women could comment, Maeve walked in on them. Her mouth dropped opened before she could stop herself. Then she shook her head, clicking her tongue. "Whut's you doin' here, Miss Arianna?" She immediately, started shooing her out of the room. "We kin take care of things in here. You go outside and gets some fresh air."

"But I want to help."

"You will help me by takin' a nice walk and lets me handle things in de kitchen." Maeve led Arianna through the house and out the front door.

Once Maeve was convinced Arianna wasn't going to bulk at the idea, she went back to face Oni and Sophie.

"Whut's dis, you be callin' Miss Annabelle, *Aree...ana*?" Oni asked.

"Dat's who she be. She's not dat devil woman no more," Maeve answered confidently. Oni and Sophie exchanged glances as if Maeve had lost her mind.

*****

Arianna stood on the porch and stared at the closed door. "I've been tossed out of my own house. What am I suppose to do out here?" She threw up her hands. Of course no one answered and she turned and walked to the edge of the porch. She let her gaze wander over the vast land of gardens, trees and brush. She sighed with a shake of her head. "This is my home." The words sounded hallow to her ears. She leaned against the railing and closed her eyes and listened to the sounds around her—the rustling of leaves, the murmuring of voices. The warmth of the sun kissed her skin and she could smell fresh baked bread.

Her lips curved. She had no memory of her life, but she still remembered the simple things. She supposed it was a start.

"What are ye doin'?"

Arianna recognized Keldon's voice, but she refused to have him ruin this moment. "I'm contemplating."

"Weel may be so, but do ye think ye might want to move out of the sun? Skin like yers will burn easily."

"I don't care. The sun knows me and I know it, and somehow that's reassuring."

"Reassurin'?"

"Uh huh." Reluctantly, she opened her eyes and looked at him. His dark eyebrows rose high on his forehead. "It gives me comfort that I'm not losing my mind. Do you know how alarming it is not to know who you are? Nothing seems even vaguely familiar except..." She lowered her gaze and looked away.

"Except what?"

She sighed. "I don't know really. What I remember is more like a dream than reality. It's like someone told me about you." She looked at him again.

"And what did this person tell ye?" Again his brows arched.

She searched his handsomely rugged features for something familiar. Inherent strength shone in his sun-bronzed face. His sea green eyes, which were clear and vibrant, missed nothing. He lacked patience at least where she was concerned. And yet the woman's voice stood out clear in her mind. *Trust the Scotsman. The man with the green eyes, he will love you and protect you.* Those words rang in her head as if someone had drummed it into her subconscious. She didn't see love in Keldon's eyes. It was more like contempt. "It's nothing. Just a dream."

A shadow of disappointment crossed his face as he turned away.

She shaded her eyes from the sun and looked toward the trees in front of her. "I thought you were going to show me around this place so I can figure out who I am."

"Ye know who ye are. Ye're Annabelle Buchanan."

"So you say." Arianna glanced at him and Keldon had the oddest feeling she didn't believe him. "But," she continued confirming his suspicion. "I feel deep down to my soul. I'm not your Annabelle. I am Arianna Ward. I am sure this is my name."

"Hmm." He still couldn't figure out her ploy. Her behavior proved suspicious with her casual attitude and flippant remarks. He could almost believe she was someone else. "Come, we'll go for a ride."

"A ride would be nice. What kind of car do we have?"

Another strange word, like the one she used from last night—the Ferris wheel. "What is this car?"

"You know a car." She waved her hand in front of her. "A vehicle you ride in. It has four wheels and runs on gasoline..."

Keldon knew his glare had silenced her, but did she really expect him to put up with her tales about fanciful machines?

"Cars haven't been invented yet," she said more to herself than to him. "Don't ask me how I know, but I do."

"I have no idea what ye're talkin' aboot," Keldon answered her as he began to wonder if the bump on the head had caused more damage than anyone could have imagined.

"I don't know why I have this image. I know there are Fords, Hondas and Nissans and— You think I'm mad?" She didn't wait for him to answer. "Forget it."

"Aye," Keldon answered. "Come along then. Leighton has saddled the horses for us."

They headed toward the stable and Arianna turned to look at him. "Do I know how to ride a horse?"

He glanced her way expecting to see a smirk, not wide-eyed innocence. He cleared his throat. "Aye, ye ride verra well.

*****

Arianna found she indeed knew how to ride. That is, after she convinced Keldon she didn't want to ride sidesaddle. She proved she could be as stubborn as he could be.

Arianna had the impression the plantation went on for miles with its landscaped terraces, shadowy gardens and ponds. Cypress trees lined the forest behind them like a wall of defense.

The plantation was self-sufficient. They made their own tools and pottery. They had a weaver, cooper, carpenter and blacksmith. They harvested cotton and indigo, but the plantation's main crop was rice. Seeing the men and woman working in the fields, she recalled the conversation she had earlier with Maeve about slaves. Did they own all the workers?

Arianna shielded her eyes, watching the workers in the fields. "Everyone looks hot and tired. Shouldn't they take a break?" When he didn't answer her, she turned to meet Keldon's hard stare. "Why do you look at me that way?"

"Ye speak in riddles."

"I speak in riddles. You should be sitting where I'm sitting."

A guttural order drew her attention to a man with light hair and thick sideburns. He sat upon his horse, yelling at the workers.

"Who is that?" Arianna asked.

"The overseer, Rafferty."

She didn't like him. Belligerent demands flew from his mouth. She'd had enough when she witnessed Rafferty bringing his riding crop down on a man, knocking him to his knees. She didn't think as she clicked her tongue and set her mount into motion. She rode over to Rafferty ready to give him a piece of her mind. She jumped down from her horse. With her fists clenched at her sides, she didn't think of her own safety as she put herself between the overseer and the helpless man on the ground.

"Don't you dare hit this man again," she spat.

Rafferty turned three shades of red, looking like he was on the verge of exploding. "Get out of my way or you'll be feelin' the crop on you!" He raised the weapon above his head, the intent made clear as he brought it down.

Arianna yelped and covered her face, but the blow never came. She lowered her arms and found Keldon gripping Rafferty's arm.

"Ye werena goin' to whip my wife, were ye, Rafferty?"

Rafferty cowered beneath the glaring green eyes. "No of course not, Mr. Buchanan?"

Keldon shoved the man's hand away.

"You must have seen," Rafferty stammered and pointed to Arianna. "She was interferin' with my disiplinin'."

"Disciplining!" Arianna glared at Rafferty wagging her finger. "You were beating the man for no apparent reason."

Rafferty pursed his lips together and glowered at her.

"We doonae want to interfere," Keldon addressed the overseer. "However, ye have been told once before that an undue beatin' isnae productive and I willnae tolerate them. Is that understood?"

"I understand, but mark my words, if you don't keep these darkies under control, they'll up and kill everyone up at your big, fancy house."

"That is yer opinion. Mine is quite different, and since I am the head of the household, ye will abide by my rules. Do we understand one another?"

"Perfectly." The man spat on the ground before he turned his horse around and rode away in the opposite direction.

Arianna breathed a sigh of relief and turned toward the man who was still sprawled on the ground. "Are you all right?" She offered her hand to him, but the man cowered, lifting his arm as if he expected her to strike him. She let her hand fall away.

"Yas'm, Miss Annabelle." He slowly rose to his feet.

Arianna could see he wasn't all right. His shirtsleeve turned a shade of red where the crop sliced through to his skin. She tried to go to him again, but he quickly backed away. She didn't move, but glanced around her. No one would meet her gaze. Feeling uncomfortable and definitely unwanted, she retreated back to her mount where Keldon waited to help her back into her seat.

They'd ridden a small distance before Arianna spoke. "I only wanted to help, but they were afraid of me." She looked at Keldon, wanting to see his expression. "Why? I was only concerned."

"That's what troubled them," Keldon answered.

"I don't understand."

His eyes darkened as he held her gaze. "Ye've never cared before. Ye've beaten the slaves for far less reasons than Rafferty has."

Arianna pulled on her horse's reins, bringing the animal to an abrupt halt. When Keldon realized she'd fallen behind, he stopped and turned around in his seat. "Is somethin' amiss?"

"Yes," Arianna calmly replied though she wanted to scream. "Everything's *amiss.* You've told me things about myself I can't believe. I feel like you're talking about another a person, a person frankly I wouldn't wish to know." Arianna mournfully sighed. "I'm a stranger in my own life. I'm scared to learn anymore about who I am. Did I ever do anything nice?" She met his gaze, begging him to say something encouraging about her personality.

"We should head back to the house."

His response didn't relieve her fear. Selfish, bitter, cruel … and these were her best qualities. No wonder Keldon looked at her with such malevolence. What horrible deeds had she bestowed upon him?

CHAPTER FIVE

After riding, Keldon deposited her back at the house as if he couldn't wait to end their time together. Leighton showed up soon after and they both left, heading for the boat. Arianna wondered if Leighton was a business partner or an annoying pest interfering with her marriage.

I sound jealous. She thought. Well, she was. *I'm married, but Keldon keeps me at arms length.* Weren't marriages based on love and trust? Obviously, their marriage wasn't of the conventional nature. They didn't even share the same bedroom. She may have forgotten many things, but she was certain a married couple slept together.

She tried to imagine Keldon's strong hands on her, his mouth kissing her…making love to her. Heat burned her cheeks. Love? The man didn't even like her. She shook her head. She had more things to worry about than wondering why her husband didn't sleep with her, but those damn words kept haunting her: *He will love you.*

She harrumphed. "He's probably a lousy kisser," she mumbled, wallowing in her misery as she walked down the unfamiliar halls.

Her steps took her to the drawing room and to the harpsichord. She pulled out the bench and sat down. Keldon insisted she never played. "What do I care what he thinks?" She closed her eyes and placed her hands on the keys. The melody came alive before she even thought of it, the slow soothing piece she'd played earlier. The melody meant something to her. She wished she knew why.

When she finished, she opened her eyes with a sigh. "If I don't know how to play, how did I manage that?" Out of the corner of her eye, she spotted a little girl peering around the corner of the doorframe. "Hello," she called to her.

The girl came fully into the room, but not too close as if she didn't want to be far from her exit of escape. Her lashes swooped down hiding her light brown eyes. "I's sorry Miss Annabelle fer disturbin' you. The music wuz so purdy. I never heard you play before."

"Don't be sorry. I'm glad you're here." Arianna didn't want her to leave and hoped she could convince her to stay.

"You are?" The little girl's mouth nearly dropped to the floor.

Arianna nodded and moved over on the bench. "Come sit by me."

The little girl hesitated.

Arianna tried a different approach. "I can't remember a lot of things. Can you tell me your name?"

"Yas'm. I be called Sally Mae."

"Well, Sally Mae would you like to learn how to play?" She pointed to the harpsichord.

"Yas'm." Sally Mae bobbed her head up and down.

Arianna patted the space next to her. "Come sit here and I'll show you."

Arianna taught her a simple tune she remembered. It was funny how she could remember things like that but nothing of her life.

After a few minutes, Sally Mae had mastered the little ditty. At first, Arianna wasn't sure what the piece was called. Then the name popped into her head. "Chopsticks." Sally Mae looked up questioningly at Arianna. She repeated with a smile, "What you're playing is called chopsticks. I think there's another more official name for it, but this one will do. Anyway, you play what you just learned, while I play the other part that goes with it. Sally Mae carefully concentrated to hit each key, while Arianna worked her magic. There were a few mistakes but over all, it didn't sound half-bad.

"Whut's goin' on here?"

Startled, Sally Mae slammed her hand down on the keys like a gavel. The effect was just as severe. Sally Mae slid from her seat. "Sorry Maeve. Miss Annabelle wuz showin' me how to play."

"You leaves Miss Arianna alone. Do you hear me?"

Arianna intervened. "I asked her to join me."

Maeve's shoulder relaxed. "Still, she has things to take care of." She motioned for Sally Mae to move. The little girl reluctantly made her way to the door. She stopped and looked back to Arianna. "Thank you, Miss... Arianna."

"You are very welcome, Sally Mae." The little girl smiled and left humming the little ditty.

"You have a kind heart, Miss Arianna. But you must be careful. Not many white folks would like you bein' so friendly with my kind."

"What do you mean your kind? We were having fun. Surely there is no harm in teaching the child to play."

Maeve eyes softened. "Where you come from things must shore be different." Before Arianna could question her, she had changed the subject. "We need to get you ready fer tonight's gatherin'."

"Gathering?"

"Yas'm. It be a small get together, but I want ter fix you up real purdy."

"Should I know these people?" Arianna felt queasy all of a sudden.

"Some, I'd say. You don't have ter worry none," Maeve told Arianna, seeming to understand her reservation.

"I can't do this, Maeve."

"You kin. Mista Keldon will help you."

She followed Maeve upstairs to her room. "Did Keldon and I marry for love?"

The woman actually chuckled. "You's not married ter Mista Keldon."

"But I thought—"

"Annabelle be married ter Mista Keldon. You've gone and took her place."

"You keep saying that. How did I take her place?"

"Don't knows dat, but I hope you's stayin'. As far as everyone knows, you be Misses Buchanan 'cause you look jest like her. But you be a sweet girl. Mista Keldon will fall in love with you. Not ter worry."

Arianna was more confused than ever. Why did everyone think she was Annabelle Buchanan if she wasn't, and how did Maeve know the truth? "I don't think I like Keldon," she confessed.

Maeve shook her head a smile touching her lips. "I'm shore you will change your mind. He's a gud man dat Mista Keldon. The ladies shore do think he's purdy."

Arianna harrumphed. "Maybe the ladies would like to have him then."

Maeve chuckled again. "Ah don't gets yourself all works up fer nothin'. Mista Keldon and you belong together."

CHAPTER SIX

Maeve helped Arianna dress. She slipped on the white soft silk under dress and a powder blue crape robe over it. Maeve fussed with her hair, pulling part of it up in the back, and curling the remaining around her face so that it showed off her delicate features.

Arianna put on the white kid shoes then ran her hand down her dress to straighten it, feeling uncomfortable with the attire. "I feel like I'm dressed up for a play." She looked at Maeve.

"You look real purdy," Maeve said as she placed a necklace around her neck to finish her outfit.

"I really look okay?"

"Breathtakin'," a deep-timbered voice answered her. Arianna turned to see Keldon standing in the doorway, dressed in his finery. Her pulse kicked up a beat. He had pulled his thick dark hair back and tied at the base of his neck. His shirt was white with a high collar and he wore tan breeches with white knit stockings that covered his well-shaped calves. To finish the attire, he wore a blue double-breasted jacket with bronze buttons.

"Madam, are ye ready?"

"Hmm?" Her eyes fluttered a moment before she met his disarming smile. Heat flared in her cheeks and she knew an unwelcome blush crept across her face. Damn her fair skin for betraying her. She'd been ogling him and if the amusement in his eyes was any indication, he was well aware of it. "Yes, I… well, yes, I think so."

He approached her then and tucked her arm under his. The impulse must have surprised him for he hesitated and looked down at her as if he expected her to pull away.

"Is something wrong?" she asked.

His gaze touched her features as if he wasn't sure. He shook his head and smiled. "Come, our guests will be arrivin' soon."

Keldon stated each of the guests' names as they entered. Now if she could just keep all of them straight in her head.

Bernard and Elizabeth Prescott arrived first. Bernard carried at least twenty extra pounds in his gut. He wore his thinning hair slicked back and his bulbous nose stood out like a clump of clay. He had a habit of sneaking a drink from a flask he had hidden in his coat. Elizabeth stood two inches taller than her husband and she wore her rich brown hair tightly wound into a bun. She looked down her straight nose at everyone and fluttered her eyes when irritated. The Prescott's were a perfect match—pompous, condescending, and if they lifted their noses any higher, rain would pour into their nostrils and drown the both of them.

Nicholas Sherborn arrived next, tall, slightly built with aristocrat features of a privilege born Englishman. When he smiled, charming dimples dented both sides of his cheeks. His alluring charms gave her the impression he left many women's hearts weeping.

Vincent Aubrey, she had already met earlier in the day. His amber colored eyes sparkled with mischief. His cultured voice betrayed he once lived in France. Arianna liked Vincent's easy demeanor and he seemed to enjoy her company as he told her of his sister, Chantal and her husband living in New Orleans. He may be one person she hadn't hurt in her questionable past.

Doc Hathaway and his wife Martha joined them also. Martha brought her servant, Grace with her. She claimed she needed Grace to help her freshen up before dinner. Arianna did her best not to roll her eyes. Truly couldn't the woman powder her own nose? Grace stayed with the other servants while they dined.

Leighton McRae, Arianna finally learned from Maeve, was a long time friend of the family and had resided with the Buchanans since Keldon was a boy. He arrived last. Arianna wondered what he'd been doing.

She knew Leighton didn't like her or trust her. He made it obvious by the way he watched her every move. She mentally added him to her list of people she must have wronged.

As the night progressed, Keldon suggested they should relax in the drawing room. Arianna stayed behind hoping to escape the tedious mingling. Maeve wouldn't let her and pushed her out of the dining room. Pushy servant.

She sighed and was resigned to endure the rest of the evening, but sniffles alerted her that someone was crying. She halted her steps. She followed the sound around the corner where she witnessed Doc Hathaway hugging Grace.

"Oh."

They both turned, coming apart. Grace gasped. Her dark eyes widened and she covered her mouth, stifling a cry.

"Go now, Grace," Doc Hathaway told her.

She scampered away like a frightened rabbit.

"Talk about uncomfortable," Arianna mumbled. "I didn't mean to—"

"You won't say anything to Martha, will you?" Doc Hathaway licked his lips. "I keep your secret and you keep mine."

"Your affair with Grace is the secret I'm keeping?"

"Affair," he huffed as if offended. "You know Grace is my daughter."

"Oh, I… oh." Arianna's eyebrows furrowed.

"You truly don't remember, do you? I thought…"

"You thought I was faking."

He cleared his throat. "I didn't mean to offend you, Mrs. Buchanan. Please don't tell Martha. She'll send Grace away. I won't be able to protect her then."

"She's your wife's slave."

"You know there isn't any other way. While she's the house servant, I can ensure her safety and a much easier life than if she was a field slave."

Arianna didn't know what to say.

"You will keep my secret," he insisted she give her word.

Doc Hathaway feared she wouldn't and that revelation didn't sit well with her. She placed her hand on his arm. "Doc Hathaway, your secret is safe with me. I would never put Grace at risk."

"Thank you."

"Now, about my secret your safe keeping for me, would you—"

Doc Hathaway stiffened.

"What is it?"

"Annabelle." Keldon's voiced boomed.

Arianna jumped. "Must you yell?" She turned to glare at him.

"The guests are waitin'." He waved his hand down the hall.

Arianna sighed and looked at Doc Hathaway. "Will you be joining us?"

"Yes… Yes, of course."

Arianna could feel Keldon's heated gaze. She wished he hadn't showed up when he did. She wanted to know what her secret was and why she forced Doc Hathaway to keep it. She had a sinking feeling it couldn't be good.

With everyone seated, Samuel poured drinks for the guests. Samuel, who preferred to walk around barefoot most of the time, was dressed formally tonight.

The talk turned to politics and Arianna tried not to yawn. She downed her second glass of wine.

"Have you heard how the war has progressed of late?" Vincent Aubrey gave the opening to the evening's conversation.

"General Ross' force marched on Washington is what I heard." Bernard Prescott nodded his head.

Arianna sat up straight. She knew this. She read about it somewhere.

"In retaliation to the burning of York," Nicholas Sherborn added.

"Where was our Army?" Elizabeth Prescott joined in.

Vincent addressed Elizabeth. "Madame Prescott, our army took it upon themselves to flee."

"Oh my. Yes, I remember reading about this," Arianna spoke up.

All eyes turned toward her.

"They made it to Virginia," Arianna continued, a smug smile spreading across her face.

"Oui." Vincent eyebrows rose.

Arianna's gaze touched Keldon's. She wanted to impress him, let him know she grasped a memory. She chuckled. "I would have loved to have seen President Madison's face. I bet he turned all shades of purple." She waved her hand. "He blamed John Armstrong for the capture and the burning of Washington. I believe he decided to name James Monroe as interim Secretary of War, am I right?"

"Where did ye hear this information?" Leighton said with such venom that Arianna would have backed up a space, if she hadn't been sitting down.

"It's common knowledge," she answered him sharply. "Check your history books, if you don't believe me." How dare he question her?

Keldon stepped in. "Enough. Annabelle, why don't ye play us a tune?" He gently helped her to her feet and led her to the harpsichord.

"I thought you said I never played before," she hissed at him, trying to break his hold.

"Aye, I dinnae think ye did, but ye proved me wrong." He put pressure on her arm until she was forced to sit. "Now, be a good lass for once and play somethin' sweet."

"Did you know your Scottish accent becomes more pronounced when you're angry?"

His eyes flashed in a now familiar display of impatience. "Just play."

Arianna flinched at the silken thread of warning in his voice. What had she done wrong, anyway? All night she'd been the perfect hostess, and she refused to be treated as a naughty child now.

He wanted her to play something sweet. Well, too bad.

Her mind raced. She wanted to pick just the right song for him, one where his hair would stand up on end.

Her eyes narrowed and a slow smile spread across her face. She ran her fingers over the harpsichord with a sweet melody, pretending to do as her ill-tempered husband bid. His smug smile riled her further. As he raised his glass of wine to his lips, she let loose, pounding on the keys.

Keldon choked on his drink.

"Goodness gracious, great balls of fire!" she screeched.

Keldon's eyes bulged and a vein popped out at his temple.

She couldn't wait to give him the finale. She stood, throwing the bench behind her. She swayed to the music and enjoyed every second of Keldon's discomfort. The words bolted from her lips so everyone could hear.

When she finished she turned and curtsied to the stunned guests. Elizabeth eyes fluttered like butterflies as she clutched her throat.

Bernard turned red and quickly pulled out his flask.

Doc Hathaway clutched his wife as she threatened to faint.

Nicholas smirked, but said nothing.

Vincent Aubrey, bless his soul, smiled and clapped his hands. "Brava! Brava! Where did you learn to play with such finesse?"

Keldon stepped in obviously believing he had to defuse the situation. "I must apologize."

"No, no. What a wonderful surprise, my friend," Vincent complimented. "Just what we needed to liven the party. No?"

Before Keldon could turn his wrath on Arianna, she exited out the French doors. "I'm not sorry," she called behind her. However, she had a feeling she'd pay for her stunt later. Maybe she should have thought her revenge through. She did have to live with Keldon, and he was less than pleased with her already.

Arianna took the lighted stone path toward the gardens. When she reached one of the benches, she plopped herself down. The cold marble felt cool beneath her.

She took a well-needed breath. Now what was she going to do? She could always apologize. "I don't want to. He deserved to be embarrassed. Who does he think he is bossing me around?" She wrapped her arms across her chest.

Enjoying her reprieve, she was put out when she heard footsteps coming down the path. "Here he comes," she uttered under her breath, preparing herself for battle. He wouldn't drag her back to the house without a fight.

Her mouth dropped open when not Keldon but Nicholas Sherborn with his flashy smile and winking dimples strode around the corner.

She stood, an uneasy feeling spread through her. She looked past Nicholas' shoulder to see if Keldon had followed close behind.

"He doesn't know I'm here," he told her.

This didn't put her at ease. "I should go back to the house. Keldon will wonder where I am." She took a step, but Nicholas blocked her. "Mr. Sherborn, I—"

He gathered her into his arms and smothered her words with a kiss, while he maneuvered his way back to the bench, lying her down upon the hard, cold surface.

Arianna was so shocked she didn't think to scream. His lips crushed against hers, bruising her mouth. She pushed at his chest, but her action only excited him more.

Finally, he came up for air when he realized she wasn't enjoying their little bout of passion as much as he was.

"What's the bloody problem with you?" He moved away and allowed Arianna to sit up.

"Me!" Her voice came out in a shrill. "What's my problem? Are you mad?"

"I know I shouldn't take such chances here, not with your husband so close. But I couldn't wait a moment longer. It has been far too long. I'm going bleedin' bonkers without you."

"This can't be happening." She shook her head bewildered over what took place. She looked at Nicholas, her eyes widening. No, it couldn't be possible.

"Come on Annabelle," Nicholas continued. "Don't be cross. I told you I had no choice. I had to report back to Captain Stevens."

Arianna stared at him, a flicker of apprehension coursing through her. "Are we having an affair?" She feared his answer, but she had to know.

"Ah, Annabelle." He brought her closer to him. "I knew you'd come around." His lips were on her again. It took all her will power not to scratch his eyes out. What in the world did she see in him? With a firm hand, she pushed him away, keeping her palm on his chest.

"You're right," she began. "I am a little cross. I haven't heard from you. You never phoned."

"Phone? What does that mean?"

Arianna realized this was another item of mystery, to everyone but her. Was she in another dimension? Maeve's explanation of how she came to be here was starting to sound plausible. She tried again. "You didn't write me."

"You know bloody well I couldn't. Do you want us to be caught? What good would I be to you if that happened, Love? You still want to get rid of your husband don't you?"

Good God! She wasn't only an adulteress, but a potential murderess, too. "We weren't really going to…uh…kill him. Were we?"

Nicholas chuckled. "You can be so incredibly naive sometimes. If he's arrested for piracy, they won't be asking him to tea."

Arianna felt sick to her stomach. This was all too much. Keldon was a pirate!

"Annabelle?"

"Yes, I'm listening," she said even though panic was rioting within her, and desperate to break free.

"Have you found out anything we can use against him?"

"I'm a spy, too?"

Her questioned seemed to amuse him. He actually chuckled. Arianna was getting a little perturbed. This wasn't funny.

"I'm sorry, Love. I'm the spy, but duty calls me elsewhere and I was hoping you might have uncovered something which could aid us." His eyes clung to hers. "How did you know about Madison replacing Armstrong, anyway? The news hasn't reached these parts yet." He didn't wait for her to answer. Instead he leaned over and kissed her cheek.

Arianna clasped her hands together so not to slap him.

"I guess you're more of a spy than you know, Love. I would like nothing more than to stay here with you, but I have to make my departure before Keldon discovers us."

He stood with a smile, showing off his dimples and white teeth. "You're one clever woman. Even I wouldn't have thought to make a scene with that simply dreadful music you played. What a perfect ploy to enable us to meet in private. I'll contact you soon, Love." His mouth swooped down to capture hers. Before she could tell him to stop doing that, he was gone, disappearing into the night, as though he had never been there.

Arianna slowly stood, her knees wobbling. Could she trust what Nicholas Sherborn told her? Was she really having an affair? She covered her mouth, stifling the scream building in her throat.

She walked toward the house, dragging her feet. "My husband's a pirate," she whispered under her breath. Weren't they cold-blooded killers, only interested in their own greed? Didn't they make people walk the plank? Arianna stopped short. Who was she to pass judgment? She was having an affair and planned to have her husband killed.

A small voice in her head shouted, *"Run! Escape! Get as far away from this madness as you can."* Unfortunately running wouldn't solve anything. Besides, where was she to go? She needed more information. She needed to know Keldon's plans.

She approached the house, keeping to the shadows. She peered in the French doors. Samuel, Leighton and Keldon were there, all the others thank goodness, were gone. The doors stood ajar and she could hear their conversation. She'd eavesdrop. The sin was no worse than the others that were piling up around her.

"We have the information for the next ship. It be carryin' silks and spices and other luxuries, the verra cargo we have been waitin' for." Leighton was pacing, obviously impatient for action.

"Ye doonae think, I ken this?" Keldon ran his hands through his hair in a detached motion. "But I feel we need to wait. What is yer mind on this, Samuel?"

"I think it wud be most foolish ter move too quick. Dere'd be other ships. We only have one life."

"Aye." Keldon nodded. "I say we wait, then."

"Blessed saints! I be far too auld to be this here patient." Curses fell from Leighton's mouth as he stormed out of the room.

From the shadows, Arianna watched Keldon light his pipe. He didn't seem put out by Leighton's childish temper tantrum.

"Leighton is cranky. No?" Samuel grimaced.

Keldon chuckled and removed the pipe from his mouth. "Aye. But he's a good friend. I wouldnae want to be at sea without him watchin' my back."

Samuel sighed. "Nor I."

"We should keep an eye on Annabelle," Keldon said between puffs on his pipe. "She may no' remember who she is, but again this could verra well be a ploy. Too much is at stake here. I am responsible for men's lives, and I have no wish to see nay one's neck danglin' from a tree."

Arianna put her hand to her throat and swallowed hard. Keldon may not have come straight out and said, *'Hey, I'm a pirate'*, but she heard enough to know Nicholas spoke the truth. She leaned against the side of the house and closed her eyes. What was she going to do? She had a duty to stop Keldon from hurting anyone else on the open sea, but something made her hesitate. Call it a crazy hunch. Keldon could be irritable, but he didn't strike her as a man without a thread of integrity. She couldn't confront him until she had all the facts.

Keldon claimed he was going to postpone his plans. Maybe she could find out what made him turn to piracy. Maybe she could change his ways. But how? The man didn't trust her. He didn't like her for that matter.

"Where did Miss Annabelle get ter?" Arianna heard Samuel ask, causing her to panic. She couldn't be discovered or she would never be able to convince Keldon to trust her. She lifted her dress and nearly sprinted back down the path to the interior of the garden. Luckily for her by the time Keldon found her, she'd composed herself at least enough so she didn't appear as if she were out of breath.

Keldon eyed her with suspicion, but she met his gaze and held her chin up. "Do ye plan on bein' out here all night? It will be dark once the servants put out the sconces."

Arianna looked up at him. "It all depends."

"Aye?" Keldon puffed on his pipe, wondering what she was going to demand.

"Are you angry with me?"

"Angry?" His eyebrows rose in question, then it dawned on him what she meant. He had been so preoccupied with his dilemma at hand, he had already forgotten about her making a scene with her unruly music fiasco. After he had gotten over the initial shock, he'd been amused by her performance. She made a spectacle of herself in front of guests. Something she would have never done before the accident. Her behavior intrigued him. "Nay. Come back to the house, it's late."

Arianna walked quietly beside him, allowing him to escort her to her room. He couldn't help but noticed her creased brow. "Is there something amiss?"

"What? No," she stammered. She opened her bedroom door, but turned to look at him as if she had an afterthought. "I'll be a better hostess next time."

His right eyebrow lifted, but before he could process her declaration, she assaulted him with another.

"You really shouldn't smoke. Don't you read? Smoking is bad for your health."

He took his pipe out of his mouth. "Annabelle—"

"Goodnight, Keldon."

He let loose a breath of disbelief when she shut the door in his face for the second time today.

CHAPTER SEVEN

Arianna couldn't fall asleep when she had a million questions. Why didn't her husband sleep with her? Was this why she had turned her attentions to Nicholas Sherborn? And did Keldon find his affections, elsewhere too? She gritted her teeth at the thought.

She hit her pillow with her fist, tossed and turned, until she thought she would go stark raving mad. She switched to her back and stared up at the ceiling, an unfamiliar ceiling.

"Who am I?"

Her only reply was the sound of rain pitter-pattering against her window. She listened, waiting to be lulled to sleep. Nothing happened. The drops fell faster and she had the urge to feel the rain against her face. What would be the harm? No one would have to know.

She could slip outside and...

The desire too strong to ignore, she threw back her covers and jumped out of bed. She quickly found her robe and put it on, securing the satin ribbon around her waist. The house would be dark so she lit the candle on her nightstand. She glanced down at her bare feet and shrugged. She wouldn't catch a chill; the night was still warm.

She opened her door and peered out into the awaiting darkness. "Not a creature was stirring, not even a mouse," Arianna whispered, stifling a chuckle. She must be quiet or she'd be caught before she made it to the door. A rush of excitement filled her as she tiptoed toward the foyer. As she passed Keldon's study, she halted. The door stood ajar and the hairs on her arm stood up. Was someone in there?

She shook her head of the silly notion. Everyone had retired for the night.

When she reached the front door, she placed her candleholder on the small wooden table. Since the candle wouldn't stay lit out in the rain, it would be useless to her.

She threw open the door, and the warm, sweet smell of wet earth hit her nostrils. "Ah, just what the doctor ordered." She stepped out and shut the door behind her.

Keldon hadn't been able to sleep and had gone downstairs to brood over his predicament. His jaw dropped open when his wife peered into the study. Dressed in white and with her shimmering pale hair cascading down her back, she looked like a spirit.

She had paused at the threshold and he had held his breath sure she had seen him, but then she turned away. When he heard the front door open and close, he rose from his seat to investigate. He spotted the candle she had left behind on the table. Why did she go outside? Curious, he walked over to the window and pulled back the curtain to see where she headed.

He blinked in surprise.

She twirled around in the rain with her face turned skyward. "What in damnation?" She'd be soaked head to toe. Blast it all. It was in the middle of the night and she wasn't properly dressed! The woman had lost her senses. He let the curtain fall and marched to the front door.

Unaware she had company, she laughed as she danced barefoot in the moonlight. He'd never seen her so free. His gaze traveled the length of her and his breath caught in his throat. Her drenched nightdress revealed every lush curve of her body. "Dear God, she is mad." He must have spoken the words aloud for her gaze locked onto him and her smile slid from her face as if the rain had washed it away.

Her hand flew to her throat. "Keldon."

"Aye." He stared at her waiting for an explanation.

She brushed a wet strand away from her face without uttering a word. Lightning cracked the sky and she looked up, her brow furrowing.

"Annabelle, what in God's name are ye doin'?"

"Isn't obvious?" She twirled around again. "Weeeeee!"

"Annabelle!" Keldon's voice boomed like thunder.

She turned to look at him. "Oh go away, fuddy-duddy." She did a pirouette and bowed as if she was on stage performing for him.

"Ach, lass, get out of the rain before ye catch yer death."

"What do you care?" This time she glided by the length of the porch and back.

He pursed his lips together. He shouldn't care. His life had been predictable before her accident. She did what she wanted, and he had his life. He should turn around and leave her to her insanity. However, she wasn't herself and his conscience wouldn't allow him to abandon her. If she remained out here, she would most likely come down with pneumonia and… "Annabelle!"

"What now?" She sounded annoyed with him.

"Stop this nonsense and come out of the rain," he demanded, deciding he needed to take a firm hold over the situation, but obviously his contemptuous tone only served to irk her.

Her chin angled up and she narrowed her eyes as she put her hands on her slim hips. "Make me."

"Make ye," he sputtered. "Make ye!" She had the gall to taunt him. He flew off the stairs.

Her eyes widened and she bolted, but he caught her by her waist before she could make her escape. He threw her drenched body over his shoulders without a care he'd be soaked, too.

"Put me down." She beat her fist against his back.

"I'm warnin' ye. Ye better stop yer thrashin'."

"Or what?" She screamed back as she pounded him one more time.

"Or this." He took his free hand and swatted her backside.

"Ouch!" She doubled her efforts, squirming and thrashing.

"Annabelle, I'm goin' to drop—" He slipped and couldn't regain his balance with her struggling to be free. He twisted, taking her full weight as he went down.

She'd knocked the wind out of him and he couldn't speak. Inches from him, he stared at her stunned expression. Then her features changed and her gaze caressed him with something almost akin to affection, but that couldn't be. This was Annabelle, the woman loathed him and he her. Only his body was having a difficult time remembering the arrangement.

She lifted her hand and stroked his face, her eyes searching his. Awareness of how her body felt pressed against him filled his every pore. Her gaze lingered on his lips and the tip of her tongue traced hers. He closed his eyes on a moan.

"Keldon, are you all right?"

No, he wasn't all right. She tormented him more now than when she had her memory. He buried his fingers in the wet tangles of her hair. She couldn't look at him with want and expect him to restrain. She was his wife and he'd take what was his. He opened his eyes, ready to plunder, but her innocent gaze threw him off guard.

"Keldon?"

Her eyes pleaded, but for what?

He was many things, but he wasn't such a blackheart to make her pay for sins she didn't remember. He pushed her to the side. On his feet, he offered his hand to her. She stared at the offer then up at him as the rain continued to soak them. He expected her to refuse, but she clasped his hand and he pulled her to her feet.

They reached the porch and to some semblance of cover from the rain. She sulked, her lips pouting as she rubbed her tender bottom. "You hurt me."

The dark wings of his eyebrows lifted. That was all she was going to say, no tantrum, no slapping, no screaming. Now he was thoroughly convinced she'd lost her mind. "What did ye think yer fists beatin' my back was doin'?"

"I hurt you?" Her eyes grew large.

Of course, she hadn't hurt him.

"I'm sorry." She placed her hand on his chest.

He lifted a brow. He couldn't remember the last time she'd touched him with kindness.

Her long drawn out sigh, attracted his attention. "I know you don't understand, but I needed this. It seemed so important. A memory or something like one was on the verge of coming to me... I remember jumping in puddles... my mom and dad laughing and joining in."

"Annabelle."

Something in his tone must have made her pause. She stopped her babbling and looked at him.

"Ye dinnae recover a memory. Yer mother died givin' birth to ye, and frankly, ye wouldnae have danced in the rain. Ye are ever fussy of yer appearance."

She stepped back and her hand fell away from him. He already missed the warmth.

"I never knew my mother?" She shook her head. "You have to be wrong. I sense it. My mother loved me." Her eyebrows furrowed and her gaze dropped to her hands as if they might hold the answers that plagued her. Different emotion flickered across her face, making her appear vulnerable.

Keldon took a step toward her, only to stop dead in his tracks. His gaze had drifted from her face to her flimsy nightdress, clinging to her slim body. He swallowed the thick lump forming in the back of his throat. Seconds before his common sense skittered into the shadows, he tore his gaze away from her breasts. He concentrated on her face, regarding her sullen expression with curiosity. For the life of him, he couldn't detect any dishonesty.

She clasped her arms, trembling.

He sighed. "Come inside, Annabelle."

She looked up at him with defiance.

He knew she was ready to argue with him again. "Please." It was the magic word.

She nodded, letting him guide her over the threshold and into the warmth of the house. She followed him into the study where she stood, watching him throw a few pieces of wood into the fireplace. Once the flames took life, he turned his attention back to her.

She shivered again.

"Let me remove yer clothes."

Her gaze riveted to his, a vaguely sensuous light passed between them. God, he wanted her.

"I mean…" His word trailed off to silence. He didn't know what he meant anymore. His hands seemed to have a will of their own as they encircled her waist and drew her near. He untied the ribbon holding her garment in place. Over the fabric, he drew his fingertips up the side of her breast. Heat spiked hitting him low in the gut as an arrow of liquid heat spiraled straight to his groin. He couldn't remember the last time he desired her so.

"Keldon?"

Her voice jolted him. What was he doing? He stepped back his hands shaking. His gaze fixed on her. She looked like Annabelle, but…

He forced himself to remember her cold heart. His eyes narrowed as distrust darkened the mood. Annabelle's cold words from the past resurfaced.

"You disgust me with your brutal touch."

"Annabelle, ye are my wife."

She laughed. "Only in name, love. I find my pleasures elsewhere."

"Keldon, what's wrong?"

She brought him back to the present, but the old Annabelle's words laid buried deep inside him, festering.

She reached for him and he could almost believe she'd changed, that this time, she'd welcome him into her arms. Her large blue eyes were vivid and questioning, as her gaze lingered on his lips.

Had she wanted him to continue, or was she simply toying with him, wanting him to beg for her, so she could push him away.

What did it matter? He had no intentions of finding out. "Stand by the fire," he ordered. "I'll go and find ye some dry clothes."

He turned and fled from the room.

He made his way through the house with the candleholder gripped in his hand. He must distance himself from Annabelle and fast. If the situation weren't so desperate, he'd have laughed. He was married to the woman for God's sake and he had every right to do as he pleased with her. She practically invited him to touch her, standing there with wet clothes clinging to her body, revealing every wondrous curve. He was only human, and it had been a lifetime since he touched her. So what was stopping him from taking what was rightfully his to sample?

He knew damn well, what was wrong. That woman he just left down stairs with her wanting glances and almost childish naiveté wasn't his wife. That is, she didn't behave according to her character. Not that he wanted her to be the cold embittered woman again, but at least he would know how to handle her. "What are ye up to, dear Annabelle? What game do ye play?"

"That is what I was wonderin'? What is all that noise ye two are carryin' on aboot?" Leighton had stepped into the hall in his nightclothes and holding a candle of his own.

"It is nothin' I cannae handle," Keldon answered hoping Leighton would go back to bed. Unfortunately, the man seemed determined to question him.

"It sounded as though ye were outside." Leighton chuckled, but he sobered as his gaze traveled over Keldon. Obviously taking in his damp hair and clothes. "Ye were outside."

"Aye. That is where I found her."

Leighton's brows shot up. "It's pourin' rain."

"Ye doonae need to be tellin' me, but the fool lassie seemed no' to care."

"What is she up to?" Leighton rubbed his chin thoughtfully.

"I havenae a clue. The oddest thing is I detect nay trickery from her."

"She wasnae meetin' someone?"

"I watched her from the window. There was nay one to be seen."

"If she wasnae meetin' anyone, what was she doin'?"

"Dancin' in the rain," Keldon answered. Just the thought of how she looked, as she spun around, letting the water wet every inch of her made his groin ache with want.

"Bah!" Leighton snorted, drawing Keldon's attention. "She's a clever one. I'll grant her that. She's tryin' to throw us off balance."

Keldon frowned. "What by pretendin' she's lost her mind?"

"What a better plan than that. This way she can spy on us because we'd think her harmless."

"I doonae know aboot that. She…" He wasn't sure what he could say to explain his feelings. "We'll be extra careful until we know for sure what she is aboot."

"Aye." Leighton nodded in agreement.

"She's expectin' me to bring her some dry clothes. I must go before she becomes suspicious."

"I'll bid ye goodnight or what is left of it. Ye best be gettin' yerself warm. Ye look a wee bit wet yerself."

Keldon nodded and entered Annabelle's room. Leighton's suggestion for warmth was the last thing he wanted. His blood scorched through his veins and he needed to contain his emotions before he went downstairs to face her again. He had no idea what had gotten into him. He despised her, but if this were true, then why the dull ache of desire? He turned toward the door.

She waited for him downstairs. All he had to do is take her.

"Ach!" He looked away and yanked a drawer open. He came across another nightdress. His hand caressed the softness of the fabric. For a fleeting moment he thought of how her skin felt beneath his hands. "Stop it!" He scolded himself and slammed the dresser drawer shut.

When he made it back downstairs and entered the study, he fumbled to keep the candleholder in his grip. Arianna had discarded her wet garments, draping a small knit blanket around her, her long legs exposed to his view. His mind was a crazy mixture of hope, desire... panic. He swallowed the lump formed in his throat and tried to look anywhere but at her smooth visible skin.

"Here, put this on." He thrust the clothing at her.

"I hope you don't mind that I used the blanket to dry off with."

He didn't meet her gaze.

"I was beginning to get chilled waiting for you."

"Why would I mind then?" he said, though he did mind. He walked over to his desk. He needed a distraction, but his pretense wasn't working. Dear God, she's naked under the blanket. How did she expect him to remain aloof, when she purposely exposed herself? He had a mind to teach her lesson and take her. She couldn't play with his emotions like this.

"Keldon?"

Was she dressed? A part of him hoped not.

"Keldon?"

Taking a deep breath to calm his nerves, he answered her. "Aye. I am listenin'."

"How did we meet?" Her voice floated over him like a soft caress.

What did she expect him to say? All he knew, he couldn't remain in the same room with her much longer, and still keep his pride. "It's late." He ignored her question. "We best be gettin' some sleep before the sun rises." He turned to face her. He wasn't sure if he was relieved or disappointed. She wore the nightgown he'd given her. "Go to bed, Annabelle. I'll take care of the fire."

She looked like she was about to protest, but in the end she nodded, leaving him to his misery.

CHAPTER EIGHT

Over her breakfast of warm oatmeal, toast and tea, Arianna studied Keldon's face, feature by feature, reacquainting herself with the man she had chosen to marry. She loved the way his dark hair waved right below his ears, and how dark thick lashes framed his cat-like green eyes. His muscles stretched beneath his white cotton shirt while his sun-bronzed skin peeked out from the collar and the cuffs.

Last night, she felt the undercurrent of attraction between them. She didn't understand why Keldon denied them. She couldn't sleep last night as she thought about the way his strong hands had touched her with such gentleness, and yet Keldon ordered her to bed as if he felt nothing. She knew his indifference to be a lie.

Had he always pushed her away? Was this why she took Nicholas Sherborn to her bed?

Keldon could feel her intent gaze upon him, and he fought the temptation to look at her. He found himself raging against a war of emotions that both confused, as well as excited him. With his heart, he despised Annabelle, but his traitorous body obviously didn't give a damn.

Half in anticipation, half in dread, he lifted his head to look at her. Their gazes touched. All the loneliness and hurt welded together in one upsurge of devoured yearning. He fought his desperation to scoop her up into his arms and carry her upstairs. As if his own reaction wasn't enough, he witnessed the same desire mirrored in the blue depths of her eyes.

A deep flush spread across her face, but she didn't shy away. "Do we always eat in silence?" She broke his train of thought.

Perhaps he misread the meaning in her eyes. He sighed. Silence didn't describe their relationship. Explosive would be more of the word he'd use.

"No' verra often," he finally answered hoping it would suffice her.

Arianna put her spoon down with a clatter. "Just what do we talk about?"

Innocence surrounded her like a halo of beauty, angering him. He wanted to shake her into remembering what they had meant to each other, which had been nothing. They argued, they screamed, but they never had a civil conversation. He opened his mouth to tell her how she destroyed the promise of their love, snuffing it out before it had the chance to flourish, but the hateful words choked in his throat. She waited, chewing on her lower lip as if she were afraid of what he'd say. He cursed. For a moment, he would have sworn he looked upon a stranger.

Leighton entered the room. He must have heard Arianna's question and since Keldon couldn't find his tongue, Leighton took it upon himself to lend a hand. "Ye speak of many things, the two of ye do." Leighton sat down.

Keldon lifted his brow and pursed his mouth together in annoyance. What was Leighton up to?

"Like what?" Arianna persisted.

"Like what yer plans are for the day," Leighton answered as he dished out a large helping of oatmeal for himself.

Keldon's eyes bore down on Leighton with a warning.

Arianna knew the look said keep quiet. Well, she didn't want Leighton to hush up. She wanted to know more about her life and unfortunately, since she couldn't remember any of it for herself, she had to rely on them. "What do we do all day? Do I work?"

Both Keldon and Leighton wore identical expressions. One would think she'd asked a humorous question. Well, she hadn't. She folded her hands and waited.

Keldon cleared his throat. "Nay, ye have never worked a day in yer life."

She didn't believe him. For heaven's sake, she had to do something with her time. She felt the screams of frustration at the back of her throat, but she willed herself to remain calm. In a defensive gesture, she folded her arms across her chest, never taking her eyes off either one of them. "Please tell me then, what do I do?"

"Ye call on yer friends and they call on ye," Keldon said, as though she should know this.

Visiting friends, all day couldn't be very fulfilling. "That's all?"

"Aye." Keldon nodded.

Arianna's eyebrows came together as she absorbed this information. She wasn't sure if she should believe him, but for the moment, she supposed she had no choice. "And what do you, two do?" She could barely wait to hear the story, for she knew they wouldn't tell her they were pirates. She leaned forward in eager anticipation, watching the two men exchange worried glances.

"We take care of the plantation." Her husband didn't quite meet her gaze.

"I thought you had slaves for that," she countered thoroughly enjoying the man's discomfort.

"Aye, but there are other things which require my attention." Keldon squirmed in his seat.

"Oh." She was silent for a moment and she was sure the men thought her curiosity had been satisfied. They were wrong. "Can I hang out with you, Keldon?"

Again, the two men exchanged bewildered glances. Leighton shrugged his shoulders, indicating he had no idea what she was asking.

"What do ye mean by hang out?" Keldon braved to inquire.

She sighed. One would think she spoke another language. "You know hang out. Let me see what you do all day. Get reacquainted with each other. Maybe being with you will spark some kind of memory." She leaned forward and lightly ran her fingers across Keldon's arm.

He jumped out of his seat and the chair flew back, toppling to the ground.

"Are ye all right?" Leighton looked at Keldon then to Arianna.

No, he wasn't all right. Keldon thought. What did Annabelle think she was doing? Touching him, asking to spend the day with him. Who was this woman? "Nay." He couldn't have her with him all day, especially with how he reacted to her last night and how she was looking at him now. Those looks were dangerous. "I have errands to run." He wasn't lying exactly. He planned to check on the heifer that was about to give birth. The poor beast was small and far too young to have an offspring. He anticipated a problem. When the heifer's time came, he needed to be there to help.

Then Keldon knew of a way to be free of her. "This is yer day to visit the women in town. Ye do yer stitchin'."

"Oh." Arianna sucked in a shallow breath and looked away. "I suppose I should follow my same routines."

"Aye, that would be best." Keldon bent down and righted the chair, leaning against the back of it for support.

When Arianna finally went upstairs to gather up what she needed for her excursion, Keldon turned on Leighton. "What was with yer misleadin' questions? Ye encouraged her to interrogate us."

"Annabelle is far better no' rememberin' how she once was. She'd be verra dangerous to us if she were her auld self. If she doesnae have her auld memories, then ye invent ones to serve our purpose."

"Ye want me to lie to her?" Keldon sat back down in his chair, not believing what he heard. He may not like or trust his wife, but he refused to stoop to falsehoods.

Leighton smiled, oblivious to how Keldon felt about his suggestion. "Aye. Ye ken me well. She's yer wife. Ye must take care of her, so she doesnae trouble us."

CHAPTER NINE

Arianna looked around Elizabeth Prescott's antebellum style home. The woman had lavishly decorated the house, with mahogany Empire furniture with sweeping crests, delicately carved rosettes and rolled arms that had an additional bellflower design. The colors were subtle, celery green and pale peach with draperies to match and yet Arianna found the home as cold and unfriendly as her so-called friend.

The only person Arianna recognized at the stitching party was Elizabeth Prescott. The other women weren't even remotely familiar. She didn't know their names and she wasn't even sure she cared. They weren't any better than Elizabeth with their *holier-than-thou* attitudes.

Horrified with the thought that these biddies were her friends, she had to force herself to smile and endure their company. They were shallow and insincere and the sooner she could distance herself from them the better. She was about to make her intended departure known, when one of the biddies said something, which actually caught her interest.

"They say this pirate is most handsome," the biddy with her light brown hair styled with ringlets, commented. "He is said to be like a ghost appearing out of nowhere. He wears a kilt and he always has his bagpipes a blaring."

"Bagpipes?" Arianna voiced before she could stop herself.

"Yes. He plays the most haunting music. Or so they say. The men are scared out of their wits that a phantom calls to them. Then the Highland Pirate boards the ships before the crew can raise their weapons."

Arianna's throat felt dry. She tried to swallow back the uneasy feeling choking her. "What do they call this pirate?"

"The Scotsman or the Highland Pirate of course. Where have you been, Annabelle Buchanan?"

Arianna felt faint. Trust the Scotsman. Those words haunted her dreams. She didn't have to be a genius to derive a conclusion. She knew Keldon and the notorious pirate were one and the same. He was the Scotsman. How long would it be before everyone knew?

"He's just a man." Elizabeth smirked. "Mark my words, they'll catch him and in the end they'll hang him for his crimes."

Arianna shuddered inwardly at the thought.

"Elizabeth do you have to be so vulgar?" biddy two, a plump woman with dark hair and a cleft chin, voiced. She obviously enjoyed biddy one's rendition of the fanciful figure.

For ten minutes, Arianna endured the agonizing maelstrom of how the Scotsman would meet his demise. She couldn't stand it anymore. "Pardon me."

All eyes fell on her with anticipation of a story.

She disappointed them. "I don't feel well."

"You do look a little peeked." Elizabeth agreed. "Would you like to lie down?"

"No," she spurted out the word before she found herself stuffed in a bedroom. "I believe it would be best if I returned home now."

Arianna raced out of Elizabeth Prescott's house afraid the woman would call her back. She spotted Samuel leaning against the carriage. He stood up straight and his eyebrows drew together. She guessed he hadn't expected her so soon. She didn't care how she used to be. She'd changed and for the better. Samuel opened the carriage door for her. She lifted her dress and hopped into the compartment.

She straightened her dress and took a deep breath, hoping to calm her nerves. "Thank you, Samuel."

His eyes widened.

"I've never thanked you before, have I?"

"No, Ma'am."

She knew Samuel came and went as he pleased. "You're not a slave, are you?"

"I be a freedman."

Annabelle smiled pleased at his response. "I'm glad."

He frowned, but didn't question her. "Is that all?"

"Yes. Please take me home, Samuel."

He shut the carriage door.

"Samuel?" He turned to look at her with his dark brown eyes. "Will you do me a favor?"

"Yas'm." Samuel nodded.

"Would you mind terribly if you called me, Arianna?"

Samuel brows rose high on his forehead.

"Please."

"Miss Arianna, then." He left her side and went to the front of the carriage to drive her home.

*****

Arianna found Keldon in the stables. He sat on a stool cleaning his pistol. She probably shouldn't disturb him, but he happened to glance up, his burning gaze holding her still.

"Ye're back early." His voice held a note of surprise.

"Am I?" She shrugged her shoulders.

"Aye. Ye usually spend all day at the Prescotts." He picked up the brush and started in on the bore of the gun.

Since he didn't openly tell her to leave, Arianna decided to stay. She found a nice spot on a bundle of hay and continued to watch him work. She wondered if he brought the pistol with him when he went pirating. She shoved the horrific image aside and cleared her throat. "I don't believe I like those women very much."

In spite of Arianna's reserve, Keldon seemed not to miss the exasperation in her voice. He glanced up at her.

"They're... well they're..." She struggled for the right words. "How should I say it..." She met his gaze then snapped her fingers. "Self-centered people."

Keldon's lips twitched. "Aye, that they are."

Arianna thought about the old saying or at least, what she thought was an old saying. *Birds of a feather flock together.* "Am I like them, too?"

Keldon tilted his head to one side, curious about her newfound revelation. Her large blue eyes held his, hope lingering in their depths. For a moment, he thought to shield her from the truth, to lie about how horrible she was to live with.

He shook his head of the fanciful thought. He could ill afford to show compassion with her. He decided to tell her exactly how she behaved. He didn't care what Leighton expected him to do. He wouldn't lie. One day she'd regain her memory and his hell would begin all over again. For protection, he'd keep his heart hardened against her. "Do ye really want me to tell ye?" He waited for her to answer, giving her one last chance to tell him no.

She pursed her lips and nodded.

"Then aye, ye're like them and worse. Ye're a spiteful uncaring woman, Annabelle." Even to him, his voice sounded harsh. Her head bowed, but not before he witnessed the raw hurt, he inflicted. A flash of guilt gripped his insides and he looked away. He thought he'd take great satisfaction in wounding her, but instead he felt hollow inside.

Her weary sigh made him look at her again.

"Why did you marry me, Keldon, if I was such an awful person? Why?"

Why couldn't she let this go? He didn't want to discuss their marriage.

"Please tell me."

He should refuse her.

"Keldon, please, I must know."

"It was arranged by our fathers." Bitterness laced each word.

"You weren't happy with the union?"

A low moan from one of the stalls interrupted before Keldon could reply.

Arianna rose to investigate, obviously forgetting her own problems for the moment.

"What's wrong with the cow? Is she sick?"

"She's in the birthin' stage." Keldon had joined her.

"She looks so small."

"Aye. That she is. I'm a wee bit worried. She may be needin' help."

She glanced over at him. "Have I ever seen a calf being born?"

He found her childish enthusiasm intriguing, making him wonder if Annabelle had been this innocent before influences and her father's indulgence made her selfish. "No' that I be knowin'."

"Then it's settled," she announced.

"What is settled?"

"I'm staying."

By her stance of hands on her hips, he realized she wouldn't reconsider. The fact she entered the barn in the first place, surprised him, but of late, everything she did puzzled him. He wondered how a simple bump on the head caused her to change and he wished this wondrous transformation could be permanent.

"Ye can stay," he said with a shrug. He appreciated the company, but he would never tell her so.

For hours, the animal labored to expel her burden. Arianna and Keldon waited, both anxious as the minutes passed with no results.

Arianna turned to Keldon. "There's something wrong, isn't there?"

"It's as I feared," Keldon commented more to himself than to anyone. He glanced at the pistol he'd been cleaning. He dreaded the thought of using it.

"I don't like how you look, Keldon. What's wrong?"

He didn't answer but moved toward the laboring animal, careful not to startle her. His examination proved he'd been right. The calf faced the wrong way, making delivery impossible. He shook his head. The poor beast wouldn't make it unless he helped.

He looked up. "Annabelle, ye need to find, Leighton for me." His eyes must have betrayed his worry. She didn't leave.

"I'm here. Let me help you. What do I need to do?"

He quirked his eyebrow up as he considered her offer.

"Don't turn me away," she pleaded.

He nodded. He'd take her assistance, but they had to move quickly, if they were going to save mother and calf. "Ye need to hold onto the mother's upper body. She's no' goin' to like what I'm aboot to do to her, but it's the only way."

"What are you going to do?" she asked as she moved into position.

"I plan on turnin' the wee calf inside her."

Arianna's eyes widened. "You can do that?"

"I'm goin' to try. Now, hold her steady."

Arianna held on tight to the squirming animal. The strain started to take its toll. Just when Keldon thought it was beyond him to save either animal, the calf suddenly turned, slipping out with its clamoring protests.

The exhausted mother immediately moved out of the way, grateful her burden was finally gone. The newborn calf, still bloody from the after birth went right to Arianna and promptly sat down on her lap. Arianna's mouth dropped open in surprise, but she recovered quickly, and hugged the calf close to her. Tears sprung to her eyes, causing Keldon to panic.

"Where are ye injured?" He was at her side, his hands roving over her.

She stilled his attention with a touch of her hand. "I'm fine," she said between sniffles. "I've never seen something so beautiful."

The calf finally realized Arianna wasn't her mother and headed in the opposite direction to find her.

Keldon smiled as the young calf latched onto his mother's udder, sucking furiously. "All births are special," he claimed even though the familiar dull ache crept through him. He remembered their child who had never had the chance to take his first breath. He glanced at his wife and he knew she remembered nothing of her questionable miscarriage.

She watched the calf, her expression serene, a smile touching her lips. He took in her disheveled appearance. Her hair had fallen into disarray, her face was smudged with dirt, and her clothes splattered with blood, but she smiled. What a captivating picture she made. He couldn't stop himself from pondering. Could he have been mistaken about her ending the pregnancy? He sighed. He may never know and maybe he didn't want to.

He glanced again at Arianna's soiled dress. He then looked at himself. What a sight they both made with their clothes and hands a bloody mess. "Yer gown may be ruined," he stated the obvious and braced himself for her to start a temper tantrum, but she just shrugged her shoulders, not seeming to care.

"It doesn't matter," she said with a sigh. "I wouldn't have missed this for the world."

Her response floored him. He had the temptation to pinch himself, to make sure he hadn't fallen asleep. She sat there contented, not caring if her clothes were beyond repair. The old Annabelle would have ranted and raved over a speck of dirt on her clothing. He shook his head in disbelief. This must be another affect from her head trauma, if only she would remain the way she was now. He could fall in love with this woman. The thought startled him. He must be careful. He must resist the pull she had on him. The way she was now wouldn't last. "Come away now. Ye need to clean up."

Arianna didn't want to leave, but she knew Keldon was right. Already the blood had crusted to her skin. She walked toward the stable doors, but noticed Keldon hadn't followed her. She stood in the doorway and looked back at him. "Aren't you coming?"

"Aye, in a moment. Ye go on ahead now. I willnae be long."

His voice sounded funny, quiet and withdrawn. She wondered why he looked so gloomy, when they had witnessed a miracle. She opened her mouth, but the way he looked at her, cautioned her not to ask. She chewed on her lower lip uncomfortable with the fact she couldn't figure him out. "Thank you, Keldon for letting me be here today."

He pursed his mouth shut, but he managed a stiff nod.

She headed toward the house, relishing in what she witnessed. A small smile curved her lips. She felt like she belonged today.

"Whut's happened ter you?" Maeve said from the porch, her eyes widening in horror as she caught sight of the blood running down the front of her dress. Arianna was sure the silly grin that was plastered to her face, made the situation worse. "You's in shock." Maeve's hands patted her down and turned her around, obviously intent on finding the wound that had caused so much bloodshed.

"No, no, no. I'm fine, really. I helped Keldon deliver a healthy baby calf."

"Gud Lord. No wonder you look a sight. We need ter get you out of them clothes and clean you up. You don't know wut I wuz thinkin' when I saw you."

Arianna followed Maeve up the stairs.

"I will draw a bath."

"It was a miracle that happened before my eyes." Arianna couldn't stop talking about the experience. "I never saw anything like it."

"Yas'm, ain't a new life wonderful," Maeve agreed whole-heartily.

*****

Keldon washed his hands, and spread fresh hay on the ground. He once again checked on the new family. He was on his way out, when Leighton slammed into him.

"What's wrong? Keldon questioned as he steadied Leighton.

"What's wrong, ye ask." Leighton's voice had a steely edge to it. "Have ye lost yer senses, lad?" He lifted his hand to reveal Arianna's bloody garment as his gaze wavered over Keldon's clothes.

"Oh that." Keldon relaxed, realizing there wasn't an emergency. "You best get rid of it. Why are ye fussin' over it anyway?"

Leighton sputtered, cursing under his breath.

"Is there somethin' else you wish to tell me?"

"Sweet Jesus!" Leighton ran his hand through his hair. "Have ye no sense? I said, take care of Annabelle, no' kilt her dead!"

Keldon frowned. "What are ye witterin' aboot?"

"The dress, lad. I see the dress." He waved the clothing in front of Keldon's face to emphasize.

"Ach, Leighton. Did ye think I ran her through, then?" Keldon was first exasperated, but he soon saw the humor of the situation and began to laugh.

Leighton didn't share his amusement. "Weel, if this here blood isnae hers, who's is it?"

"She helped me birth the calf." Keldon pointed behind him, revealing the new offspring.

"We're talkin' aboot Annabelle here," Leighton said. "It be easier for me to believe ye kilt her."

"She did help."

Leighton scratched his head, his worn face holding a frown of disbelief.

"I know what ye're thinkin'." Keldon shook his head. "Our Annabelle wouldnae have dirtied her hands let alone her clothing, but I witnessed it. She helped without a whimper or a complaint."

Leighton stared at him. "Have ye lost yer mind?"

"Leighton, do ye no' think a person can change?"

Leighton's eyes narrowed. "Tell me yer no' thinkin' Annabelle has really changed, for ye be a damn fool to think so."

"Aye, but ye witnessed it, too."

"I've seen that she's put on a good show, I'll grant ye that. But mark my words, the sky is forever blue, and the grass is green and there be nay changin' it. Annabelle be the same person deep inside and doonae be forgettin' it."

CHAPTER TEN

Arianna spotted Sally Mae heading toward the house and quickly called to her. The child stopped and walked the few spaces back. Arianna didn't miss the fear that flickered across the little girl's face and hurried to put her at ease. "It's okay, Sally Mae."

"Maeve says ter let you be and not bother you."

"You aren't bothering me," Arianna assured her. "Didn't you like playing the harpsichord with me?"

"Yas'm." A smile spread across her face.

"Why don't you join me," Arianna suggested. It's such a beautiful day. We could plan a picnic and then afterwards, if you want, I can show you how to play another tune."

Sally Mae looked over her shoulder. Concern puckered her brows. "But I's not done yet," she stammered. "I's in charge of de upstairs," she added with pride.

"You're just a child."

"I kin do de job," Sally Mae defended her position.

"I'm sure you can." She hadn't meant to offend her. Sally Mae could be no more than eight or nine. "You should have fun, too. Don't you ever play with the other children?"

"There ain't no time ter play." Sally Mae shifted to one foot then the other as if she wasn't sure what she should do. "Shud I go now?"

Arianna nodded. What else could she say to the little girl? She did however know what she wanted to say to her husband.

Arianna stormed into the house with determination. She headed to his study, knowing she'd find him there. She threw open the doors. He sat behind his desk. The jerk didn't even look up. Arianna cleared her throat. "May we speak?"

Keldon wondered if he should prepare himself for a battle. Maybe her memory had returned and she wanted to make up for lost time. He leaned back and his breath caught in his throat. Pale blonde hair loose from its bounds tumbled carelessly down her shoulders. Her cheeks colored like a sunset on fallen snow and her scowl did nothing to hamper her beauty.

She flipped a strand of hair away from her face and placed her hands on her hips. Keldon had the distinct feeling he was about to be reprimanded.

"She's just a little girl."

There was defiance in her tone as well as subtle challenge, causing him to take heed.

"She should be playing and having fun like any other little girl her age. All she does is work all day." She threw up her hands.

Keldon had no idea what she was talking about or why she thought he'd care. "Are ye feelin' all right?"

"What? Am I feeling... Are you hearing me? I'm talking about Sally Mae."

"Sally Mae?" He still didn't understand.

"You know, the cute little girl, who is in charge of the upstairs chores. You do know who she is, don't you?"

"Aye, I know who she is. I doonae know what ye are accusin' me of."

Arianna took a deep breath. She strode over to the desk and met his gaze head on. "You can't do this to Sally Mae or any of the other children for that matter." She leaned toward him but pointed behind her. "They should be enjoying the outdoors."

"Are ye thinkin' of sellin', Sally Mae?"

"No! God no." Her eyes flashed with outrage. "I could never sell a person. That's appalling."

He was more confused than ever. Slaves were a part of her life. She never cared what happened to these people. He leaned forward now. They were only a breath away. "The slaves are yers, no' mine."

"What... I..." Arianna sputtered. "I own another human being? That's impossible." She shook her head and moved away from the desk. "It just can't be." Her eyelids fluttered and she swayed on her feet.

Keldon whisked around the desk and held her steady. "Ye better have a seat." He led her over to the high back chair.

Her hand lingered at her neck and her mouth stood open as if words were stuck in her throat. Keldon poured her a drink from the decanter.

She lifted the glass to her lips and downed the contents.

Keldon lifted his eyebrows in surprise.

She held out the glass to him. He hesitated.

She jerked the glass at him.

With a shrug, he filled it for her and she did a repeat performance. This wasn't like her, not that anything she did of late was. Maybe she should lie down until the shock of what he told her wore off. "I'll find Maeve."

In his absence, Arianna must have poured herself a few more drinks. She looked up when she saw him. She quickly threw back her head, emptying another glass. She held the decanter against her chest.

"Ye have had more than enough, I believe." He strode toward her.

"No, I haven't." Her words were slurred. "No why? 'Cause I'm not stinking drunk yet and I need to be to escape this living nightmare called my life."

Keldon wrestled the decanter from her, but the effort pulled her from the seat. He caught her before she fell on her face. He easily scooped her up and she threw her arms around his neck. He motioned for Maeve to follow him with a quick jerk of his head.

"Where... *hiccup...* taking me?"

"Up to yer room. Ye need to lie down for a while." She snuggled close, burying her head in the crook of his neck.

His muscles stiffened. "What are…" His voice failed him, as she pressed her lips against his skin. "Dear Father in Heaven," he cursed.

How he opened her bedroom door was beyond him. He made it to the bed and threw her from his arms.

She flipped her long hair away from her face. Her eyes were glazed from too much alcohol, but he didn't miss her intent as her gaze scorched a path down the length of him.

"I want you to make love to me," she announced.

"What are ye aboot lass?"

"I'll leave you ter handle her then." Maeve chuckled as she headed for the door.

"Doonae leave," Keldon commanded.

"No, you should leave," Arianna countered as she moved from the bed as if stalking prey.

While Keldon was busy trying to control where Arianna's hands were groping him, Maeve abandoned him. "Stop it." He threw her back onto the bed.

Her chest rose and fell as she leaned back on her elbows to look up at him. "Why, Keldon Buchanan, I do believe you're afraid of me."

She had no idea. "Doonae be absurd," he told her with a harrumph.

"No? Hmm. Your accent thickens when you're flustered, too. Interesting."

"Doonae…" He took a deep breath. "Doonae be ridiculous."

"I tell my husband I want him to make love to me and he tries to run away. I know you want me." Her eyes traveled the length of him again.

He kept his hands balled at his side. He swore under his breath as he turned away. "Annabelle, please stop this."

"If you won't sleep with me, then at least kiss me."

Keldon whipped around and stared at her.

"Kiss me and I'll let you go," she repeated.

"Ye've had too much to drink." Keldon decided.

"Yep. I have… *hiccup*… too much to dink … I mean drink. It's the only way to forget what a terrible person I am?" Her lips pouted pitifully. "Kiss away all the nightmares." She closed her eyes and puckered.

His mind shouted for him to walk away before he made a mistake he couldn't take back.

He ignored the plea of good sense. On the open sea, he thrived on danger. Why not here, now? He couldn't help but see her in a different light and God help him, he wanted what he saw to be true. He took the steps that separated them. Cupping her chin, he searched her upturned face, her lips posed in an offering he couldn't refuse. He covered her mouth with the hunger of a starved soul. He heard her small intake of breath as she shifted closer and deepened the kiss. He wrapped both arms around her, crushing her to him. His body rippled with tension, but he was terrified to give into the desire, to trust her fully. He must stop. Now! He broke the embrace and she winced as if he nipped her flesh. He backed up, eyes wide and hands trembling.

Retreat. Escape. His mind screamed. He whirled on his heels and stalked out of the room.

Arianna sighed and collapsed on the bed, touching her hand to her lips, the kiss still singing through her veins. She closed her eyes and smiled.

*****

Arianna didn't know how long she slept. She sat up and the room spun. She ignored her tipsy state and headed for the door. She had an announcement. She gripped the banister as she descended the stairs. The floor weaved in and out, but she managed not to break her neck. She headed out the doors and headed over to the kitchen. There she found Oni and Sophie busy with their tasks for the day. They both looked up when she stumbled in. She ran her hand threw her tangled strands and straightened her dress. She stared at her bare feet wondering when she'd taken off her shoes. She looked up again, remembering her purpose.

"Stoop what your doin'." Her tongue felt thick. She smacked her lips together. She must make the announcement. She concentrated. "I own you no more." She waved her hand dramatically around the room, stumbling forward, but she didn't fall. She covered her mouth and she giggled. "I must go now." She left the two women and went to look for Maeve and Sally Mae. Before she found either one, her attention swayed. The lure of the harpsichord called to her and she entered the drawing room. She sat down on the bench and played the haunting tune from her past. The song meant something to her… a connection to… She didn't know.

Keldon found her as she started on her fourth rendition of the same melody. He strode over to her and gripped her shoulder. She looked up, ignoring his scowl. "Weel 'ello Mr. Boocanun." Arianna grinned from ear to ear as a little chirp sound escaped her lips in a bubbling hiccup.

Keldon had a long talk with Oni. He had headed toward the stairs to find his wife, when he heard her playing the song, *his* song. She didn't realize how she tortured him with the sweetness of the melody. "I thought, I told you to rest a wee bit."

"Ya know, I wuv the way ya talk."

"Annabelle, ye're changin' the subject."

"You're upset," she said in a singsong voice. "I know 'cause your brogue thickened."

"Ye are mistaken."

"Am not. But do you know what? I don't care what you think even if you are a good kisser. 'Cause you don't know me. You don't even call me by my real name." She turned away and pounded out the chords as she sang. "My name is Arianna and I'm living a nightmare. My husband is cute, but he's a…"

"Annabelle!" Keldon raised his voice over her racket. "Ye have Sophie in tears."

This stopped her and she looked at him. "Sophie, the real young one who's going to have a weeeeee bairin? Isn't that how you Scots say it?"

His lips puckered in annoyance that she wouldn't pay attention. "She has it in her head that yer goin' to sell her. Oni said ye told them so."

"Sell her?" Arianna's eyebrows furrowed. "I'm not going to sell her. I've set her free." She waved her arm and nearly toppled off the bench.

Keldon righted her before she broke her neck. He stared down at her with his hands on his hips. His eyes narrowed.

"You told me I owned the slaves," she said. "John Adams didn't own slaves."

"John Adams. President John Adams? I doonae understand. What does he have to do with this?"

"I was just thinking is all. John and Abigail loved each other, did you know that?"

Keldon took a deep breath for patience. "Anna—"

"Don't call me Annabelle." She wagged her finger at him. "And let me finish."

"Then do so and be quick aboot it."

"John and Abigail worked their own land and hired people if they needed help. We should follow in his footsteps. So I freed everyone so they could make their own choices. This is America." She frowned and hiccupped. "I can free the slaves, can't I?"

"Aye. But where are they to go? They cannae verra weel march out of here and call it a day."

"They can apply for a job. God knows they couldn't want to work in a rice paddy all their lives. Yuck."

"Ye ken weel, the fair people of Charleston willnae have a person of color work for them."

"No, I don't *ken*," she mimicked him. "I don't *ken* any of this! You tell me I own another human being. I know this is wrong, so how could I be so despicable? Everything you've told me so far, it's as if you are describing someone else. I'm a stranger in my own life!"

Keldon couldn't argue with her. She was a stranger to him, too. She looked and sounded somewhat like Annabelle, but she by all means, didn't act like her. What could he say? The facts remained. She had been all those things and more.

He ran a hand through his hair. "I can only tell ye what I ken. Maybe ye losin' yer memory as you did, it's given ye a chance for redemption."

Arianna didn't have the opportunity to reply.

Samuel escorted Nicholas Sherborn into the room.

Arianna tensed, every muscle bunching beneath her skin at the sight of Nicholas Sherborn. She may be a little tipsy, but the memory of her last encounter with Mr. Sherborn stood fresh in her mind.

"Good-day, Mrs. Buchanan." Nicholas bowed slightly as he removed his hat. His light trousers and a blue jacket flattered him.

Arianna shook her head. She refused to find him attractive. She was a married woman. He needed to leave at once. "What are you doing here?"

Keldon placed a hand on her shoulder. "Annabelle, there is no need for rudeness. Please go upstairs. We'll speak later."

How foolish she felt. Obviously, Nicholas was here at Keldon's request not to meet with her. Her eyes narrowed. Nicholas wanted to harm Keldon. "I think I'll stay." She lifted her chin and met Keldon's icy gaze head on.

Nicholas hid a smile behind his hand.

Obviously, Keldon wasn't amused. He leaned near and whispered, "Please doonae make a scene in front of our guest or ye'll be sorry."

"You wouldn't dare do anything to me," she snarled right back, but seeing his green eyes flash with anger she decided not to call his bluff. "Okay, Okay, I'm going."

Keldon escorted her to the door and waited for her to go down the hall before he turned and walked back into the room. "You wanted to see me?"

"Can we speak freely?" Nicholas nodded toward Samuel who was standing with his arms folded against his chest.

"Aye that we can. Samuel can weel be trusted." Keldon then motioned for Nicholas to take a seat, while he went to the table to pour a drink for them.

"I have the information you have been waiting for." Nicholas didn't waste time.

Keldon wasn't facing Sherborn so he was able to hide his expressions. He hadn't decided if he could trust this man or not. Sherborn showed up, wanting to join his band of would-be privateers. Until Sherborn proved his worth, he was reluctant to reveal information about his intentions. "And what information do ye have for me?"

"A Spanish frigate loaded with supplies is headed in our vicinity. We could intercept her with ease."

Keldon had finished pouring the drinks and handed one to Nicholas before he answered. "We have to know a wee bit more aboot this frigate and its captain. Did you obtain the information?"

Nicholas smiled. "Of course. The captain is Nathan Cordellos. In his prime, he would have been a worthy opponent, but now he is an old worn out man. The Spanish will not expect anyone to attack them. They have undermanned the ship in hopes of fooling everyone into thinking they're not carrying anything of value. Since you have only attacked British ships, the Spaniards won't expect such an assault. It would be like taking candy from a baby and quite profitable, I might add."

Keldon took his pipe out of his pocket and put it in his mouth. He thought about what Sherborn offered him. This would prove Sherborn's loyalty if he chose to trust his information. He could take all the precautions necessary. Keldon removed the unlit pipe from his mouth. "Will ye be goin' with us?"

"Wouldn't bloody well miss it, now would I?" Nicholas smiled as he raised his glass in a salute.

CHAPTER ELEVEN

Arianna sat in the middle of her bed and braided her hair. She worried about what unsavory deeds Nicholas Sherborn was convincing her husband to do. Whatever the plan may be, it would be a trap. She had to think of a way to stop him.

Keldon would never listen to her; he didn't trust her. If she admitted to the affair with Nicholas, it would only make matters worse.

Tap, tap, tap.

She lifted her head and listened.

Tap, tap.

She turned toward her window. Her whole body tightened like a bowstring.

Nicholas Sherborn peered in at her, grinning from ear to ear.

The audacity of the man was unnerving. She had no other choice but to let him in before someone discovered him dangling from the ledge.

"What do you think you are doing? How did you get up here?" Arianna said as she helped him inside.

He didn't answer her until he had both feet planted on the hardwood floor. "I climbed up the trellis like I always do. I had to see you."

"You must be crazy."

"Only mad about you." He reached for her but she ducked and moved out of his way.

"Listen, you have to leave. It's not safe."

"Keldon won't bother you. As we speak, he is discussing the plans to take the frigate."

Arianna put space between her and Nicholas' roaming hands. To save Keldon, she needed answers. "Is this how you'll capture him?"

"No." He sighed. "It's a real shame, I know. I can't wait until he's out of our way. I'm as anxious as you are to marry."

Her stomach churned. She'd promised to marry him. She couldn't believe it, but why would the man lie? She stared at Nicholas. His light brown hair and charming dimples were appealing, but there was no heart fluttering, no *I-can't-wait-to-see-you-again* feeling. She felt nothing for him. She couldn't inform Nicholas of her change of heart, at least not yet. She needed information, so she could insure Keldon's safety.

She grimaced. Before her accident, she wanted Keldon dead, had planned his demise without a thought.

She touched her fingers to her lips. Both Nicholas and Keldon had kissed her. Nicholas' caress had infuriated her, but Keldon's kiss had spilled through to her soul. No matter what happened between her and Keldon in the past, it didn't matter now. Her heart knew she belonged with him.

She turned her attention back to Nicholas. "If you aren't planning to take him in, what is the plan?"

"Take him in?" Nicholas frowned.

"You know, arrest him," she explained further.

"Oh. Keldon must trust me first. Then the British will step in and justice will be served."

"Are you sure we're right about Keldon? Maybe he has a good reason for—"

"Pirating," Nicholas finished. "Think of what you're saying. The man has terrorized every British ship in sight."

"We're at war with the British. They've attacked our ships and they haven't allowed us to trade peaceably. They think they can dictate with whom we can trade. Keldon has confiscated items we need to survive."

"Are you bloody insane? He's not out to help anyone. He's a murdering thief."

Arianna paled. "He's committed murder?"

"Did you think he asks for the goods and the captains of each ship tip their hats and gladly hand over their cargo without a fight? Keldon Buchanan has murdered without a qualm. The only life he holds sacred is his own."

Arianna blinked. The new information was like a slap in the face. Could what Nicholas just told her be true? Could Keldon really be so despicable? She didn't want to believe it. *Trust the Scotsman.* She couldn't shake the feeling this was important to remember.

"Annabelle, you were the one who came to me with your suspicions. I need to know. Whose side are you on?"

Arianna's gaze locked with his and she realized Nicholas might say he loved her, but he'd forfeit her life if he thought he couldn't trust her. Her whole life was a pack of lies. What was one more? She sauntered toward him and batted her eyelashes. "I'm with you, of course. Can you fault me for wanting proof of Keldon's deeds?"

"If anyone deserved the rope, Keldon Buchanan is our man." Before Arianna could move out of his reach, Nicholas grabbed her arm and pulled her close. "Give me a little kiss and I'll be on my way."

He didn't wait for her, but satisfied himself before she could object. Then he was at the window, daring his escape. He looked at her one more time with his devilish grin and impish dimples. "You're beautiful. I wish I had the time to make love to you. But alas, duty calls." Then he was gone.

Arianna's head spun and it wasn't from the alcohol she had consumed earlier. Nicholas Sherborn was like a whirlwind. She felt exhausted after each encounter with him. With a heavy heart, she sat down on the bed. She rubbed her temples, feeling a horrendous headache coming on. "You deserve a hangover."

Maeve knocked before she entered. "Miss Arianna, kin I's ask a favor of you?"

"Sure. You name it."

"Will you reassure Sophie dats you ain't goin' ter sell her. She's been cryin' and dat ain't gud fer de chile she be carryin'."

"I didn't mean to cause any problems, but it seems that is all I do."

"I know you has a gud soul."

"I'm afraid you're the only one, who believes that."

CHAPTER TWELVE

Arianna cringed, hearing Sophie's sobs and knowing she'd been the cause. Oni sat next to Sophie on the floor, rubbing her back and trying to console her. Maeve inhaled deeply and walked over to them. She knelt down in front of Sophie. "Now, now," she soothed. "Miss Arianna be here ter tell you herself, dat she ain't goin' ter sell you."

"It ain't dat," Sophie spit out before she doubled over in pain. A pool of water formed beneath her.

"Lordy," Oni exclaimed. "De chile be comin'."

"Now?" Arianna's eyes widened in alarm.

Sophie screamed as another onslaught of pain gripped her.

"We got ter get you back ter your cabin. Kin you walk?" Maeve asked. Sophie managed a nod between sobs.

"Maybe she should stay here," Arianna suggested.

"Oh no." Maeve shook her head. "Don't worry none. We'll take gud care of her." Maeve and Oni lifted Sophie to her feet, each supporting her weight on their shoulders.

"I'll go with you." Arianna didn't know if she'd be any help, but she would try.

"No, no. You must stay here," Maeve told her.

Arianna followed them to the door and watched them carry Sophie away. She caught the worried glances between Oni and Maeve and a cold dread settled on her heart. What weren't they telling her?

As hours slipped by with no word about Sophie, Arianna wished she knew where they'd taken her. She'd march down there and find out herself.

The house was like a tomb with no one around as if they all deserted her. She settled on waiting for Maeve in the drawing room. She sat at the harpsichord. As she played, the tension ebbed from her body. The music soothed her like nothing else did.

"Dat's so purdy."

Arianna ended the song on the last note and smiled. "Thank you, Sally Mae. Have you been in the house the whole time?"

"No'm. I jest come in."

"Do you happen to know how Sophie is doing? Did she have her baby?"

Sally Mae looked down at her feet, shuffling them back and forth. "No'm, she ain't birthed yet."

A dull ache of foreboding seeped into Arianna's chest. She'd been right. Something was wrong. She walked over to Sally Mae and gently lifted her chin. "What's happening? Is Sophie going to be all right?"

Tears glistened in the child's eyes.

Not good. Not good at all.

"No, Miss Arianna. She ain't fine. The baby won't come out. I think she's goin' ter die."

Arianna suppressed the panic welling inside of her. She didn't want to scare the child. "Don't worry about Sophie. She's not going to die. Women have babies all the time."

Sally Mae shook her head. "No, she's goin' ter die. Maeve is prayin' over her now. She made me go."

"Why would Maeve pray unless what Sally Mae claimed was true? She shook her head. Sophie couldn't die. She was young and healthy, so full of life. "Sally Mae, tell me where Sophie is. I have to see her. Maybe there's still hope."

"You kin make her well?" The little girl's face lit up.

"I don't know. I need to find out what's wrong first."

Sally Mae took Arianna's hand and led her to a rundown cabin, well hidden behind the large Cypress trees. The door stood open for all the good it did. The air was thick, the heat stifling.

Arianna spotted Oni sitting on the floor rocking back and forth with her eyes closed, humming a chant. Maeve hovered over Sophie, who withered in pain. Her shift was soaked and her skin glistened with sweat.

"What's going on?" Arianna took a step closer to the bed.

Maeve and Oni both stopped their meditation and stared at her. Maeve strode over to her.

"Miss Arianna, you shudn't be here," she whispered.

"Sally Mae told me Sophie was dying," she whispered back.

Maeve's eyes betrayed the truth before she even spoke. "Dere's no more ter be done?"

"Why? What's wrong? Why isn't a doctor here?"

"Dere ain't no doctor dat will helps de likes of us."

Arianna didn't understand, but she didn't want to waste time questioning Maeve. "What about the baby?"

"Dat's whut's de problem. The chile, be turns de wrong way. She kin't deliver."

"There must be something we could do?"

"No Miss Arianna, there ain't nothin' we kin do." Tears sprung to Maeve's eyes. She turned away and went back to Sophie.

Arianna couldn't accept Sophie would die. There had to be something. There had to be a way. Then an idea came to her. Without a word, she left the small cabin and ran as back to the main house.

She spotted Samuel leading two horses back to the stables. She looked skyward. "Thank you, Lord." She ran inside the house, knowing where she'd find Keldon. She burst into the study, the door flying against the wall.

Keldon looked up. Arianna's bedraggle appearance made him frown. Strands of hair had fallen free from her long braid, and her clothes hung in an askew fashion.

"You have to come with me," she demanded as she approached him. She took the glass of whiskey from his hands and placed it on his desk. She then grabbed the decanter, before she pulled on his arm to follow. He allowed her to lead him out of the house, curious of her urgency. Once they started down the beaten path, he knew where they were heading, but didn't know why.

She stopped in front of one of the cabins. "She's in there," Arianna said like this explained everything.

"Who's in there?"

"Sophie. She desperately needs your help. She went into labor and the baby is turned the wrong way."

"This still doesnae explain why I'm here."

"You have to turn the baby," she blurted out, her eyes pleading.

Keldon ran his hand through his hair. "I cannae do that. Have ye lost yer senses?"

"You saved the calf," Arianna insisted. She touched his arm, a wistful gesture Keldon didn't miss. "You can save Sophie and the baby, too."

She looked up at him with hope and trust. She believed he could work a miracle, but what she suggested was insane. He removed her hand from him. "I'm sorry, I cannae do it." He turned away intent on heading back to the house, but Arianna's next words halted him.

"Coward!" Arianna hissed.

Keldon stopped dead in his tracks.

"You care more for your animals than you care for the people you are responsible for."

He turned on her then. His eyes were like shards of green ice, ready to tear into her. "Ye dare say, I doonae care." He walked the few spaces back to where she stood.

His handsome face grew hard and resentful as he towered over her.

Maybe she'd pushed him too far.

"It's because I do care that I cannae do this. I doonae want anythin' to happen to Sophie."

His deep voice held a strange edge of passion that moved her and she placed her hand on his arm.

He looked down at her. "What I did for the wee calf is all too different. I cannae verra weel treat Sophie like a heifer. She's a person and I couldnae live with myself if I killed her."

"If you don't do something, she's already dead," she implored, never letting her gaze waver. She knew in her heart, Keldon was Sophie's only hope. If he walked back to the house, Sophie would die.

Keldon broke the gaze, nervously running his hand through his hair.

Arianna waited as she watched him work through what she asked of him.

He took a deep breath and looked at her again. "Ye're goin' to have to help me. Are ye up to that?"

"I'll do whatever you say."

He grunted something unintelligible under his breath and they entered the cabin.

Arianna insisted Keldon scrub his hands thoroughly. Then she poured his good whiskey over them. He thought she was daft, but she explained it was to fight infection. He decided he didn't have the time for her to clarify how she knew this. Time was of the essence. Sophie weakened by the second. If by some miracle, he turned the child around, he feared she wouldn't have the strength to push.

He walked over to the bedside. "We're goin' to try and make that stubborn bairn of yers turn the right way. Ye're going to have to help me, lass. I willnae lie to ye. What I'm goin' to do will hurt somethin' fierce, but it's the only way. Do ye ken?"

Sophie nodded and Arianna took hold of her hand. "You squeeze as hard as you need to," she told her.

*****

Four hours later, Sophie delivered a healthy baby boy. After Arianna bathed the baby, she wrapped him in a small blanket and handed him over to his mother. "He's perfect, Sophie. What are you going to name him?"

Sophie kissed the top of the tiny baby's head. "Elijah." She then looked at Annabelle, her mistress, who she had once feared. Maeve had been right; Annabelle no longer existed. "Thank-you, Miss Arianna."

"I didn't do anything."

"Yas'm you did. You brought Mista Keldon here ter save me and my chile." She looked at Keldon now. "Thank you." Sophie's eyes had misted with tears of joy, for she and her child were alive.

"Ye're verra welcome, Sophie. Ye rest now." Keldon motioned to Arianna that it was time for them to leave.

On the way back to the house, Arianna quietly slipped her hand into Keldon's, giving it an affectionate squeeze. He was so startled he missed his step. He glanced at her questioningly, but Arianna didn't turn to meet his gaze. Question

He didn't know this woman who cared for others and went out of her way to help them. He sighed wearily. If only she would remain like this, but he kept waiting for the old Annabelle to resurface and wreck her vengeance.

He glanced down at their clasped hands, liking the feel of her small hand in his. He laced his fingers through hers, giving her hand a quick squeeze, too.

CHAPTER THIRTEEN

Arianna leaned on the counter as she watched Maeve and Oni prepare for the day's meals. "Where's Elijah's father?"

Both women stopped what they were doing and exchanged worried glances. Arianna didn't understand why they hesitated to tell her.

Oni cleared her throat. "You done sold Thaddeus."

"Sold him?" Arianna stood up and closed her eyes, mortified over her past transgressions. Would she ever learn something about herself that wasn't so revolting?

Maeve put a comforting arm around her. "It ain't your fault."

Arianna knew Maeve held fast to her conviction that she was someone else, but it wasn't possible. How could she have switched places with another person? She had to face the facts. She'd been an awful, conniving and uncaring person. She should thank the Lord that the blow to her head knocked common decency into her. "Whom did I sell him to?" she asked determined to correct the wrongdoing.

"Mista Prescott," Oni answered.

"I'll tell him I've changed my mind and want him back."

Again, Oni and Maeve exchanged glances.

"What's wrong?" Arianna was almost afraid to ask.

"Mista Prescott, he never sells his slaves. They die dere." Oni sadly shook her head.

"We'll see about that."

Maeve's eyes narrowed. "You have a wicked gleam in your eyes, Miss Arianna. Wut's you plannin' ter do?"

"Hmm?" She looked at Maeve. "Do? I plan on fixing this."

"Wut's you mean fixin'?"

"You told me you had powders that would help a headache. Just how potent can you make the remedy?"

*****

Once the Prescott's home loomed before Arianna, she lost some of her confidence, but she couldn't back down now. Everyone was relying on her to bring Thaddeus back to Blue Run.

On the way over, she informed Samuel of her plans. Well some of it. She purposely left out the parts he might find objectionable. She didn't want him to stop her. Samuel didn't come right out and call her a fool, but his raised brows said it all.

Straightening her dress, Arianna looked at Samuel. "Wish me luck."

Samuel's mouth twitched. "You's goin' ter need it, Miss Arianna. I ain't ever seen Mista Prescott part with nothin', slave or otherwise."

"I plan on being very persuasive." With her package in hand, she made her way up the steps.

Arianna had inquired beforehand. Elizabeth wouldn't be home until later today. She'd gone to visit Biddy-Number-One for tea.

Arianna would have Bernard's complete attention.

She took a deep breath and knocked at the door. A tall black man wearing formal attire with white gloves and all, answered. "May I be of service to you, Mrs. Buchanan?" he said in a clipped speech.

"I have some business to discuss with Mr. Prescott. Please let him know I'm here?"

"Yes. Please do come in." He led her to the drawing room before he left her to find Bernard. She sat down on the sofa, but stood again. "Stay calm," she whispered under her breath. "You can do this."

"What do I owe the pleasure, Mrs. Buchanan?"

She whirled around and forced herself to smile.

Bernard waddled over to her and took her hand with a polite kiss.

She fought the urge to wipe his slobber on his jacket. "I'm here on my husband's behalf. He asked me to bring you a gift, thanking you for your last business transaction."

Bernard cleared his throat and pulled at his collar. "He told you?"

Arianna had no idea what arrangement Keldon and Bernard had. She was making this up as she went. "Only that he appreciated your business and he wanted to show his gratitude." She then opened her package. Arianna couldn't have been happier when Bernard licked his lips and raised his hands greedily for the bottle. "Would you care to sample it?" she asked, hoping he would.

"Yes, yes by all means." Bernard Prescott snapped his fingers and the servant who had answered the door, was there to take the bottle from him.

"Please join me." Bernard offered her a seat.

The servant filled the glasses and left the room, closing the doors behind him.

Bernard closed his eyes and sniffed the amber liquid. He smiled and took the first swallow. "Yes, yes this is very good." He opened his eyes. "Your husband has exquisite taste. Tell him I would like to do business with him again."

"I will. And I will also let him know you were pleased with the gift." She nodded toward the glass he held in his hand.

Bernard took another sip. "I'm curious, Mrs. Buchanan, why aren't you with Elizabeth and the other ladies today?"

Arianna leaned back in her chair, ready to put her plan into action. "I needed a change. I thought we could chat for a while." She lowered her eyelids ever so slightly and at the same time, she crossed her legs lifting her dress above her ankles. Maeve told her this would be scandalous behavior. She needed to distract Bernard, rankle him a bit so he couldn't think straight.

He cleared his throat and yanked at his collar. Who knew ankles were such a turn on. Bernard downed the rest of his drink.

Oh yeah, he was flustered. "Would you like another?" She didn't wait for him to answer. She stood and walked over to him. She let her hand linger on his before she took the flute from him. She noticed his Adam's apple nervously bobbed up and down as he swallowed. She poured the drink, overflowing the glass on purpose. "Oh my! I can't believe how clumsy I am."

"It's quite all right." He pulled out a handkerchief, trying to clean up the mess.

Arianna poured another glass for him. This time she added the powder Maeve had given her. Maeve assured her it would only make him drowsy. She didn't want him knocked out. She needed his cooperation.

Finished, Bernard sat back down and Arianna handed him his glass. "Aren't you going to join me?" he inquired.

Arianna almost let out a sigh of relief as she watched him down the drink. "I believe I will." She refreshed Bernard's glass, too. "To good friendships."

With a nod, Bernard touched his glass to hers. "Um friendship."

She didn't like the gleam in his eyes as his gaze traveled the length of her. She hoped the powder worked fast.

Bernard blinked rapidly and laughed. "I'm a little light headed."

She frowned. She wanted fast, but maybe she'd used too much. This wouldn't do. He needed to stay awake long enough for him to sign the papers she brought.

"Now Bernard... You don't mind me calling you Bernard, do you?" She sat close to him and placed her hand on his thigh.

"Nooo." Bernard leaned a little too close and Arianna pushed him back.

"May I take Thaddeus home today?"

"Thaddeus?" Bernard blinked a few times.

"Yes, Thaddeus. You remember the young slave I sold you."

"Oh 'im." Bernard frowned. "He's been more trouble. It's no 'onder ya wanted to get rid of 'im," he slurred.

"Where is he?" Arianna kept her voice under control.

"Had to 'each 'im a lesson." Bernard leaned back and closed his eyes.

Arianna shook him and his eyes popped back open. "Wh—"

"Where is he?" She repeated, desperate to have the information from him before he fell asleep.

"He's... He's... Now where is he? Oh yeah... He's in the hole." Bernard's eyes rolled back in his head and he fell forward into Arianna's lap.

Horrified, she tried to lift him back up, but she knocked him to the floor. "Oh my God!" Now what was she going to do? She wouldn't be able to pick him up, but she couldn't leave him. Besides, he hadn't signed the papers.

The doors to the drawing room crashed opened. Arianna whirled around with a gasp. Keldon stood there his gaze pinning Arianna down with a shimmering wave of pulsing fury. "Have ye lost yer senses completely, Annabelle?"

"How—"

"Maeve told me."

"Traitor," she mumbled.

"Ye cannae do as ye please, Annabelle and think there are nay consequences. Where is Bernard?"

Arianna glanced down at her feet.

"Nay." He shook his head. "Ye have done it already." He rushed over and looked down at Bernard Prescott, slumbering at her feet. "What did ye plan on doin' with him?"

"I wanted him to sign the papers so Thaddeus could come back home." She pulled out a parchment she had folded up in her pocket. "Unfortunately, Bernard passed out cold before I had the chance."

He grabbed the paper, scanning the contents. His eyes narrowed and his jaw stiffened. How in the world did she think this would work? His gaze leveled on her. "Ye need to go home, now." His voice was low, steady, but one wrong word from her and he'd throttle her.

She put her hands on her hips and lifted her chin in defiance. "I refuse to leave without Thaddeus."

"What did ye say?"

Arianna flinched. "I said I'm not leaving."

Keldon's hand snaked out, but she sidestepped and he missed.

"I don't believe I stuttered," she answered as she ran behind the sofa. "I won't leave without Thaddeus."

Keldon lunged to the left and she ran too, keeping her distance from him. When he caught her, she'd be sorry.

"Listen, Keldon." She made her way safely around the sofa once more. "Keldon, please, I must bring Thaddeus home."

She'd gone too far with this charade and he wouldn't let it go on a moment longer.

She ran around the sofa again, but this time he didn't. He jumped over it and tackled her to the floor. He landed on top of her, but she kicked and clawed until he grabbed both her hands and held them above her head. Her nostrils flared as she glared at him.

"Now, ye will listen …" He felt her heart beating against him, felt every luscious curve as his body heated. He wanted to throttle her and kiss her at the same time. He refrained from both. "Ye will go home, now!"

"Please, Keldon," she pleaded, her beautiful blue eyes pooled with tears. "Bernard put Thaddeus in the hole. I don't know what that is, but it can't be good. I can't leave him. I did this to him. Don't you see? I have to correct my mistake."

Keldon stared at her without saying a word, mystified over her ever-changing personality. Her declaration confused him. "Why? Why him? What is it ye want with him?"

"Want with him? Nothing. He has a son. A father should be with his child, don't you agree?"

"Sophie's wee bairn belongs to Thaddeus?" This was the first he'd heard of it.

"Well yes. I thought you knew."

Keldon released her and sat down next to her. Arianna scooted out of his reach.

"Let me understand. Ye want to bring Thaddeus, a slave, back home to be with his wee bairn?"

"Didn't I say as much?" Arianna's chin tilted up. "I know what you're thinking. I've changed. I have. Please let me prove it."

Keldon's anger evaporated. Annabelle didn't want the slaves to have families. She purposely separated them, sold them to whoever gave the highest bid.

"Well? Will you help me?" she interrupted his thoughts.

He stood and offered his hand to her, lifting her easily to her feet. His dark gaze raked over her, looking for any hint of deception.

She didn't shy away.

"Aye, I'll help ye," he finally answered her.

*****

Samuel discovered from the other slaves, the hole was actually that. Bernard had a hole dug in the ground with a door bolted above, shutting out the light. He used this manmade prison for disobedient slaves. Thaddeus had been in the pit for two days now for not keeping his eyes averted, when Mrs. Prescott gave her orders.

Keldon broke the lock and lifted the lid to the prison. Thaddeus stood and shaded his eyes against the flood of light that assailed him.

"Are you all right?" Arianna leaned down to ask.

Thaddeus nodded. Confusion etched his features and Arianna couldn't blame him. She might not have put him in this hole, but her action brought him here.

Keldon lowered the ladder. "Can ye climb, lad?"

Thaddeus' gaze shifted to Keldon. "Yas'm."

"Then be quick about it," he ordered.

Thaddeus hesitated. "Iz dis here a trick?"

Samuel stepped forward. "You be given freedom boy and you are still wonderin' ef you shud take it. Gets yourself up here now, before I decides ter shut de door again."

Immediately Thaddeus obeyed and climbed up the ladder.

Arianna gasped.

Thaddeus turned and looked at her with his one good eye, the other swollen half shut. He licked his parched lips. The way his clothes hung on him, he hadn't had a decent meal in a long time. "What did he do to you?" She lifted her hand to touch his face, but he flinched. She didn't miss the loathing in his gaze before he lowered his lids. She knew she couldn't blame him. She sent him here to be beaten and starved. She sold him as if he was nothing, like his feelings didn't matter. She took him away from the woman he loved, ensuring he'd never know what happened to her or their child. No wonder his gaze betrayed his hatred.

Arianna looked away, but not before Keldon noticed her chin trembled as she inhaled. He almost felt sorry for her, but he pushed those thoughts away. They didn't have time to waste. Thaddeus needed to be off the Prescott's land before Bernard woke up.

"Samuel, I'm relying on ye to bring them back safely to Blue Run."

Samuel nodded understanding the hurry.

Keldon started in the opposite direction, but Arianna grabbed hold of his arm. "Aren't you coming with us?"

"Nay. I must insure Bernard willnae be pressin' charges against ye. If ye forgot, a slave is property and the offense for stealin' one is most severe." He shrugged free and headed for the main house.

*****

On the way back to Blue Run, Thaddeus leaned against the seat, pretending to be asleep. He didn't fool Arianna.

"You have a son," she said softly.

Thaddeus' dark eyes flew open, wary and untrusting. "I has no chile."

"Sophie says differently," Arianna insisted.

Thaddeus leaned back, closing his eyes again. His Adam's apple bobbed up and down as he swallowed hard.

Arianna knew Thaddeus wouldn't ask about Sophie and the baby. He feared she'd do something to them. Pain squeezed at her heart. She'd atone for her sins even if it were the last thing she did.

Once they arrived back at Blue Run, Arianna stepped out of the carriage first and faced Samuel. "Bring Thaddeus to the kitchen, please," Arianna insisted. She wanted to make sure he had his cuts cleaned thoroughly and had a good meal before he returned to his quarters.

Samuel didn't argue.

As soon as they entered the dining room, Oni ran over to Thaddeus and threw her large arms around him squeezing him so tight she nearly knocked the wind out of him.

She released him then and really looked at him. "Lordy, you look a sight, but you's really here."

"Oni, let the man sit down," Arianna said as she went over to see what was cooking in the large black pot. "Will you make sure he's cleaned up and given a hot meal?"

"Yas'm, Miss Arianna. Right away."

Arianna glanced at Thaddeus. He wouldn't meet her gaze. She would have liked to stay, but she knew Thaddeus wouldn't relax if she hovered. She left him alone with Oni, knowing the woman would take good care of him.

"Wut's dis? You called her Miss Arianna?" Thaddeus wearily took a seat as soon as Oni and he were alone.

"Dat's wut we call her now, since Miss Annabelle went back ter de devil."

"Wut are you's talkin' about?"

Oni handed Thaddeus a wet cloth to clean himself. "Now don't be worrin' yourself none." She dished out a large portion of stew and placed it before him.

His mouth watered. He hadn't eaten anything for two days and any meal at the Prescotts' wasn't worth mentioning. Not even the dogs would eat what they served their slaves. Thaddeus stared at the healthy portions of meat and vegetables. He wanted nothing more than to take a large spoonful, but he had to think of Oni. "I kin't eat dis. You will gets in trouble."

"No, it be okay. Miss Arianna insists we eat gud. She's redone de menu, insistin' meats and vegetables be added. I even had me some fruit jest de other day. It near makes my mouth water jest thinkin' about it."

Thaddeus shook his head, still hesitant, but Oni placed her hands on her large hips and waited for him to take a bite. After the first one, he couldn't help himself. He wondered if Sophie... How could he have forgotten to ask about her? "Oni, tells me de truth. Sophie be all right?"

"Lordy. How could I be so slow? Sophie and de chile be fine."

Thaddeus sighed with relief, but quickly frowned again. If Sophie was all right, why wasn't she in the kitchen working? Thaddeus flew to his feet. "Where iz she?" he demanded to know.

"Wut's wrong with you?" Oni frowned at him.

"She ain't workin' with you. So where iz she?"

"Misses Arianna insisted dat she take some time with de baby. She's not ter works for a few weeks."

Thaddeus sat back down with a thud. "Miss Annabelle said dis?"

"No, No. Miss Arianna says. Ain't you been listenin', boy? Miss Annabelle be gone."

This was so unbelievable for Thaddeus. He was sure he must have died in that hole. Slaves having meals fit for their masters, Sophie being able to rest for a couple of weeks to take time with the baby... these things didn't happen.

"I have some clean clothes for you." Arianna had entered and walked over to Thaddeus. "Maeve is sure they'll fit." She placed the folded garments on the table. "You might want to clean up a bit before you see Sophie. Should we draw you a bath?"

Thaddeus' jaw dropped. She'd let him see Sophie. Didn't Miss Annabelle send him away because he'd been with Sophie in the first place? He looked at Oni. Maybe her story had some credibility.

"Miss Arianna," he said the name just to see if she would answer.

"Yes, Thaddeus."

Maybe she was a different person as Oni claimed. "Thank you."

Arianna smiled with a nod. "You're welcome."

*****

When Keldon had made it back to the Prescotts' house, Bernard was still snoring away peacefully. He carefully lifted him back onto the sofa and propped him up. He then took a seat in the chair and patiently waited for the man to wake up.

He didn't wait long. The disoriented Bernard moaned as he rubbed his head. He looked at Keldon and blinked. "Keldon?"

"As I was sayin' we will call it even," Keldon began as though he had been carrying on a conversation with Bernard.

Bernard scratched his head. "You'll have to excuse me, Keldon, I must have dozed off. What were we discussing?"

"The signin' of the papers. Bernard, what is wrong with ye? We agreed ye'd give me Thaddeus."

"Why on earth would I give you a slave?" Bernard sat up.

"Weel have it yer way, then." Keldon stood, his full height towering over Bernard. "I guess ye leave me no choice. Name yer second."

Bernard hands trembled. "Name my second? Are you calling me out? What in the world is going on? What have I done to offend you?"

"Please, doonae insult me further. Ye know what ye've done and I willnae be standin' for it."

Bernard licked his parched lips. "I've obviously insulted you in some way, but as God as my witness, I don't know what it is I've done. When did you arrive?" He frowned as he ticked off the events. "Your wife was here. We had drinks and... and... then the next thing I know, you've called me out. I'd say something doesn't sit well here." He sat up and winced.

Keldon glared at him, hoping to intimidate Bernard without bloodshed involved. He could save Annabelle with an excuse she wasn't well since her head injury, but Thaddeus would be at the Prescotts' mercy. Bernard would take out his rage on the slave. The hole was proof enough. "Weel?"

"Where's the paper you want me to sign?" Bernard chuckled nervously. "If we can call it even, giving up one troublesome slave is fine by me."

CHAPTER FOURTEEN

The sun had set hours ago without Keldon's return from the Prescotts. Arianna wanted to go back for him, but Samuel insisted they wait at Blue Run.

While she abided her time, she thought about her relationship with Keldon or rather the lack of one. She understood why he didn't like her before the accident, but she'd changed. She wanted him to trust her. If only she knew what exactly had gone wrong with their relationship in the first place.

Their marriage had been arranged. Maybe Keldon wasn't attracted to her. As she thought of this, she knew it wasn't the case. His kiss, the way his sexy mouth brushed over hers, sending an explosion of pleasure through her veins. He wanted her as much as she wanted him. Could she have imagined the passion? She'd been a little tipsy at the time and he did run from the room. Not exactly the behavior of a healthy virile man.

Could he be involved with someone else? She couldn't dismiss the thought. She was having an affair. Maybe Keldon was, too. However, every time Keldon left the house, he was with Leighton or Samuel. Maybe he didn't like women at all. "No, it can't be the case, could it?"

Whatever the truth may be, she had to know.

Keldon's emotions rioted inside of him and he couldn't face Arianna tonight. He couldn't face the emotional trap she'd laid out for him. A week ago, he detested her and could care less what happened to her. Now he didn't recognize this compassionate woman who respected him and others.

He'd be lying to himself if he denied there wasn't an attraction between them, but the draw still baffled him. How many times in the past had Annabelle told him she loathed his existence? A bump on the head couldn't change her desires and yet when he kissed her, she responded, clinging to him as if he were her lifeline. By an act of God, she somehow became everything he wanted in a woman and it scared the hell out of him. He didn't want to reopen all the old wounds leaving him vulnerable. If she regained her memory back, he wouldn't survive her rejection this time around.

The divorce papers would arrive soon and he could leave this place and Annabelle's tempting ways. All he had to do is keep the wall he formed around his heart from crumbling away.

He let himself inside the house. Maeve had extinguished the candles for the night. He wouldn't be disturbed. He walked into the study. He needed a drink and just maybe if he drank enough, he would no longer see his wife's beautiful face in his mind. He must remember how she treated him in the past, so not to fall prey to her charms again.

He took the first swallow of the strong potent liquor, welcoming the burn.

Arianna heard the front door open and shut and knew Keldon had arrived home. She jumped out of bed and ventured downstairs determined to confront him. He'd come clean tonight and tell her if they could salvage their relationship.

The house was drenched in darkness, but she knew Keldon hadn't gone to bed. She knew she'd find him in his study. She walked in. The moonlight streamed through the open window allowing some light. He lounged on the high back chair, his long legs stretched out before him. He nursed a dram of whiskey, but he held the decanter in his other hand.

She sensed he stared at her with those intensely cat-like green eyes of his, but his face remained in the shadows and she couldn't read his expression.

"We need to talk," she announced before she lost her courage.

"Talk?" he replied, his laugh raking her. "That is a new one. I doonae think we ever talked." He lifted his glass to his lips.

Arianna sighed. He wouldn't make this easy, but she refused to give up.

"Well, I would like to now."

"And what is it ye would like to talk aboot?" He twirled the liquid in his glass before downing it.

"Us." Arianna waited for him to laugh at her again, but silence met her ears. She wasn't sure if this was a good sign or not. She couldn't stop now. They must hash out whatever was wrong with their marriage and find out if they could have a future. "So, are you…you know… Do you like… Oh, I'll just say it. Are you gay?"

"Gay? Ye want to know if I'm happy."

She heard the confusion in his voice, making her wonder if she used another foreign word. It wasn't bad enough she'd lost her memory, but she'd also lost the means of communication.

"Do you prefer men to women?" she clarified.

This time Keldon did laugh. "Is that what ye think?" He found her observation of him comical, since she couldn't have been farther from the truth. "Let me assure ye, the feel of a warm and willin' woman is what I most prefer." He heard her take a breath. He wondered if she sighed in relief or disappointment. Could he dare think she might finally want to be with him?

He mentally reprimanded himself. Annabelle made her feelings known to him a long time ago. However, curiosity had him wondering where this conversation was heading. Since her accident, she baffled him with her caring motives and now she questioned his sexual preferences. He had married a woman who despised him. She'd been predictable with her vicious acts and lashing tongue. He knew what to expect from her and could react accordingly, but now he wasn't so sure.

"I thought," she continued, "since we didn't share the same bedroom... Well, I... You said we had a marriage of convenience. I thought..."

"Ye thought I was interested in men," he finished.

They were silent for a long moment before Arianna took a few steps closer.

Keldon's breath caught in his throat. From where she stood, the light from the moon shone through the thin material of her nightdress. He could make out every contour of her body, every lush curve, every place he would like to put his hands on. If this were her way to test his manhood, she would soon find out how attracted he was to a woman.

He swore beneath his breath, annoyed how his body betrayed him. He must rebuild the wall and keep her out. He had to remember the conniving, cold and bitter woman who destroyed everything in her wake.

He squeezed his eyes shut. God help him.

"Did we ever..."

She kept stumbling over the words and he could imagine the blush deepening the color of her face.

"Did we ever sleep together?"

He cleared his throat and sat up a little straighter. Maybe she really didn't remember how it was between them. "Annabelle..."

"Arianna," she said with exasperation.

He couldn't understand why she kept insisting she wasn't Annabelle. How much simpler this would all be if she wasn't. "Arianna," he said, patronizing her. "What we had before... Weel, it was nothin' passionate."

"We never loved each other," she stated not asked.

He thought he detected disappointment in her voice, but he wasn't sure. If he could see her face, judge her expression... He shook his head. He could light a candle but the shadows were easier to hide from the truth.

"Keldon?"

"Ye never loved anyone, except yerself."

"Do you always have to hurt me?" Her voice quivered, but he chose to ignore it as he mocked her.

"Do ye want me to speak the truth or no'?"

"I guess, I do."

She fell silent again and he wondered for the hundredth time what she wanted. She seemed determined to tell him.

"Keldon, I don't want to live like this. I don't want to be at odds with you." She moved closer still and now he could see her lovely face. Her blue eyes brimmed with tears. "Is it possible we could start over? Is it too late?" she implored, her lower lip trembling.

Start over? Did he hear her correctly? Years ago, he would have welcomed the chance, but now there were too many hurts and too many betrayals. No matter how much he wanted her, he wouldn't allow himself to believe she offered a fresh start. "It's too late for that. Ye made these arrangements. I offered my heart to ye in the palm of my hand. Ye took it and squashed it like a wee bug, without compassion, without remorse. As far as I'm concerned, I like our arrangement just the way it is." There he had said the hateful words, but in his heart he wanted to draw her near, hold her and tell her he wanted nothing more than to love her. He bit the inside of his cheek to stop those words from escaping his lips.

Arianna heard the bitterness spill over into his voice and knew in her past she'd hurt him deeply. His animosity left her weak and vulnerable. She shouldn't be surprised that she destroyed their relationship. Now everything made sense. The way he'd distanced himself from her. The reason he had his own room. He only tolerated her. He didn't love her and it was her fault.

Her voice caught, as she tried to apologize. "I'm so sorry. I'm so, so sorry." Then she turned and quietly walked out of the room.

The unbearable silence that followed her retreat weighed heavy on Keldon's shoulders and he didn't understand why. He'd clawed his way through his wife's thick skin and finally hurt her. So why wasn't a silken cocoon of euphoria wrapped around him instead of this self-doubt and bitterness?

He poured himself another dram. He was about to quench his insatiable thirst, when he heard the front door open and close. Who left? He strode to the window to investigate.

His wife's glorious pale hair stood out like a moonbeam in the surrounding darkness.

"Where in the devil does she think she's goin' and her no' even dressed? Does the woman have no sense to even put on decent clothes before she leaves the house?" As he tried to speculate where she might head, his imagination went wild. She was meeting someone. Anger singed the corners of his control and he slammed down his glass.

He bolted out of the study and swung open the front door. Hurrying, he made his way to the stables. He peeked inside careful not to make a sound.

She hastened to saddle her mount and he knew he'd been right. He clenched his fists. She was meeting someone and he'd soon find out with whom. He hid in the shadows as she made her departure. He gave her only seconds before he mounted his horse, not bothering with a saddle for fear he would lose her.

He followed at a safe distance. Then he realized she rode in circles never going far from the house.

She finally halted her horse at the gardens and dismounted. Keldon did the same and crept close enough so he could see what she was doing.

He waited. Any moment the man she was meeting would appear. He balled his hands into a fist. "I'll kill him." He pushed the reasons why he cared to the back of his mind. He wasn't jealous. He was… It didn't matter. He would not tolerate her carrying on an affair under his very nose. No husband would.

But ye said ye dinnae want her.

Damn his conscious for pointing out the obvious.

After ten agonizing minutes, he realized she wasn't meeting anyone. He felt foolish lurking in the shadows like a spy.

Arianna sat down on the ground with her knees curled up to her chest. He was baffled over her odd behavior. Why was she out here, if she wasn't going to meet someone?

She answered his question in her next breath. She knelt and raised her hands skyward. "Dear Lord, help me." Her voice choked with a sob. "I'm so lost. I'm afraid, I'm afraid..." She kept her hands outstretched, waiting for what seemed to be an answer to her prayer. When none came, she lowered her hands and her shoulders slumped in defeat.

Her cry for help pulled at Keldon's conscience, making him feel ashamed. He had been relentless with his cruelty. He had convinced himself she deserved what he gave her. He'd paid her back for all the heartache she'd caused him. Now he felt mortified over the callous words he had thrown at her.

He shook his head. He couldn't take the words back and he knew he couldn't go to her and tell her he was wrong. It was better to leave matters the way they were.

He intruded on her privacy long enough and turned to leave. Preoccupied with his thoughts, he wasn't watching where he stepped. The snap of the twig sent a deafening echo into the once silent night.

Arianna was on her feet at once with a quick intake of breath. "Who's there?"

He could hear the shiver of panic in her voice. As much as he didn't want to reveal himself, he knew he had no other choice.

"It is only I, Annabelle." Keldon moved into view.

Immediately a flood of relief crossed her face before the questioning quirk of her eyebrows rose high on her brow. "Did you follow me?"

"Aye."

"Why?"

He didn't want to tell her for fear she'd think him a jealous fool. He repeated the thought. Was he jealous? If this were true, wouldn't it mean he still cared for her? He cleared his throat and tried to shrug off the disturbing notion. "I wanted to make sure ye were all right. Now that I have seen that ye are, I'll leave ye to yer solitude." Anxious to be as far away from her as possible, he turned away.

Arianna stood there for only seconds before her brain registered what he had said to her. He had been worried about her, worried enough that he came after her. Surely this meant he still cared. "Please, wait!" She ran after him.

Keldon froze.

Half in anticipation, half-in dread, Arianna watched a he slowly turned around to face her. They stood staring at each other while silence loomed between them. A breeze blew a strand of her hair across her face. She went to brush it away, but Keldon reached out and gently twirled the silky softness around his fingers. She stood still, barely taking a breath for fear he would pull away. It was such a gentle touch. The most intimate caress she'd received from this man, who was supposed to be her husband.

Her gaze snared with his and her pulse flickered and leaped at the way his eyes blazed with unspoken desire, but then he lowered his lids. His hand slipped away, but she couldn't let him walk away. Her hand snaked out in a desperate plea. He didn't struggle to pull free, but looked at her once more. She lowered her lips to his palm, kissing his flesh with sweet tenderness. "I'm so sorry for all the pain I have ever caused you. Please forgive me," she implored him, tears sliding down her cheeks. "I promise you to my dying day, I'll never hurt you, again."

She saw the flash of indecision on his face. She couldn't blame him for his mistrust. He told her she'd thrown their love away. She couldn't remember doing it. She couldn't remember her life before the bump on her head and maybe it was a blessing in disguise. She was able to see him clearly now without the prejudices, which must have forged her decision to cast him aside. She cared and respected this man. It didn't matter he was a pirate. She didn't believe the rumors about the Scotsman. There was more to the story and she would find the underlying cause of him venturing out to sea.

What she couldn't ignore was her heart. She was in love with him. She knew they belonged together and he was here before her. Not all could be lost.

She took a step closer, until she rested her head against the corded muscles of his chest. She breathed in the spicy masculine scent of him as she wrapped her arms around him, praying he wouldn't push her away.

Keldon could barely breathe. Such pleading, such heartfelt sincerity he had seen in her luminous blue eyes.

Keldon wanted to believe her, but he couldn't brush aside years of hurt with a few idle promises.

He squeezed his eyes shut, hoping to rid himself of his desire for her, but it was of no use. He could feel the swooping pull at his innards, his heart's erratic pounding.

He *wanted* her.

He *needed* her.

His arms encircled around her, feeling her body melt against his. He could smell the flowery scent of her hair and the softness of her warm body. She lifted her head to look into his eyes and her rosy full lips parted in invitation. He told himself he would only kiss her once, and it would end his tormented desire.

Fool. He had already gone down this road before and it had cost him dearly and yet he didn't heed his own warning as passion overrode caution. His mouth all but consumed hers in a rush of frantic kisses. His hands locked against her spine, molding her to the contours of his body. She trembled and clung to him. He was like a man who'd gone without water too long. He needed more of her. He parted her lips, touching his tongue to hers, losing himself in the silky warmth of her mouth while waves of pleasure poured through him quenching his thirst.

His heart pounded against his chest, a beat strong, thick and unrelenting. His breath caught as desire so intense it felt like pain engulfed him. He dragged his mouth from hers, inhaling deeply. He gazed into her eyes recognizing the passion mirrored there. Fresh urgency plowed through him, forcing him to take this moment for all it was worth—before the binding thread of yearning disappeared. They needed to go back to the house... Now. It nearly killed him to break their embrace.

"Don't go," she said, not hiding the desperation in her plea.

In one forward motion, he drew her to him, showering her with reassuring kisses. "I was only goin' to retrieve the horses." His deep voice was raw with emotion.

"No."

He cupped her face and looked down at her. "I thought—"

"Here, in the open with all of nature around us, just you and me, no past to harbor our intentions."

He gave her a quick nod, knowing exactly how she felt. They wove a spell around them and to go back to the house threatened the enchantment. He stepped away from her, only to remove his coat and lay it on the ground.

She sat down on her knees and looked up at him. With her outstretched hand, she beckoned him to join her. He took her invitation and knelt down in front of her. This was all so new to him and he was afraid to proceed. Never had Annabelle displayed any interest in him touching her. From the beginning, she cringed at the thought of their coupling.

Her brow furrowed and she licked her lips nervously. She truly didn't understand his hesitation, the look of uncertainty, he was sure, lurked in his gaze. She rested her hand on his arm—a gentle touch—an invitation that sent the blood surging down to his groin. He looked into her eyes, recognizing the same smoldering desire.

"Touch me Keldon." She moved closer, running her hands over his broad chest before she unbuttoned her nightgown and slipped it over her head.

He drank in her beauty as his hands traced a path over her skin, exploring her waist, her hips. A shiver of anticipation ran down his spine.

"I want you," she told him, her voice thick with emotion.

He never dreamed he'd hear her say those words. He wanted to take things slow, savor every moment, but he feared the heat between his legs threatened to take over.

Trembling, he touched her breast, his fingers massaging until her nipple puckered. He lowered his mouth, tasting her sweet scented flesh.

She slid her fingers through his hair, urging him to continue.

He moved to her other breast and gave it equal consideration, his wet mouth closing over the peak. He lowered her to the ground. He cradled her in his right arm, while he gently ran his other hand down the length of her slim body. He lingered on the soft curls that kept her womanhood from view. He parted her legs, but she put her hand on his to stop him. He looked at her and saw tears pooling in her eyes. He didn't understand what he'd done. "Do ye want me to stop?" He held his breath, fearing her response.

She shook her head and inhaled deeply trying to compose herself. "No... No, I... I'm scared." Her gaze touched his. "I'm afraid, I'll disappoint you. I don't remember how we were together."

Keldon swallowed the lump in his throat and caressed her cheek. "Ye need no' worry," he assured her. Then he convinced her with his burning kisses. Soon he felt her fears ebb away as she relaxed, leaving only craving hunger. "Let me love ye." His fingers feathered down her stomach, waiting for her to give him permission.

She nodded against his chest, this time letting him touch the tender flesh. He held her as his fingertips drove her to new heights of passion. He could feel her heart pounding as she clutched his arm, her body readying to receive him.

She reached up and her lips flickered over his, encouraging him. He removed his garments and took her in his arms again, flesh to flesh. He breathed warm soothing kisses down her neck. "Ye are all I have ever wanted." He lifted his head to look at her. "I have waited so long to be with ye in this way." Her brow furrowed with confusion and he knew she didn't remember how they had been together. How she recoiled from his touch. He prayed she never would again. "Doonae fret, we are startin' over this night." He kissed every inch of her, biding his time until he could fill her completely.

Arianna didn't know how much longer she could wait to make their union complete. Everywhere he touched her felt like an electrical current racing through her skin. His tongue tantalized her until she thought she'd die from his caress. She needed him to satisfy the hunger growing deep inside her. She slid the palms of her hands up the side of his chest, as she rubbed her hips suggestively against him. "Please," was all she was capable of saying, but Keldon knew what she wanted; he wanted it as much as she did. He lifted her hips and she clasped her legs around his waist as he plunged into her depths. A bolt of fire lanced through her, but his mouth covered hers, drowning out her gasp. As quickly as the sharp pain had hit her, it was gone. She relaxed surrendering completely, eagerly meeting each of his intimate embraces. His emotions ran free, as her passion equaled his own. He took all she had to give and silently demanded she give more. Struggling for breath, a slow throb pulsed through her body.

"Arianna!" Keldon cried out as the tremors moved along his manhood in tiny convulsive jerks. She held on tight to him as her body followed suit.

She pressed a kiss at the pulse of his neck and he pulled her toward him so she lay tucked against his side. She shifted in his arms and looked up at him seeing the future so clearly. She was truly his. "Keldon, do you realize you called me Arianna."

"Aye." The tenderness in his gaze shattered them both. He leaned over and crushed his mouth to hers. She felt him harden against her and she nudged her hips forward.

This time they took their time to explore, to arouse and give each other pleasure.

Later, they watched the sunrise over the horizon as a new day was born. For the first time, Arianna felt she actually belonged.

CHAPTER FIFTEEN

Keldon led Arianna's horse by the reins so she could ride with him. They both craved the closeness they'd shared last night.

When they reached the stables, Keldon dismounted first to help Arianna down. He held onto her longer than deemed necessary, but she didn't seem to mind the intimacy. He traced her face with his finger, memorizing every detail of her features. Then he leaned down and kissed her.

He'd been married to her for five years and yet last night he felt like it was the first time. As he deepened the caress, he remembered the way he made love to her, the way she responded to his every touch. She had given herself to him without reserve and he hoped she would let what was simmering between them grow into something more. Just thinking about how she felt in his arms made the stirrings of want begin again. However, he had pressing business he needed to take care of today. He affectionately kissed the tip of Arianna's nose before he let her go.

He pulled his coat closer around her. "Ye head up to the house and get yerself dressed. I'll be there soon to join ye for breakfast."

She gave him a tentative smile and nodded.

At the door, Arianna turned and looked at the man she'd fallen in love with and maybe it was for the very first time. He sensed her lingering and he turned his head, giving her a lopsided grin. She smiled and blew him a kiss before heading out to face the day.

Arianna passed a scowling Leighton on her way up to the house. "Good morning, Leighton," she greeted cheerfully. She didn't wait for his reply but kept going. She could feel his heated gaze following her, but she didn't care. Nothing could ruin her day when her heart was full of joy.

Leighton's brow creased as he walked over to the stables. He could hear Keldon whistling that damn tune of his. "There'd be too much happiness aboot this mornin'," Leighton grumbled. When he entered the stable, Keldon turned to greet him before he continued his whistling.

"I passed by Annabelle on my way here. She was up and aboot in her nightclothes." Leighton waited for Keldon to explain the rest.

"Aye," was his only reply. He then continued his whistling, as he rubbed down the horses.

"Ye seen her then?" Leighton frown deepened.

Keldon stopped whistling just long enough to answer. "Aye."

Leighton cleared his throat with harrumphed. "Will ye stop that infernal racket?"

Keldon looked up. "What the devil is the matter with ye?"

"With me? I was wonderin' where ye've been, but now I ken verra weel. Ye've been cavortin' with that woman." Leighton pointed behind him.

Keldon stopped what he was doing and walked over to Leighton. "That woman as ye have referred to, happens to be my wife."

"Defendin' her now. Are ye? Has the woman bewitched ye?"

"I believe it's none of yer business." He purposely turned his back on him and continued with his task.

"Weel ye answered the question sure enough." Leighton moved beside him with determination. He wouldn't be put off. "Annabelle isnae good. Ye ken this as much as I do."

"Arianna has changed," Keldon snapped back.

"Arianna, is it now. Ye best stop thinkin' with, yer lower extremities and think with yer head. She be a verra bonny lass, but she has nay heart. How quickly ye be forgettin' this, when she offers ye her favors."

"That's enough." Keldon's eyes blazed with anger. "You doonae understand."

"Aye. That be true enough, but I do know that I love ye like a son. I say these things to protect ye. She doesnae care for anyone, but herself."

"I thank ye for you concern, but I ken verra weel what I'm doin'. Is there anythin' else you'd be wishin' to speak to me aboot?"

Leighton still fumed, but he was wise enough to bite his tongue on the matter. "Vincent Aubrey will be by this mornin'?"

"I'm aware," Keldon answered stiffly.

"He may have some information aboot Nicholas Sherborn's story. If his information proves to be true, we set sail within the week. I'll head back to the house."

"Ye do that."

After Leighton left, Keldon went back to the horses, still miffed over the confrontation. Leighton had a valid point, but the man hadn't witnessed what he had. Annabelle had changed. Last night, he had seen her soul mirrored in her eyes. She was *Arianna* with a kind and compassionate heart. Maeve told him she was different from the start and now, he believed it, too. He loved the new woman she'd become. "Arianna." The name rolled off his tongue and he smiled.

*****

Vincent Aubrey arrived early and waited in the foyer until Arianna came downstairs to greet him. She assured him Keldon would be in shortly and invited him in for breakfast. How could he refuse a beautiful woman's invitation? She wore a cream colored dress with burgundy roses and her hair wrapped in a braided twist—simple, but fetching.

"So how do you know my husband?"

"Aah I'm forever in your husband's debt of course."

Her gaze swept over him with what appeared to be skepticism. "Of course. Do you care to tell me why you are in my husband's debt?"

He chuckled as he pulled out the chair for her at the table. The delicious aromas of bacon, eggs, fresh bread and coffee hit his nostrils. "I suppose I should explain." Though he wouldn't tell her everything. "Your husband saved me and my crew from certain death. For this I do owe him my life."

Arianna passed the plate of scrambled eggs to him. He felt enchanted by Keldon's wife. She was possibly the most beautiful woman he'd ever seen. He hadn't met her until last week and he was pleasantly surprised. He had heard horror stories about her from Leighton and he'd been convinced she sported horns from her head. The exaggeration on Leighton's part spoke of the man's unfounded prejudices. Vincent's lips curved into a grin as Arianna spoke of her husband with fondness. Her blue eyes shone with admiration at the mere mention of his name. Keldon was a lucky man. His wife loved him without reservation. This much he was certain.

"What brings you out to see us so early this morning?" Arianna asked as she handed him a plate of freshly baked bread.

"Just business of the most tedious type. I'm afraid I would bore you with the details of it."

Arianna highly doubted it. Pirating could be anything but boring. She had a hunch Vincent wanted to discuss Nicholas' information about the Spanish frigate. She needed the information, too. Only she didn't have the foggiest notion how she was going to get it.

"I enjoyed the music you entertained us with the other night. The... what was it called? Ah yes, *Great Balls of Fire.*" There was a twinkle of amusement in his amber colored eyes, making Arianna giggle.

"The music was a little unconventional, but I just couldn't resist."

"Well, I rather enjoyed it. My sister, Chantal used to play for hours at a time. I really hate to admit it, but her music could be such a bore at times. It was quite refreshing to hear something lively. Did you write the piece yourself?"

Arianna smiled. "No, though I don't remember who did."

The conversation had little chance to progress before Keldon appeared. Arianna noticed he'd brushed his hair and changed his clothes. His gaze touched her, making her heart race at the memory of last night, the physical awareness of the way he had held her, touched her.

They were lost to each other for the moment, until Arianna heard Vincent clear his throat. She glanced at Vincent's *know-all* expression and felt the heat burn her cheeks. Had Keldon and she been so obvious?

"Good morning, Keldon, my friend." Vincent turned his attention on her husband. "You have decided to join us, no? Your wife has been a most gracious host."

Keldon lifted one dark eyebrow. "Has she now." He pulled out his chair and took a seat.

I thought we could discuss a few things after breakfast," Vincent added.

"Do ye bring good tidings, Aubrey?"

"That I do good friend. That I do."

Arianna suddenly lost her appetite. The good news could only mean one thing. They would set sail to do their unsavory deeds of larceny.

*****

After breakfast, Keldon and Vincent Aubrey took the boat into Charleston. Arianna grew tired of waiting for their return and headed down the beaten path to visit Sophie. She could hear the baby's wails as she approached.

Arianna poked her head inside the cabin. "Hello," she raised her voice to be heard over the wailing child.

Sophie turned to look at her and relief spread across her face. "Miss Arianna. I don't know whut ter do with him. He cries all day." Sophie looked exhausted. Her hair was standing on end and her eyes were puffy and blood shot. She didn't look like she had slept for days.

"Why don't you let me take him for a while," Arianna offered.

Sophie stopped pacing and stared at her.

"I promise, I will be careful with him," Arianna coaxed, believing Sophie thought she couldn't handle the infant.

"Sorry, Miss Arianna. I don't mean ter gawk, but you want ter hold my little Elijah?"

Arianna didn't understand why Sophie found this odd. "Of course I want to hold the baby." Then she added, "as long as you don't mind."

"No, I don't mind." Sophie walked over to her and handed her Elijah.

"Now, don't you worry about anything," Arianna assured her. "You go and lie down. I'll take care of the little one for you."

Arianna held the crying baby cradled against her, while she paced back and forth across the small cabin floor. "It's all right, Elijah. Don't cry," she cooed. Then she started to hum a sweet lullaby. The melody was soothing and peaceful and finally the baby's wails turned to whimpers before ceasing altogether. He stared up at her with his big brown eyes. She gently wiped away his tears with her thumb and kissed his forehead. "Would you like to hear another song?"

The baby cooed, making her smile.

Sophie had been asleep for a while and Elijah finally drifted to sleep, too. Arianna sat down in the only chair that was in the room. Reluctant to put Elijah down and have him awake again, she decided to hold him for a while longer.

*****

Keldon watched Arianna from the doorway, completely mesmerized by his sleeping wife. She looked at ease cuddling the infant close to her chest. Against his will, old memories came back to haunt him, making him remember the child they'd lost.

Arianna stirred, her eyes fluttering open. "You're back."

"Aye. How's the wee lad?"

"Growing. He's so beautiful, Keldon," Arianna said as she gently caressed the sleeping child. She looked up and met his gaze, her eyebrows furrowing as if something bothered her. "Do you want children, Keldon?"

He swallowed hard. She didn't remember. "Aye. Verra much so." He held his breath waiting for her to say something to the contrary. The old Annabelle had made it very clear she never wanted to have a child, but this new woman she'd become, he didn't know what she would say.

Arianna's lips curved. "I think we better try a little harder then."

"Are ye up to tryin' tonight?" He hurriedly asked, not wanting to give her a chance to change her mind.

"On one condition."

He nodded for her to continue.

"That we share one room from now on."

Keldon thought he would never hear those words. He cleared his throat. "A simple enough request. Will I be movin' into your room or will ye be joinin' me?"

"I'll join you."

CHAPTER SIXTEEN

Arianna closed the door to her room. Happy to know she didn't have to sleep in there anymore. She still had a problem with Nicholas Sherborn. She never knew when he'd show up for a visit. She had to end the affair, but she didn't know how. Since Keldon wasn't ready to confide in her, she needed Nicholas for information.

She walked across the hall to Keldon's room—their room now. Her gaze landed on the bed and her heart thudded in her chest. Keldon would lie down next to her and... She chewed on her lower lip as she worried. She glanced around Keldon's room with its bold colors and stark furnishings. Her belongings mingled in among his but she felt like an intruder. She hugged herself. "I'm being ridiculous. We've been married for five years." Still her nerves were on edge. She couldn't help it. She didn't remember any of those years. As far as she was concerned, last night had been their first time together and she feared the magic wouldn't be there.

Maeve walked in carrying her vanity tray. "Lets me brush your hair so it's all shiny."

Arianna knew it would be useless to argue with the woman. For no matter how much she assured Maeve she could do things for herself, the woman seemed determined to ignore her.

Arianna sat down on the chair that stood beside the bed, letting Maeve begin her task. "You have beautiful hair."

Arianna wasn't really listening. Her thoughts turned toward her dilemma. She needed a concrete plan to stop Keldon from his life of piracy before Nicholas Sherborn had him killed. Unfortunately, she hadn't a clue what she was going to do. She didn't even know where he hid his ship, but she had a sneaky suspicion Maeve might. She seemed to know the comings and goings of everyone and their business. She glanced over her shoulder. "Maeve, where does Keldon dock his ship?"

Maeve paused for only a second before she continued brushing Arianna's long hair again. "Ship? I don't know whut you be takin' about."

Maeve's slight hesitation proved suspicious. Arianna turned in her seat, looking into the woman's soft brown eyes. "You know what he's been doing? You know he's a pirate."

"I know no such thing," she insisted. "Where'd you get a fool notion like dat?"

Arianna ignored her denial. "He can't keep going on this track. It's dangerous. If he's caught, they'll hang him. I can't have that happen. Not now when we have a chance for a future. I love him, Maeve."

Maeve squeezed her hand. "I know you do."

"Then you have to help me."

Maeve was well aware of the danger. After all, she was no fool. She also knew that Keldon had only begun this hazardous business of the sea because Annabelle had been so terrible he couldn't stand living with her. Perhaps by God's will the forces brought Arianna here to save him. "Whut's do you plan on doin'?"

"Stow away. I have to try to make him change his ways before it's too late."

Maeve's eyebrows shot up. "Whut's stowin' away goin' ter do? It will gets you kilt, is whut," she answered her own question.

"I'll be perfectly safe. Once I make my presence known, Keldon will be there to protect me."

"You's crazy. Mista Keldon more than likely will be so furious with you, he'll want ter throws you overboard."

"I'll take my chances. We're talking about Keldon's life. I know he won't willingly tell me about his transgressions, but if I see what he does, he'll have no other choice than to confide in me. Then I can tell him about—" Arianna paused, clamping her mouth shut, but that only proved to Maeve she was hiding something.

"Whut gots you all torn up inside?"

"Oh Maeve. There is something I've done and I am so terribly ashamed of it."

"Kins it be fixed?"

"I hope so." She looked at Maeve's kind and understanding face. She knew she could trust her. "I was having an affair," she blurted out, still not believing it herself. "I swear, I don't remember and I most definitely have no intentions of continuing it."

"Honey chile, Miss Annabelle wuz havin' an affair not you."

"Please, Maeve. I must accept my past deeds and find a way to make up for them." She knew Maeve wanted to say more, but the woman pursed her lips together.

"This man wants to do Keldon harm," Arianna said hoping this would sway Maeve.

"You gots ter tell Keldon, then."

"I want to, but I'm afraid Keldon won't believe me. I'm afraid he'll only see my deceit and hate me forever this time. Don't you see? I have to build his trust in me first. Then I'll tell him."

Maeve shook her head. "I don't know."

"This man won't do anything on this venture," Arianna rushed to tell her. "He told me he wanted Keldon to trust him so he could lead him into the trap without him suspecting anything." Arianna hesitated when she realized how upset Maeve had become. She had a hunch it wasn't only for Keldon's safety. She worried about someone else. Then it dawned on her who Maeve feared for and Arianna used the fact to her advantage. "Samuel is in danger, too. He'll hang along with the rest of them." Arianna then remained silent chewing on her lower lip, while she waited for Maeve to make her decision.

Finally, she nodded. "I will see whut I kin do."

The knock on the door made both of them jump. Maeve recovered first. "It be Mista Keldon and I'm not finish with your hair."

"That's all right." Arianna took the brush from Maeve's hand.

*****

Keldon had paced downstairs, for what seemed like hours. He promised to remain there until Maeve told him Arianna was ready, but the wait became insufferable. He felt like a new groom, waiting for his blushing bride to be prepared. He hadn't been this nervous on their wedding night.

He was anxious to be with his wife. *His wife.* How wonderful those two words sounded to him. He entered the room. "I'm sorry to rush ye, but—" His eyes took in Arianna's radiant beauty, blushed cheeks and timid smile. His mouth suddenly felt dry and he forgot what he was going to say.

Maeve walked over to him. "You be right on time. Come in." Maeve made her exit, shutting the door behind her.

Arianna stood and waited.

Keldon could hear his own heart beating against his chest. He never remembered Annabelle... Arianna...being so beautiful. How strange. He now thought of his wife as Arianna. He approached her and slid his fingers through her long hair. The strands shimmered like moonbeams. "So soft," he whispered. He pulled her close and captured her lips to his. He felt her tremble in his arms and he leaned back to search her face. "Ye're quiverin'."

She swallowed. "I can't help it."

He took a deep breath against the panic welling inside him. He had been worried that she would change her mind. Afraid she would think they'd made a mistake. He closed his eyes trying to will the disappointment from his mind. "Do ye want me to stop?"

"No, don't!" Desperation rang in her words and his eyes snapped open. "No," she repeated again in ragged whisper. "Don't ever let me go."

Keldon's heart pounded against his ribcage. She wanted him, as much as he wanted her. He lifted her easily into his arms and brought her to their bed.

She looked up at him with trusting eyes.

"Ye are so beautiful." His hand moved over the thin fabric of her nightdress, lingering on the swell of her chest. He sensed she was nervous. He was, too. "Do ye want me to snuff out the candle?"

"Do you want to?"

He shook his head. "Nay, I want to see all of ye. It has been such a long time since ye have been in my bed."

Arianna took a deep breath. "Leave the light on then." He leaned down to kiss her, but her words halted him. "Will it hurt this time?"

His eyebrows drew together. "Did I hurt ye last night?"

"No. Well, a little the first time." She blushed from head to toe, a becoming crimson color. "But I was talking about you."

"Me?"

"There was a little blood on your jacket and I thought maybe I did something to hurt you."

Keldon wasn't sure what to make of what she told him. There shouldn't have been blood. She wasn't a virgin and yet he recalled how tight she had felt when he had entered her. For a moment, he let himself think about what Maeve had suggested, that Annabelle was no longer here, that this woman, who was before him was someone else. God, he could almost believe it.

"Keldon?" She sounded worried.

He shook his head to clear his thoughts. Obviously, he had too much wine before he came up here to be thinking such fanciful notions. "Nay lass, ye dinnae hurt me."

"Good." She sighed with relief, but still she chewed on her lower lip.

He took her hand and placed her palm against him. "Do ye feel it?" he asked. "It is my heart ready to leap from my chest." He then brought her hand to his mouth with a kiss. "Doonae be afraid."

Naked passion warmed her gaze. "I trust you." She curled her fingers around his shirt, pulling him closer. She kissed the base of his neck, her lips feeling cool against the warmth of his flesh. "I love the way you smell," she murmured.

"And how is that?"

She inhaled. "Salt air, pipe tobacco and…"

"And?"

"Don't laugh."

He touched her chin tilting her head back. "I willnae laugh."

"It's a unique scent that is only you, all male."

He cradled her head and with one smooth movement covered her mouth with his own.

She helped him remove his shirt. He trembled as she worked her way from his neck to his abdomen then down to the waistband of his trousers. He burned with desire from her sweet touches. He ran his hand down her back, gathering the thin material she wore, freeing her of its confines. Completely bare to his eyes, he eased her down to the softness of the large bed. He drank up her beauty, memorizing each curve of her body with the touch of his hand. He then leaned down to kiss her rosy lips, letting his tongue touch hers, intertwining and mating as one. Her hand trailed down to cup him, kneading his hard member. His gut clenched tight and his willpower dwindled fast. He didn't want it to end this way. He put his hand over hers to halt her caresses.

She looked at him her brow creased with worry. "Don't you want me to touch you?"

"Aye, so much so I fear I'll no' please ye first."

"What do you mean?"

She really didn't know. "Ah my innocent lass." She sighed as his lips feathered over hers. "Let me take care of ye tonight and then later, ye may have yer way with me." He leaned down to kiss her again, but she placed a hand on his chest.

"You promise?"

He chuckled. "Aye, ye have my word."

She nodded letting her hand fall away.

He made love to her with his tender caresses, bringing her close to rapture only to slow his pace, his palms burning a path down her, as his mouth took the full flower of her breasts. His hand slid between her legs, his fingers gently stroking, caressing fanning the flames of desire. He left her only to remove the rest of his clothing. She welcomed him back into her embrace, their bodies coming together with reverence of love. Holding tighter, he took her past desire with his steady thrusts to the trembling world where passion touched their souls.

CHAPTER SEVENTEEN

Anticipation thickened the air around her as Arianna counted the minutes before Keldon would take her in his arms, again. He stirred a deep sexual hunger within her until she thought she'd go mad with want for his touch. For the life of her, she couldn't understand why she made her bed in the room across the hall, or why she started an affair with Nicholas Sherborn. "Sherborn." The blood drained from her face as she remembered he could ruin everything. He was a danger to Keldon and to her, especially if he realized she didn't return his affections. She couldn't let Nicholas catch on that she'd changed her mind about their relationship, at least not until she secured Keldon's safety.

She frowned. Keldon continued his life of piracy, but she supposed she shouldn't have thought otherwise. He wouldn't stop simply because they slept together.

Blast it, anyway! They were trying to have a baby. She wanted their child to grow up with a mother and a father. Keldon was too self-assured, thinking he could out sail every ship after he plundered their goods. No one could run forever and when they caught Keldon, they'd hang him for his arrogance.

She bit her tongue whenever he said he had a meeting to attend. She wanted to yell at him and tell him how stupid he was to risk everything for a few coins. The plantation was lucrative. Keldon told her she had inherited land and money from her father. They didn't need the money and even if they did she wouldn't have cared; she wanted him. She didn't know she could love someone so completely. His mere touch worked magic. Passion would consume her until she was lost in his world. There, it didn't matter what he did for a living, but reality did. He had to stop and soon, or they'd lose everything.

Their time together in matrimonial bliss became limited. Keldon had late night meetings and trips into town. Men, she didn't recognize visited Blue Run all times of the night. In a matter of days, Keldon would set sail. Once on the open sea, she didn't know what the future would hold for them. So much could go wrong, but she dare not dwell on those possibilities. She had to hope she could gain Keldon's trust, and finally, shed all secrets.

This is why she'd set up this plan. She hurried down the stone path to wait in the garden as Maeve had instructed her to do. Samuel would meet her there with his decision.

She paced with worry and wrung her hands. Then she spotted him walking toward her, but his worn, dark face revealed nothing. His dark gaze bore into hers, assessing her of her worth. He looked away then. "You must meet me on de 'morrow, de moment dat Mist' Keldon leaves de house. You do jest as I says and I'll be gettin' you on de ship."

Arianna released the breath she had been holding. "Thank you, Samuel for helping me. You won't regret it."

"You make sure dat I don't. Ef any harm comes ter Mista Keldon 'cause of treachery, you will wish you wuz never born."

"I am doing this to protect him," she defended herself. She met Samuel's gaze head on daring him to find any sign of deceit.

"You love him?" He scratched his head and his eyes widened in amazement.

"Of course, I do. I only want the best for him."

"Maeve mentioned dere be traitors among us."

She nodded. She couldn't tell Samuel who he was. He wouldn't keep her secret. His loyalty would demand he tell

Keldon immediately. She'd have to add one more lie to the many. "There is, but I don't know who he is."

"How'd you come ter know someone means him harm den?"

"I was walking in the garden when I heard a low hum of conversation. I didn't mean to eavesdrop. I had planned to circle around and head back to the house, but I took a wrong turn, bringing me closer to where the two were conversing. Their agenda included Keldon dangling from a rope." The lie tasted bitter in her mouth, but there was no going back now.

"Why didn't you go ter Mista Keldon with dis information?"

She straightened her shoulders. "You know he wouldn't have listened to me. He doesn't trust me, but I'm different now. I'm not that treacherous woman who didn't care who she trampled. I can't erase what I did to Keldon in the past, but I can ensure he will have a future. I would never do anything to harm Keldon," she pleaded with Samuel to believe her. "If I'm on the ship, maybe I'll recognize the voices I heard and be able to point out the traitors to you."

After a horribly long moment, Samuel finally sighed. "I know you's different. One, you wud have never stood dere defendin' yousself ter me." He nodded his head. "I believe you. You go back ter de house fer now. I will give Maeve clothin' fer you ter wear. You will have ter looks like de others." Samuel rubbed his chin and looked thoughtfully at Arianna. "You be tall enough ter pass as a cabin boy, efs you hides your hair. I'll see whut I kin do about gettin' you a cap. I will see you 'morrow." Samuel turned on his heel and disappeared into the foliage.

For a long moment, Arianna stayed rooted in her spot, too afraid to move less Samuel return and tell her he'd changed his mind. She sat down on the bench with a sigh of relief. Phase one of her plan was in motion. Tomorrow, she'd be on the ship with Keldon.

*****

"Don't make me do it," Maeve said to Arianna with the shears poised near her beautiful hair.

"You have to, my hair's too long. I'll never be able to hide it under the cap Samuel gave me." Arianna didn't know why Maeve had to be so difficult.

"Dere must be another way. I kin't do it." Maeve put the shears down on the dresser and Arianna turned to look at her.

"Listen, I'll do it myself if I have to. I was hoping you would help me cut it evenly. It's not a big deal." She shrugged. "Besides, my hair will grow back."

Maeve still wasn't sure. "Why don't I braid it and..." Arianna shook her head before she could finish explaining her plan.

"I can't take the chance of my hair falling free." Arianna took the shears from her. She was about to cut the first strands, when Maeve put her hand upon hers.

"I suppose ef you's dat determined ter cut your hair, I will try ter makes it look neat."

"Thank you, Maeve."

CHAPTER EIGHTEEN

As soon as Keldon left the house, Arianna donned her disguise. She met Samuel at the appointed meeting place near the small pond in the garden.

She didn't feel safe until she was onboard Keldon's ship, the *Good Intent*. She hid behind the water barrels and the boxes filled with supplies.

She questioned Samuel about *The Good Intent,* wanting to know all there was about the ship. He told her it was a masted sailing vessel rigged with a longbow sprit. It had a shallow draught, so it would be able to move with ease even in low tide. The flag that Keldon chose to fly was the typical black with skull and crossbones in the center, but to the right of the skull was a bagpipe and on the left, there was an hourglass. Samuel explained the bagpipes signified Keldon's love of music and the hourglass symbolized the days of their lives. She prayed their hourglass would remain full.

Arianna worried even though Samuel insured her of her safety. Samuel stocked and readied the supplies. There was no reason one of the men would stumble upon her. Once they were out to sea, she hoped to mix in with the crew. She would just have to wait patiently for the ship to set sail.

She settled down and waited, her lids felt heavy and she let them fall, telling herself she'd only rest her eyes for a moment, but it seemed she fell asleep. She awoke again to the sound of Keldon's booming voice, ordering his men to lift anchor.

This was really happening.

She shifted her weight to a crouching position and peeked around the bulky water barrel. The men scurried around in the dim darkness. Her gaze riveted to Keldon's tall lean frame garbed in his Scotsman kilt of green, gold and orange. He looked powerful, handsome and deadly all in one. Her heart swelled with pride as she watched him take command and he by no means, stood idle. He helped his men finish the tasks that would put them out to sea.

Arianna felt the ship lurch forward. Then pick up speed as the ocean water pushed against the sides and the wind skimmed the open deck.

She watched the crewmembers at work, wondering if any of them had visited Keldon at the house. She spotted Samuel, Leighton, Vincent Aubrey and— Dear God! She immediately slid further back into her hiding place. Her heart went into sudden shock. How could she have forgotten about Nicholas Sherborn? Of course, he would be on the ship. It was his plan to take the Spanish frigate, in hopes Keldon would trust him.

Once Nicholas found out she was onboard, she had no doubt he would corner her for answers. A rush of dread whirled inside her as Arianna racked her brain for a plausible explanation Nicholas would accept.

"Miss Arianna?" Samuel hissed.

"I'm here." She scooted forward.

"You kin come out now."

She crawled over to Samuel, hesitating to go out in the open. "Are you sure?"

"Shor' as I kin be. Jest keep your hair covered and don't be talkin' ter no one. I have a place where you kin wait down below. We won't catch up ter de other ship fer days. Even ef all goes well, it kin be very tricky. You best stay below jest in case dere be fightin's goin' on."

"Samuel, is there a lot of bloodshed when you take over another ship?" She dreaded the answer, but she had to know the truth.

"No'm dere ain't. Mista Keldon don't believe in killin' unless dere be no other way. Now, let's stop de chatterin' before we gets ourselves caught."

She nodded and they made their way down to the lower deck without a hitch. The place Samuel had in mind for her to hide in was dark and stuffy. She thought about taking her chances up above, but in the end, she knew she'd be foolish to risk it. She had to stay hidden until they were far enough out to sea, so that Keldon wouldn't be able to turn back without jeopardizing the whole expedition.

Arianna would wait to put forth plan B—well before they attacked the Spanish frigate. Keldon wanted to start a family. Being a pirate and a father couldn't go hand in hand. Since their night in the garden, Keldon had been most attentive. With as much heated passion as he displayed, she could already be pregnant. If he didn't want to run the plantation, then there had to be another line of business, a legitimate one that would interest him.

She stood and paced in the small enclosure. The sway of the ship and the stale air made her stomach turn. She needed fresh air. Surely, it had been a few hours since they had set sail. She made her way up the stairs to the bright sunshine, realizing the day had begun, while she'd been sitting in the dark hole below.

"Hey, ye lad get a move on." Arianna turned toward a large burley man with dark eyes, long hair and sideburns. She realized he addressed her. She gulped and pulled her cap lower, until it covered her ears. "Did ye hear me lad?" the man yelled to her, again.

Arianna didn't trust her voice. She nodded her reply.

"Well then get yer bony arse up here and help Higgins with the ropes."

Arianna nodded again even though she had no idea who Higgins was, but one look from the scowling man giving the orders, made her think she'd better find him.

Lucky for her, she heard Vincent Aubrey call to Higgins. Her eyes widened as she caught sight of the tall scraggly looking boy. He looked more out of place than she did. She headed over to him, keeping her face hidden from Vincent's view. She couldn't take the chance he'd recognize her.

"Boy! No watch out!" Vincent's warning came a second too late.

Arianna stepped in the center of the loop as Higgins yanked on the rope. The twine constricted around her ankle like a noose, dragging her down and knocking the wind out of her. Higgins oblivious to what happened continued to drag her across the deck.

"Higgins stop," Vincent ordered as he ran to help her.

Higgins turned and the color drained from his face. "Bloody 'ell." He loosened his hold.

Arianna breathed a sigh of relief. Being unceremoniously hauled up by her feet was bound to call attention. This was exactly what she didn't need.

Vincent knelt down beside her.

She lowered her hat, covering her view. Why didn't she have the sense to stay down below?

Vincent removed the rope from around her legs. "Are you all right?"

Arianna kept her eyes averted. "I'm fine," she answered in a gruff voice. Her ankle throbbed and her skin felt like it was on fire, but she needed Vincent to leave her alone before he recognized her. She scrambled to her feet, but once she put pressure on her right foot, she knew she was in trouble. She pitched forward and Vincent caught her.

She cringed as his hands landed on her chest.

"What in the world." He steadied her and lifted her chin, forcing her to meet his gaze. "Good God, Mrs. Buchanan?" he whispered.

She nodded slowly. He helped her to move away from the others. Oh, she was in for it now.

"Does Keldon know you're onboard?" he asked.

She shook her head and pleaded with her eyes for him not to say anything.

"You can't keep it a secret," he said as he nervously looked around him, noticing that Higgins watched them.

"Is he all right, sir?" Higgins called.

Vincent quickly answered. "No harm done, that can't be taken care of. Continue what you were doing, Higgins. I'll take the boy down below to wrap his ankle."

Vincent half led, half carried her to one of the cabins. There was a large bunk to the left of the room, a table and chairs to the right of it. He made her sit down on one of the chairs, before he knelt down to inspect the damage. He gingerly lifted her foot and rested it on his knee.

"Pardon me, Mrs. Buchanan, but I must remove the boot to make sure the ankle is not broken."

Arianna wasn't going to protest. Her foot throbbed.

When he removed the boot, she nearly bit her lip through, trying not to scream. He probed and poked until he was sure no bones were out of place. He dragged the other chair over and made her prop her foot up. He stood back and rubbed his chin thoughtfully. "Now what do we do with you?"

"Are we far enough from home that Keldon won't be able to send me back?"

"What is this about?" He frowned. "What mischief are you up to? Why are you here?"

"I have the right to know what kind of man I'm married to. I wanted to see for myself, firsthand how he conducted business."

"Hmm. What exactly do you think we're doing? Or should I ask?" he added with a small smile.

"You shouldn't ask," she replied.

"You have your suspicion and maybe you are right." He studied her for a moment.

"What?"

"I'm wondering how you sauntered past the men undetected. Even in your ridiculous outfit, you are too pretty to be a boy. Surely the men must be blind."

Arianna knew she blushed and cursed her fair complexion.

Vincent grinned. "Oui."

"Yes?" Arianna eyebrows furrowed.

"Oui. Yes, to your question. We are far enough from home. Keldon won't turn around. I suppose, you will have to take this adventure with us." He tilted his head, his eyes betraying his worry. "As much as I enjoy your company, I am not sure how your presence will affect the other members of the crew. It might be for the best if we keep your identity a secret."

She sighed. "That was my plan. It didn't work out so well."

"No." He chuckled. "You made quite an entrance."

"Keldon's not going to be pleased with me, is he?"

"I would say not, but again, you are a lovely sight to behold. He might not be too angry with you."

"Maybe I should go to him." She attempted to stand, but Vincent immediately put a restraining hand on her shoulder.

"You best stay put. I'll bring Keldon to you. This way I can ride the storm of his fury, he's sure to bestow. When he's calm enough, I'll send him down."

"That's nice of you to do that for me, Mr. Aubrey."

"Vincent, please." He smiled. The man was charming, especially when his amber eyes twinkled with amusement.

"Vincent then and you must call me Arianna," she insisted.

"Arianna?" He sounded baffled. "But I thought your name was Annabelle. No?"

She sighed wearily. "Yes, so I've been told."

"Now you have me more confused than ever."

"You see, I had a fall recently and my memory is not as it should be. I don't recall any of my life before a week ago and to be perfectly honest with you, I hope I never remember it. From what I've learned, I was not a very kind person."

"If I may say so, it is most difficult for me to believe it. I must confess I have heard interesting rumors about you. I imagined in my mind that you had two heads and horns protruding from them." He chuckled making Arianna smile at the ridiculous picture he conjured.

"You make me sound like a devil."

"Ah, people talk and sometimes they are most unkind."

"In my case they may have had every right to talk."

"Then you must have changed for I find your company very pleasant and Keldon must too. I haven't seen him seem so... How should I say this... Well, most content. I envy him," he confessed, then cleared his throat as if he'd said too much. "I'll go talk to Keldon now." He took her hand in his and bestowed a kiss. "Everything will be all right, Arianna. I will make sure of this."

*****

Vincent shielded his eyes from the sun as he came topside. Spotting the tall Scotsman, he made his way over to him.

Keldon acknowledged him with a nod then yelled for Higgins to loosen the sails.

Dragging Keldon away would prove difficult, but Vincent kept up with him, lending a hand when needed.

Keldon pivoted and bumped into Vincent. Keldon's eyes narrowed. "Is there somethin' ye wanted, Aubrey? Ye've been my shadow for the last half hour."

"You have an unexpected visitor aboard," Vincent blurted out before Keldon could be called away again.

Keldon chuckled. "Weel did ye set out the fine china for tea?" When Keldon realized he was the only one laughing, his eyebrows came together in a frown. "A visitor, ye say. Ye mean a stowaway."

"Oui. Before you get yourself upset—"

"Get to the point, Aubrey. I doonae have all day to figure out yer riddles."

"Always in a hurry, my friend. All right, then. Your wife is in your cabin."

Keldon blinked in surprise. "Ye are mistaken. I kissed Arianna goodbye and left her safe at home."

"She's down below."

Keldon didn't answer.

"Did you hear me?"

"Aye, I heard ye fine. I am havin' a wee bit of a problem believin' this is possible."

"Well, since I brought her down below myself, after her fall, I—"

Keldon grabbed Vincent's shirt, worry creasing his brow. "Fall? Is the fool lass all right?"

Vincent pried Keldon's fingers from his shirt and glanced behind him. You might want to keep it down."

Keldon took his meaning. He glared at anyone who was brave enough to meet his gaze.

Vincent continued, "Arianna is fine. She twisted her foot. Nothing was broken."

"And how, may I ask do ye know this?" he growled. His face turned red and the tick in his cheek warned Vincent one wrong word from him and he would be feeling Keldon's fists.

"Now listen, I had to make sure the foot wasn't broken. No?"

Keldon took a deep breath and nodded. "Aye," he managed to say, through clenched teeth. "Now that I know she is fine, she'll be ruing this day." He turned on his heel, grumbling under his breath. "I doonae have enough to worry aboot, now I have to worry aboot her, too. What did the fool lass think she'd accomplish by sneakin' aboard his ship?"

Vincent ran ahead and intercepted Keldon before he could go down below.

"Move aside, Aubrey," he warned.

"You must give me your word you will not be too severe with her."

"This is none of yer concern. Now move aside before I move ye myself."

"Then I'm going down below with you. I will not have you mistreating her."

Keldon opened and shut his mouth with a harrumph. "Ye cannae be serious. What do ye think I'm goin' to do to her?"

"I am not sure, but if your scowl is an indication…" He shrugged, letting the implication speak for itself.

Keldon smoothed out his features. "If I give ye my word, that I will no' lay a hand on her, will ye let me pass?"

"Your word has always been good with me."

"Aye. Then ye have it. Now, kindly move aside."

With a sweep of his hand, he gave him wide berth.

He watched Keldon disappear into the inky blackness, hoping he had not made a grave mistake.

"What was that about?"

Vincent glanced over his shoulder to see Nicholas Sherborn standing there.

"You two look like you were about at blows with each other."

Vincent shook his head. "The captain has something unexpected to take care of. It's nothing that he can't handle."

*****

Keldon ran a hand through his hair. Arianna was down below in his cabin and here he had felt guilty telling her he had to leave her this morning. He fabricated a story about Vincent needing his help with a family emergency. She had sweetly kissed him and told him she understood. He had been pleased that he didn't have to make a desperate plea. He knew it had been too easy, but she distracted him by crawling into his arms and kissing him until he forgot his worries. The minx knew she'd see him soon, no wonder she'd been so easily appeased.

With his hand on the door handle, Keldon drew in a deep breath before he entered his quarters.

Arianna looked up innocently with her doe-like eyes. He still couldn't believe it, but there she was, dressed in an outfit that hung on her. She posed a ridiculous picture, but all he could think about was tearing the cap off her head and burying his fingers in her long silky hair as he ravaged her lips. She'd lured him in like a siren's call and he couldn't resist her.

"Keldon, don't look at me so."

"And how am I lookin' at ye?"

"Like you want to devour me whole."

He chuckled. "Ye are close."

His Scottish accent thickened, a sure sign he wasn't pleased with her. She swallowed hard, questioning her judgment about taking this voyage.

He closed the door and locked it. She knew he would never hurt her, but his scrutiny made her uncomfortable. She couldn't read his expression.

Without a word, he approached her. He knelt down in front of her and lifted her foot. Her skin was raw and swollen, already turning three shades of color. For possessing such large hands, his touch was surprisingly gentle.

He looked up. "Does yer ankle hurt much?"

His pale green gaze always knocked her for a loop and it took her a second to realize he asked her a question.

Only, it wasn't the inquiry she expected. Where was the reprimand for her stupidity? She had a whole line of answers to shoot back at him for that question.

She cleared her throat. "It looks worse than it feels. I wasn't looking where I was going and—" She swallowed her words as his mouth captured hers in a hungry kiss. Arianna's eyelids fluttered closed and on a sigh she gave into the passion he offered. He then released her, making her lurch forward from the sudden abandonment.

Keldon stood and backed away from her. He opened his mouth to say something then turned away mumbling under his breath. He paced back and forth. He ran his hand through his hair then finally he stopped and stared at her.

Why was she here? How did she know of his ship? And what did she plan to do with the information? Old doubts flooded through his mind. He couldn't just ignore them like a love, sick fool. "Ye best be tellin' me why yer dressed like a lad out fer his first sea voyage."

"I wanted to be with you and I would miss..."

He narrowed his eyes and her gaze fell away. "Please, doonae lie to me, Arianna."

"Oh Keldon, please don't be angry with me. Listen to me with an open mind and I'll tell you the truth."

He nodded and leaned against the bunk. "Go on then."

"I know who you are," she stated.

He lifted an eyebrow, waiting for her to continue.

"You're the Scotsman. Everyone in town has been talking about you."

Keldon couldn't help but chuckle. "I'm the talk of the town, am I?"

She threw him a frown. "Be serious. It's not a claim to fame you should want. No matter how glamorous and romantic they make you sound, you are still a criminal in their eyes."

"Romantic?"

"That glimmer in your eye isn't amusing. I have the mind to slap some sense into that thick skull of yours."

"Do ye think ye're capable?"

She ignored his challenge. "You just don't get it do you. You think this is all fun and games. Well it isn't. You and your motley crew are playing a dangerous game on the high sea. This isn't *Disneyland*, you know. You won't be getting off the *Pirates of the Caribbean* ride at the end of the trip. This is for real. If you're caught they'll hang you." She was out of breath by the time she had ended her tirade.

"What is this Diz-knee-land? And we are no' pirates of the Caribbean. We have a purpose other than plunderin' ships. The British brought this upon themselves. Our country cannae freely trade with other countries. My band of pirates—as ye want to call them—and I are verra weel the blessin' to the country. We bring the goods in as needed. The cargo wouldnae have gotten through otherwise. You ken?"

"No I don't *ken*," she said sarcastically. "Do you really believe what you are saying? You think slaughtering innocent men and stealing their livelihood is okay because you give it back to society."

Keldon brows shot up. "Slaughterin'? We defend ourselves of course, but we do all that is in our power no' to murder a soul. Ye have my word on the matter." He moved away from the bed and knelt down beside her. "Do ye care for me?" He desperately wanted to know, for though she had shown him a physical attraction, she had never declared her love to him.

"What kind of question is that?"

"A verra good one. Do ye?" He wanted the truth.

"Of course, I do. Why do you think I am here? I want you alive. I want you to be the father of my children. I want to grow old with you."

A smile spread across his face. "I be wantin' those verra things, too. I have been on American soil since my thirteenth year and it is my home. I have an obligation to my men and to this country." He was surprised at his own declaration. When he had started this quest, he had wanted to do something reckless, something Annabelle would hate. But his marriage had taken on a new meaning and he knew his purpose.

"Then do this the right way. Obtain a..." She waved her hands in the air searching for the right words. "Obtain a pardon from whomever you get a pardon from, and help with the cause if you feel you must. You won't have to worry much longer anyway. There will be a treaty made soon."

"A treaty?" He lifted one dark eyebrow, wondering how she would know of this.

Arianna didn't seem to hear him. Her eyes glazed as if she were in a trance.

He took hold of her hand, but she didn't acknowledge him as she told him her eerie premonition. "Fighting will break out in New Orleans before the information reaches anyone."

"What are ye talkin' aboot?" Keldon asked, trying to gain Arianna's attention.

"In December when the American and British peace commissioners sign the Treaty of Ghent. It'll put an end to the war of 1812. Unfortunately, the British General... can't think of his name. Anyway, he'll lead his men into an attack on New Orleans. General Jackson will hire sharpshooters from Tennessee and Kentucky. The battle will only last about a half an hour or so and it ends up being a slaughter for the British. Over 2000 of their men will be killed. We fair much better. Eight killed, thirteen wounded. Jackson will be celebrated." Arianna stopped her rendition of the war and blinked. "Oh my God, how do I know this? I read it somewhere, had to memorize it or something." Her eyes widened in fear. "What is wrong with me? I have these flashes of places, of things like their lost memories, but they couldn't be, could they?"

"Ye have been sayin' such strange things since that bump on yer head." Keldon feared more than just her personality had been altered.

"I know and it's driving me mad. An image or an event pops into my head, like this one. I know sometime in September of this year a man by the name of Francis Scott Key will be inspired to write, the *Star Spangled Banner*. The song will one day be our national anthem." She sang a few lines.

"Catchy."

"This isn't funny."

"I wasnae tryin' to be."

"Then listen, please. As sure as I am sitting here, I know what I just told you about the war will happen, too."

"Like how ye know aboot the thing ye called a *car* will be invented?"

Arianna nodded. "I don't know how I know. I just do."

He nodded. "Somehow ye have gotten the second sight."

Arianna squeezed his hand. "Then listen to me now, for the life you are leading will end in tragedy."

He didn't have a chance to comment before there was a knock at the door. "Captain," the man on the other side of the door called out. "We've spotted a ship. She's not flying her colors. There may be trouble ahead."

Keldon stood. His conversation with Arianna would have to wait. "I'll be there right away," he called out.

"Aye captain." They heard the man's retreating steps.

"Ye stay put," he said to Arianna. "I ken verra weel ye have a curious mind, but ye cannae be in the way. Promise me ye will stay in my cabin."

"What if the ship is sinking?" Arianna said, sarcasm dripping from her words. "Should I still stay put then?"

He threw up his hands. "Ye are impossible ye know." Half, kidding, he added with a wag of his finger, "If I see yer bonny arse up above, I'll shoot ye myself." He leaned down and kissed her on the forehead. Then headed out the door to find out what awaited them.

Up top, Keldon headed over to Vincent and Leighton. "What do ye see?" he asked, as Vincent handed him the spyglass.

"Have a look for yourself."

He knew Vincent had already made his assessment. By the tone of his voice, it didn't bode well.

He frowned. If the other ship caught up with them, they'd be in for a fight. He wasn't pleased to have another complication thrown his way.

His men were well trained for confrontations and he had no worries about their capabilities, but one never knew when you might come across a ship that was able to outman them. On top of it all, he worried about Arianna. He'd never forgive himself if something were to happen to her. "Prepare the men," he said grimly as he handed the spyglass back to Vincent.

"Can we out run them or should I sharpen my blades?" Leighton asked.

"I plan on tryin' to out run them. Their ship is smaller and therefore lighter and swifter. If they plan to board us and if the wind doesnae change, they'll be upon us in a few hours."

The men were silent while they worked to keep the *Good Intent* ahead of the other ship. As soon as it deemed possible, Vincent made his way back to Keldon. "What about our visitor below?"

Keldon eyes narrowed. "Why are ye so preoccupied with my wife?"

Vincent raised his hands in defense. "Nothing, other than concern for her welfare, my friend."

"Doonae fash yerself none. I'll defend her with my life, if need be."

Vincent smiled.

"Why are ye wearin' a silly grin?"

Vincent shrugged. "You told me not too long ago you weren't on good terms with your wife. I wanted to know if I should stand guard over her, but it seems you have reconciled, no?"

"Ach, Aubrey, worry aboot savin' yer own arse." Keldon strode away with Vincent's chuckle grating on his nerves.

Nicholas wasn't blind to the events unfolding. He noticed Keldon and Vincent whispering to one another. Nicholas hadn't been convinced before, but he was now. Keldon had someone down below. If it hadn't been for the blasted pirate ship chasing them, he would have already had the mystery solved, but for now, he had duties to perform to keep the enemy at bay. "This venture should have been a smooth run," he mumbled under his breath.

Nicholas' gaze landed on Higgins. A slow smile spread across his face as a plan formed in his mind. He called to the boy. "Hold my line, will you?"

"Sure." Higgins took hold not even asking why.

Lucky for him the lad was too eager to please. He edged his way around and slipped down below unnoticed. He hurried to Keldon's cabin. He expected he would have to break the lock, but to his surprise, it opened with ease.

For half a second he stood there in shock. "What the bloody, infernal..."

The heavy lashes that shadowed Arianna's cheeks flew up and a soft gasp escaped her. She was standing on one foot, while she wrapped a torn sheet around her ankle.

"What are you doing here?" Disquieting thoughts began to race through his mind. He never imagined the captive would be Annabelle Buchanan.

She nervously lowered her foot to the ground. She leaned heavily on the chair and avoided putting pressure on the injured leg. "I couldn't stay at home," she told him. I needed to see for myself how Keldon ran his ship."

Nicholas gave her a hawkeyed assessment. Was she playing him the fool? She fidgeted with nervous unease and her eyes darted to the door as if she thought she could make a run for it. She wasn't going anywhere. Nicholas glanced down the passageway to make sure no one had followed him. Then he closed the door and faced her. "You wanted to see the slaughter?"

"God, no! I had to see for myself what kind of man my husband is. I had to see for myself that he is as cruel as you say."

"What is the matter with you?" He frowned at her, sensing something wasn't right. "You know how he is. You were the one who told me of his cruelty."

"I told you he was cruel?" Her breath caught in her throat.

Nicholas was silent as he assessed the woman that he had cared about and who had at one time shared in his goal to rid the world of Keldon Buchanan. Now he wasn't sure he could trust her. She had changed. "You did tell me of his cruelty, as sure as I am standing here. However, if you don't believe he's capable of treachery, ask him about Richard Hawkins and then tell me he isn't beastly."

Arianna's brow furrowed. "Richard Hawkins? Who—" Her words strangled in her throat as the ship lurched to the right. She barely kept to her feet. "What's going on?" she asked when she had regained her balance.

"Looks as if we are in for a bloody fight." Nicholas pulled out his pistol from underneath his belt buckle. "Stay down below," he ordered as he headed back up top.

Arianna plopped down in the chair. Why had she lied to Nicholas? Keldon had been anything, but heartless. He was strong, loyal and genuinely cared about people. Even with her, when she had no right to expect kindness, he was never spiteful. A wave of apprehension swept through her as she realized what she must have done for all of them to end up here.

She put Keldon in danger by fabricating a story, lies to destroy his character and she had the audacity to drag Nicholas into the foray of deceit. As much as she wanted to make Nicholas out to be the bad person in all this, she knew he wasn't. She had used him, played with his emotions. She didn't love Nicholas and probably never did.

The ship lurched again, bringing her to her feet.

She couldn't sit down here and wait. If there were a fight, she wouldn't be the helpless victim. She hobbled over to the chest, which was at the end of the bunk and against the wall. She threw open the lid, hoping there was some sort of weapon hidden within its depths. The smell of pipe tobacco hit her nostrils as she rummaged beneath the woolen blankets. As she had hoped, she found a pistol. She lifted the heavy gun and looked it over. She had no idea how to use it, but to have it in her hand made her feel safer. She was about to close the lid when she noticed the slingshot and a pile of rocks. Now this was something she could handle.

She wrapped the rocks in one of the linen shirts and grabbed the slingshot. She hobbled over to the opened door and slowly made her way to the upper deck. She poked her head into the open.

The smell of exhilarated fear hung heavy in the air as both sides fought to win. Arianna found a hiding place among the boxes and tried to spot Keldon within the throng of fighting men. She caught sight of the boy Higgins first, fighting for his life and looked to be losing the battle. Arianna took the slingshot and one of the rocks. She aimed carefully and pulled back on the strap. The rock flew through the air and smacked the man, who was defeating Higgins, on the side of his left temple. Arianna feared the man was unaffected from the blow but he turned toward her, teetering on his feet. She watched as his eyes rolled back in his head and he went down hard.

Higgins scrambled to his feet, scratching his head in confusion. His eyes darted back and forth, obviously wondering where his would-be-rescuer hid.

Leighton came into Arianna's line of sight next. The man moved with ease, throwing his sword with little or no effort at all.

"Impressive, Leighton, but how about a little help?" She took another rock and aimed. The men were moving so fast that her aim wasn't true, but it served its purpose. The man fighting Leighton grabbed between his legs, cursing as he crumpled to the floor. Leighton promptly hit the man over his head, putting him out of his misery.

Leighton chanced a look behind him and spotted Arianna with her slingshot. His eyes narrowed as if trying to recall who she was.

"Look behind you, Leighton," Higgins called.

Leighton whipped around, his sword swinging down.

Vincent Aubrey's gaze landed on Arianna, his eyes widening in disbelief. He made his way over to her. "You must go down below. You will only be in the way."

"No way am I sitting this out. I can help." She raised the slingshot, took aim and fired.

The rock hit another man between the eyes.

"Yes!" She said bringing her fisted hand down in a triumphant display.

"My, my Arianna aren't you full of surprises. I stand corrected. The enemy is feeling your sting." He bowed to her. "As you were, my lady." He turned and jumped back into the foray.

Arianna finally spotted Keldon. Her breath caught in her throat as she saw him jump out of the way, as the cutlass brushed deathly close to his mid-section. She fumbled with the slingshot. Panic welled in the pit of her stomach as she tried to load the slingshot, afraid she would be too late to help Keldon. She took aim and fired, but the pirate moved safely out of the way as he lunged again at her husband. Keldon jumped out of the way, but lost his footing falling heavily to the ground, his sword sliding out of his reach. The man's ugly face slid into a smile as he neared his victim. Arianna had to think fast or Keldon would be cut in two.

The gun!

She pulled it out of her waist pocket. She had no idea how to use it, though. She glanced up to see Keldon roll out of the way, as the cutlass lashed down inches from where his head had been. Keldon was close to her now and she chanced yelling to him, while the pirate was busy pulling his weapon free from the floorboard.

"Keldon, over here."

He turned. She couldn't hear his words, but it didn't take much imagination on her part to know he wasn't pleased with her.

She tossed him the pistol, which he gratefully caught. As the pirate came barreling down upon him, he turned and fired the single shot. The man fell with a crash on top of Keldon. He quickly threw the dead weight aside and jumped to his feet.

"Get below, ye wee fool!" he shouted as he picked up his sword in time to fight his next adversary.

"*Get down below, ye wee fool,*" Arianna mimicked. "Make me, you stubborn Scotsman," she mumbled under her breath. She grabbed another rock from her supply and searched for the next victim.

A noise behind her made her whirl around. She gasped as a dark bearded man plunged down with his blade. She rolled away and he splintered wood. He yanked the sharp edge out of the crate and whirled around, his snarl raising one corner of his lip. Her eyes darted back and forth, looking for an escape. The pirate threw his knife at her as she made a dive for safety. She heard the sharp metal whiz by her head and the *thunk*-sound, as the blade entered the box above her. She scrambled to the other side of the boxes, hoping to make it around, but the pirate anticipated her move and was there to greet her.

"Ye slip of an urchin. Where did ye think ye was goin'?" he grounded out. He moved closer and Arianna backed up a step.

"You... you yellow-livered...spawn of the devil!" Arianna shouted back. A niggling of a memory came to the forefront of her mind. *Pirate movies.* She shook her head and pushed the thought away. She had to stay focused.

The bearded man only laughed, showing his mouth full of decaying teeth.

"So much for sounding fierce." She tried to make a run for it, but he grabbed her shirt, yanking her back. He held her close, his breath hot and putrid as he spoke. "Now little swab, let's see's how brave ye be." He balled his fist and pulled back his arm. Arianna closed her eyes waiting for the deathblow, but there was none. The man suddenly went limp and released her. She stumbled back, watching him fall. She winced when she stepped hard on her injured foot. Her gaze whipped around. Keldon stood there with his sword in his hand. Before she could feel grateful for his rescue, she saw another man running up behind him, his knife poised to kill. "Keldon, watch out!" she screamed. He whirled around his sword jabbing through the pirate's side. Keldon yanked his arm back and the man fell to the ground, a pool of blood already spreading underneath him.

Arianna grabbed her stomach as she felt the bile rise. She leaned to the side as the yellowish-green fluid spewed in every direction. Wiping the foul taste from her mouth with the back of her hand, she had the fleeting thought that she should have listened and stayed in the cabin.

"Are ye all right?"

Arianna nodded. "Go, go. I'm fine."

Keldon gave her shoulder a quick squeeze before heading toward Nicholas who was pinned down by three men.

"Let's even this up a bit, hey Sherborn." She heard Keldon yell as he swung his sword. Keldon fought by Nicholas' side. Metal clanked and sliced the air until they were the only two standing. Nicholas barely had time to voice his appreciation before Keldon moved on.

"They strike the colors!" Vincent Aubrey shouted. Arianna had no idea what that meant, but immediately the fighting ceased.

She breathed a sigh of relief, when she saw that Keldon remained unhurt and was issuing orders to round up the prisoners from the opposing ship. She noticed the enemy fared far worse than Keldon's men had. His crew had few wounded and fortunately no casualties. The other ship had lost seventeen men and the survivors looked worse for wear.

Arianna learned from Higgins that strike the colors meant the enemy had volunteered to surrender. She sat on top of one of the cargo boxes to see what was going to happen to the captured men. She made a quick survey and was pleased to notice there wasn't a board extending over the edge of the ship. She hoped this meant Keldon wasn't going to have the men walk the plank.

Keldon stood on crates and faced the prisoners who were waiting to hear their fate. "I am the Captain. Ye may have heard me referred to as the Scotsman or the Highland Pirate." The murmuring gave proof they had. "Ye have a choice this day. Join my crew, or ye can take yer chances with the long boats. If ye sail straight, ye'll find land soon enough. Ye'll be given plenty of provisions to see ye safe. It's yer choice. Think it through."

Some stayed and others chose to leave, taking their chances that they would reach land safely. Arianna felt a sense of pride on the way Keldon handled the situation. He had a practiced eye making quick decisions and his natural charm and gift of persuasion aided in winning loyalty from the men on the other ship.

She also kept an eye on Nicholas Sherborn, the other man in her life. He too, held a sense of prestige. He helped organize the supplies, handing out the satchels as the men stepped into the long boats. She supposed she could see why, she might have been attracted to him. Nicholas mirrored Keldon in many ways, their style, and their compelling presence, which demanded respect.

But what did Nicholas see in her? He told her he wanted to marry her.

Keldon looked her way, his gaze meeting hers.

All thoughts of Nicholas vanished.

"Later," he mouthed.

Anticipation thickened the air in her lungs as she imagined what he had planned for her. She wanted to go to him now, but she knew she couldn't. Her identity needed to remain a secret.

Keldon sent some of the crew over to the other ship to set it into motion. In less than two hours, they were on the way again.

Arianna went down to Keldon's cabin to wait. The throb in her foot had her gritting her teeth. She scooted to the center of the bunk and placed a pillow under her foot. She began to relax as she allowed the sway of the ship to hug her. She melted into the corner of the bed and it wasn't long before she was lulled to sleep.

CHAPTER NINETEEN

Keldon had two very good reasons why he sent Leighton over to the other ship. One, he was the best man to make sure everything went according to plan. Two, it prevented him from figuring out the new cabin boy was Arianna.

After Keldon cleaned the blood and sweat from his body, he left Vincent Aubrey in charge. He would take over again in the pre-dawn hours.

He entered his cabin expecting Arianna to be awake. Instead, he spotted her small frame snuggled comfortably on his bunk. "She's made herself at home, the wee imp," he said softly as he removed his shirt and then poured himself a drink.

Arianna stirred, eyelids fluttering open. She tried to sit up but winced.

"Yer ankle is troublin' ye still?"

She nodded. This time she successfully sat up and leaned against the headrest of the bunk. I've wrapped it like I learned in first aide class."

Keldon sighed. "There ye go, again. First aide class?"

"I never took a first aide class?"

"No' that I know of, but again there be things I am just now learnin' aboot ye." Keldon poured her a drink, and took a seat next to her on the bunk. She tried to refuse. "This will take the edge off of yer injury. It's what I learned in my first aide class."

Arianna's lips twitched.

"Drink it up," he insisted.

Raising the cup to her lips, she choked it back as if she downed poison. "There." She nervously glanced at

Keldon, his intense gaze making her squirm uncomfortably. "You're doing it again."

"What am I doin'?"

"You're looking at me as if you want to devour me."

He chuckled. "Only 'cause I do. Ye taste good right here." He leaned forward and kissed her neck."

"Mmm."

He caressed her face. "What I am to do with ye? I should by all means tan yer backside, but I see yer beautiful blue eyes lookin' at me and all I want is to ravish every inch of ye." He glanced at the cap she wore and shook his head. "Will ye remove that absurd hat of yers now?"

She lowered her eyes and slid the hat off.

"By thunder!" He jumped from the bed hitting his head on the railing above. "Ouch!" His hand flew to his head. He stared for a full two seconds. "There's practically nothin' left of yer beautiful tresses. What have ye done? Yer hair is a mite shorter than mine. Who did this monstrous thing to ye?"

Arianna looked up sheepishly. "No one did this to me. I needed a disguise. I couldn't very well mingle with the crew with my hair flowing down my back. Surely, they would have noticed."

She was right. Her lustrous hair would have been a dead giveaway that she wasn't a lad. "Ye shouldnae have been on the ship in the first place," he growled.

"My hair will grow back." Arianna ran her fingers through her chopped strands.

"I ken that verra weel." He sighed as his gaze wavered over her delicate features, taking note of the two red blotches on her cheeks. He hadn't meant to shame her. "Ach. Ye're still a bonny lass. The shortness of yer hair only startled me." He approached the bunk once more. Being careful not to bump his head again, he sat down beside her. "Although yer hair was soft to the touch, it wasn't why I care for ye so."

Arianna really looked at him now. "You care for me?"

Her surprise made him smile. "Aye, with all my heart," he said as he took the empty glass from her and placed it on the floor. He gathered her into his arms and leaned down to kiss the tip of her nose. "I adore every inch of ye."

She smiled and placed her hand on his firm thigh, slowly inching her way underneath his kilt. "I have been wondering, since the first time I saw you in your highland outfit— what exactly do you wear underneath it?"

Keldon chuckled and his eyes twinkled mischievously. "If yer hand goes any farther, ye'll find out soon enough."

"I'm prepared to take the dare."

"Ye've become a brave lass." He gasped as he felt her hand grip him.

"Hmm. Maybe you should wear a kilt all the time."

"Sweet Jesus." He closed his eyes.

Arianna watched the pleasure on his face as her fingers circled him. He was thick, velvety smooth, no wonder he filled her so completely.

She helped him remove his clothing and with swiftness she could never match, he removed hers. He stretched out next to her and her gaze slid over him, admiring his muscular body. A trail of hair started at his navel and traveled down to his groin, framing his member.

He rolled over, but she placed a hand on his chest. "Uh uh. It's my turn." She smiled at his surprised expression. "You promised, remember?"

He settled on his back. "So I did."

She pleasured him, as he had done her, leaving none of his flesh untouched. She smoothed her palms over his chest as she kissed a trail down the hard plane of his stomach. She heard his intake of breath as she took him in her mouth.

"Ye're killin' me, lass."

He died many deaths before she granted mercy and lowered herself on him, accepting the thick fullness of him. Thrill after thrill filled her, as she possessed his body.

His gaze caught hers and held. He grabbed her hips. A slow throb pulsed through her as shudders racked him.

She lowered herself stretching the length of him. She rested her chin on her arm and looked at him. "Just what I needed." She sighed with satisfaction.

His chuckle vibrated against her. "I'm glad I could be of service to ye then." His hands slid over her back.

With a sigh, she enjoyed his loving caresses. It wasn't too long before her lids grew heavy and she drifted to sleep.

*****

Keldon had his pipe in his mouth and he carried his ancient bagpipes with him. Vincent watched his friend closely and noticed the tension that emanated from him had melted away to contentment and he had a good guess why.

"You have made amends with your wife? No?" Vincent asked.

Keldon removed his pipe from between his lips and returned the smile. "Aye. All is weel... for now." They were silent for a moment, as they listened to the water lap against the side of the ship. The night was clear and calm and they both hoped the good weather would last. Keldon looked at Vincent again. "Ye best get some rest."

He nodded. "See you in a few, Buchanan."

*****

Nicholas knew Keldon would be busy above deck for a while. Even so, it was dangerous to sneak into the captain's quarters, but he thrived on risks and taking one to see how Annabelle fared was nothing he couldn't handle.

He quietly entered the room, closing the door behind him. He made his way to the bunk, where she slept peacefully. He sat down beside her and touched her long slender arm. She rolled toward him in slumber and he couldn't resist planting a kiss on her lips. She responded and put her arms around him. He nuzzled his mouth against her neck and she moaned with pleasure as she murmured her lover's name.

Nicholas stopped cold and pushed her away. His sudden movement caused Arianna to wake fully. She grabbed at the blankets and held them to her chin, her eyes betraying her wariness.

"Bloody inferno! You share his bed, again," Nicholas accused barely able to keep his voice controlled.

"He's my husband," she shot back.

"I bloody well know who he is. You don't have to remind me. But you told me it was over between the two of you, long before we started our affair. You lied to me. Are you playing me for a fool?"

"No. No," Arianna pleaded. "Let me explain."

He didn't like her tone and he sensed he wasn't going to like her explanation either. He tried to stop her, but she was determined to tell him anyway.

"I don't remember what we once shared," she blurted out.

He frowned. "What are you saying?"

"I don't have a memory of anyone or anything until a little over a week ago."

He narrowed his eyes. "What do you take me for?"

"Just listen. I fell and hit my head. I lost my memory. You're a stranger to me, as much as my own husband has been. I'm slowly beginning to learn who I am, or who I used to be. So far, what I've discovered isn't pleasant. Frankly, I don't know why you care for me, other than maybe we shared a common goal of sorts, and an ill advised one at that." She took a breath. "Nicholas, we were wrong about Keldon. He's not the vicious killer we portrayed him to be. Didn't you see that today?"

"He's fooled you for now, but he'll soon show his true colors. I know what he's done. Have you failed to ask him about Richard Hawkins?" Her silence told him she hadn't mentioned the man's name to him. "I see. And what should I expect from you? Will you tell Keldon of my plans? Should I plan on being marooned somewhere for being a traitor or worse?"

"I don't want anything to happen to you. You're not a bad person."

"Well thank you so much."

"Nicholas, please," Arianna pleaded.

Anger burned through his veins. Their relationship was over and he didn't understand why. "Please what, Annabelle? Please forgive you for tricking me. Please forgive you for making me fall in love with you when you didn't give a damn. Am I getting close?" Her eyes pooled and he looked away. "Christ. Just answer my question and I'll be gone. Are you going to tell Keldon about me?"

"I won't betray you, Nicholas. I owe you that much, but you must give up this quest. We were wrong about Keldon. He's a good man and he'll give up this life of piracy."

"You seem sure of yourself," Nicholas spat as he wondered how she came to this conclusion.

"I am sure," she insisted. "After this adventure, I will convince him to change his ways."

Nicholas was silent as he stared at the woman he thought he'd been in love with and realized he looked upon a stranger. She claimed Keldon was a decent man and it held a ring of truth to it. Keldon had shown mercy to his foes and in the battle, he came to his rescue. If anything, he owed the man for saving his life.

He pinched the bridge of his nose with frustration. "For the love we once shared, I'll give Buchanan a chance." He leveled his gaze on her. "If after this adventure, he swears to never pirate another ship, I'll give you my word that I'll not seek revenge on him." Without waiting for her to respond, he turned on his heel and stormed out of the cabin.

He went above deck and stood in the shadows, gritting his teeth together tightly as he tried to regain control of his emotions.

He listened to Keldon play the haunting music from his bagpipes. How he loathed Keldon Buchanan, but curse it all, he respected him, too.

Before he had met Keldon face to face, it had been simple. He hated him for changing his life forever. He had made a pledge to take his revenge, anyway he could. He purposely sought out Buchanan's wife. He was going to use her to bring Keldon down, but he found Keldon could care less about his wife, or at least that was what he had thought. To his own dismay, he had fallen into his own trap and fell in love with the beautiful Annabelle Buchanan.

She had started out to be a vibrant distraction and he thought he could forget about what Keldon had done. However, Annabelle then voiced her demands. She wanted revenge of her own. She claimed Keldon mistreated her. Now he wondered if that had ever been true. At the time, it was easy for him to believe her. He wanted to judge Keldon Buchanan a dishonorable man.

He plotted with Annabelle to set a trap for Keldon, knowing in the end the man would dangle from a rope. Their plan was falling smoothly into place. Only now, Annabelle claimed not to remember any of it. She didn't remember sharing her dreams with him, or that they had planned to run away, once Keldon was out of their lives. If he didn't know better, he would swear Annabelle Buchanan was a different person all together. To make matters worse, working side by side with Keldon made him see the man in a different light.

Keldon's crew held only admiration for him, not fear. He witnessed the way Keldon dealt with his enemies. He had treated them fairly. Could what he had heard from Richard Hawkins' crew been an exaggerated fabrication of what had really happened? For the first time, he doubted the truth of the story.

He had made a muck of his life and all in the name of revenge. He was in love with a woman who was never his and he had wasted months plotting to bring down a man who didn't deserve to die. "What am I to do?" Nicholas hadn't realized the music had stopped, or that he had spoken aloud until he heard Keldon's booming voice.

"Who's below? Show yerself."

Nicholas moved away from the shadows. "It is only I, Captain, Nicholas Sherborn."

"Sherborn." Nicholas saw him settle back and his voice loss its terseness. "It is late. Ye should get some rest."

"I was heading down below." Nicholas turned to leave, but Keldon called him back.

"Ye fought well today. I will no' be soon forgettin' the fact. I am proud to have ye aboard." Keldon's face showed the admiration he felt.

"Thank you, sir," Nicholas answered feeling like a loathsome rat.

*****

Keldon played his bagpipes again. The music drifted down below to where Arianna lay awake. She whispered the words that belonged to the sweet melody, for she knew the song well, though Keldon had insisted she shouldn't have. He had even insisted she couldn't play the harpsichord and yet she could. These things plagued her. It didn't make any sense.

The words to the melody flowed freely from her lips. She racked her brain, trying to remember how she knew them. Nothing about her life seemed to fit. It was like she was living it all for the first time.

She closed her eyes and listened to the music that seemed to call from her past... another time. Arianna fell asleep with those thoughts drifting in her mind. She dreamt of people who she recognized, but she couldn't recall their names. She tried going to them, but they walked a different path, locked away in another world where they couldn't see or hear her.

CHAPTER TWENTY

With her injured foot wrapped, Arianna could put pressure on it with only mild discomfort. She placed her cap low on her head, covering her ears and tucking most of her hair underneath the rim. Satisfied no one would question her as anything but the cabin boy, she left the quarters and went up above to make herself useful.

Macab, the ship's surgeon would have his work cut out for him as he took care of the wounded from yesterday's skirmish. Macab was a big burly man with carrot-colored hair and a gruff voice. As soon as he spotted Arianna, he put her to work finding out which men needed attention the most.

Haunted and unsure faces peered back at her. She offered them something to drink and cleaned out the wounds the best she could.

Macab set to work on stitching up a man's leg. The gash ran from the knee down to his ankle. The man bit down on a leather strap grimacing in pain, while two crewmen held down his arms. Arianna cringed as she walked past, heading for the young boy huddled near the crates. The boy stared, his eyes wild with fear.

Arianna disguised her voice, by lowering it a few octaves to keep up her facade of being the cabin boy. "Don't be scared," she said, hoping to put the young boy at ease. "I'm only going to clean your wounds." The boy's eyes darted back and forth as if looking for a way to escape.

"Leave that one be," Macab yelled to her. "The boy doesn't want any help."

Arianna would have obeyed the surgeon's orders, but the boy was holding his upper arm and she could see the blood oozing between his fingertips. She couldn't leave him.

"I just want to take a look at that arm," she coaxed, pointing, hoping to make him understand.

The boy shook his head and yelled, "Rester!"

Arianna's brows furrowed. "I'm sorry, I don't know what you mean. You must let me clean your arm or an infection will set in."

The boy turned away, hugging his knees close to his chest.

Arianna took a step closer and the boy shrieked, jumping to his feet, poised for battle, but then he swayed on his feet. Arianna watched in horror as the boy's eyes rolled back in his head and he collapsed to the floor.

Arianna ran forward and knelt down. The boy's chest rose and fell evenly, but she feared he passed out due to a lack of blood. She unbuttoned his shirt and with a gasp of surprise, she flipped the material close again. Her gaze flew to the boy's face—long lashes, smooth cheeks. "You're a woman," she murmured. She quickly buttoned the shirt and glanced around to see if anyone had noticed.

Macab caught Arianna's gaze and walked over to her. "Well the lad has finally succumbed. Let's get his shirt off so I can take a look."

"No!" Arianna blurted, losing the deepness of her voice. The surgeon eyed her, suspiciously. She didn't know what to do, but she knew she couldn't let the surgeon remove the unconscious woman's shirt. A little more calmly and in a deep voice again, Arianna made a suggestion. "I'll tear the sleeve, so the boy doesn't catch a chill."

Macab shrugged. He obviously didn't care one way or the other. He just wanted to take care of the wound and move on to his other tasks. He took out his needle and thread. "What a scrawny lad, this one is," he commented when he lifted his patient's arm. "He's near skin and bones."

"Don't you have to disinfect the cut?" Arianna hovered over Macab's shoulder.

His eyes narrowed. "Why don't you check on someone else? I can take care of this one."

Arianna was reluctant to leave, but she couldn't think of an excuse not to. When she had the chance, she caught Vincent Aubrey's attention and hurried over to him, pulling him to the side.

"Is something amiss?" he whispered, concern lining his features. "Your foot is bothering you. No?"

"No, no. I'm fine, but there is someone you must speak to."

"Who might that be?"

She leaned close and whispered, "One of the men from the other ship isn't a man at all and I think she only speaks French."

Vincent shook his head. "Another woman aboard, what are we to do?" His lips curved into a grim smile. "Show me where she is."

By the time they reached the young woman, she had awakened and was threatening Macab with one of his instruments.

Vincent quickly moved in and rapidly spoke the girl's language.

The young woman hesitated, realizing she understood Vincent. He continued, calmly talking to her, soothing her.

Tears pooled in her eyes and she finally let the weapon slip from her fingers.

"Damn crazy bugger," Macab cursed as he retrieved his surgeon's blade.

Vincent ignored Macab and spoke to the girl again.

She eyed Arianna closely, tilting her head, making Arianna squirm under her scrutiny. Obviously, Vincent revealed her identity.

Then in two strides, the woman threw her arms around Vincent. His eyes widened and he looked at Arianna for help.

Arianna grinned with a shrug. "It must have been something you said."

He pursed his lips together, but he returned the embrace, patting her back.

"I had no idea the bugger was a lass," the surgeon proclaimed in his defense. "I wasn't trying to molest her. I was only checking for any other wounds. What a shock to find two..." He cleared his throat. "Well let's just say she wasn't no lad."

"It's all right. I'll take it from here," Vincent assured him.

"Aaah good riddance, I say." Macab returned to his duties without a backwards glance.

Arianna moved closer to Vincent and the young woman who held onto him as though her life depended on it. "What did you say to her to make her trust you?"

"I told her what I had to. I told her that you were also a woman. I also let her know I would protect her, as I would you." He nervously cleared his throat with a chuckle. "Literally, I insured her I would slit any man's throat that laid a hand on her."

Arianna gaze riveted to his. *God, the man wasn't jesting.* "Oh."

*****

The young woman was Bernadette LaQuil and her presence aboard, the Good Intent spread like wildfire. Arianna kept a low profile having no wish for the attention Bernadette was receiving. The men hovered, some leered, but Vincent was good to his word and demanded the men behave.

Vincent learned the full story of Bernadette's plight, starting with her abusive father. Once she'd been old enough, she ran away with a young man thinking she would start a new life. He betrayed her also. Bernadette claimed a woman proved open prey to any man's desires. She decided she would become the hunter and disguised herself as a man. Since she didn't have money to pay her passage, she signed up on a working ship, hoping to find a port where she would call home.

Unfortunately, pirates had captured the ship she'd been on and the only way to survive was to join them.

Bernadette was only nineteen years old, living a lifetime of hardship and regret. She wasn't use to men treating her kindly and it didn't surprise Arianna that the young woman latched onto the only man who had ever shown her a shred of decency. She became Vincent's constant shadow, but if his gentle words and tentative glances were any indication, he didn't mind Bernadette's attention.

When the other men tried to approach Bernadette, she would give them a fierce scowl and yell at them in a very colorful and creative French vocabulary. The men may not understand what she spat at them, but they didn't miss her intent.

Vincent would shake his head at her and smile. "Ah, my little brave bear, I am the man. I protect you. No?"

Bernadette hung on his every word.

"She's infatuated with you," Arianna said.

Vincent's gaze riveted to Bernadette, who was helping Higgins with ropes. She glanced at Vincent, her lips curving into a smile.

Vincent turned away clearly flustered. "She's like a sister to me."

Arianna touched his arm. "Then be careful with her. Don't crush her heart."

CHAPTER TWENTY-ONE

Arianna sat at the table stitching one of Keldon's shirts. She heard the door to the cabin open then close. She knew who entered and smiled when his large hands covered her eyes.

"Guess who?" he whispered near her ear. His other hand skimmed her breasts.

"Hmm. I'm not sure." She inhaled deeply. "You smell of pipe tobacco and the sea. Is this Vincent?"

He growled. "He better no' be so familiar."

"Oh Keldon, how could I not know." She put down the shirt and turned in his arms accepting his kiss.

"Do ye know what ye taste like?" he asked.

"No, what?"

"Like wicked temptation and sinful pleasures."

"Is that so." She wrapped her arms around his neck and he pulled her up out of her seat so she leaned against him.

She nudged her hips. "My, my, what have we here?"

He brushed his firm mouth back and forth over hers. "Maybe I'll show ye."

"Maybe you better."

His eyebrows shot up and he smiled. "Aye." He picked her up and carried her to the bed, his lips working magic on her senses.

"It feels like we've stopped moving." She arched her back as he trailed kisses down her neck.

"Aye, we wait now until the Spanish frigate is spotted."

She gripped his arms and he looked at her. "Keldon, do you have to do this?"

He brushed her hair away from her face. "Shush now. Ye doonae need to fear, Arianna. My crew knows what to do."

"But what if something goes wrong?" Her voice caught in her throat.

"Nothin' will go wrong." He sucked her lower lip into his mouth and she was caught between a sigh and a moan. "Doonae worry so much." Then he closed his mouth hard over hers and she melted into his embrace.

*****

On the evening of the third night the lookout spotted her. The Spanish frigate had kept their steady course unaware the *Good Intent* had entered into view and was now pacing them.

As the sun set the fog rolled in, hiding the Spanish ship behind its wall of haze, but Keldon shouted the orders for their plan to go into effect. Arianna thought he had lost his mind to venture out now.

She took a step forward, but Vincent put a restraining hand on her arm. "You must stay back."

"He's going to be lost out there."

"Keldon knows these waters like the back of his hand."

"Well, that's all he'll see once he's out there on this suicide mission."

"I'll be watching his back," he said and headed for the long boats.

"Yeah, who'll be watching yours?" she whispered. She didn't want to watch this, but she'd go crazy if she waited down below.

Keldon gave the order to have the long boats lowered. Keldon, Vincent Aubrey, Nicholas Sherborn and a select group, made their way toward the armed Spanish frigate.

Arianna couldn't see a thing, but she could hear the first cries of battle. The not knowing was unbearable. She leaned against the ship's edge, staring out through the eerie, deathlike mist. She clutched her hands together in prayer.

"You seem worried." Samuel came to stand next to her at the railing.

Arianna nodded, not taking her eyes away from the depths of the white swirling fog.

"Well, dere's no need, I assure you. Mista Keldon be de finest of dem all. He will return."

Arianna nodded, grateful for Samuel's company. They stood by each other, adding comfort as they waited for the Captain's return.

Bernadette was also standing vigil, but everyone knew her anxiety didn't lie so much with the captain, but with Vincent Aubrey. Her prayers no doubt were for his safety.

Bernadette never thought she would want the attentions of a man. Most of her life she'd feared them, but Vincent Aubrey treated her like a lady. She loved how his muscles flexed and relaxed with the flow of his movements and how his body spoke of power, endurance, strength. His skin was tawny-velvet with dark stubble on his chin and his eyes were the color of whiskey shimmered with golden depths. She sighed. Her heart raced when he drew near.

She wasn't a naïve country girl. She knew what lust looked like and Vincent's eyes didn't smolder with passion when he gazed at her. She hoped in time she'd persuade him to change his mind. He meant everything to her and desperation to keep him gave her strength. Surely, if there were a God, he wouldn't let her find such a wonderful man, only to have him slip away.

Keldon and his men had boarded the frigate, claiming control almost immediately.

Vincent approached one of the crewmembers and ordered him to point out his captain. "Quien es el capitan de este barco?"

"Qué quieres de nosotros?" the captain asked as he came forward already fearing the answer.

Vincent turned to Keldon to translate. "He wants to know what we want from them."

Keldon chuckled. "Tell him that we only want their cooperation and if they follow our orders, no harm will come to him or his crew.

Vincent nodded and turned to the captain. "Nomas tu coperasion. Si siges nuestro ordenes no les asemos dallo a ti ni a tu hombres."

Keldon watched the captain, his gaze assessing him. Slowly his eyes widened in horror. He made the sign of the cross, repeatedly. When he spoke, his voice was barely above a whisper. "El es el Fantasma de los piratas."

Vincent lips slid into a wide grin. "Si, el es El Capitan Highland Piratas."

The captain began to speak rapidly, fear motivating his commands.

Vincent reassured the captain again, that no harm would come to them if they followed the orders given. Finally after careful deliberations, the man agreed to the terms offered.

"The coins are below as we were informed they would be," Nicholas relayed to Keldon.

"Good. Make haste then."

Nicholas nodded and shouted for a few men to help with the task.

Vincent glanced at Keldon with a spark of amusement touching his lips. "It seems, my friend, your reputation has preceded you. They've dubbed you the *Phantom Highlander*. You appear out of nowhere to capture your prize. You then disappear into the deep waters without a ship of your own."

Keldon's deep laugh vibrated through the night air, sending shudders through the already intimidated crew. "Imaginations do run high. Let us take what we came for and...." Keldon leveled his gaze on the captain. With an exaggerated wave of his hand, he said, "disappear... desaparece!"

The captain flinched and turned away to hurry his crew.

*****

Finally, Arianna thought she saw something move in the ever, shifting haze. She grabbed Samuel's arm and pointed. "Do you see? There to the left."

Samuel squinted into the night, then a slow smile spread across his face. "It be them!"

Arianna and Bernadette waited to the side, while the men lifted the heavy cargo onto the ship.

As soon as Bernadette spotted Vincent, she ran over to him, throwing her arms around him and kissing him. His shocked expression caused the crew to snicker.

"Ye have a love sick pup on yer hands," Leighton said in passing.

The remarked not only embarrassed Vincent, it sent him into a panic. He quickly removed Bernadette's arms from around his neck.

Keldon was at the wheel and Arianna made her way over to him. She wanted to throw her arms around him, too, but hesitated until she saw him beckon her. She ran into his strong welcoming embrace. Tears sprung to her eyes, making her feel foolish, but she couldn't help it. She had been so worried.

"It is all right, lass. No' a soul was hurt."

"Lass, is it!" Keldon and Arianna both turned to see Leighton. His face turned red and his hands clenched into fists. "I thought her face was familiar," he accused. "What is wrong with ye, Keldon that ye let the witch venture on yer ship?"

Keldon protectively shielded Arianna behind him. "Ye mind yer mouth. Ye best be givin' Arianna the respect she deserves or ye'll be answerin' to me."

"We'll all be answerin' to the devil himself by the time she's through with the likes of us."

"If I need yer advice, I'll ask for it. Ye ken?"

Leighton's whole body tensed. "Yer a fool, Keldon Buchanan." He turned his back on him, stomping away.

Keldon protectively pulled Arianna back into the folds of his arm.

"God, he hates me," Arianna's voice was a thin whisper.

"Nay. He doesnae know ye, Arianna. Give him time." He gave her a hug and a quick kiss on top of her head, but it didn't make her feel any better.

Arianna spotted Nicholas Sherborn down below. He briefly glanced up at them, nodding toward Keldon in a questioning gesture. Then she remembered her last conversation with Nicholas.

"Keldon?" She looked up at him.

"Aye," he answered as he gazed ahead of him.

"Who is Richard Hawkins?"

She felt every fiber in his body tense at the mention of the name and he glanced down at her startled.

"Who is he, Keldon?"

He hesitated for a moment, choosing his words carefully. "He's long been buried."

"What happened to him?"

Avoiding the issue, Keldon met her question with one of his own. "Why is there a need to be knowin'?"

"I heard his name mentioned and wondered who he was, is all."

"He's no one. Ye need no' concern yerself with him." He shrugged. "Now come here and keep me warm. We have a long journey still ahead of us."

"Aren't you worried the Spanish frigate will come after us?"

His mouth twitched at one end and then into a roguish grin. "Nay. Who would be fool enough to venture out in this thick muck?"

CHAPTER TWENTY-TWO

They traveled to *Willow Bend*, a small river community located in Louisiana where Keldon had an antebellum style home. Keldon allowed his men to use part of his land to make permanent homes and shops for trade.

A skeleton staff was hired to help Arianna and Bernadette clean and organize their temporary base. They dusted every piece of furniture, scrubbed the floors and changed the linens. Arianna discovered a harpsichord under one of the coverings and was thrilled by the prospect of playing it.

Vincent Aubrey and a few men stayed behind, while Keldon, Leighton and Nicholas went ahead to meet with officials and naval officers in New Orleans to begin the negotiations for the trade. Once they dispersed the cargo and paid the crew, Keldon and Arianna would set sail again for *Blue Run*.

Vincent did his best to distract Arianna with cards or amusing stories. Weeks passed and she couldn't believe it had been a month since she'd been home to see Maeve, Sally Mae, and everyone else at *Blue Run*. She missed them terribly.

Usually she could camouflage her loneliness with mindless work around the house, but today she couldn't seem to shake the feeling of melancholy. She rose from her seat and went over to the window, pulling back the heavy drapes. She turned when she heard someone enter the room. Bernadette looked at her with genuine compassion in her eyes as she strode over to stand at her side.

Arianna's gaze traveled over Bernadette's attire. She wondered if the woman owned anything other than a pair of baggy pants and oversized shirts. "I was daydreaming," Arianna told her.

Bernadette pointed to her chest where her heart was and then she pointed to the window. "Triste... sad?"

Arianna nodded. "Yes, I am sad. I miss Keldon, terribly."

"Oui," Bernadette said, obviously understanding perfectly.

Even though Vincent was here, he might as well not be, for all the attention he paid Bernadette. It wasn't as though he ignored her, but Arianna couldn't help but notice he treated her as if she were a child.

Arianna may not know French, but she had no problem recognizing an aching heart. "You're in love with Vincent, aren't you?" Arianna asked using the same sign language that Bernadette had used, by placing her hand on her heart, while emphasizing Vincent's name.

Bernadette smiled. "Oui." She nodded with a sigh.

They looked at each other for a long time trying to think of a way to communicate with one another about their gloomy disposition. Then for no reason at all, they started laughing. They were laughing so hard that they had to sit down on the sofa to catch their breath.

"Are we pitiful, or what?" Arianna exclaimed as she took large gulps of air. "Here we are feeling sorry for ourselves. I don't know about you, but I needed to laugh."

Bernadette had no idea what she had said, but she answered her in French all the same.

Arianna gave her a quizzical look and then they both started laughing again.

Vincent had heard the merriment and obviously couldn't resist finding out what was so funny. When he walked into the room, both women fell silent and just stared at him. Then they looked at each other before they burst out laughing all over again.

"We're sorry…" Arianna managed to say between chuckles. "We were just talking…"

"You were?" His eyebrows quirked as he regarded each woman.

Arianna dabbed her eyes. "It's difficult to explain, but believe me we had a conversation."

"I see." He scratched his head. "I have to admit, I am most pleased to see smiles on your faces." He rapidly translated to Bernadette, which was his habit.

Arianna glanced at Bernadette, then to Vincent, a plan formulating in her head on how she could bring these two together. Vincent clearly cared for Bernadette. He was handsome, charming and most importantly—single. Maybe if she gave him a nudge, he would see Bernadette as a woman and not as a child. She cleared her throat drawing their attention. "I was wondering if you both could show me how to dance."

"Dance?" Vincent raised his eyebrows.

"You do know how to, don't you?" Arianna prayed he did.

"Well of course, but I don't…" Vincent began but never had a chance to finish. Arianna was on her feet, leading the baffled Bernadette toward him. She placed Bernadette's hand in Vincent's, making her blush from head to toe. The poor girl had no idea what was going on. Vincent cleared his throat and quickly explained Arianna's request.

Bernadette's gaze riveted to her, and one lovely brow arched in question, but Arianna didn't say more as she hurried over to the harpsichord and sat down on the bench.

"Now you will need some music." Arianna chanced a look at the couple.

Bernadette's cheeks were bright pink, and Vincent pulled at the neck of his shirt, but at least his lips curved.

"Shall we?" He started out slow, but soon he twirled her around the room.

Arianna could tell Bernadette was thrilled to be so close to Vincent. Her cheeks were rosy pink and her eyes lit up every time her gaze met his.

"You dance beautifully, Little Bear," Vincent complimented her, adding to her embarrassment.

Vincent was amazed Bernadette knew how to dance, but again his little bear was full of surprises. She was young, but educated, knowing how to read and write, mostly due to her own persistence to better herself. Life had dealt her a cruel hand, but she was a survivor. He had to give her credit for not giving up. He'd come to respect and care for her deeply. He wanted to keep her safe, give her a chance to start over. He wasn't sure how he was going to accomplish the feat, but he was determined to see it through.

He moved his hand to her waist, surprised at how tiny she was. Her baggy clothes hid her attributes well. He impulsively pulled her closer, relishing in the way her softness moved against him. She gave him a small tentative smile, nothing seductive and yet he couldn't tear his gaze away from her face. Her eyes were warm and expressive with long lashes to frame them. His gaze automatically dropped to her full lips—sensuous lips made for kissing. He frowned, wondering how his thoughts had taken him where he had no right to be. Hadn't he sworn moments before, he would protect her? He had no right to seduce her. Holding her like this was wrong. She was a child for heaven's sake.

He closed his eyes, trying to distract himself from making a mistake, but her sweet scent enveloped him, betraying him. His eyes snapped opened and he swallowed the lump in his throat.

He tried to throttle the dizzying current that raced through him by diverting his gaze, but the desire didn't diminish. He feared it was already too late. He had witnessed a longing in the softness of her brown eyes.

Arianna continued to play not realizing they had stopped dancing.

He gingerly caressed Bernadette's cheek. She wasn't a little girl, but a woman. Blithely ignoring the voice of reason, which told him to let her go, he lowered his head, letting his mouth cover hers.

Nothing could prepare him for what the onslaught of that gentle drugging kiss would mean. Every curve of her body molded against him, his arousal painfully obvious. He wanted more, so much more, but he pulled away with a tearing reluctance, still feeling the sweet throbbing of her lips.

The music had stopped. He quickly pushed Bernadette away, taking several steps back, as if the distance would be enough. "You must pardon my actions," he said shakily before he turned and fled the room.

Bernadette lowered her head the light in her eyes going out like a flickering light.

Arianna stood and went to her, placing her arm around her shoulders. "It'll be all right. I'll think of something to turn him around."

*****

Arianna awoke early and made her usual morning jaunt down the brick walk lined with exotic wild flowers. She passed the cherub fountain in need of repair. She'd have to add it to her list of things to do.

Willow Bend had many majestic oaks but oddly, there was only one willow tree. She leaned against it with its weeping bluish-green leaves. She breathed in the clean morning air, while enjoying the warmth of the sun before it rose too high in the sky, making the heat unbearable. She hadn't been out there long before she heard footsteps coming down the walk. She glanced back to see who had risen so early to join her.

"It's a beautiful day," Vincent greeted her as he looked toward the panoramic view of turquoise waters.

"Yes, it is." She studied him for a moment, wondering if she should mention what happened yesterday or leave well enough alone. "Has Bernadette risen, yet?"

Wariness entered his expression as he glanced her way. He cleared his throat. "I am not sure."

A flicker of a smile rose at the edge of Arianna's mouth. He was nervous and preoccupied, all very good signs, which indicated he was smitten. Now, it was persuading him to admit it. "So, what do you think of her?"

"Think of her? Whatever do you mean?"

So he wasn't going to make it easy. So be it. She would lay it on the line. "As a man, how do you feel about Bernadette?"

Vincent chuckled and pulled at his collar. "She's a mere child."

She shook her head. "She doesn't think she's a little girl and I don't believe you do, either."

"I see." He became defensive with the truth so blatantly out in the open.

"And what else do you seem to know?" He purposely folded his arms across his chest as though he could protectively hide his true feelings behind them.

"I know that Bernadette is in love with you."

"She… How is it that you know this when you cannot speak French? She couldn't possibly have told you."

"We women can sense these things, just as I also know you're in love with her, too."

Vincent opened his mouth to deny it, but he shut it without uttering a word.

Arianna saw the flicker of emotions cross his face, the realization of the truth, but then his expression turned grim. He shoved his hands into his pockets and his shoulders hunched.

"What's wrong?"

"I never want to hurt my little bear. She has had enough heartache in her life." He sighed wearily. "I have a price on my head and cannot offer Bernadette a permanent home." He looked at her now, his amber eyes filled with sorrow and perhaps regret. "I love her and because I do, I will never make my feelings known to her. I must hold fast to my conviction and let her go."

"There must be a way to clear your name."

He took a deep breath and adjusted his smile. "You cannot clear a man who is guilty."

Dropping her gaze, she turned away. "I'm sorry, I just…" She never finished what she was about to say, for what was the use? The harder she tried to avoid the truth the more it persisted. Vincent was guilty of piracy, but so was Keldon. It didn't matter how honorable their reasons were. What they did was against the law and if caught, they would hang.

Vincent put his hand on her shoulder. "Don't be sad. I am aware that you were only trying to help, but there is not much hope for me."

"Nor for Keldon, either."

Vincent must have realized his mistake for he hurried to make excuses as if he could now sugarcoat the truth. "So far no one has identified the Scotsman."

"But some do suspect, don't they?" She didn't have to wait for him to reply for she could see the answer in his eyes.

"Please do not worry yourself so. Keldon has been most careful."

Arianna nodded, but couldn't help but think of the crew's flag, the emblem of the hourglass. Keldon could take all the precautions, but eventually their time would run out, finding him on the wrong end of a rope.

She chewed on her lower lip, wondering how their conversation had turned so dismal, but since it had, she'd venture to take it a step further. Perhaps Vincent would be more forthcoming with information than her husband had been. "Did you know Richard Hawkins?"

Vincent eyebrows rose. "You are full of surprises this morning. I haven't heard that name for a long time."

"And?"

"He's been put to rest."

"Yes. I know this. Why won't anyone tell me who he was?"

"He was someone we have all tried to forget about for various reasons. I take it you have asked Keldon about him. No?"

"I ask him and received the same response you gave me. What are you both hiding?"

"It's not what you think."

"Then tell me." She saw him hesitate and she quickly took his hand. "Please."

He finally nodded. "It happened when we first started our... shall we say challenging experiences. I was a captive aboard Hawkins' ship when Keldon's band attacked. It was their first run. The takeover hadn't been difficult, but Hawkins being a pompous man tried to overpower Keldon. Hawkins went for Keldon's pistol. They both fought for the power of it. Hawkins lost. It was as simple as that."

Arianna's brows furrowed. "It was an accident then?"

"That it was, but Keldon has felt responsible for the man's life ever since. He felt he should have known better than to have turned his back on the captain of the ship. We had a decent burial for the man, not that he deserved it. Even though Keldon didn't have to do this, he personally sent a percentage of his booty to Hawkins' widow."

"What did you think of Captain Hawkins?"

He was more than willing to let her know, his voice holding such venom that Arianna inwardly flinched. "He

captured my ship and half starved my men! He showed no
mercy and for that I can't bring myself to mourn the man's
passing."

She shook her head not understanding all this. "But
Keldon felt differently?"

"Ah well, Keldon is a complicated man. I don't believe
he thought of the consequences of his actions. The first
time someone dies at your hands, it hits hard."

"Does killing become easier after that?"

Vincent sighed. "No, but you're prepared. For some
reason, Keldon wants to be a freebooter, but he doesn't
want to harm the men aboard the ships. With the least
amount of bloodshed as possible, we subdue the crew,
only resorting to killing if our life is in danger. Keldon, at
times is too honorable for his own good, but like all of us,
I suppose he has his reasons for taking to the sea."

Arianna was silent as she digested the information,
more confused than ever. Why did Nicholas Sherborn
want her to know about the incident with Hawkins? It
didn't make sense. It was an accident. Obviously, she was
missing something. "Captain Hawkins was the only one
who was killed?"

"Oui," Vincent slowly nodded. "Why is this so
important?"

"I was only curious." She shrugged, not wanting
Vincent to become suspicious. Even though she had a
good idea, Vincent didn't know anymore than she did
about Nicholas' association with Hawkins. "You said every
man has his reasons for setting out to sea. If you don't
mind my asking, what were your reasons?"

"Nothing gallant, I'm afraid. I was bored and thought
the sea daring, adventurous and maybe just a little
charming." He smiled meekly with a shrug. "My sister,
Chantal warned me that I would be miserable once the
picturesque fantasy wore thin."

"Your sister sounds like a very wise woman. You should listen to her more often."

"Oui. That I should."

The sun rose higher in the sky and she shielded her eyes from the glare. "Do you want to head back to the house for breakfast? All this talk and fresh air has made me incredibly hungry."

"You have read my mind."

Arianna turned and swayed, the sudden movement causing her head to spin.

Vincent's hand shot out and steadied her. "Arianna, are you all right?"

She opened her mouth, but she couldn't answer. The ground felt like it had dropped beneath her feet and the world dimmed. The next thing she knew she was sprawled on the ground with Vincent hovering over her, patting her hand rapidly and speaking French.

"English Vincent." She tried to sit up. "English."

"Oui, Oui. Are you all right?"

The whirling sensation was eased, but she felt far from fine. "I don't know what happened. I felt so dizzy."

"Has this happened before? Have you been ill and not told me?"

"No… Well, not like this anyway. I must be coming down with something. Every morning this week I have felt queasy to my stomach and…" She closed her eyes, as a new wave of dizziness threatened to overtake her again.

"Every morning?" he asked.

"Yes, but after a few hours, I feel perfectly fine."

"Ah, I see."

"See what?" She opened one eye and looked at his smiling face, wondering what he could possibly be so smug about knowing.

"If I may be so bold, I might be able to tell you. I was lucky enough to be born into a family of all women. I have five sisters to be exact. And well how should I put this, have you missed your... uh…" He cleared his throat. "Well could you possibly be in a family way?"

"A family way?" Then it dawned on her what he was implying. She tried to remember when she had her last monthly. If she had taken the time to see the signs her body had given her: no period, the tender swelling of her breast and the queasiness. She should have known.

"It is true then?" Vincent asked as he watched her expression.

"I believe so." Arianna's face lit up. She was going to have a baby.

"I am most pleased for you and Keldon," he said as he helped her to her feet. "Come now. Let's get you back to the house. You need your rest." He stayed close, just in case she should feel faint again. "When is the baby due?"

She had been trying to calculate the dates when he asked. Unfortunately with her hazy memory, she wasn't certain when her last period was. Then she had an unsettling thought she couldn't ignore. She had carried on a liaison with Nicholas Sherborn. When was the last time they slept together? Had it been long enough to make a difference? Could she be certain she was carrying Keldon's child, or was she actually carrying Nicholas Sherborn's?

Vincent gave her a startled look and immediately brought their walking to a halt. "Mon Dieu, you are a ghastly shade of white."

"I don't feel well." She sat down on one of the nearby rocks and fought the urge to be violently ill. She didn't know whose baby she carried. Panic was on the verge of choking her and she waved her hand in front of her face hoping to draw in air. How could she have allowed this to happen? She should have realized the position she put herself in, the situation she caused because she wasn't faithful. Her gaze riveted to Vincent. "When do you suppose Keldon and his men will return?"

"It shouldn't be much longer." He took her hand and patted it. "Now, don't you worry. Keldon will be home soon. You must try to relax."

Relax! She couldn't relax. She had to speak with Nicholas and find out the last time they'd slept together. She prayed he would tell her what she wanted to hear.

\

CHAPTER TWENTY-THREE

Keldon stared at the poster with a grim smile before he folded it and put it in his coat pocket. A costly warrant on his head was the last thing he needed right now. They would have to lie low for a while until the document wasn't such a pressing issue.

Luckily, so far it hadn't interfered with them unloading their goods. They made a sufficient amount of money and with the gold coins they confiscated from the frigate, they should be fine for a long time.

Keldon arrived at the restaurant early. There was a sparse group tonight, which suited him fine. He ordered dinner of soup, lamb chops, sweetbread, and the vegetable of the house. He was already nursing a glass of claret, by the time Leighton and Nicholas showed up.

"Have ye heard the news, Keldon?" Leighton asked as he pulled out a chair and took a seat. "Remember that nonsense we thought Annabelle was witterin' aboot? Ye know aboot John Armstrong bein' replaced? Curse me if she wasnae right. Armstrong was blamed for the burnin' of Washington. Just like she said. Now how do ye suppose she got wind of such news?" Leighton poured himself some wine and offered the bottle to Nicholas before he continued. "She's a spy and I have no doubt that the wee witch is the one who put the bounty on our heads."

"Stop with yer rantin', Leighton. Arianna is nay a spy." Keldon's expression was taut, hoping his old friend would drop the subject.

"*Arianna, Arianna.*" Leighton mimicked, completely ignoring the warning signals. "I am a wee mite sick of hearin' that name, when we all know she be christened with the name, Annabelle."

"I prefer Arianna. She's changed and the name suits her." Keldon twirled the wine in his glass.

Nicholas shook his head. "You might want to lower your voices."

He was right, Keldon thought. There was no need to draw unwanted attention to them.

"I ran into a gentleman today." Nicholas sipped his wine and sat back in his seat.

Keldon never thought he'd actually like Nicholas. He had been a means to an end, but he turned out to be a decent addition to his band of would-be-pirates. He put in a good day's work like the rest of them and he didn't shy away from danger. "Who?" Keldon asked.

"A gent, who was stationed at Fort McHenry. He's been humming this little ditty. He said everyone was singing it because of this gent. Now what was his name?" He tapped his chin then snapped his fingers. "Oh yes, Francis Scot Key. The chap has bloody well written a song he calls the *Star Spangled Banner*. It's a rather catchy little tune, if I must say so." He started to hum it, causing Keldon to choke on his wine. Nicholas leaned forward and slapped him on his back. "Are you all right?"

"Francis Scott Key, did ye say? It cannae be."

"Do you know the chap, then?" Nicholas asked.

Keldon realized Leighton and Nicholas were staring at him. He couldn't tell them Arianna's prediction. Leighton would condemn her as a witch and Nicholas most likely would think him daft.

"Nay. His name sounded familiar for a moment." Keldon bit his tongue, but it didn't stop him thinking about some of the other things Arianna had revealed to him. Maybe there was a reason she had the sight, a reason he shouldn't ignore. "We'll head back to *Willow Bend* tomorrow."

CHAPTER TWENTY-FOUR

Arianna wrung her hands as she waited for the ship to dock. Keldon had finally returned and she wanted to share her good news about being pregnant, but her doubt of who the father might be overshadowed her joy. She never thought she would say this, but she also hoped Nicholas was also among the crew. She had to speak with him alone. She closed her eyes and said a prayer while she tried to ignore the heaviness surrounding her heart. Her whole future with Keldon rested on Nicholas' answer.

She opened her eyes and spotted Keldon immediately. There was no mistaking the tall, handsome man with the cat-like green eyes. For the moment, she let her worries roll off her shoulders. She didn't care who watched, she ran to greet him, throwing her arms around his neck. He swung her around returning her hug with a fierce one of his own. She breathed him in—pipe tobacco, salt and musky male scent that was all him. She was reluctant to release him.

He stood back and eyed her closely, while he rubbed his chin. "Yer hair is a mite longer now. I like the way ye have curled it."

"You do?" She was pleased that he had noticed her extra primping she had done solely for him.

"Aye, verra much so. It's most flatterin'." He gave her his lopsided grin. "Did ye miss me?"

She playfully hit him. "You know I did. What took you so long?"

"We had a wee bit of trouble and had to lie low seein' that we had a price on our heads."

"They know who you are?" Arianna's eyebrows knitted together.

"No' exactly. They know of the Scotsman Ghost but no' of his true identity." He pulled out a flier and handed it to her. Arianna relaxed when she saw the ridiculous sketch. She burst out laughing. "Do they think you're a leprechaun? Who gave such a ridiculous description?"

"Someone I am grateful to say hasnae actually seen me." He took the flier. Folding it, he put it back in his coat pocket. "So my wee lass, what have ye been doin' while I was away?"

"Mainly worrying that you were caught and I was never going to see you again. When I wasn't doing that, I cleaned the house, redecorated, tried my best to communicate with Bernadette and played chess with Vincent. I'd say I probably bored the poor man to death, but he was ever the gentleman."

"Aye, Vincent is a good friend." Keldon leaned down and kissed the top of her head.

"So when are you going to greet me properly?" Her gaze snared with his and her heartbeat quickened as she thought of him making love to her and kissing every inch of her skin. She licked her lips as she did a slow slide with her eyes.

His eyebrows lifted in surprise. "Ye're wicked gaze betrays ye lass. If ye keep it up, I'll have the mind to take ye here and now."

She grabbed his hand. "Then let's hurry back to the house or I might let you."

*****

Arianna woke up and bolted out of bed. She grabbed the porcelain bowl before the bile left her mouth.

Her retching woke Keldon and he rushed over to her not sure what he could do to help.

Still hugging the bowl, she looked up at him.

"Are ye all right, then? Ye're as white as the sheets. Can I be gettin' ye somethin'?"

"I'm fine. Go downstairs and have breakfast."

"Fine? Ye doonae look fine to me."

"Please." She looked at him. "Go." She waved her hand at him in dismissal.

He stood there looking down at her, not sure if he should leave her.

"Keldon, you're staring. Please, go downstairs.

He let loose a breath, half in disbelief that she dismissed him, and half frustration that she wouldn't let him stay with her. "Fine," he mumbled. "I'll go have myself a bite to eat and no' care ye are sicker than a dog."

"Good."

He harrumphed and turned on his heels. "Damn stubborn lass." Feeling rejected, he headed downstairs.

"Bonjour, my friend." Vincent's face held a smirk as he waited for Keldon at the bottom of the stairs. "I was sure, I would not see you quite this early." His chuckled turned into an embarrassed cough as he realized he was the only one laughing. "Has something happened?"

"It's Arianna; she isnae weel. She made me leave the room while she..." He waved his hand in front of his mouth. "Ye ken?"

"Oh, that. She will be fine in a half an hour or so. We better see that breakfast is ready. She will be ravishingly hungry by then." He started to walk away, but Keldon's hand snaked out and held him steady.

"What is this? Arianna has been ill daily and ye can only think of yer stomach." His guttural burr sounded like a growl.

"Don't be cross. It is nothing to worry about. I assure you."

"Nothing to worry aboot. Ye dinnae see her pale face. Ye dinnae see her leanin' over the pot."

Vincent chuckled. "Well you better get use to it. She may be doing that for a few months. Chantal had the morning sickness all through her delicate state."

"Delicate state? What in… What are ye sayin'? Are ye sayin' that Arianna is carryin' a wee bairn?"

"Oui. Oh my! Didn't she tell you?" Vincent's eyes widened.

She hadn't told him and Keldon wondered why. Did she change her mind about starting a family? The death of their first child came hurdling back to him, to haunt him with the suspicion that she had deliberately ended the pregnancy. Would she try something drastic again? He couldn't live through that kind of heartache a second time.

"Keldon?"

Keldon didn't answer Vincent. He ran back up the stairs, taking them two at a time. He threw open the bedroom door, slamming it behind him. Arianna was lying on the bed and she lifted her head to look at him. He went over to her and he gently brushed her short strands of blonde hair away from her eyes.

"Why dinnae ye tell me?"

Arianna sighed. "Vincent told you, didn't he? I wanted to be the one." Darn the morning sickness anyway for giving her away. She hadn't wanted to tell Keldon until she had the chance to speak with Nicholas. This felt like a lie, but she forced a smile for Keldon's benefit.

Keldon pulled her into a hug. "Ye've made me the happiest man alive."

She closed her eyes. For the moment, she relished in his happiness.

As soon as she felt better, she left the house in search of Nicholas Sherborn. She didn't know how long he intended to stay at *Willow Bend* and she could pretty much count on him not seeking her out to say goodbye.

She spotted Nicholas' lean frame resting against the side of Buchanan's Mercantile and Trade. He was clearly surprised to see her, but he tipped his hat and smiled, showing his charming dimples. "Mrs. Buchanan, to what do I owe the pleasure?"

Arianna swallowed hard and squared her shoulders. "I need to talk to you in private. It's vitally important."

His eyebrows raised and his mouth curved. "Come now, do you really think that's wise?"

"I have no choice." She sensed his hesitation, but she wouldn't let him brush her aside so easily and held her ground. "I think what I have to say, may very well concern you. And you owe me."

"Owe you!" His voice rose an octave, clearly indicating his irritation.

Good, it was about time she put a chink in his composure instead of the other way around.

"Are you all right out there?" one of the men yelled to Sherborn.

He waved him off and lowered his voice "If you must insist, let us part from prying ears. I'll escort you back to the house and you can speak your mind."

"Fine."

Nicholas glanced at her as they walked. "Whatever you have to say must truly be dire."

She cut him a sharp look. "What? Why do you say that?"

"You're wringing your hands." He pointed with a nod, daring her to argue the point.

Arianna looked down and quickly pulled her hands apart wiping them on her dress.

Once they started down the path leading to the house Nicholas looked at her again. "I believe we can speak freely now."

"I'm going to have a baby."

She didn't miss a step as she made her announcement, but his gut clenched with unease. "Congratulations," he said carefully.

"That's all you're going say?" She threw up her hands in exasperation.

"Bloody hell! What exactly did you want me to say? You tell me you don't want to see me anymore or least that was my impression. So I wonder why I would care that you and your husband are about to start a family?" His lips thinned with displeasure.

She placed a hand on his arm bringing him to a halt. Her eyes searched his for God knew what. He wanted to pull away, but her next questioned stopped him cold.

"I wouldn't have sought you out, but you see, I had no other choice." She took a deep breath. "Could the baby possibly be yours?"

He stood there, while her words sunk in. Was the baby his? Could it be possible? He thought back to the last time he made love to her. For about half a second, the thought of having a child pleased him. A smile spread across his face, but when he looked at Arianna—the way she chewed on her lower lip, he knew with a pulse-pounding certainty she he didn't want this baby to be his. His smile vanished and relief spread through him as he realized he was no longer in love with her. He had fallen in love with a woman who ignited his own passion of hatred and vengeance. He'd been wrong about Keldon Buchanan. They both had. He didn't want revenge and it was obvious she didn't either.

"It doesn't matter if I am the father or not." He shrugged. "Anyway, chances are Buchanan is. You shouldn't worry overmuch."

"How can I not? How can I expect Keldon to care for a child who may not be his?"

"He need never know. Forget the past," he pleaded with her. "Forget our time together. I know I will." He caressed her cheek. "Your different now. It's like I had an affair with another woman." A smile touched his lips and he let his hand fall away. "Let it go."

How easy he made it sound. How easy it would be to do as he asked. For truth be-known, she didn't recall ever being with Nicholas. He thought he made love to a different woman. Well, the intimacy they must have shared was lost to her all together.

He took her hands. "Be wise and never reveal our involvement. Nothing good will come from it. Why cause, undo pain when there is no need to?"

Arianna wanted to believe Nicholas was right, but she had a nagging feeling the past would one day come back to haunt them all.

*****

Leighton finally arrived and took a seat in front of Higgins. He was glad the lad had seen fit to show up. Of course, it helped matters that he dangled the pouch of coins in front of his face for his trouble.

"Weel lad?"

"She met with Sherborn at Buchanan's Mercantile and Trade." Higgins licked his dry lips and looked nervously over his shoulders.

"Weel?"

"They just talked."

Bah! Talked? If they be meetin' of course they'd talked. I be wantin' to know what was said."

Higgins squirmed uncomfortably.

Leighton decided he would risk losing a few more coins to loosen the lad's tongue. "I'll offer ye double, if ye ken anythin'."

Higgins' glanced at the pouch Leighton shook in his hands. "I'd say they were real comfortable like with each other. They went walkin'. Sherborn held her hands at one point."

Leighton grinned. "Thank ye lad. Ye have done real good, ye did." Now, he had ammunition to fire at Keldon, force him to open his eyes and see his wife as she truly was.

Pleased, Leighton joined the other men in a drink, but one drink turned out to be many before the night was over.

He passed out sometime in the early morning, while the others continued their merriment.

CHAPTER TWENTY-FIVE

"I want to take ye back to New Orleans with me," Keldon announced at dinner.

"Is it safe to go back? They have a warrant out for your arrest." She wouldn't allow him to take unnecessary chances if she could help it.

"It's safe enough." He smiled over the rim of his glass. "Besides people see what they want to see and no' a mite more. They're lookin' for a Highland Pirate, a short stocky fellow. They willnae be lookin' for a distinguish gent."

"Hmm, yeah I get it. Something like Clark Kent and Superman."

Keldon's eyebrows arched.

"You don't know who Clark Kent is, do you?"

"No' that I know."

"Clark Kent is Superman, a man with super human strengths. He fights evil. Clark Kent puts on a suit and a pair of glasses and..." Arianna could see she had lost him. "Well anyway it's like you say, people see what they want to see."

"Ye have a fanciful imagination. A man with super human strengths..." He shook his head.

I didn't make up the comic book character?" She tried to explain. "Superman isn't the only super hero, you know."

Keldon wasn't interested in super heroes at the moment. He was more interested in her second sight. "Ye know I have been thinkin' of the things ye be knowin'." He met her gaze with a long and interested search. Her blue eyes were vivid and questioning, but he didn't have all the answers. He only had the inkling she was different in some way and it was important he pay attention. "Some of the events have actually happened, just as ye said they would."

"Then I am not losing my mind." She sighed in relief, making him realize she had been dwelling on the possibility. She leaned forward anxious to know the truth. "What I told you really did come to pass?"

"Aye, some. I want ye to meet with a gentleman who might be interested in what ye be knowin'. Would ye be willin' to do this for me?"

"But what if I'm wrong and I say something that might be harmful?"

"He doesnae have to take yer advice. We are people of free choices. But if my hunch is right, ye'll be a help to his cause."

"I guess I'll talk to him. Who is this man?" Arianna asked as she sipped her tea.

"General Andrew Jackson."

She choked. "The Andrew Jackson?" She put the teacup down.

"He is the only General Andrew Jackson, I know of. Does the name mean somethin' to ye then?"

"Only that he will lead our men against the British in the battle of New Orleans. I told you about him. Weren't you listening to me?"

"I do remember ye talkin' aboot some general, but at the time ye had me preoccupied." He winked at her. Then seriously, he added, "Then ye will talk to him. If there is anythin' that could aid him, ye must help."

"I will tell him what I can."

"We'll leave early on the 'morrow. Changes on the ship should have already been made."

"What changes?"

"Oh, like the name. We couldnae verra weel come into port with the known pirate ship of the Highlander."

"I suppose not."

They finished their dinner and Keldon pushed himself away from the table. "Come here." Keldon motioned to her with the crook of his finger.

"I don't know." She chuckled. "The gleam in your eye makes me think you want to devour me."

"Ah perhaps I only wish to claim my dessert. Aye?"

She sauntered over to him and he welcomed her into his arms so that he cradled her on his lap. "So, I'm a tasty dessert, am I?"

"Dinnae I tell ye? My favorite."

When Keldon bent his head, she met his lips halfway, a kiss full of passion and need. His hand moved down her arm to her midsection. Unfurling streamers of sensations hit him—happiness, apprehension. He wanted to make love to her, but the memories of doubt crowded his thinking, like a hidden current. He had to know the truth. He had to be sure she wouldn't do anything drastic about the pregnancy. He tore his lips from hers so he could see her face clearly. "Ye are content to be startin' a family? Aye?" He knew she didn't understand the strange urgent unease about him since she didn't remember the loss of their first child. He held his breath afraid of her answer.

She cupped his face her gaze never wavered. "I want nothing more than to be carrying your child."

Keldon felt the tension leave his limbs and he surrendered to the crush of feelings that drew him to her. He rubbed her stomach as though he could feel the baby growing beneath his hand. "Our baby will be strong." He looked at her with longing. "I sense this."

"I hope so and I pray the child will be born with your dark hair and cat-like green eyes."

Wrapping both arms around Arianna, he pulled her to him not realizing her trembling was not solely passion, but fear she carried someone else's child.

CHAPTER TWENTY-SIX

No one knew General Jackson was anywhere near New Orleans. He was on his way to secure the army's position in Spanish Florida. Secretary of War, James Monroe was opposed to this action, but Jackson was sure he could capture Pensacola with little or no trouble at all. If his plan succeeded, it would open the door to invade Florida.

Jackson agreed to meet with Keldon Buchanan and his wife—a personal favor from a mutual friend of trade. He vouched that Keldon had vital information he shouldn't ignore.

Jackson stood tall. Arianna could see why Jackson led an army. He had an air of authority about him, a *don't-mess-with-me* attitude or you'll be sorry. Jackson eyed Keldon closely as if deciding for himself if he should think of him as an enemy or adversary. He then looked at her with appreciation, his expression softening for a moment before he cleared his throat. He offered them a seat and Arianna began to tell him what she knew. "I don't have all the details just the outline of the events," she admitted.

"You want me to stop the battle from happening. How do you suppose I do this?"

"I don't know. Send word to General Pakenham. Inform him of the Treaty of Ghent."

"Mrs. Buchanan, I cannot in all good faith, send word of an event of which I have no knowledge."

Arianna sighed and leaned forward. "So many will die and for nothing. It'll be a slaughter."

"You come to me with this information, Mrs. Buchanan and you seem sincere in your belief of these fantastic claims, but I can't just take your word. I worked with concrete proof and so far all you've given me is conjectures. How do you know this? From whom did you acquire your information?" Jackson looked at Arianna then to Keldon.

"We cannae say," Keldon answered. "Ye must understand we are only here to help."

Arianna noticed the flicker of skepticism cross Jackson's features. He didn't believe them and why should he?

She folded her hands on her lap and glanced at Keldon. "We have to tell him the truth." She ignored Keldon shaking his head no and looked at Jackson. "We didn't come here to waste your valuable time. The truth of the matter is that I'm unsure of how I know. It's more like an intuition."

"Pray tell, Mrs. Buchanan surely you are not trying to tell me that you're a medium and can tap into the future." A chuckle escaped him.

Arianna pursed her lips, wishing she had listened to Keldon. Now Jackson was going to think she was a crackpot. Maybe this had all been a mistake anyway. Maybe what happened was supposed to be and she couldn't save Pakenham and his men even if she tried. Or maybe her warning prevented a complete annihilation by saving the men under Jackson's care. No matter what the outcome might be, she wanted a clear conscience. She had to give the information to Jackson. After that it would be out of her control.

"I think our meeting is over." Jackson stood expecting them to do the same.

"If I reveal something that proves I'm telling you the truth, will you at least consider what I've told you?" This caught his attention and he motioned for Arianna to continue. "I know you haven't received orders to attack Pensacola, but you will—on November 7th, 1814."

"How did— Only the men who are apart of my unit know of this plan and they wouldn't dare defy me by breathing a word of this to anyone."

"That's right, they wouldn't, *Old Hickory*."

Jackson was silent for so long that Arianna wondered if she had pushed too hard, but then a slow smile spread across his face and he sat back down.

"Old Hickory, is it? Only my men call me that. Maybe, I should hear the information one more time."

Keldon and Arianna exchanged knowing smiles. They had accomplished what they had set out to do.

*****

Leighton awoke with a horrendous hangover and staggered back to *Willow Bend*. He was furious when he discovered Keldon and Arianna left for New Orleans. They wouldn't be back for a few days. Vincent and Samuel didn't understand what was so dire that Leighton needed to talk to Keldon. All but the minor details were needed for the goods to be delivered. Leighton being snappish as ever refused to enlighten them of the trouble. Nor did he explain why he wanted Nicholas Sherborn found and held.

"Mista Leighton." Samuel entered the study with the news he dreaded to tell him.

"Weel, what is it? Where's Sherborn?"

"Dat's whut I come ter tell you. He ain't nowhere. And we found dat de long boat is missin' along with the boy Higgins."

"Curse me! I should have known, he'd flee."

"Higgins?"

"I doonae give damn aboot Higgins. It's Sherborn." Leighton paced a few moments before coming to an abrupt halt. "This could be good. Aye. It's just what I want. Sherborn fleein' shows his guilt."

"Guilt fer whut? He was offered his cut and wuz free ter go."

"Did I ask ye for yer opinion?"

Samuel shook his head as he left Leighton to his ranting.

CHAPTER TWENTY-SEVEN

Arianna snuggled closer to Keldon and he pulled the covers over them as he planted a kiss on the top of her head. "The meetin' went verra weel with General Jackson."

"Uh huh," she answered, but he could tell she was distracted.

"What is troublin' ye?"

She tilted her head to look at him. Dark shadows filled the blue of her eyes and the knowing arch of her brow creased. She lifted her hand, cupping his face as her thumb gently caressed his cheek. "Promise me you won't take anymore chances with your life. No more pirating, I couldn't bear losing you."

He chuckled, a deep throaty chuckle, but became serious when he realized she wasn't joking.

"Promise me," she insisted.

He gently kissed her brow, smoothing away the worry lines. "Aye, I will promise ye. No more piratin', I give ye my word."

Arianna was grateful for his promise, but she worried he'd come to resent her for it. He loved the sea. His eyes lit up when he was at the helm. She chewed on her lower lip. She couldn't have it both ways. He either was happy and alive with never going out to sea again, or he could continue his destructive path doing what he loved best. She shook her head. *He couldn't go out to sea with the price still dangling over his head. It would be suicide.* She had to hope he'd find something suitable for him on land, something within the law.

She looked up at him again. "Is it possible for us to head home now?" she asked, suddenly, feeling homesick.

"Are ye no' havin' a good time?"

He had shown her New Orleans. Its French ambiance and Spanish influenced architecture with wrought iron fences. The city was both beautiful and haunting, but most of all, she enjoyed being swept away by Keldon's charm and experiencing how it was to be his wife. "I love being with you, but I miss Maeve, Sally Mae, and the others. I won't even recognize baby Elijah."

He gave her an affectionate squeeze. "If that is what ye wish, I'll will be verra glad to take ye there."

"Thank you."

"There's no place like home. Aye?"

Arianna's brow wrinkled. How strange, the phrase made her think of ruby slippers.

*****

Keldon had some last minute business to take care of, giving Arianna ample time to set her plans into motion. She sent a note to Jackson requesting to meet with him one last time.

She breathed a sigh of relief when he sent a driver to pick her up. This time the meeting took place in a building at the far side of town. She entered the one room building at the same time as a man was leaving and ended up colliding into him.

"Beg your pardon, mademoiselle," the tall stranger said as he steadied her. "I wasn't looking where I was going. Are you quite all right?"

Arianna was dazed for a moment then she really looked at the man who had nearly knocked her over. He was tall, slender and handsome with dark hair and eyes that bordered on being green-hazel in color. "I'm fine, thank you."

"Then I will bid you, adieu." The stranger went on his way, though he gave her a second glance.

It took Arianna a few seconds to collect herself before she went inside to greet General Jackson. She knew the commotion had not escaped him.

"Would I be presumptuous to ask who that man was?" Arianna inquired as she turned to look out the window at the man one more time.

"No, not at all. The man is Jean Lafitte."

"The pirate?" Arianna spun around.

Jackson chuckled. "So, you have heard of him. Though, he being a pirate is a matter of opinion. Mr. Lafitte would deny any claim of such a title with his life. He thinks of himself as a... well, shall we say a businessman. Do you know much about him, Mrs. Buchanan? Is he another one of your men of history?" he teased.

"He is. Did he come to offer his services to you?"

Jackson frowned. "The man did indeed, but I sent him on his way."

"You might want to reconsider. Though he is a pirate, he is first a gentleman. His word can be trusted. The British officers by now should have tempted him with a pardon and financial rewards to help them attack New Orleans. You don't want that to happen. We need him on our side."

"I'm afraid I may have spurned the man. He will not approach me a second time."

"You must find a way to meet with him again. He is vital for your fight against the British."

Jackson rubbed his chin as if contemplating over what she proposed. "To work with a well-known pirate and trust him... this is a lot to ask, but again you seem to know more about this war than I do. I'll see what I can do."

"Thank you."

"Now, Mrs. Buchanan, what do I owe the pleasure of your company?" He walked her back to his makeshift desk and offered her a seat.

"I have a favor to ask of you."

"Oh?" Jackson didn't hide his surprise. "Go on."

"My husband and I have a dear friend who seems to have gotten himself into a bit of trouble with the law. He is a good man and we would like to see he has a second chance."

"What has this man done?"

"Have you heard of the Highland Pirate?"

"Ah yes. Seems to have frightened many captains into thinking he's a phantom of sorts."

She gave him a wry smile. "Yes, something like that. Would it be possible for you to see if a Letter of Marque could be granted to this pirate?"

"Hmm. This friend has stepped over the bounds. He has attacked a Spanish frigate just recently. Am I not right?"

Arianna nodded, her heart pounding in her chest. If Jackson refused to help, Keldon would always have a price on his head.

Jackson sighed. "I am personally pleased he decided on a Spanish ship to attack, but others will not see it that way. When the Highland Pirate took ships for his own personal gains, it was considered an injustice that was set against the United States of America."

"He's never attacked American ships and he has always brought the goods he acquired to American soil. So as I see it, the Highland Pirate has worked for his country and his fellow Americans."

She watched his lips twitched as he fought not to smile. He pretended to contemplate over her dilemma, but she had the feeling he already knew what course of action he would take.

"I will send word personally to President Madison in this pirate's behalf. You do know I will have to have his true name."

"Yes, of course…"

He held up his hand obviously realizing her hesitation. "You don't need to give it to me now. Let me see what can be done. If the charges are dropped, the letter will state the Highland Pirate had the right from the beginning to be an American privateer."

"Thank you. May I hope when the Highland Pirate is cleared of charges, his men will be also?"

"Well of course."

"Wonderful." This meant Vincent Aubrey would also be in the clear and would be free to marry Bernadette.

"Is there another friend you are worried about?" Jackson lifted his eyebrows.

"Yes, and having his name cleared will make it possible for him to marry a woman whom he holds dear."

"Well then I wish him luck, also."

Arianna stood, as did the general. "Thank you." Even though Jackson didn't say he knew the Highland Pirate's identity, Arianna suspected he did.

"Again, my dear it has been a pleasure." Jackson nodded.

"And mine." Arianna was at the door when the general asked her one more question, confirming her suspicions.

"I hope your husband appreciates you?"

Arianna turned and smiled at him. "Yes, he does and the feeling is quite mutual."

*****

Keldon carried in their luggage they had acquired in New Orleans, while Arianna told Maeve about her adventure. They were so thrilled to see each other that they couldn't stop talking.

Keldon shook his head. If he didn't see it with his own eyes, he would have never believed his wife would befriend one of the slaves, yet there she was as though Maeve was her best friend. "Friends," he said beneath his breath. The word popped into his head, but it rang true. Arianna thought of Maeve as her friend. He smiled. He knew they were heading outside to the kitchen. He'd let the women have time alone and he would check on other matters.

Sally Mae squealed in delight when she saw her mistress had returned. Arianna opened her arms and Sally Mae immediately ran to her, hugging her waist.

"We missed you somethin' fierce."

"I missed you, too, little one." Arianna said kissing the top of the little girl's head before she released her.

Oni's eyes misted with tears and she too hugged Arianna with her large warm arms. "Glad you's home, Miss Arianna. Weren't de same without you."

"Well, it wasn't the same without you, either. I missed your good cooking, too."

"Well's, I best be fixin' you somethin' then." She hurried over to her worktable to finish preparing the meal.

Then Sophie came rushing in, carrying Elijah. "They were right. You come back, Miss Arianna." Her smiled broaden as Arianna returned her greeting.

"How's that baby doing?"

"Most fine."

Arianna held out her index finger for the chubby little infant to grab. "May I hold him?"

"Shor' thing, Miss Arianna." Sophie gladly handed over her child.

"He's grown so big. And how is Thaddeus?"

"He's proud as any father kin be."

"I have something I want to share with all of you. I'm going to have a baby, too." Everyone at once started talking, offering congratulations.

Arianna smiled but when her gaze met Maeve's it faltered. She needed to speak to Maeve and in private. Arianna handed Elijah back to his mother. "We'll talk later. I have so much I want to tell you, but I still need to unpack." She looked over to Maeve. "Would you mind helping?"

"Shor' thing."

Arianna breathed a sigh of relief when she found Keldon wasn't in the bedroom. She shut the door and turned to face Maeve.

"Whuts eatin' you chile?"

"Maeve, where do I begin?" She paced the room as she spoke. "No matter how I want to run away from my past, it just keeps haunting me."

"Whut does?"

"I'll just come right out and say it. I had an affair with Nicholas Sherborn. I don't remember being with him but I can see no reason why he'd lie to me. We obviously slept together, but I assure you it is over between us. Anyway…" She took a deep breath and faced Maeve. "But here's the problem. You see, I don't remember when my last time of the month was, so I have no way of knowing whose child I do carry."

Maeve shook her head sadly. "You still not comes ter terms with your new life. Dear, dear, Miss Arianna. How hard it must be ter not know. You must open your heart and accept whut wuz freely given ter you."

"I don't understand."

"I will say it as I know it, but I kin see you ain't goin's ter believe me." Maeve sighed. "You have ter trust yourself. Shor'ly you know whose chile you carry, ef you allows yourself ter believe. Miss Annabelle wud never have a babe grow in her belly, especially ef it wuz Mist' Keldon's. I know dis fer a fact." Maeve brushed a strand of Arianna's hair away from her eyes. "Your chile will have Buchanan blood runnin' through its veins."

Arianna knew Maeve harbored the fantasy that she was another person, but how could she be? Even if it were possible and somehow she'd switched places with Annabelle Buchanan, where did Annabelle go? Wouldn't this mean she was now living her life?

Arianna shook her head. No matter how much she wanted to believe Maeve, she couldn't. The idea she suggested was impossible.

CHAPTER TWENTY-EIGHT

After three weeks of bad weather, horrible food and company, which was less than desirable, Leighton and the others arrived back at *Blue Run*.

Arianna did her best to stay out of Leighton's way, since his unpleasant looks made her feel uncomfortable. However, she was thrilled to see Vincent and Bernadette. She immediately invited them to have dinner at the house.

"I have missed your company, Arianna. How do you fair?" Vincent asked. "Pregnancy definitely has agreed with you. You appear to be the picture of good health. I take it your stomach does not ail you nearly as much."

"The morning sickness happens rarely now," she told him as they walked down the hall.

"Oh, I am so glad to hear this."

Arianna turned to Bernadette, dressed in her baggy clothing. Some things apparently never changed. "And how are you doing?"

"I... uh... good, thank you," Bernadette answered in English, surprising Arianna.

"You understood me?"

Bernadette nodded. "Vincent teach me the English." She looked at him and smiled, warmly.

Arianna raised an eyebrow and he sheepishly gave her a shrug. "It was something to pass the time. Where is Keldon keeping himself?" he inquired clearly eager to change the subject.

"He'll be along soon. He was checking on our overseer. He seems to have been mistreating some of our workers, yet again."

They entered the room and Sally Mae jumped and sprinted away from the harpsichord. "Sorry Miss Arianna.

I wuz jest cleanin'." The little girl stammered her gazing shifting uneasily to Vincent then to Bernadette.

Arianna knew the child was fascinated with the harpsichord. "Sally Mae, it's quite all right. I told you already, you may play the harpsichord anytime you wish." Arianna turned to Vincent and Bernadette. "I'm teaching Sally Mae how to play. She's very talented, too."

"You taught her?" Vincent eyes widened with disbelief. "The girl's a slave. No?"

"Please don't tell me I have misjudged you. I thought of you as a fair man."

Vincent put his hands up as if to fend off her verbal assault. "Arianna, please let me explain. I was only surprised, not that I disapproved. Pardon me, but I have never believed in the institution of owning another human, but it seems the South does not hold my opinion."

She felt the heat rise in her cheeks. "I'm finally seeing my own folly. I'm sorry I jumped down your throat."

He chuckled. "Jump down my throat? I have never heard it put quite that way."

"I meant I apologize and to make up for it, we'll play you a piece that I have been teaching Sally Mae." She looked at the little girl. "Are you ready to have an audience?" Sally Mae nodded and took her seat and Arianna sat down beside her.

The little girl nervously chewed on her lower lip.

"You can do it," Arianna encouraged. "We've practiced this a hundred times."

Sally Mae stumbled over the piece at first, but gained confidence as she heard Arianna singing the haunting words.

After dealing with the bothersome Rafferty, Keldon had been in a sour mood, but when he heard Arianna's lilting voice, the tension seemed to melt away. She sang his favorite song. At first, he wondered how she came to know it, but now it seemed the melody had always been a part of her... a part of them. He stepped in the drawing room and his deep voice joined hers.

No one missed the devotion in their eyes as they sang the unforgettable melody in perfect harmony.

The song ended and Vincent and Bernadette clapped their hands.

"That was superb!" Vincent bowed to Sally Mae. "You my dear are most talented."

Sally Mae giggled and put her hand over her mouth.

Vincent looked at his two friends. "You two make beautiful music together. It is as though your voices were meant to blend into one."

Sally Mae stood and excused herself to find out if dinner was almost ready.

Keldon kept his attention on his wife, but he directed his question to Vincent. "Is everything taken care of at *Willow Bend*?"

"The deliveries went without a hitch. Though, we all had to put up with Leighton's bad temper."

Keldon nodded. "Aye. He's been in a sour mood of late. Maybe I should put in a word?"

"Leighton is Leighton. We kept clear of him while he was sober. I tell you, the men were trying to force grog down him every night." Vincent chuckled.

"And what of the other matter?" Keldon asked.

"The frigate was stripped and being careened as we speak. When we're finished with her, no one will ever know she belonged to the Spanish."

"Dinner is served," Maeve announced at the door.

"Thank you, Maeve," Arianna replied.

"Oni made your favorite dish," she added, smiling.

Arianna clasped her hands in girlish delight. "She made the trout fillet coated in milk and fried with butter?"

"Yes'm."

"Did she add the almonds?"

"She did jest dat."

"My mouth is already watering." Vincent chuckled.

"You'll have to be excusin' my wife," Keldon said. "She thinks of nothin' but the next meal. I doonae ken how she's still so thin."

Arianna nudged Keldon. "Don't tease me." She looked down at her disappearing waistline.

"I wouldnae think of it. Come on, dear. Let us proceed to the dinning room before ye have Vincent drooling at the mouth.

The dinner Oni prepared was indeed wonderful. Arianna savored every buttery mouthful.

Vincent entertained them with old family stories of what they were in store for when their child was born. He had them laughing so hard that there were tears in their eyes.

"Where do your sisters live?" Arianna asked.

"Four still live in France. I don't see them much, but we do write, or rather they write to me. I am terrible about correspondence; however, my family is always in my thoughts. My sister, Chantal and her husband Gerard live near New Orleans. Chantal had her first baby last spring. She's a beautiful little girl with the rosiest cheeks. Chantal just wrote me saying Gerard's mother was planning to visit and I should make a special effort to join them, a family reunion of sorts. I'll have to see what I can do."

"You sound close to your family." Arianna leaned forward enjoying the stories Vincent told.

"Oui, I am. They mean everything to me."

"Then why is it that you have not settled down yourself?" The minute she said this, she wished she could have bitten her tongue off for being so insensitive. Poor Bernadette looked like she wanted to cry.

"Ah, but it is not so simple." He tried to make light of her question. "The woman who would meet my every need is already married to my best friend, unless he wishes to part with her." Vincent looked questioningly at Keldon.

"Watch it my friend or ye may verra weel be sorry," he warned good-heartily.

Vincent sighed and looked at Arianna once again. "So you see, I must pine away for you then."

"Vincent, you are incorrigible. Has anyone ever told you this before?"

"Most often, merci."

Arianna wasn't immune to Bernadette's feelings and her heart went out to her when she saw how Vincent's casual words had wounded her. Obviously, nothing had changed between her two friends. She had hoped that Vincent's attention toward Bernadette meant he had decided to court her. Didn't the man realize the torture he bestowed on the poor woman?

Bernadette was pretty, with her wavy light brown hair and light golden brown eyes, but she dressed as though she was ready to hoist a long boat into the water and sail away. This had to change. Bernadette needed a makeover. She needed a woman's wardrobe to show off her slim figure and a hairdo to flatter her petite features.

A slow smile spread across her face. Vincent was attracted to the street urchin, transforming her into a lady would cause him to lose what little self-control he still possessed. They wouldn't be playing fair, but if this was the only way to make Vincent lower his guard, then so be it.

CHAPTER TWENTY-NINE

Vincent and Bernadette would be their guests for only another day. They'd have to work fast if they were going to shake Vincent up a bit. Maeve volunteered to help with the process. They ushered Bernadette into Arianna's old room and locked the door behind them.

"I not know this good idea," Bernadette kept saying, but Arianna was determined.

"Trust me. Men are sometimes very slow to realize what is good for them. All we have to do is make Vincent notice you in a different light."

"He sees me. No?"

Maeve led Bernadette to the chair as she spoke. "He sees you as someone he needs ter protect. You need ter let him see you as a woman dat knows whut she wants." Maeve pointed to her outfit.

Bernadette blushed. "I no have purdy dresses."

"But I do," Arianna offered. "I want you to feel free to use any of them until we have a chance to have your own gowns made."

Bernadette didn't know what to say. She never had so many people fussing over her. Bernadette wanted Vincent to look upon her with devotion, but doubted the possibility. He cared for her, but he kept his affection restrained, leaving her frustrated and lonely. She had tried everything short of throwing herself at his feet. She looked at Arianna. Could she really make her wish come true. Tears stung her eyes and she brushed them away.

Arianna misunderstood Bernadette's mood. She quickly tried to make her feel better. "Please don't cry. I didn't mean to offend—"

Bernadette placed her small hand on hers, halting her apology. "I accept your help. But you are very, very tall. No? I don't think your dress fit."

Arianna frowned. "You're right. I hadn't thought of that."

Maeve came to the rescue. "I kin make it fit, ef it be all rights with you, Miss Arianna."

"You go right ahead and I'll start with Bernadette's hair." Arianna pointed to the chair and Bernadette gratefully sat down, willing to do anything to make Vincent a permanent part of her life.

After all day of prepping, bathing, dress altering and arranging her hair, Bernadette was ready. Arianna went downstairs first to greet the men. She wanted Bernadette to make a grand entrance.

Keldon waited at the bottom of the staircase for her. He hadn't seen Arianna all day and if the pout was any indication, he missed her. She gave him a quick kiss winning her a smile.

"Where's Bernadette?" Keldon asked, as he wrapped Arianna's arm around his.

"She'll be down shortly." She smiled impishly.

Keldon leaned near to whisper in her ear. "What are ye up to, lass?"

"Nothing," she answered, innocently. She slipped her arm free from Keldon's and went to greet Vincent.

"You are looking as charming as ever," Vincent commented as he took her hand. He leaned down to bestow a kiss and stopped midway. His mouth dropped open as his gaze riveted to the top of the stairs. His gaze all but gobbled up Bernadette.

Vincent closed his mouth the moment he realized it was agape. Dear Lord in heaven, his little bear had gathered her wavy light brown hair away from her face, revealing her high cheekbones. The dark blue dress she wore flattered her olive skin and exaggerated her tiny waist. "An angel," he whispered. He swallowed the lump that had formed in the back of his throat. Common sense skittered into the shadows as her gaze held his. He moved around Arianna and waited at the bottom of the steps.

Finally, she was in reach. He had a tangible urge to touch her and make sure she was real.

Bernadette smiled. "You like?"

There was no denying his little waif was a beautiful, attractive woman. Vincent's mouth curved into a smile. "I like very much, my little bear." He offered his arm.

Bernadette glanced hesitantly to Arianna, who nodded for her to accept. Bernadette then looked at Vincent and gave him a dazzling smile as she slipped her hand through the crook of his arm.

Keldon moved beside Arianna. "Yer doin' no doubt."

"Isn't she beautiful?"

"Aye that she is, but no' as beautiful as ye."

"Shush." Arianna nudged him playfully.

*****

Bernadette and Vincent stayed late into the evening. Arianna enjoyed their company, immensely, but she was exhausted. Keldon walked her to their bedroom. When he didn't follow her in, she turned toward him expectantly. "Aren't you coming to bed?"

"No my sweet, but ye go. I know ye are tired from all yer matchmakin'."

"It went well, don't you think." She walked over to him and he opened his arms to her.

"Aye, verra weel. Vincent could barely follow the conversation all evening, for he couldnae tear his gaze away from Bernadette." Keldon kissed the tip of Arianna's nose.

"You must be tired, too." She looked up at him with her blue eyes, her gaze focusing on his lips.

"Aye, but no' enough," he growled. "If I followed ye into our bed chamber just now, I would want my way with ye."

She put her arms around his neck. "I wouldn't mind." She yawned and they both laughed. "Maybe you are right. I am a little tired."

"I willnae be long. I want to have a smoke."

"I wish you wouldn't smoke that pipe. It's not good for your health."

"Doonae worry so much. A little tobacco dinnae hurt my Grandda and he lived for a verra long time." He gave her a quick hug as he kissed away her frown. "Now, off to bed with ye."

Keldon took a leisurely walk out to the stables. He lit his pipe and drew in the tobacco in small puffs. He thought of how contented he was with his life. He was married to a woman he adored and she was going to have his baby. He couldn't have been happier.

*****

After leaving the Buchanan's, Vincent drove the carriage at a slow pace, wanting to be with Bernadette as long as possible. He glanced at her sitting next to him. She was sitting up straight with her gloved hands folded on her lap. Her serene face held a trace of a smile. She was beautiful and it wasn't because of her new clothes she wore, or the way she had cleverly arranged her hair. He thought she was lovely before Arianna and Maeve dressed her in finery. He had refused to acknowledge the fact before tonight because he knew he would never be able to let her go. He silently cursed Arianna for meddling with his life, though only half-heartily.

He would think of a way to change his life so he could ask Bernadette to marry him without giving her reason to regret it.

Bernadette felt his intense gaze upon her and she glanced up at him. She trembled, though it wasn't from being chilled. It was because of the way he stared with such longing in his eyes.

"Are you cold, Little Bear?" Vincent asked. He didn't wait for her to answer. "Come closer and I will warm you." He patted the space that separated them. Bernadette only thought about his offer for half a second before she accepted it. She moved close and he slipped his right hand around her shoulders, while keeping his other hand securely on the reins. "Is that better?"

"Oui. Much, much better." Bernadette closed her eyes and relished in the pleasure of having the man she loved so close to her.

CHAPTER THIRTY

Leighton purposely stayed out late because he knew there would be a full house tonight. He couldn't sit and be cordial for one more evening with Annabelle looking so blissfully full of herself. The lying deceitful woman was breeding on top of it all. As soon as he cornered Keldon alone, he'd knock some sense into him and he'd see Annabelle left *Blue Run* with her bastard child in tow.

As Leighton neared the stables, he saw Keldon there, leaning against the wall smoking his pipe. Leighton couldn't believe his good fortune, alone at last and at his mercy to hear him out. He dismounted, leading his horse behind him.

"Have no' seen much of ye, Leighton." Keldon nodded his greeting.

"Aye. I havenae cared for the company of late."

Keldon's eyes narrowed. "Ye best be careful," he warned.

"I will." He sighed with a heavy heart. "If ye will listen with an open ear."

"Speak what ye must and be done with it."

"She was caught with Sherborn." Leighton decided not to mince words.

"Who was?"

"Doonae play me as a fool, Keldon Buchanan. Do ye think it is easy for me to tell ye of these things. Yer like a son to me. I would never want to hurt ye, but that woman ye took as yer wife isnae good. Ye use to know that, yet ye somehow have forgotten."

"Leighton, I wish ye would give her a chance. I doonae know how to explain it. She isnae as she was before. She's a different person."

"Ye're a love sick fool to be believin' that. Doonae be takin' my word on the matter. It be better she hang her own self. Ye ask her what she be doin' with Sherborn on the eve that he stole the long boat and disappeared. They were holdin' hands like lovers. I never knew why ye trusted Sherborn. Be it here or back in Scotland, he is still Sassenach."

"Stop."

"Ye stop. Higgins saw them together. If that doonae look suspicious all by itself, then ye tell me why would a man leave his share of the booty behind and sneak away in the middle of the night no less?" Leighton could see the doubt cross Keldon's face. "What man does that? A guilty man," he answered his own question. "Do ye ken, now?"

"I ken nothing." Keldon pushed himself away from the barn wall. He didn't want to hear anymore, but Leighton wasn't finish.

"I hear she's carryin' a wee bairn."

Keldon stopped cold.

"Now, I would be askin' myself, just whose babe she be carryin'. Remember she made sure she dinnae carry yer first born. Why would she want to now?"

Keldon didn't look back. He couldn't for doing so would mean he believed what Leighton was insinuating. He kept walking toward the house, but his mind raced. Could Leighton be right? Could Arianna be carrying Nicholas Sherborn's child? He didn't want to believe it. He didn't want to believe she would betray him, not now, when he had opened up his heart to her.

He went inside the house and took the stairs two at a time, frantic to have the answers. He threw open the door to the room they now shared and forced himself to walk over to the bed.

Arianna didn't stir from her slumber as he watched her sleep. It was difficult to believe she would delude him yet again. She looked so sweet and angelic, but with Leighton's accusing words, it dug up the memories he thought he'd buried. There could be a hundred reasons why she met with Sherborn, only he couldn't think of a single reason why she would need to hold his hand. A cynical inner voice brought another question to mind: *Why did she try to hide her pregnancy?* Why didn't she tell him the moment he arrived back from New Orleans? It had been Vincent who slipped, revealing the truth.

Keldon pulled up a chair and sat down next to the bed, willing her to open her eyes, so she could explain away his suspicions. He clasped his hands, trying to remain calm, but like an awakening giant, anger rose in him. In a heartbeat their stormy past began to cloud his judgment, making him forget the way she had felt in his arms, the way she had looked at him when they made love.

She had deceived him before and without a qualm. She knew how to play the game and she always seemed to hit where it hurt. Only this time he had been so sure she was sincere. He had been so sure she loved him.

Arianna rolled over, her eyes fluttering open. "Keldon?" She sounded so tired that he almost told her to go back to sleep, but desperation stopped him. He couldn't go another moment without knowing the truth.

"Aye," he said so calmly that it surprised him.

"What are you doing? Why don't you come to bed?"

Arianna closed her eyes and would have probably gone back to sleep, but he hovered over her. She opened her eyes. "Keldon?"

He didn't answer.

"Keldon?" she asked again concern lacing her words.

If only she'd have as much concern with his heart. "I had an interestin' conversation with Leighton." His voice held an ominous inflection, forcing her take notice.

She sat up. "What's wrong?"

Keldon needed to see her face when he asked the question. He didn't want shadows hiding the truth. He moved away, only long enough to find the flint box and light the candles. He then looked at her trying to keep his emotions in check. He managed to keep his voice low, but his words whipped like steel. "Whose bairn do ye carry?"

For a moment all time seemed to halt, as the fine line that held their lives together seemed to unravel. As he watched her face pale and her lower lip tremble, he felt as though a cutlass had severed him in two, his essence slipping away. Without her saying a word to him, he knew she'd betrayed him.

"Why would you ask such a thing?" she breathed. Fear touched her eyes and she clutched at her nightdress.

"Tell me, I doonae have a reason to doubt ye and I'll no' ask ye again." He prayed she would say the words that would make this nightmare go away. He prayed she would tell him she had been with no other, even if it was a falsehood. However, the words that could have saved their happiness failed to leave her lips.

Arianna knew his heart was breaking and she could do nothing to stop it. She had been untrue to him and she refused to fabricate another lie on top of it. Not anymore because she knew the deceptions would never end. She lowered her head, feeling the shame she had been living with wash over her. The fragile ground they had gained in starting a new relationship slipped away as though she stood in a pit of quicksand. "I can't." She choked on the words, feeling trapped with no escape.

They were both silent for a long time, neither one wanting to break the quietness, for doing so would mean they would have to deal with the shattering reality.

Keldon leaned against the nightstand. "Is the bairn ye carry, Sherborn's?"

How could she explain herself to him, when she didn't understand the betrayal herself? The heaviness she felt pressing on her chest made it difficult for her to breath. "I don't know." A sobbed escaped her, filling the room with a deafening echo.

"Ye doonae know!" Keldon whirled on her his guttural burr thickening as anger took over. His green eyes bore into hers. "Ye mean there were others?"

"No! God no! I mean, I don't know if the baby is yours or..." She just let the sentence trail off to silence because she didn't want to admit the horrible possibility that the child wasn't his.

"Tell me this," Keldon asked as he took a seat in front of her. "Did ye lie down with me because ye thought ye might be carryin' Sherborn's bairn?"

Arianna shook her head frantically. "I wouldn't do that to you."

"Ye wouldnae do that to me! Yet ye are willin' to admit that ye have been with another! What would stop ye from goin' a step further!"

"I didn't know I had been with Nicholas, until he told me. I don't remember having the affair. It happened before I received the bump on my head." She tried desperately to defend herself, but the words sounded hollow even to her.

He stood so abruptly his chair flew behind him. "It's gettin' to be a wee bit too convenient that ye keep usin' the bump on yer head as an excuse." He began to pace.

"I'm not making this up. As soon as I knew of Nicholas, I made him stay away from me. I have been faithful to you ever since. I swear to you. I swear to God."

Keldon stopped pacing and swung around to face her. "Doonae be takin' the Lord's name in vain in this matter of adultery." He stood at the edge of the bed, looking down at her with a harrowing expression as he witnessed her tears streaming down her cheeks. He wanted to believe the affair was over and that it had meant nothing. He wanted to trust that she had been faithful since they declared their love to each other, but he was too hurt. He wanted to lash out. He wanted to hurt her as much as she had hurt him.

He questioned everything now—Sherborn's interest in joining up with his crew and then his sudden disappearance. "Sherborn took ye from me, yet he dinnae leave with ye. He wormed his way into my house and worked with me. What else was he after?" He was upon her then. He grabbed hold of her shoulders with a squeezing grip, the black rage blinding him. "Tell me."

"Keldon, you're hurting me."

"Tell me! Was he after my life as weel? Dinnae he know that takin' ye away from me would have been enough to make my life worthless? Tell me, I say!" he repeated, squeezing even tighter.

"Keldon, please." She sobbed.

He finally realized what he was doing and released her.

She moved away to the far side of the bed.

He dragged in a breath his nostrils flaring. She'd betrayed him. He looked down at his trembling hands then to her huddling in fear. His gaze clashed with hers startled and upset. He was mortified at his actions. He lost control and he could have killed her. "What am I doin'?" He ran his hand through his hair as he closed his eyes and tried to ignore the ache that had settled behind his heart. He had never raised a hand in violence toward a woman and he wasn't going to let his anger toward her cause him to do something he would regret for the rest of his life.

He couldn't stay, not when the old pain shimmered deep inside him resurfacing to choke him. He wanted desperately to trust she spoke the truth, that what they had was real. He wanted to believe Nicholas meant nothing to her, but he'd forgiven her so many times before he had lost count. How could she expect him to exonerate her for betraying him? How could she expect him to raise another man's child?

With one smooth motion, he turned and stormed out of the room, slamming the door behind him.

CHAPTER THIRTY-ONE

Arianna dozed in and out of sleep where haunting dreams plagued her. She dreamt of people she didn't know and yet they seemed close to her. She dreamt about a fortuneteller with a desperate warning, *"Trust the Scotsman. He may feel mistrust for you because of the other woman's black heart."*

"Miss Arianna, Miss Arianna." Maeve shook her.

Arianna tossed and turned, screaming out.

Maeve shook her, again.

She sat up in bed with a ragged intake of breath. "Where am I?"

"Dear, dear chile. You's home." Maeve patted her hand.

"Home?" Her voice broke and she put her head back down on the pillow and closed her eyes. "Please leave me alone."

"Miss Arianna, you slept past the mornin'. I's worried about you."

"I'm fine," she told her.

"No's you ain't. I's not blind. I know dat dere be somethin' terrible wrong with you and Mista Keldon. Him mopin' and you hidin' up here. Why don'ts you tell me?"

"There's nothing to tell." She hugged her pillow to her chest, rocking back and forth. Her resolve wore thin and she broke down. "I've lost him and it's my fault. I betrayed him."

"How did you betray him? You ain't hurt no one."

"Oh Maeve. I don't know whose baby I'm carrying?" Tears spilled down her face and she wiped them away.

Maeve sat down on the bed next to her and gently patted her back. "You poor, poor chile. You never gone and betrayed him. I told you. Miss Annabelle did. Dat dere chile you carry be Mista Keldon's."

"Maeve, I can't believe your fantastic story of how I switched places with the evil Annabelle like there was some twist of fate at work. Please leave me alone," she pleaded.

Maeve knew there was no convincing her, especially in her present state of mind. With a heavy heart, she left the room. If only Arianna would believe who she really was, all this could be resolved. Maybe she could shake some sense into Keldon. It was worth a try.

She found him in the study, nursing a glass of whiskey. He hadn't been to bed and still wore the clothes he had on yesterday. His hair was unbound and wild as his bloodshot eyes. Maeve took a deep breath for courage. "Mista Keldon, kin I say somethin'?"

He acknowledged her with a nod.

"You have ter trust your heart." She ventured a little closer. "You know dat Miss Arianna loves you. She not hurt you fer nothin'."

His eyes narrowed to where they were just slits below two dark eyebrows. "Oh but ye are wrong, Maeve. She's already hurt me more than ye will ever know. I willnae trust her again." His green eyes flashed, revealing his tormented soul. "Now leave me. I want to be left alone.

CHAPTER THIRTY-TWO

Arianna hadn't seen Keldon for days. He rose early and took his meals late. When he refused to sleep in the same room, Arianna moved her belongings back to the other room.

"You shud not give Mista Keldon the consideration. It's his own stubbornness that keeps him sleeping in a chair."

"It's my fault he's miserable, Maeve. I broke his heart. I won't stay in his room when I know he doesn't want me there."

"Ah..." She waved her hand at her in frustration. "You's jest as foolish as he is."

Keldon wanted to seek out Arianna's company. He yearned for her smile, her laugh. He wanted to hold her in his arms. He missed her, but he refused to go to her. He wouldn't play the fool.

He spent most of his time outside in the fields or down by the water, anywhere he didn't have to be tortured by seeing her dispirited blue eyes, imploring him to forgive her. He wouldn't do it, not this time.

After a week of this torture, he decided it was time, to venture out again. He set up a meeting in Charleston with Vincent to discuss their departure. With Arianna's betrayal, his promise to stay on shore didn't matter any longer.

"We put out to sea at the end of the week," Keldon announced as he approached.

Vincent raised an eyebrow. There were black smudges under Keldon's eyes and few days' growth on his usually smooth face. "What is troubling you, my friend?"

"It is nothin'." Keldon avoided meeting his gaze.

"Ah, it is as I have expected. You are having trouble with your lovely wife. Do not worry. I know of these things from my brother-in-law. A woman in their delicate state can be quite moody. It will not last. Why Chantal—"

"Enough!" Keldon cut him off sharply.

Shocked at his rudeness made Vincent fear something had happened. "Is Arianna having trouble with her pregnancy?"

"If ye doonae mind, I am in no mood to be discussin' my wife. We have more important matters of concern, which I would verra much like to go over with ye."

"As you wish, but let me buy you a drink. You look as if you need one."

"Aye."

"I almost forgot." Vincent halted him and pulled out an envelope from his coat pocket. "The boy was on his way to deliver this to you. I took the liberty of being responsible for it."

Keldon stared wide-eyed at the envelope, realizing what he held.

"Are you going to open it?"

"Nay, I already know the contents."

"Is it bad news?"

Keldon shook his head. "Nay, 'tis my freedom."

CHAPTER THIRTY-THREE

After everyone was sound asleep, Keldon sat down behind his desk and opened the envelope. He stared at the divorce papers. He couldn't believe he'd forgotten all about them. He should be rejoicing. He could leave and never look back.

He shoved the papers in his desk, slamming the drawer shut. "It's what ye wanted, Buchanan," he mumbled to himself without conviction.

He rose from his seat and headed toward the stairs, berating himself for wanting to see Arianna one last time before he set out to sea. He entered her room and walked over to the bed. He stared down at her so peaceful in her slumber with her bewitching face—fine bone structure, full kissable lips. Her thick lashes rested on her cheeks, a dark contrast to her hair that framed her porcelain skin like shimmering moonbeams.

He held his breath as his groin jerked, betraying him. He could pretend he didn't desire her, but it would be a lie. He wanted to touch her, feel every curve come alive as he caressed her. He wanted to bury himself as deeply as he could within her and not come out. How could he hate her and love her at the same time?

With an aching heart, he backed away from her, knowing if he didn't he'd do something stupid like kiss her.

He turned to leave, but froze at the sound of her voice.

"Please wait." The pleading in her voice made his heart catch and he cursed himself for the maddening inability to break free from her.

"Are you leaving?" she whispered.

He sensed with those words the true meaning behind them. She asked if he was going to return. He honestly didn't have the answer.

He turned to look at her.

She was sitting up in bed, waiting.

"I'm settin' sail." Then he decided to add, "For a while."

"Oh."

Was it relief he heard in her voice? He was not sure. The shadows hid her face. He couldn't stay any longer. It was difficult enough to be near her when she slept, but with her awake and to hear her sweet voice, it was too much to endure.

"Keldon?" She called out to him, hoping to stall him for just a little while longer. She wanted to tell him she loved him and that she was so sorry for everything. She yearned to tell him she would do anything he asked of her, if only he would give her one more chance. However, she knew groveling wouldn't earn her respect in his eyes. He didn't trust her and they needed trust to make a marriage work. She held back what her heart wanted and the true words went unsaid. "Please be careful."

His only response was the gentle closing of the bedroom door.

CHAPTER THIRTY-FOUR

Vincent wasn't sure what he was going to tell Bernadette, but he knew he couldn't leave without some kind of explanation.

Their relationship had started to take on a new meaning, but it was still fragile. He had lain low, feeling out the residence of Charleston to see if they suspected him of being a pirate. It appeared they thought him a gentleman. His refined schooling his parent's forced on him came in handy for something after all.

Vincent wanted to settle down and he would have to tell Keldon. This run would be his last.

He found Bernadette in the garden. She wore a gown of moss green, matching jacket and her hair pulled up above her head in a twist. Very fetching, he thought. She was beautiful, slim but with soft curves. God help him, he wanted her.

She must have sensed him for she turned her head and looked up with a smile. "How did your meeting go?" she asked in English. She still had trouble mastering some of the words, but she was improving every day.

"That is what I've come to talk to you about. I…" How could he ask her to wait for him? She deserved so much better and yet he couldn't let her go.

She closed the distance between them and she reached for his hand. He looked at her questioningly. A hint of a smile shadowed her sweet face. "You go to sea again?"

She didn't want him to go, he knew that, but he also knew she wouldn't hold him back. He gently caressed her face. "Oh, my Little Bear. I never thought leaving you would be so difficult."

Hope lit her eyes as she searched his. "You will miss me, then? No?"

He nodded. "Oui. Very much so, but I cannot stay. I do promise you that I'll be back. I rented the house for a year. May I hope that you will be here on my return?"

Knowledge flashed in her eyes, understanding what he asked her and she nodded. "I be here waiting for you always."

A primitive force inside him demanded he sweep her into his arms and declare his love. Only protocol, held him back. He wanted to do everything right by her. She deserved to be treated with respect that had been denied her from others. He raised her hand to his lips bestowing the gentlest of kisses, sealing the promise to return. "Then I shall not tarry."

CHAPTER THIRTY-FIVE

Keldon was relentless on the sea and with his crew. Any vessel that looked apt to board Keldon demanded it. Loaded down with valuables, the Good Intent was forced to head into port to lighten the load.

The men couldn't have been happier with their good fortune. Keldon put on a good show of being contented, but the ones closest to him knew his soul was troubled.

Samuel and Vincent could only speculate that his troubles existed with Arianna, but no matter how many times they approached him, he cleverly avoided their attempts to draw out the truth. Keldon had become so withdrawn they were afraid for his welfare. They knew he couldn't possibly go on with the relentless pace he set for himself. As for the anger, he held onto—he was on the verge of exploding. It was only a matter of when and where.

"We set sail on the evenin' tide," Keldon announced to Vincent only moments after they stepped foot on dry land.

"Keldon, the men need a few days rest. We haven't seen land for a month. You must give them time to take care of personal matters."

Keldon's features darkened. "I doonae want to tell ye, again. We leave with the evenin' tide. If you think you cannae handle spreadin' the word of it, I'll be glad to relieve ye of yer duties."

Vincent's jaw dropped open. He stared at him for a full two seconds. "Be glad I know you are hurting, my friend, or I'd teach you a lesson in good manners." He might still consider it since he seemed bent on picking a fight.

"Just do as I asked."

"Aye, aye, Captain." Vincent saluted him.

Keldon cursed under his breath, but didn't say any more.

The crew under protest reluctantly did as their captain bade and set sail once more. The weather turned out to be cold and wet, putting everyone on board in an irritable mood. They hadn't spotted any other prey for days and Keldon was beginning to think Vincent had been right about staying put for a while. He was about to announce they turn the ship toward dry land, when the man on watch gave the cry.

"Captain, vessel on the portside."

Keldon strode to where he could get a better view. Vincent followed close behind.

"Can you see her jack?" he asked.

"She's flyin' the British flag, *The Waterfront* is her name." Keldon handed the spyglass to Vincent. "Take a look for yerself."

"Ah, she's a beauty. You think we can take her. No?"

"Aye, cannae see a reason why we wouldnae be able to. She hasnae even noticed us, yet." Keldon looked behind him and shouted the order. "Bring a spring upon our cable, we have *The Waterfront* in our sights."

"Aye, aye," Leighton replied.

They were in pursuit.

When *The Waterfront* realized the danger, the captain sounded the alarm, but it was already too late. Though the British ship was making way, the *Good Intent* was the faster of the two. At a last attempt, *The Waterfront* tried to use the chase guns on the closing schooner, but Keldon countered the attack. They closed in. They were beside *The Waterfront* now, and if they could just get the grappling hooks over the bulwarks, they would have their prize.

The cry of success finally came. "We have them, Keldon," Leighton shouted.

Keldon's crew quickly boarded the vessel their weapon's in tow. Within fifteen minutes, the fighting was virtually over and *The Waterfront* was theirs for the taking. Keldon watched over the disgruntled Captain Stevens, while the men went to work to see what treasures the ship held.

Stevens stood nearly as tall as Keldon with hair the color of straw and eyes as dark as sin. The man wasn't intimidated and refused to keep his mouth shut. "You know you will not get away with this. We'll run you down. I know these waters and we'll find you and hang every bloody one of you unsavory scoundrels."

"I think my men are up to yer challenge," Keldon countered with self-reliant ease that enraged Stevens further.

Vincent approached with the news of the find. "The jobs completed, Captain and you will be pleased to know we found something well worth our trouble. They were carrying hard currency."

Captain Stevens overheard and continued his verbal assaults. "You better leave that where you found it. That's a hanging offense."

Keldon's smile held no warmth when he addressed Stevens, once again. "Weel since we are goin' to hang one way or another it might as weel be for somethin' that's worth mentionin'."

"You will rue this day," he seethed with contempt, his dark eyes nearly bulging out of his head.

Keldon chose to ignore him and in a voice for all to hear, he made his announcement to his prisoners. "We thank ye all for yer warm hospitality, but we must be goin'. So if ye will kindly make yer way to the long boats, we'll lower ye below."

"You're bloody mad!" Stevens' eyes widen in horror. "Surely, you don't mean to set us afloat in this unfavorable weather."

"I do recall that ye told me ye knew the waters weel. A wee bit of rain willnae hurt ye and besides ye claimed ye would hunt us down. It may be slow goin' in the long boats, but ye can give it a good try." Keldon nudged the red, faced captain, adding to his insult. "Now, move."

Vincent was in charge of lowering the long boats and had already started the monotonous task. While he was busy, Leighton took some of the men back to the *Good Intent* and started releasing her hold on *The Waterfront*.

Keldon could see no apparent trouble. Everything was running smoothly. Then in a blink of an eye, it all went to hell when he spotted the man who ruined his life. He felt his features contort in anger until he knew he wore a glowering mask of rage. "Nicholas Sherborn!" he spit out the name like a horrible obscenity. He'd kill the man. He'd rip his heart from his chest and feed it to the sharks.

Nicholas' eyes widened, but he stood his ground, his fists clenched at his side.

Damn him. He should be groveling, asking for forgiveness. A pulsing fury clouded his judgment and Keldon went after him. He leapt over obstacles and pushed everyone out of his way, but before he could get his hands around Nicholas' neck, a burly sized man stepped in with a vicious blow to the side of his head. He lost his balance and slammed into something hard and unyielding. He blinked rapidly as a blinding light sent him to his knees.

Then everything went dark.

Out of the corner of his eye, Vincent saw Keldon go down. Then yells erupted and there was mass confusion, as the captives broke free. Vincent noticed Sherborn's face among the muddle of chaos, but was too far away to apprehend him. He drew his sword and shouted the order, "Raise your arms, men!"

British outnumbered them and it didn't take long to see Captain Stevens' crew would win out. Vincent hadn't seen

Keldon rise and a nauseating wave of dread hit him. In all the time he had fought side by side with Keldon, he had never seen the powerful man fall. Had they killed him? He had to know for sure. He swung his sword and tried his best to move toward where he last saw Keldon, but at every attempt, he was blocked. In the end, he had no other choice but to retreat to the *Good Intent* or be caught himself.

Vincent stared at *The Waterfront*, as she slowly faded from his view. They should be cheering for their clever decamp, but instead they left with a heavy heart.

"We kin not go back." Samuel clasped Vincent's shoulder. "Mista Keldon wuldn't want us too. We endanger every one efs we did."

"I know this, but it doesn't make me feel any better. If he was still alive, we left him to a fate we all have had nightmares about."

*****

The British scrambled to weigh the anchor and get their ship into motion. In their hurry, they managed to pierce their own ship. Though the damage was minimal, the vessel started to take on water. They had to turn toward land, which infuriated Captain Stevens beyond reason. The Highland Pirate left with the currency in his possession and he had a damaged ship. Someone would pay for this. Violent images lurched inside his head as he thought of what form of torture he'd use on the man who cost him this embarrassment.

"Captain?"

"What do you want, Dugan?" Stevens snapped.

"Do you want us to clap the irons on the Highlander?"

"What?" Stevens looked at his man for the first time. "What did you say?"

"Do you want us to clap the irons on the Highlander?" Dugan repeated.

Stevens couldn't believe it. In all the confusion, he had assumed the man had escaped. He started laughing, hysterically.

.

CHAPTER THIRTY-SIX

Sophie showed Arianna the welts Rafferty had given a small boy, who was no more than eight years old. "Please take care of him Sophie. I'll be back."

"Where's you goin'?"

"I've had enough of Rafferty's abuse." She set out to the fields with determination. She wanted the horrid man off her land and she wanted him gone today.

Rafferty saw Arianna approaching, but he made no move to meet her halfway.

"Did you beat a little boy?" Anger splintered and flashed as she met his gaze. The arrogant bastard smiled.

"If you means the nigger boy, I did." He spat at her feet.

She clutched her fists at her side to refrain from slapping the man's face.

"You are worse than any vile thing that has ever slithered on God's green earth and I want you off my property."

"You ain't orderin' me around. I take orders from no woman."

"You won't have to. You're fired."

"I don't think you heard me." Rafferty grabbed her upper arm. "I say what goes here. No woman tells me otherwise."

"Let me go." She struggled with his grip but he laughed and tightened his hold.

His gaze raked over her as a dark evil sneer spread across his face.

"I said: Let. Me. Go!" She grounded out each word.

"No, I don't think I will." She screeched when he pulled her against his sweaty body. "Now don't make a fuss. I ain't ever had no complaints before from a lady."

"Stop it." She turned her head away.

"I know why you're struggling so much, but never you mind. It don't bother me none that you have a baby growin' in your belly." He rubbed against her his arousal evident.

Arianna's eyes widened in fear as she realized she shouldn't have confronted him alone. Rafferty didn't respect anyone. She lashed out with her free hand, slapping him across the face.

"Oh so you want to play rough, do you? I can oblige." He slapped her with such force that she lost her balance. Sprawled on the ground, Rafferty was upon her, roughly pawing her with his hands. He squeezed Arianna's tender breast so hard tears sprung to her eyes.

"Get off of me!" She fought back in desperation. "Do you plan on taking me in front of all these witnesses?" She tried desperately to make Rafferty see what he was doing.

Rafferty's sinister laugh sent a chill down Arianna's spine. He didn't care. He was going to rape her and she had a sinking feeling he liked the idea of an audience.

"Do you think anyone of those darkies will come to your rescue?" he spat at her. "Don't count on it. They know better. If they touch a white man, it means a sure death to them." Gripping her hair in his fist, he leaned down and forced his mouth on hers. She bit down on his lip, holding on with her teeth, until she felt the blood spurt and the flesh pull away.

Rafferty screeched in pain. "Why you little—" He struck her.

Arianna saw stars. She blinked, forcing herself not to lose consciousness.

"I'll teach you a lesson you'll never forget." He pulled back his fist to hit her again.

Arianna shut her eyes, waiting for the blow but nothing happened.

Rafferty grunted and went limp, toppling head first into the dirt.

Arianna scrambled away from the horrible man.

Thaddeus knelt down beside her. "You be all right, Miss Arianna?"

Arianna's hands shook and the side of her mouth hurt, but otherwise she was unharmed. "I'm fine." She looked up at Thaddeus. "Thank you."

He held out his hand and she gratefully took it. She glanced at Rafferty with a shudder. He would have raped her if Thaddeus hadn't stepped in. She turned toward Thaddeus, her eyebrows furrowing. Rafferty would press charges and Thaddeus would suffer for his bravery. She couldn't let this happen. "Thaddeus, would you help me bring Rafferty back to the house?"

"Dat might not be a gud thing ter do."

"Don't worry, we'll tie him up. Then I need you to go into town and bring back the authorities." She paced as she thought. "Yes, the plan will work. It must."

"Plan?" Thaddeus frowned.

"No one must know you were involved. Once Rafferty comes to, he will want satisfaction and I refuse to let him have his way because of the unfairness of the law." Arianna looked around at the other men and women who stood as witnesses. "Everyone, forget what you saw today. It didn't happen. You never saw Thaddeus raise a hand to Mr. Rafferty. If you all cooperate, I will take care of the rest."

Rafferty wasn't pleased when he woke up with his hands and feet bound. He struggled desperately to free himself, but without any luck.

When Arianna walked in with the authorities, Rafferty cursed. "You're makin' a grave mistake!" Rafferty yelled. I demand me rights. I was struck by one of those niggers and I demand you find out which one!"

Arianna shook her head and looked at George Alten, the magistrate in charge. He was in his early forties, balding and not in favor of a man who couldn't hold his liquor. He was even less inclined to forgive a man for scaring a pregnant woman half to death with his vulgar actions.

"As you can see, he has delusions which are simply not true." Arianna had doused Rafferty with whiskey, broken a few items around the room to help manifest Rafferty's unstable mind. She now dramatically waved her hand around the room emphasizing the destruction.

"The bitch is lying!" Rafferty screamed.

A small vein throbbed over Alten's right eyebrow as he glared. "You will mind your manners, Mr. Rafferty."

"See what I mean?" Arianna shook her head.

"Yes. Go on."

"When I told Mr. Rafferty we had to let him go, he became wild with rage. I am just fortunate he tripped and knocked himself unconsciousness or I don't know what else the man would have done."

Alten cleared his throat. "You leave everything to me, Mrs. Buchanan, I'll see to it personally. This man will not harm you or anyone else for that matter."

"Thank you, sir."

The magistrate snapped his fingers and two of the men he had brought with him dragged the screaming Mr. Rafferty out of the house and hopefully out of their lives forever.

Exhausted, Arianna collapsed onto the sofa with a sigh. She closed her eyes letting the tension ease away.

"Miss Arianna?"

"Yes, Thaddeus."

"Now dat you don't has Mista Rafferty ter take care of things, who's going ter take his place?"

Arianna sat up. She hadn't thought that far ahead. "This does put us in a predicament." She paused for a moment, tapping her chin with her forefinger. "I know absolutely nothing about running a plantation." She looked at him then. "But, you do. You could be in charge."

Thaddeus shook his head in disbelief. "Dat ain't never been done. No slave kin be in charge."

"Well it's time for a change. You're strong; you know the work and the people will respect you. You're the best man for the job. I want to hire you."

His mouth dropped open in disbelief. "Miss Arianna, you kin't hire me. You own me."

"I may not know how to legally free you, but if you are willing, I want to hire you, anyway. Why is it I can't do what I want?"

Maeve walked over to her. "Maybe there be a way around it."

"How?"

"There's badges fer hire. Its ter say we has a trade ter offer and lots of plantation owners use dem badges ter make extra monies when de seasons slow, but sometimes they lets de tradesmen keep some of de pay."

"Hire badges, hmm. Perfect." She looked to Thaddeus. "I will pay you at Mr. Rafferty's rate?"

"I don't know whut ter say."

"Say, yes."

His face broke into a wide grin. "Yas ma'm."

CHAPTER THIRTY-SEVEN

To Arianna's dismay, Bernard and Elizabeth Prescott decided to pay a visit. She led them into the parlor while Maeve took care of preparing the tea for them.

Elizabeth seemed to carry most of the conversation, while Arianna prayed she wouldn't have to endure their company for long.

"Annabelle?" Elizabeth repeated. "Are you paying attention to anything I have been saying?"

"I'm sorry I guess I'm a little tired. Please go on," she said to Elizabeth, though she wished the woman would shut up. Her voice ground on her nerves and if she had to listen to her for too much longer, she was going to scream.

"The quilt we all have been working on will go up for auction on Saturday. We added the final changes. I must say the other women and I have missed you terribly. Won't you come back and join our little group?"

"I might," she lied. She didn't intend to join the little group of snobs. "Since Keldon's been away on business, I just haven't had the time."

"When is that husband of yours returning?" Bernard asked looking around the room as if he might appear out of the woodwork.

Keldon never told Arianna what he had said to Bernard the day they rescued Thaddeus. She suspected by the way Bernard acted her husband intimidated him considerably.

"I expect him back soon." Another lie. She was getting good at this. She wondered what the Prescotts would say if she told them she didn't know if Keldon would ever return. "Would you like some more tea?" She leaned forward with a gasp, her hand flying to her stomach.

"What's wrong?" Elizabeth asked.

Arianna smiled. "I felt the baby kick."

"Dear, it isn't proper to speak of your delicacy in public."

"You're in my house. I'll speak of my *delicacy* if I want to."

Elizabeth fluttered her eyes. "When are you expecting the new arrival?"

"I believe, May," she begrudgingly answered her. She didn't want to share this moment with anyone, especially not with the Prescotts. Why couldn't they go home and leave her alone.

"Keldon must be ecstatic?" the nosy Elizabeth continued.

Arianna's smile vanished. If only this were true, but the reality of the fact was harsh. Keldon didn't want the child, not when he wasn't sure if it was his. Arianna couldn't trust her voice to answer, so she nodded and poured the tea.

Thaddeus appeared at the door, but hesitated.

Arianna smiled, warmly. "Thaddeus, do come in."

He removed his hat. "Sorry ter be disturbin' you, but I wuz wonderin' ef you still be wantin' me ter clear de section near de house?"

"I would, if you have the time to do so today."

"Shor'ly, ma'am." Thaddeus then turned to the Prescotts. "Hope yous folks have a nice visit." Then he went on his way.

Arianna could barely keep from laughing when she saw the Prescotts' jaws drop in unison.

"Well, I never. How dare he address us." Elizabeth touched her hand to her chest.

"He was always an insolent pup." Bernard looked at Arianna. "You mustn't give him so much freedom. A good day at the workhouse in Charleston would teach him respect."

"You feel beating a man is the answer?" Arianna's voice was low and trembling with anger, but Bernard seemed not to notice.

"It's in their nature to be uppity and a whipping keeps them in line."

Arianna mentally counted to ten trying to maintain a calm appearance. The pompous ass was the one who needed a beating.

"You aren't one of those activists, are you?" Elizabeth shook her head. "Mr. Drayton has sided with them, you know. He's no better than that... What's that colored man's name, Bernard?"

"Cuffee"

"Yes, he not only wants to free the slaves, but he wants to relocate them as well."

"Sounds like a good idea if the men and women want to go," Arianna said.

"How can you say this? Why, who would take care of the fields? Who would serve us?" Elizabeth huffed.

Who indeed. Arianna stared at them. They couldn't be her friends when everything they stood for sickened her.

"Really Arianna, when did your views change so drastically?" Elizabeth clucked her tongue. "Is this why you let poor Mr. Rafferty go?"

"Poor Mr. Rafferty." Her voice rose. Then it dawned on her why they were here. Obviously, they had heard about Rafferty's sudden departure. "Did you come all this way to tell me how to run my household?" Arianna could feel her blood pressure rising.

"We're worried about you," Elizabeth said. "We ran into Rafferty and he told us that you fired him. He claimed you took the word of a slave over his, on a matter of indifference."

"Mr. Rafferty has a strange way of putting things. I let him go because he is a dirty, lying bully who would stoop to anything if he was allowed."

"Well, I never," Elizabeth huffed.

Bernard patted his wife's hand, but he addressed Arianna. "Please tell us the rumors are false. You didn't put Thaddeus in charge?"

"I did. He's a hard worker and I trust him."

"He's a man of color?" He nearly choked.

Arianna had heard enough of their indignity and stood. "This conversation is over. I believe you both have better leave."

The Prescotts stood. Bernard took his wife's arm, but Elizabeth shook free. She looked down her nose at Arianna. "Let it be known, you've been warned."

"As you have, my dear." Arianna gave her a sweet smile and batted her eyes. "Now get your bony behind out of my house."

Elizabeth sputtered not able to speak.

Maeve appeared as if on cue. "I will shows dem out."

Bernard lifted his chin as he led his wife out of the room.

Arianna fell back onto the sofa in relief.

A few minutes later Maeve returned. "They be on their way. I believes Mrs. Prescott's nose wuz out of joints."

"She should count herself lucky, she left without me punching her in the nose."

Maeve chuckled. "I wuds like ter see dat."

Arianna smiled, feeling better now that she let off some steam. "Mr. Prescott mentioned a Mr. Cuffee. He didn't seem to like him. I can bet I will. I need ink and paper."

"Whut's you cookin' up in your mind?"

"I don't know yet, but when I do, I'll share it with you."

CHAPTER THIRTY-EIGHT

Doused with cold water, Keldon inhaled deeply and his eyes flew open. His head pounded against his skull, making his stomach roll. He felt disoriented and blinked trying to focus. He jerked his arm, but realized his hands were bound above his head with the rope attached to a wooden post. His back lay bare, his shirt ripped from him. This couldn't bode well.

"We've been waiting for you to join us."

Keldon's gaze riveted to the man who spoke. His eyes narrowed—Captain Stevens. Then the memories came barreling down on him. The takeover of *The Waterfront*, Nicholas Sherborn… a blinding pain…

"We thought you would sleep all day." Captain Stevens paused. His gaze traveled the length of Keldon as if contemplating his next move. "Hmm… What exactly are you supposed to be? Are you a Highlander turned against us?" He deliberately tugged on Keldon's kilt as he circled him. "Or are you a pirate? Either one would still put you in an awkward position?"

Keldon didn't answer.

"Looks like your crew decided to leave you. You'll have to enjoy our accommodations." The captain obviously enjoyed the power of his position with the way he paraded like a peacock.

Keldon curved his lips, though he knew the smile didn't reach his eyes. "I have to tell ye," he thickened his brogue for Steven's benefit, "that thus far, I am no' pleased with the hospitality ye've showed me."

"You won't be feeling so cocky after we're through with you today." He spoke calmly, but his eyes blazed with anger and hate. "You being a pirate, you probably are aware of the flogging techniques."

Keldon inwardly cringed, but he by no means would let this pompous little man see it. "Floggin'? Nay, cannae say I am. See, I never had to use such a... *technique* as ye call it."

Stevens turned and jerked his head to someone who stood behind him. "Come forward. Don't be shy."

Keldon hid his surprise under half closed lids as Nicholas Sherborn stepped into his line of sight. The bastard wouldn't even look at him, fidgeting and shuffling his feet. If his hands weren't bound, Sherborn would cease to breath.

Captain Stevens sent Sherborn on the mission to flush out the identity of the Highland Pirate. He thought Sherborn would have been the best one for the job, since he had a good reason to want the pirate hanged for his deeds. However, Sherborn had come back to the ship empty handed, stating he had run into a dead end. Stevens hadn't believed him then and he didn't now. "Do you know this man?" Captain Stevens asked Keldon, as he tried to read his face for any sign of recognition.

"Should I?" Keldon replied, his green-eyed gaze challenging him.

Stevens was still not convinced. He suspected the two encountered one another, but what he was interested in was if Sherborn deliberately protected the Highland Pirate. "Well, well, is it games you want to play? I would be most happy to oblige." The captain turned to Sherborn. "You'll do the flogging."

The color drained from Sherborn's face. "Sir, I don't understand," Nicholas began, but the captain waved his hand to silence him.

He then handed Nicholas the weapon. "I'll know if you hold back and if you do, you'll feel its bite. Do I make myself clear?"

Nicholas blanched, his gaze shifting to Keldon's.

Nicholas' horrified expression thrilled Stevens. He was good at exacting pain in any form. It was one of his secret pleasures—be it by his hands or mental manipulations. It didn't matter to him. The end results were always the same—death. "Step behind our captive, Mr. Sherborn."

"This is madness!" Nicholas said as he took his position.

"Madness, Mr. Sherborn? This is justice. He's a thief, a murderer—the enemy. He deserves death. He waved his hand in a flippant manner. "You may proceed with one swift blow to get my point across."

Sherborn hesitated for only a second, his mouth pressed into a fine line. Then he raised his arm and brought it down.

Keldon's whole body lurched forward, but he didn't call out. *Damn the man.* Stevens inwardly cursed. Keldon must have bitten the inside of his cheek to prevent himself from humiliation. He'd fix that. He would soon learn his silence would cost him. "That my friend," Steven's grounded out, "is flogging, just so you understand." He circled him to see the damage the blow had caused. He ran his fingers lightly over the red swell that marred the otherwise perfect skin. An explosion of pleasure spread through him as he imagined the man's back a crisscross of mutilated flesh. It took all his control not to take the whip from Sherborn and finish the job.

With a ragged breath, he walked around to face Keldon, again. "The quartermaster is the one who usually administers this punishment. He might use the cat o' nine tails of an unwound whip of nine strands or sometimes the ends are tarred knots, musketballs or fishhooks. It's really quite a barbaric ordeal." The captain leaned very close to

Keldon. "Now you felt the first lash and there are ten more Mr. Sherborn will give you, or we can forget this little punishment of yours if you tell us your true name and where we can find the rest of your crew."

"I'll no' cooperate with ye. Do what ye must."

"Are you mad? Your crew left you! What loyalty do you owe them now?"

"Ye can save yer breath with yer lies. My crew would only leave me if they had nay other choice."

"Don't be a fool," Stevens persisted. "I can decide your fate. Give me what I want and I'll have you killed, quickly."

"It be better to die a man, than a snivelin' dog." Keldon purposely looked away from the captain and stared straight ahead. "We have nothin' more to discuss."

Fury raged through Stevens like a wildfire, making him incapable of speaking for fear if he moved, he'd kill the man where he stood. He took a ragged breath, letting the black rage clear from his vision. He wanted Keldon's death to be a long and agonizing departure from this world. He wanted him to beg to be killed. They had a long journey ahead of them. He'd make sure he broke the Highland Pirate before they pulled into port.

When Stevens finally composed himself, he replied in an even voice, "As you wish." He turned his attention to Sherborn. "You heard the man."

Nicholas paused and Stevens turned on him. "Do it now!"

Keldon braced himself as the whip came down on him over and over again. He'd already measured what kind of man Captain Stevens was and he had concluded the man a bully, taking great pleasure in seeing men suffer at the hands of his rank. Even if he were a man who would betray his crew, which he most definitely was not, Captain Stevens would show no mercy. He closed his eyes and tried to focus on something other than the tearing of his flesh.

One lash... two lashes.

Keldon surprised himself when Arianna's sweet face came to mind. He left home to be away from her, but somehow through the unjust punishment he found solace in thinking of her.

Three, four, five lashes.

He remembered how it felt to slide his finger through her soft hair. He remembered how her voice sounded as she sang a lovely melody. He held onto the way her lips felt pressed to his, but the pain became unbearable. He thought he would disgrace himself by calling out, but again Arianna's image floated toward him and gave him the strength to endure.

Seven...

His skin angrily pulled away from his body and he could hear the crew taking pleasure in his humiliation, their laughter ringing in his ears. Shut it out, he told himself. "Arianna," he breathed her name as if she was his only salvation.

CHAPTER THIRTY-NINE

Changes were made to *Blue Run* and Arianna was proud of the accomplishments. She worked from sun up to sun down, ignoring Maeve's fussing that she did too much. Work helped her forget for a while how much she missed Keldon and how she worried for his safety.

It had taken her awhile, but she'd learned every man, woman and child's name. She knew all their responsibilities and what they entailed.

She wanted everyone to have a hire badge and started an apprentice program rotating the workers from the fields. She'd been appalled when she saw how raw the worker's skin became from working in the flooded rice paddies. And the clothing they wore—horrendous. She chose four women, who knew how to sew. They would be in charge of making everyone on the plantation three changes of clothes. Three didn't seem nearly enough, but it was better than the one they did have.

"Miss Arianna," Sally Mae called.

She looked up and wiped her brow. She was hot and sweaty from melting tallow for candles and soap. "Is something wrong?"

"No, no. Maeve sent me ter tell you the *Gud Intent* has been spotted."

Every emotion possible assailed her. Would Keldon be aboard? Was he coming back to her? Or would this be his last goodbye?

Her nerves were on edge, making her stomach churn. She looked down at herself and cringed. She needed to change. She hurried to the big house. She needed to brush her hair, too. The tangled mess wouldn't do.

She grabbed Maeve on her way upstairs to help her. "I'll wear the blue gown. Blue's his favorite color." She glanced down at growing midsection, knowing she couldn't hide her condition any longer. She chewed on her lower lip.

Maeve frowned at Arianna's expression of doom. She clicked her tongue. "Ef he comes back, it don't matter."

She looked at Maeve, willing herself to smile. "I know," she said the words, but they were hollow. "I'm afraid to hope."

Maeve went over to her and took her hand. "Everything will work out. Now, let's not keep him waitin'."

They were standing on the porch, when they saw the two men riding hard, dust flying around them like a cloud of smoke. Arianna knew immediately neither man was Keldon. There was no shock of dark hair. The riders' shoulders weren't broad and their stance not as powerful as his.

"He didn't come back." Arianna's voice faltered.

Maeve took her hand in hers, squeezing it.

Leighton and Vincent were off their horse almost before their mounts had time to stop. Leighton's face flashed like a warning beacon with it on the verge of turning purple with rage.

Vincent grabbed him and held him back.

Arianna gripped Maeve's hand tighter.

"Ye witch!" Leighton spat at her as he struggled to be free of Vincent's grip. "Are ye satisfied now? He's dead. Keldon is dead!"

Arianna paled. "Dead? No!" She leaned against Maeve for support, shaking her head in denial. He couldn't be gone. Without thinking, she laid her free hand protectively on her abdomen.

Leighton laughed bitterly. "That is what killed him. Ye ken? He spotted Sherborn on the ship we took. All his concentration was blinded by hatred ye caused him. He dinnae see the fist that knocked him out cold. I knew it. It be true all along. Ye are carryin' Sherborn's bairn."

Arianna wanted to deny the claim, but she couldn't because she didn't know. Her gaze met Vincent's questioning look. Clearly he hadn't heard about her sordid deeds. She wanted to die from the shame of it. "I once told you that I had done things I was not proud of. Before the accident, according to Mr. Sherborn, we'd been intimate. I swear I don't remember any of it."

"How convenient ye bi—" Vincent squeezed Leighton's arm so tight, that the words were lost in his screech of pain.

"We are not helping Keldon by making accusations against his wife," Vincent angrily berated him.

Arianna's eyebrows drew together in confusion. "Help him? I thought you said—"

"We don't know of his outcome. We couldn't get to him and had to leave him behind."

"You left him?" She couldn't believe what she was hearing. "You left him to die?"

"We had no choice," Vincent replied, his voice tormented. "We were out numbered." He lowered his head not wanting to meet Arianna's accusing eyes.

"You left him!" Her anguish peaked, shattering the last shreds of her control. She ran down the steps to Vincent. She threw herself at him beating at his chest. "How could you do that?"

Vincent let go of Leighton to fend off her attack. He wrapped his arms around her.

She desperately fought him, but he held her tight until her anger turned to a retched sob. "How could you leave him?"

"For the rest of my life, I will regret my decision." Vincent held onto her.

"Weel..." Leighton clapped his hands slowly. "What a verra charmin' performance, Annabelle. But ye doonae fool me. Ye no more care aboot Keldon, than ye do one of yer slaves."

Maeve spoke in Arianna's defense. "Then Mista Leighton, we know dat she be lovin' dat man of hers somethin' fierce."

Leighton lost some of his composure, staring at Maeve as if she lost her mind.

Arianna pushed herself away from Vincent. She had to pull herself together. If Keldon was still alive, he needed their help. Straightening her shoulders, she glared at Leighton. "You may have every right to accuse me of not caring in the past, but I have changed. I, however, have the right to point the finger at you. You left Keldon defenseless against the enemy. You left him to die."

Vincent put his hands on her shoulders, but she shook them off.

"Don't patronize me. I want action. I want to go back for him. Maybe, we're not too late."

Vincent shook his head and tried to approach Arianna again. He reached out his hand to comfort her, but her blue eyes impaled him and he let it fall away. With a deep sigh, he tried once again to explain. "Dear Arianna, we would like nothing more than to rescue him, but he would not want us to risk our lives to do so. Captain Stevens would be on the lookout for the *Good Intent*. Our men won't brave a suicide mission."

"Then we go after Keldon in the Spanish ship you captured and I'll ask Thaddeus if he would help."

"Thaddeus?" Leighton's eyebrows rose.

"Miss Arianna?" Thaddeus had come around from the back and couldn't help but hear the unpleasant exchange of words.

Arianna walked over to him. "Thaddeus?"

"Sorry ter intrude, but dis here letter came by messenger. He says it was important dat you sees it right away." He handed it over to her.

Arianna turned the envelope over in her hand, but other than her name, there wasn't any indication of who sent it. She hastily tore it open and scanned what was written.

"Oh God." She sat down on the porch step, resting her head in the palms of her hands. Vincent approached her and she handed him the letter.

CHAPTER FORTY

The man meant nothing to Nicholas and yet here he was taking a chance with his own life. He moved painstakingly toward the back of the ship. He kept telling himself that he was doing this because Buchanan had saved his life; he owed him. He hated owing anyone, especially a man he worked so hard to despise. He almost hoped that Keldon would refuse his help. Then he could wipe his hands clean of the whole mess.

He suspected Keldon had found out about his transgressions with his wife. There was no missing the hatred that blazed from his eyes before Brock had knocked him out cold and he was captured.

Nicholas experienced a gamut of bewildering emotions as he wondered why it mattered so much what Keldon Buchanan thought of him. Somewhere down the line, he had grown a conscience. To add to his transgressions against the man, he'd publicly humiliated Keldon when he'd been forced to flog him. However, he worried more about the wounds he inflicted on the man's heart than the ones on his back.

The Waterfront was seaworthy again and they would set sail in the morning for home. Once they set foot on British soil, he had a hunch Stevens would make sure Keldon never made it to Newgate, but would meet his end much sooner. Nicholas was determined to see this didn't happen.

The captain left one guard on duty. He was arrogant enough to believe they wouldn't have any trouble from the captive since Keldon had taken on a fever from the lashings he received three days ago. Nicholas prayed

Keldon was lucid enough to travel or his efforts were going to be for naught.

Arnold Davenport, a young man in his early thirties with red hair and slightly overweight, drew the short straw tonight and stayed behind. He leaned against the post and looked like he was about to fall asleep. Without a moment's hesitation, Nicholas was upon Arnold before the man realized what happened. With a single blow to the head, he fell to the ground. He'd have one hell of a headache when he woke up.

Sherborn took out the keys he had secured earlier from the captain's cabin. He opened the door to the storage room and waited for his eyes to adjust to the darkness. Heat fetid with sweat and sickness hit his nostrils, making him gag, but he walked in anyway.

He spotted a still form in the corner of the room. With careful steps, he approached not sure what he would discover. Keldon had been weak after the flogging, but Nicholas hadn't seen him since. He only happened to overhear the surgeon tell the captain Keldon was feverish. He didn't dare inquire further about his welfare or the captain would become suspicious.

He cautiously knelt down beside Keldon, gently placing his hand on his lower back to see if he was still breathing, a mistake which almost proved fatal. Keldon rolled over so fast Nicholas didn't have a chance to react as the man's fist plowed into his face. He had clearly under estimated the Scotsman.

Nicholas managed to separate himself from Keldon's fist and move a safe distance away. He knew if he didn't talk fast, he was going to find himself beaten to a bloody pulp. "Keldon." Nicholas tried to draw his attention, hoping he would be able to reason with him. "I've come to help you."

"Help! Ye have helped me plenty already." Keldon spat. "I'm aghast that ye have the audacity to suggest ye are helpin' me. What? Are ye plannin' on finishin' the job ye already started?"

"I'm aware of what you're thinking, but I don't have the time to convince you of my sincerity. If you want to live, I suggest you use your fists to fight your way out of here."

"I thought that was what I was doin'." He took a menacing step toward Nicholas, who immediately stepped back.

"You don't have much time," Nicholas told him. "We have to act now before the men return from their night out on the town." This seemed to catch Keldon's attention. He hesitated and Nicholas hurried to explain. "I know these parts. There are enough uninhabited areas that we could easily lose ourselves in its folds."

"How do I know this isnae a trick?"

Nicholas hoped he wasn't making a grave mistake, but he had to convince Keldon that he could trust him. He slowly crouched down, careful not to make any sudden moves. With his forefinger and thumb, he pulled out his knife that had been concealed in his boot. He then put the knife on the floor and slid it toward him. "If I betray you, use the knife to cut my bloody throat."

A chill ran down Nicholas spine as he watched a slow smile spread across Keldon's face. "It will be my pleasure to do so, too," he replied all too readily.

Nicholas had no doubt Keldon meant the statement as a promise. He wiped the blood from his lip on the back of his shirtsleeve. He nodded before he headed for the door, knowing Keldon would follow.

Nicholas was relieved to see Arnold remained unconscious. He glanced back at Keldon and for the first time really noticed his attire. He frowned. Keldon was a man who stood out in a crowd without questionable attire. He still wore the kilt. His shirt was filthy and blood stained. "You're going to have to change out of the garments you're wearing." He looked at the unconscious man and without speaking Keldon already knew what he'd suggest.

They quickly stripped the man and Keldon slipped into the uniform. The fit wasn't perfect with the sleeves too short and the pants even worse, but it would have to suffice. He left his blood-soaked shirt, which was beyond repair, but he refused to leave the kilt. He folded it and concealed it against his chest.

While Keldon had been dressing, Nicholas dragged the guard into the storage room and locked him in.

Nicholas' brows rose in amazement that Keldon could even stand after his ordeal, let alone punch him with the strength he exhibited. He touched his sore jaw, still feeling the sting.

"Are ye goin' to stand there all night or are we gettin' off this ship?" Keldon grunted as he left Nicholas gaping at his departing back.

Nicholas followed as he shook his head. He wondered who was rescuing whom.

They hadn't gone far when they spotted two of the crewmen. Keldon and Nicholas quickly hurried to conceal themselves behind the boxes lined on the deck. Keldon pulled out the knife Nicholas had given him. They waited until the men moved on by before they crept slowly toward the plank. They were almost there when one of the crewmen called out.

"Who goes there?"

"Bloody hell," Nicholas cursed beneath his breath and quickly stepped in front of Keldon as he turned to face the man who strode toward them.

"Brock," Nicholas greeted him. "Do you want to join us at the tavern?"

"Just come from there. I've had too much to drink as it is." Brock chuckled as he rubbed his large protruding belly. "I think I'm going to turn in. You two have a good night of it." He turned and walked away.

Nicholas breathed a sigh of relief. "Let's get out of here," he said, taking over the lead.

Traveling proved slow through the foliage, but they had to put as much distance from the ship and them as possible. Nicholas knew Captain Stevens well and he wouldn't let his captive go so easily. He would send out a search party and if they were caught, he had no doubt they would both be swinging from the nearest tree.

They traveled in silence, Nicholas glancing behind him every so often to see how Keldon held up. He looked wretched. Sweat poured down his face and his breaths were labored. The man needed to rest before he collapsed.

"We're stopping," Nicholas announced.

"Why? Are ye tired?" Keldon barely puffed out.

Nicholas swallowed his pride, deciding it wasn't worth the man dying before he could rescue him. "Yes. I need to rest."

Keldon's lips thinned. Sherborn lied, but he knew he couldn't continue at this pace. He needed to sit down, even if it was only for a moment.

Sweat drenched him and yet he found himself shivering. He knew this was the effect of the beating he took. The only medical attention he received had been a quick look over by the ship's surgeon, who ended the visit by dousing his wounds with salt water.

Pain radiated up and down his spine, his flesh burned from the infection raging through his body, and his stomach ached from lack of nourishment. He didn't know how much more he could take. Every step he took was an agonizing feat, but he would never let Sherborn know this.

Nicholas eyed Keldon closely, obviously making his own assessment. He took out a flask he had in his inside pocket of his jacket. He handed it to him. "Drink some of this. It'll take the edge off the pain." Keldon didn't argue. He gratefully took a swig, savoring the burn as the liquid ran down his throat.

The tension between the two men was like a loaded dueling pistol with a hair trigger temper. Finally, Keldon couldn't take it anymore. "Why did ye come into my life and ruin all I have ever wanted?" Keldon's words were sudden, raw and angry. He glared at his adversary, his eyes blazing with unresolved loathing. "Do ye make it a habit to have a man trusts ye? Then go aboot seducin' his wife?"

"I'm not proud of what I've done, but at the time I thought I was justified. And no, I don't make it a habit of shagging other men's wives, but your wife was all too willing."

Keldon flinched at Nicholas' words. He didn't want to hear anymore, but Nicholas wouldn't let him off so easily.

"Annabelle and I had a goal. I thought we both wanted it. She seemed to abhor you as much as I did and we fed off that hatred. We would have destroyed you, too. We were so bloody close, but something changed. It was almost like Annabelle become another person. You even called her by another name—Arianna. It seemed fitting, I suppose." His shoulders lifted in a shrug. "Arianna forced me to see you as you really were. As much as I didn't want to, I couldn't refute what I witnessed. You weren't what I expected. You were a man of honor and not the fiend I had conjured up in my mind. I had set out to destroy you, but in the end it was I who had lost."

Keldon's anger wavered as he tried to comprehend what Sherborn confessed. "Why would ye think ill of me?" He needed to know, wanted to understand.

"Because you stole my security. You took away the only person who meant anything to me, who had cared for me when my parents died. I believed you had blatantly murdered, Captain Richard Hawkins."

The shock of this discovery hit him full force. "Hawkins was kin to ye?" He shook his head and stared at him in astonishment. "I never meant to kill the man."

"I know and isn't this the irony of the whole mess."

Keldon grasped what had driven Nicholas to do the things he did. Maybe he even deserved Nicholas' hatred, but it didn't mean he had to forgive him. Nicholas had taken too much. He had taken the woman he loved, destroyed his trust and stripped him of his pride. "Do ye know she is with child?" Keldon asked.

"I know."

"Is that why ye ran away, then? Ye knew it was yers?" There was a sudden thin chill hanging on the edge of his words.

"Bullocks! I didn't run. I left and there is a bloody big difference between the two. As for the child being mine..." He shrugged. "It doesn't matter. I will not claim it. Arianna wouldn't want me to."

"She doesnae want ye to claim yer own bairn?" Keldon raised his voice at the ridiculous logic Nicholas seemed to possess. "If the bairn is yers that is how it is. Ye cannae be changin' the fact."

"I bloody well can do as I please. You're a real wanker aren't you? You already decided the baby is mine, when in all probability the child she carries is of your blood."

Frustrated, Keldon ran his fingers through his hair and took another swig from the flask. The effect of the alcohol deadened the throbbing pain in his back, but it was failing miserably to dull the pain he felt in his heart. "Tell me this, Sherborn, would ye be able to raise another man's bairn? Would ye be able to hold yer wife, knowin' she'd betrayed ye with another?"

"I don't know if I can answer you truthfully, for a man can easily say what he would do when he hasn't endured the situation himself." He paused for a moment. "I'll give you an answer though, if you wish."

Keldon grudgingly nodded.

"If I loved her enough, I believe I could."

He was surprised by Nicholas' answer. Was he being so shallow that he couldn't put the past to rest and move forward? He wasn't sure. Though he did know, life without Arianna would be like floundering in an agonizing maelstrom of despair. Was his love strong enough to forgive her? Could he learn to trust her again and care for a child who possibly wasn't his?

He never had the time to answer his own questions. Four men burst through the clearing, their weapons drawn.

CHAPTER FORTY-ONE

"On your feet," the leader, a man with a thick French accent and long black hair, ordered. Seeing they were surrounded, Nicholas and Keldon had no other choice other than to obey. The men weren't from *The Waterfront*. They didn't know if they should be happy over this fact, or if they should be silently saying their prayers. Keldon decided he had no desire to fall prey to another man's wishes. He didn't come this far to fail now.

"I can take the two beside me," Keldon whispered. "If ye can handle the other two."

"I was assessing the men myself. I have no wish to be a prisoner." Letting out a horrendous shout, Nicholas launched his attack.

Keldon didn't waste any time, either. He threw his punch into the man nearest him, sending him sailing through the air. He immediately connected his fist with the other man's chin, knocking him unconscious with the first blow. Satisfied he concentrated on the first man he attacked for he was already on his feet, lunging toward him.

In a matter of minutes, the four intruders were lying unconscious at Keldon and Nicholas' feet. Breathing heavily, Keldon collapsed to the ground and Nicholas immediately went over to him. "Brilliant! Your back is bleeding, again."

"Then that accounts for the frightful pain that I be feelin'. Do ye see the flask? I could use a drink aboot now."

Nicholas searched the ground. Recovering the flask, he handed it to him.

"Are ye hurt?" Keldon said as he glanced at him.

"No, but I could use a drink myself. My nerves are in a jumble." Keldon passed the flask and Nicholas took a long swallow. "I wondered where these men came from?" Nicholas commented. "Highly unlikely they were out for a late night stroll."

"No. They were not," a deep voice, answered from behind them. Keldon stood and Nicholas closed his hands into a fist, both men were ready to fight again if the need arose. When they faced the new comer, they faced not only one man, but twenty or more emerged behind him.

"Bloody hell!" Nicholas exclaimed.

Keldon's heart sank. They weren't going to fight their way out of this situation, unless they planned to die in the process.

The tall dark-haired man who held the presence of authority took a step forward. "Do you mind telling me what you two are doing out here in the middle of nowhere?"

"Just having a quiet drink among friends," Keldon replied. From their dress, he knew the men were pirates. He only hoped that from one pirate to another, he could talk his way into having these men help them, rather than kill them.

The dark-haired man's eyes narrowed. "My men are in top condition and yet they lay unconscious. How is this possible when you look like you're on the verge of collapse?" He waved his hand at Keldon.

"They didn't give us a chance to explain." Keldon shrugged.

"And I should? You're wearing British uniforms and I am not fond of them these days." He turned to the young man standing next to him. "Check the prisoners for weapons."

The young man stepped forward. He didn't look old enough to be away from his mother's apron strings. He searched Nicholas first. When he didn't find a weapon on him, he approached Keldon. "This one has somethin' in his shirt."

"Well see what it is," the man in charge demanded.

Keldon let the boy remove the kilt from beneath its confinement. "It's a dress of sorts." The young man curiously looked at the item he held in his hand.

"It be a kilt, lad," Keldon corrected.

"Kilt?" The man in charge walked closer to see for himself. He eyed Keldon. "How did you come by this?"

"It is mine, as it was my father's and his father's before that. The clothes we wear now were… borrowed." Keldon swayed, feeling a bit lightheaded.

"Are you ill?" The one in charge gave him a scrutinizing once over.

"Nay ill, but damaged," Keldon told him. "I have suffered from the hands of the British." Keldon turned slightly so the man saw that the back of his shirt was blood soaked from his injuries.

The man understood immediately what had transpired. "Why would they have treated you so unkindly?"

Keldon shrugged. "Mayhap, they dinnae like me plunderin' their ship."

The dark haired man didn't say anything at first, but then his handsome face broke into a grin. "The British are quite funny about such acts."

Keldon relaxed. He'd been right to trust his instincts. The man was a pirate.

The dark-haired man became sobered as he glanced at Nicholas. "What of him? He sounded British to me."

Nicholas tensed his eyes glancing uneasily toward Keldon. Keldon looked at him and saw the fear in his eyes. He knew Nicholas thought he was going to betray him. It was tempting, but instead he slapped Nicholas on the back nearly toppling him over.

"Him?" Keldon replied, jovially to the stranger. "Nicholas cannae help who fathered him, but ye have my word—he can be trusted."

"My friend here," Nicholas flashed him a look of gratitude, "He would never say as much, but he is in dire need of some medical attention."

"Come back with us and I'll have my surgeon look at you." The man in charge nodded. He then snapped his fingers and ordered a few of his men to collect their unconscious shipmates who were just now beginning to moan their way to consciousness. He then turned his attention back to Keldon. "What name do you go by when you are plundering ships?"

"The Highland Pirate."

The dark-haired man leaned back his head and laughed. "The phantom, I have heard you called. I am Jean Laffite, my friend."

"Your reputation precedes you." Keldon bowed, slightly. "It is an honor to have been captured by you."

"And it is an honor to have done so."

"As a friend of the sea," Keldon said. "I have to give you fair warnin', the British Captain we spoke of, willnae have taken kindly to my departure. He most likely willnae give up pursuit so easily."

"Not to worry, my ship is well hidden. I assure you, he will be hard pressed to find it."

CHAPTER FORTY-TWO

Vincent carefully read the note Arianna handed him.

"Weel what does it say?" Leighton was too impatient to wait.

"It seems Jean Laffite would like to have an audience with us. He has Keldon, but because of certain circumstances, he is unable to bring him directly here. He states Keldon isn't well enough to travel. Laffite will be sending someone in a few days to escort us to him."

"Laffite sent the letter?" Leighton asked.

"Not exactly."

"What do ye mean, not exactly?"

Vincent cleared his throat. "Nicholas Sherborn sent it."

"What kind of fool trick is this?" Leighton's curt voice lashed out. "Keldon is surely dead then, for his betrayer wouldnae send for us."

"We must go. How can we not?" Vincent leveled his gaze on Leighton.

"If ye go, ye might as weel dig yerself a hole and put yerself in it because that's where ye'll be soon enough."

Arianna stood and faced Leighton's wrath. "I'll go to him."

"Ye'll go?" Then Leighton added sarcastically, "Ye mean, ye'll go to Sherborn. I ken verra weel now what yer plan be."

She ignored his last remark. "I'm going and if it is a trap, Leighton, you'll be able to celebrate my demise."

"That is weel and good, but how do ye plan on gettin' to the meetin' place with nay crew to man the ship?"

"We'll persuade as many of the men as we can," Vincent offered, ignoring Leighton's disapproving frown.

"Miss Arianna." Thaddeus drew everyone's attention. "I will go with you and I know dere be others dat will help. Ef you says de word."

"What spell have ye cast, witch?" Leighton looked at Arianna. His lips thinning with anger, his nostrils flaring. "Ye have all the slaves doin' yer whim, when nay long ago they would have spit on the verra ground ye walk on." He took a menacing step toward her, but Vincent intervened, blocking his path.

"That is enough from you, my friend," he warned gently, but there was no doubt there was a threat beneath the words. "You are unjustly accusing Arianna and I'll not stand for it."

"Ye doonae understand. Ye dinnae live with the witch. Ye ken?"

"You's wrong," Maeve defended Arianna to Leighton. "Dat evil woman you talk of be dead."

"Ye doonae know what ye're sayin'." Leighton waved his hand at Arianna as he ranted. "Ye're all so willin' to believe that *Annabelle* has become this *Arianna*, but I willnae be fooled."

"I never said I was another person, Leighton." Arianna moved around Vincent to face him. "I only want you to give me a chance to prove I've changed."

"Aye. Ye proved yerself weel enough when ye spread yer legs for Sherborn. I know that wee bairn is his, for ye wouldnae be carryin' it otherwise."

"What is that suppose to mean?" she demanded to know.

"Years before ye dinnae hesitate to rid yerself of Keldon's bairn."

For a second she froze as self-doubt gnawed at her. "You're lying," she choked out the words, her face draining of color as her chest tightened. She teetered on her feet and Vincent grabbed a hold of her, supporting her weight. "I wouldn't." She spoke in a broken whisper and shook her head. "I never would do such a thing."

"Ye did. Ye have never cared for Keldon. Ye have proved it over and over again."

"Miss Annabelle be de one who done it not Miss Arianna." Maeve again came to her defense.

Arianna looked at her for confirmation. "Was there another child?"

Maeve hesitated, pursing her lips together.

"Maeve, you have to tell me." She bit her lip until it throbbed like her pulse. She desperately needed Maeve to tell her it wasn't so, but the spark of hope was quickly extinguished when she witnessed how Maeve's shoulders sagged.

Maeve nodded. "Yas'm, but it wuz Miss Annabelle's chile not yours."

Arianna felt like her world was ending as a new anguish seared her heart. How could she have rid herself of her own child? A suffocating sensation tightened her throat. She smothered a sob as she covered her mouth.

Vincent turned to Leighton. "We have heard enough from you, today. If you want to help Keldon, you'll find out how many of the men will go with us."

"Ye plan to go into the trap? After all I've told ye." There was a cynical tone in his voice as he threw up his hands in disgust.

"Oui. I cannot stay here and do nothing. I must go, but that does not mean you have to join us. Thaddeus has already offered his help. We will manage." Without looking back, Vincent turned his attention to Arianna, ushering her inside the house. He led her to the drawing room and forced her to take a seat. She finally looked up at him. Her eyes pooled and huge tears rolled down her cheeks. "Why are you still here? How can you even want to talk to me after all you've heard?"

"You are my friend. No?" he said as he took a seat next to her.

"Yes, but—"

"Shush now. What you have or have not done in the past does not matter to me. I see now a beautiful and kind-hearted woman."

"But all those horrible things I did," she stammered in bewilderment. "It is no wonder I've chosen not to remember them."

"Then keep it that way. Don't cloud your thoughts with what you cannot change."

She lowered her head assaulted by a terrible sense of shame. "What you ask me to do won't be easy. Everyone hates me and with good reason. I don't like who I was. How can they forgive me when I don't think I can forgive myself?"

He gently lifted her chin so she met his gaze. "Often many things we do are not easy to forgive, but you will have to do your best." He touched his fingertips to the corner of her eyes and wiped away the tears. "Stiff upper lip now, we have to make ready to sail."

She nodded and swallowed an upsurge of sobs.

*****

Bernadette and Vincent waited for Arianna outside in the carriage, but after twenty minutes and she still hadn't emerged from the house, they began to worry.

"I'll check on her," Bernadette offered.

"Oui, please do so. I don't want to rush her, but the day is dwindling.

Already Laffite's man waits for us."

Bernadette found Arianna in the study. She was lovely in her light blue dress with darker blue ribbons to match. She wore her hair in a mass of curls over her forehead and ears and the longer tresses drawn up into a loose bun. She sat behind the desk, staring at something in her hand.

"Arianna?" Bernadette approached, realizing she was crying again. "Are you all right?"

Arianna looked up, wiping away the tears that were only replaced by others. Arianna knew she needed to pull it together and move on, but what she found in her husband's desk had devastated her.

She wiped her eyes again, took a deep breath and met Bernadette's worried gaze. "We better go." Without explaining, she folded the papers and put them in her dress pocket.

CHAPTER FORTY-THREE

They set sail for Lafitte's home in the bayous near New Orleans with forty-nine men, half of which were recruited by Thaddeus. Leighton at the last moment decided to join them, mumbling obscenities under his breath of how he must have lost his mind to join them on the voyage of doom.

The ship needed a new name after its complete overhaul. She was christened for what they all needed right now, *Hope*.

Weather held and they made good time.

Nicholas Sherborn spotted the ship on the horizon and came to greet them as they docked.

He was shocked Arianna was among the able seamen, though he shouldn't have been. With her courage and determination, he could see her manning the ship herself if she were forced to do so. Not one person of the former crew gave him a kind glance and he appreciated Arianna greeting him with a wave of her hand.

"You seem to be faring well." Nicholas addressed Arianna as his gaze lingered for only a moment on her swelling midsection.

"Thank you. I hope you don't mind if we skip the pleasantries, but I must know how Keldon is?" She looked up at him with her pain stricken eyes.

"I have to be honest with you—"

"That'll be a first." Leighton interrupted with a sneer as he met them on the walkway. Nicholas wisely chose to ignore his snide remark.

"We thought it was best for Keldon to stay put in one place. He has relapsed." He held up his hand and rushed on. "The surgeon said there is no need to worry. He needs rest is all, so he can regain his strength." He shook his head. "He's a bloody stubborn man. We almost had to tie him to the bed. He wanted to set out to sea when he could barely stand. He feared he'd overstayed his welcome, but Laffite can be most convincing. Another stubborn man, I am afraid. I knew you would worry not knowing Keldon's fate. I persuaded Laffite to let me send word to you."

"And I do appreciate your generosity. May I ask what happened? How did Keldon escape Captain Stevens and end up with Jean Laffite? And how did you and Keldon come to be together?"

Nicholas couldn't suppress a chuckle. "So many questions and I'll answer them soon enough. Come with me for now. Laffite has been a kind host and has offered us the best accommodations."

*****

Keldon slept in a fit of restless slumber. His face was pale and drawn and he had lost a considerable amount of weight. If Nicholas hadn't assured Arianna he would survive, she might not have believed it. She stood in the doorway for a long time before she forced her feet to move. She was certain Keldon wouldn't want her to be there, but how could she stay away. She sat down on the bed and tenderly caressed his bearded face. His skin felt warm against her palm, too warm. "Oh Keldon." His name caught in her throat.

Keldon's eyes fluttered open, but the fever that raged through him left him disoriented. He thought he heard Arianna's voice, but that was impossible. She wasn't here. He was alone and always would be. His heart sank so low he could feel the pulse all the way down to his toes.

"Keldon?"

His eyes fluttered open again and his eyebrows furrowed. "Arianna?" He reached out his hand and touched her face.

She leaned into his palm with a kiss. "I'm here."

Phantom or not, he pulled her to him wanting to feel her against him. He hugged her gently before he fell back to sleep. For the first time since his ordeal, he slept soundly.

CHAPTER FORTY-FOUR

Nicholas had not exaggerated. Jean Laffite had seen to their every comfort before he had left, stating he would return in two weeks. There was plenty of fresh food and every room was furnished for comfort.

Nicholas relayed the whole story of what had transpired, including his hand in the lashing. Arianna's heart wept as she thought of the pain and humiliation Keldon endured.

Arianna walked into the bedroom with her tray of supplies. Keldon looked up, his gaze meeting hers before he looked away again.

"Leave me be, Arianna."

This had been their conversation for the last week. He wanted her to leave and she insisted he let her care for him. "No, I don't believe I will."

His gaze riveted to her.

"And you can stop your green-eyed glare. I'm not leaving until you let me dress your back. I need to treat the wounds to keep the infection at bay or would you rather they festered and you can wallow in your misery a while longer."

He snorted and crossed his arms across his chest.

"Well?" She arched one eyebrow in challenge.

Finally he gave in, making a production as he rolled over on his stomach.

She cut the bandages away. "Your back looks better." Finally the flesh didn't appear so angry and raw. New pink skin replaced the scabs and the puckered tissue smoothed.

Since the first day, Keldon didn't offer to take Arianna into his arms again. She tried to talk to him, but he distanced himself, refusing to remove the invisible barrier he put forth.

She caught him watching her at times. She recognized the longing in his gaze. Her body heated with each visual caress. She wanted to go to him, but once his eyes fell upon her swelling stomach, his mouth would harden and he would turn away. With a sinking heart, she realized he would always look upon her as the woman who betrayed him and the child would be a constant reminder of it.

If there'd been any hope he would accept the baby, she would endure his cold silence. She could tell him she loved him but he wouldn't believe her. She grasped the reality of the situation—there would never be a *happily-ever-after* for them and she needed to plan for her future, one without Keldon.

"You can turn over now, I'm all finished."
*****

Laffite arrived home after his successful run, anxious to put up his feet up and relish in his glory. He brought back fine wine, tobacco and fresh meat and vegetables to celebrate his good fortune. His cook was already preparing the feast.

Wanting a few moments alone before he returned to business, he walked around the back of the house to enter through the side doors of his study. He expected the room to be empty, but instead, he found a beautiful lady with blonde hair eyeing his small library of books. She turned toward him now her blue eyes showing her unease. Laffite never forgot a face; he remembered her. She had changed somewhat. Her hair was longer and he didn't miss her expanding condition.

"So, we meet again." Laffite removed his hat as he bowed.

Arianna only had a fleeting look at him—the time when he nearly knocked her down in his hurry to leave his meeting with Andrew Jackson.

Laffite was a tall and striking man. He entered the room with an imposing presence one could not ignore. He moved around his desk to stand in front of her. "You must be Buchanan's wife. No?"

Arianna hadn't found her voice yet and could only nod.

"And how is he? The last time I saw him, he was not himself."

Arianna cleared her throat and forced the words to leave her mouth. "Much better, thanks to you." She felt strangely awe-struck by the man and covered up her self-consciousness with conversation. "How was your voyage? Did you take many ships?" As soon as the questions left her mouth, she wanted to kick herself.

Laffite's eyes twinkled amused rather than offended. He flashed her, his charming smile. Women would be drawn to him, but she sensed the appeal could also prove lethal.

"We did very well. We will have a feast tonight to prove it." He came closer to her and she felt a whisper of apprehension course through her as a prey would feel when stalked. She took an involuntary step back, bumping into the bookcase. "Now Mademoiselle..."

"Madame," Arianna corrected him.

"Ah yes. Madame Buchanan, would you join me in a glass of wine?" She let him lead her to the small sofa before he went over to the bookcase and took down the decanter he had hidden on the third shelf.

"I really don't want any wine, thank you. It's not good for the baby."

Laffite raised an eyebrow. "I had not heard of this, but if it is what you wish..." He shrugged. He only poured the rich liquid into one of the crystal glasses before he came to sit down beside her. "Now Madame Buchanan, how do you know General Jackson?"

She cleared her throat. "I don't know him, not really."

"I see, but you requested a private meeting."

"I wanted to obtain a Letter of Marque for my husband."

"Ah, oui." His eyes lit up as if he remembered something important. He removed an envelope from his coat pocket and handed it to her. "I believe this is what you have been waiting for."

"But how did—" Arianna began only to have Laffite interrupt.

"Jackson entrusted me to give it to you." He took a sip of his wine. "It was an interesting meeting. It seems it was you who convinced Jackson to renegotiate my demands. In exchange for their cooperation with my terms, my men and I will help keep the British at bay." He took another sip of his wine as he studied her. "I make you nervous, no?"

"I…" she knew she couldn't fool him so why try. "Intimidated, would be more like it."

"I do not wish for you to be uncomfortable. No harm will come to you. You have my word."

She nodded.

"Good, for I only wish to thank you for your assistance," Laffite continued. "One thing has puzzled me. Why would you come to my defense? We do not know each other."

"You're right, but it's difficult to explain."

"Try me."

"Keldon would say I have the sight. Maybe, I do. All I can tell you is—I know things. It's like I've read about your adventures from a book."

He let out a warm chuckle. "A book?"

"Whether you choose to believe me or not, you'll be dubbed the gentleman pirate."

His gaze touched and held. "You are quite serious."

"I am."

"Then who am I to doubt a woman who possesses the sight?" He paused as if weighing his next question carefully. "This battle of New Orleans, will we win? I do so hate to lose."

She hesitated for it wasn't all clear, but without having anything to back up her apprehension, she kept it to herself. She nodded. "Yes, we'll hold New Orleans."

Laffite's face broke into a grin.

CHAPTER FORTY-FIVE

Vincent didn't agree with Arianna, but he helped her make all the arrangements. She would stay with his sister, Chantal and her husband, until the baby was born.

"I wish you would reconsider." Vincent tried, one last time to make her see reason.

"There isn't any other way around it." She closed her trunk before she turned to face him. "If I stay, all I'm doing is causing Keldon more pain."

"And what about you, my friend?" He couldn't help but worry about her.

She tried to be brave, but the light in her eyes had faded.

She sighed wistfully. "I have to let him go."

Vincent wrapped his arms around her. How he wanted to beat some sense into Keldon for being so blind. The man held happiness in the palm of his hand and yet he chose to let his stubborn pride destroy it. "Chantal and Gerard will take good care of you."

"I wish I didn't have to impose."

"You'll be most welcome. You stay with my sister. After the baby is born, then you can decide what you must do. Perhaps by then, your stubborn husband will stop being the fool and come to his senses."

She gave him a wry smile. "I must ask you to promise me one thing."

"You only need to name it."

"I beg of you, don't tell Keldon where I am. He may not love me anymore, but his honor will make him feel obligated to see to my welfare."

"As he should."

She shook her head. "He divorced me, but he didn't kick me out of our home."

Vincent frowned not understanding. "What do you mean, he divorced you?"

"Back at *Blue Run*, I found the papers in his desk. It seems he divorced me some time ago. Whatever his reason may have been, he kept it a secret from me. Maybe because we had started to build a new relationship, he thought we would have a chance." She sighed miserably. "However, I ruined any chance of it happening."

"I'm sorry," he said, not knowing what else he could say.

"So you see why I don't want you to tell him where I am. I won't take his charity. I can play the harpsichord for a living. I could give lessons to children. I can make this work." She took hold of Vincent's hands. "You must not tell him," she said, demanding him to give his word.

He sighed. "Oui, my friend. You have my word."

*****

Keldon was in the study nursing his afternoon drink, a ritual, which was beginning to resemble a bad habit. He glanced up as Arianna walked in, his eyes glazed, already too deep in his drink. She took the glass from his hand and he didn't have the strength to argue. She then handed him two envelopes.

"What is this?" he asked. His tongue felt thick in his mouth.

"It's your freedom."

His eyebrows lifted high on his brow. "Arianna—"

"Let me say my peace." She took a seat across from him and folded her hands over her stomach. "I know you have let me stay these months out of obligation and it isn't that I don't appreciate the fact, but it cannot go on. I have brought this unfortunate situation upon myself. I could live with it, but there is another person I have to worry about now." He watched her unconsciously put her hand on her stomach. "No matter what my wrong doings are, this baby is innocent."

"Arianna, I am no' a cruel man. I wouldnae mistreat the wee bairn. I would make sure it had all its needs satisfied."

"I have no doubt that you would support the child—financially. However, a child needs love. I have thought this over carefully. The letters you hold are your way out, and I want you to take it." She looked at him, caressing him with her gaze.

Desire clawed at him, but he refused to give into it. No matter how much he wanted to kiss her and let his fingers slide through her hair, he couldn't because if he did, he would be lost within her charms. A man had to have some pride. He looked away.

Her sigh spoke of sadness, but he could comfort her. "This child that I carry could very well be yours. You don't know how much I want it to be. If I'm lucky, the baby will be born with your dark hair and cat-like green eyes, but if the baby has light hair, I'll never know." A sob escaped her lips and Keldon fought the urge to wrap his arms around her and tell her everything would be all right. He wanted to be able to tell her he would love the baby she carried. That it didn't matter if the child was of his blood, but he couldn't bring himself to speak the words.

Arianna rose from her seat and came to him. She leaned down and touched her sweet mouth to his before he knew what she'd been about to do. He tasted the wet salt of her tears and felt the quivering of her lips. He knew without a doubt that she had given him a farewell. It wasn't until she left the room he realized he was crying, too.

CHAPTER FORTY-SIX

Arianna had left Keldon alone to wallow in his misery. He stayed up all night wondering what he was going to do with this freedom she offered him. He had thought if she was gone from his life, he would feel relief, but he felt like the air had been whooshed out of him and he'd never catch his breath again.

She had to walk out for him to realize he didn't want her to go. He would learn to trust her again. He vowed he would love the child she carried. He just needed some time. That's all he was asking.

He drank the last of his whiskey straight from the bottle, clumsily putting it down on the table. None-too steadily, he walked out of the room and went to find her.

He knocked at her door, but she didn't answer. He knocked louder. "I know ye're in there. I have a few words to say to ye."

Silence.

"Arianna?" He put his hand on the doorknob, turning it easily. Upon entering the room, he saw that the bed was neatly made as though she had never slept in it. "Where is she?" he said aloud.

"She's gone."

Keldon whirled around to see Vincent leaning against the doorframe.

"Gone? Where?" he demanded to know. He knew she offered him freedom, but he hadn't expected her to leave the moment she granted it.

"I can't say, my friend. She left early this morning."

Keldon's mind raced as he pieced together his last conversation with her. She truly left him. His heart sank. Could it be possible that she had left with Nicholas

Sherborn? He rubbed his temples. Did she say she was leaving with him? Wouldn't that just serve him right since he pushed her away? He looked a Vincent, again. "Did she leave alone?"

"What are you asking me?"

"Ye verra weel know what I be askin'. Where is Sherborn?"

"He's not with her, if that is what you think." He matched Keldon's clipped speech.

"I have to find her." Keldon tried to go around Vincent, but he blocked the doorway. "If ye willnae move on yer own volition, I shall be only too glad to move ye myself."

Vincent still didn't budge. He planted his feet and folded his arms in front of him. "She doesn't want you to go after her."

"I said, let me by." He tried physically moving Vincent, but he continued to hold his ground.

"Let her go, Keldon. If you can't love her completely, let her go."

Keldon took a step back as if he had been slapped. He turned away and ran his hand through his hair. "Let her go, ye say." Keldon walked over to the window. "What will I do without her?"

Vincent sighed. "We'll set sail."

He turned to look at him. "Set sail? To where?"

"There's a war to be fought. We must join Laffite's men at New Orleans."

"We doonae have a ship or men for that matter."

"We do. Didn't I tell you that Thaddeus and some of the other slaves... pardon me, they're free men now; we all came aboard the Spanish frigate. She looks a mite different. We raised the gunwales for greater battle protection. The renovations were made below deck to accommodate the men. She's named *Hope*."

"*Hope*," Keldon said as he parted the curtain and looked outside. What else did he have to do? Defending New Orleans seemed the best course to take. As soon as the battle ended, he would look for Arianna. He glanced at Vincent, again. "What is this ye say aboot freemen?"

"Arianna freed all the slaves. Some went with a man named Paul Cuffee to Sierra Leone with a promise of a new life. Some stayed behind."

"Blessed saints." He shook his head, a small smile curving his lips. "Aye, I should have known, she would do such an act." He straightened his shoulders and took a deep breath. "Weel Vincent, let's put the wolves to sea."

Vincent saluted him. "Aye, aye Captain."

While Vincent rounded up the men to ready the *Hope* for her voyage, Keldon went to his room to change. When he took off his coat, the papers Arianna had given him fell out. He hadn't opened them. He did so now, his eyes widening as he read the document:

James Madison, president of the United States of America,

To all who shall see these present, Greeting:

BE IT KNOWN, That in pursuance of an act of congress, passed on the 25th day of September one thousand eight hundred and twelve, I have Commissioned, and by these presents do commission, the private armed Schooner called the Good Intent or any vessel confiscation of the burden of one hundred and forty-five tons, or thereabouts, owned by Keldon Buchanan ..."

It was like a dream. The document couldn't be real, but he had it in his hands signed by President James Madison himself.

He had a Letter of Marque absolving him and his crew from any past crimes of piracy. With this document, he had the authority to continue his quest as he saw fit in the name of the United States of America. Arianna had attained this for him. When? How?

Then he looked at the other papers and realized at once what they were, the divorce documents. He'd forgotten about them. He was no longer married to Arianna and she knew it. "Arianna, where are ye?"

Silence.

He sat down heavily on the bed with the forewarning of what his life would be without her.

Vincent found him there and frowned as he walked in. "What's wrong?"

Keldon looked up. "Here." He handed him the papers. "See for yerself. Arianna has obtained a Letter of Marque."

"What…" Vincent had taken the papers and was now looking them over. "But how?"

"I doonae know."

Vincent couldn't contain the happiness he felt. "Do you know what this means?" He didn't wait for Keldon to respond and answered his own question. "It means, I can ask Bernadette to marry me without feeling guilty that I could leave her widowed in the next breath."

He glanced at Vincent. He had been so preoccupied with his own grief he had failed to realize his best friend's dilemma. "Ye really do love her, then?"

"Oui. From the first, but I had fought my feelings because I believed I was not worthy."

"Any woman would be honored to have ye."

Vincent's smile was wan. "Thank you for the compliment, but when you have no permanent home to speak of and no steady income, how could I dare to hope she'd marry me?

He sighed. "But that's all behind ye now."

"Thanks to Arianna."

Keldon couldn't meet his gaze. "Aye." He was silent for a moment. "Did ye know I divorced her?"

Vincent nodded. "She told me."

"I dinnae do it because of her betrayal." For some reason, he felt he needed to defend his actions. "The divorce was something I had done long before, when I thought I dinnae care for her any longer. It was when she was so, uncaring and... weel different. I received those papers on the day we discussed our departure. Ye handed them to me and later I put them in my top drawer of my desk."

"Why didn't you give them to her, if that was what you wanted? Why did you lock them away?"

"I doonae know," Keldon answered, though he did know. He didn't want the divorce. He fell in love with Arianna, the person she became. He wanted a life with her, but now it was too late. Arianna had seen the papers. No wonder she left him. What had he expected her to do when they were no longer promised to one another?

Not one kind word had he given her once he knew of her involvement with Sherborn. Without complaint, she nursed him back to health, knowing he'd divorced her.

He didn't even grant her the decency to hear her explanation. Every time she had extended her hand, he had stubbornly hit it away. He blamed her for a life she didn't remember and finalized everything with those damn documents. He refused to forgive her and with his actions, he denied himself the chance to heal. He denied them a chance for a future together.

CHAPTER FORTY-SEVEN

Jackson proclaimed martial law in New Orleans as soon as it deemed possible and with his main force he set up camp. Keldon and Vincent were making their way to Jackson's camp with two other men that had vital information to present.

Jackson seemed pleased to see familiar faces. "So, you decided to join the fight, Buchanan." He reached for his hand.

"Aye. We're here with my ship the *Hope*."

"Excellent, excellent." Jackson glanced at Keldon's attire of trousers, vest and linen shirt. "I am glad you decided to put your *kilt* away for this adventure."

Keldon hesitated for a half a second. Jackson knew or at least suspected he was the Highland Pirate. Then it dawned on him how Arianna could have obtained a Letter of Marque. Jackson had helped her. He cleared his throat. "I thought it would be best. I wish I could say differently, but we have heard rumored that a Highlander unit is to fight and I dinnae want to be mistaken for the enemy." He nodded toward the two men that had traveled with them. "These gentlemen have information ye must hear."

Jackson listened to every detail about the British force seizing plantations and made the announcement to his men without reservations. "Gentlemen, the British are below, we must fight them tonight."

With five thousand men and with the aid of the 14-gun schooner, the *Carolina*; Jean Laffite's band; and Keldon's *Hope*, they made their attack on the British in the dead of the night.

The British were stunned by the boldness the Americans displayed and they were forced to retreat to safety so that they could wait until their troops were brought in from their fleet.

Jackson used this time to his advantage and had his men retreat to the *Chalmette Plantation* situated on the banks of the Rodriguez Canal. The land separated the British camps from New Orleans. Jackson ordered a mud rampart so the Mississippi River was on the right and the Cypress swamp on the left. It would prove impossible for the British to get by them.

Unaware of what lay ahead, General Pakenham on the British side put forth his plans of attack. They made their move on December 28th.

With the help from the *Louisiana* and the *Hope*, once again they blasted the British flank with broadsides from the river. Pakenham bombarded the Americans with artillery, but Jackson's gunners were able to still stand their ground against them.

Keldon had a purpose in life that he had forgotten. He wanted to live and he wanted to protect what was his. He wanted to win back the family he'd driven away. So he fought and when he had time to rest, he dreamt of a lass with moonlit tresses and who sang to him with her beautiful lilting voice. She was part of his soul and his hope for the future.

CHAPTER FORTY-EIGHT

January 8, 1814, at dawn when the fog was the thickest, Pakenham had his men cross the Mississippi River downstream. He planned to attack Jackson's troops on the riverbank opposite the Rodriguez Canal. Once they were in position, they would then attack each side of the American lines.

"If only the fog hadn't cleared," Pakenham muttered. "Damn the troops for taking so long to cross the river."

"General Pakenham, we don't have the ladders or the fascines." One of the soldiers came toward him with the information.

He paced with frustration then turned on his man. "Where are they?" When the soldier had no reply, he lost it. "How do you plan on scaling the ramparts without the damn ladders?"

"Sorry sir, but in the rush this morning the Unit in charge—"

"Get out of my sight." He waved his hand at him in dismissal. "And prepare to fight."

As Keldon approached Jackson, the General handed him a mug. "It's hot," he warned.

"Thank ye, General." Keldon took a welcomed sip. The coffee was strong, but it was what he needed to warm his insides. "I spoke with the Haitians like ye asked. They wannae fight as well."

"Good." Jackson nodded. "Former slaves now fighting as free men." He took a seat by the fire and Keldon joined him. "We have everyone now that your wife said we would have on our side. The Kentucky and the Tennessee frontiersmen with their deadly long rifles, and Laffite and his outlaws. Don't tell him I said that." He chuckled.

Keldon smiled, knowing Laffite insisted he was a businessman. "The British still have twice as many men."

"Yes." Jackson sighed. "Do you not have faith in what your wife has foreseen?"

"Aye, I do have faith." He nodded, knowing that even if Arianna happened to be wrong, Jackson's ragtag force had enough determination to win this campaign.

"Together, Buchanan. Together, we create a united force to be reckoned with. Do you not agree?"

"Do ye think that Pakenham would listen to reason, if we made him aware of what we know?"

"I have already tried to communicate with the man, hoping to stop this madness. He wouldn't listen. I have no wish for unnecessary bloodshed, but I cannot let New Orleans be taken. There is no other way, but to fight."

"Do ye believe fate is written and there be no changin' it?" Keldon couldn't help but wonder. Arianna knew of what would come of this war, but she hadn't foreseen *their* future. She didn't foresee he would pine for her or else she would not have left his side. Of this he was certain. She left because she believed there could not be a future for them, but she was wrong.

Jackson sighed. "Maybe history cannot be changed. Maybe we just have to follow it through, no matter the consequences. Perhaps, we are all fated to do time's bidding."

As expected, fate was not kind to General Sir Edward Pakenham. His tactics were flawed because of the continual mistakes his men made, as well as his own decisions. He placed his troop in a dangerous position, making them perfect targets as they marched across the open ground without any cover. The men fell by the score and his senior generals were shot at the beginning of the battle, leaving the men without anyone to direct them. Still, Pakenham was determined to win the encounter. He ignored the first two wounds he received and continued his march, but the third wound was severe. He stumbled and fell.

A quick assessment was made, confirming the inevitable. An artery in his leg had been severed. Pakenham knew there wasn't much time. A change in command was vital. He grabbed hold of the man that would replace him. "Continue the attack," he choked out his last command as his breath caught in his throat and death took him.

"What do we do, sir?" The young man at the new General's side asked. "Do we go on as General Pakenham ordered?"

"No. Enough have perished. We take the survivors and pull out."

"But sir, General Pakenham said–"

"I believe that I am the General now and I gave a direct order."

"Yes sir."

With the shout of surrender, Keldon was put in charge of searching for survivors, American and British alike. The going was long and tedious. There were more he found dead, than alive. He was ready to abandon his search, when a sound drew his attention. He pulled out his weapon and headed into the foliage. He caught a glimpse of a man fleeing and went after him, tackling him to the ground.

The man struggled to free himself, but Keldon had the upper hand and pressed the barrel of the gun to the back of his head. "Doonae move or I'll be forced to blow yer head clear off." The man froze and Keldon removed his knee from the man's back. He stood above the British soldier with his weapon ready if he needed to use it. "Now, slowly get to yer feet."

The man stood and turned to face his attacker. The moment of recognition sunk in. Keldon cursed. "Sherborn, are ye bound to always cross my path?"

Nicholas managed a lopsided grin, his dimples denting his cheeks. "How have you been, Buchanan?"

Keldon lowered his gun. "I be doin' a mite better than ye, it seems. These parts are swarmin' with Americans tryin' to capture all British that still have life in them."

"So, I've witnessed. I've been trying to make my escape."

"Then why are ye still here?"

"In midst of the fighting, I was knocked unconscious from an explosion that left the man beside me without half his face. When I came to, the fighting had already ceased and my unit had retreated without me."

"Aye." Keldon nodded.

"Captain Buchanan, are you all right?" Evan McLeary, a young man with Jackson, called out to him. In a matter of seconds, Sherborn would be discovered.

Keldon's gaze never wavered from Nicholas as he quickly shouted back to McLeary, letting him know he was fine. "Take the men and head back to camp. There are no survivors left."

"Aye, aye, Captain," McLeary, answered.

Keldon then spoke to Nicholas. "Ye best keep goin' in that direction." He pointed to the right of Nicholas. "Ye should find yer unit soon enough."

He nodded. He was about to leave, but Keldon spoke again. "Can I have yer word that I willnae have to lay eyes on ye again?"

"You bloody well can count on it." Nicholas Sherborn saluted Keldon before he hastened away.

CHAPTER FORTY-NINE

Six weeks after the battle at New Orleans, Keldon sailed the *Hope* to *Willow Bend*. Half of the men, including Vincent and Samuel chose to stay with him and see what they could do with the land. Leighton decided to return to the plantation with the others.

Keldon still had the hard currency to help with the renovations of *Willow Bend* and he would make sure his part of the money would be used to expand the mercantile. The store would be his main source of income. The thrill of sea had lost its appeal.

Thaddeus set sail for *Blue Run* to bring back Sophia and Elijah. Keldon entrusted him with his heartfelt letter to Arianna. While he waited for Thaddeus' return, he threw himself into his work, relentless in proving himself worthy to ask Arianna to be his wife once more.

Vincent and Bernadette wanted to be married as soon as their house was finished. Vincent worked on it day and night. He had confided in Keldon that waiting to be with Bernadette as man and wife was pure torture, but he was determined not to touch her—except for a few stolen kisses—until they were married. Vincent hadn't told him everything about Bernadette's sordid past, but Keldon had a hunch the woman had been through a lot in her young life. Vincent was a good man and he held fast to courting Bernadette properly.

After a long and agonizing month, Thaddeus finally returned with Sophie and the baby. Oni, Maeve and Sally Mae made the voyage, too. Keldon's heart fell when didn't see Arianna among them.

"Thaddeus, it is good to see yer face." Keldon greeted him.

"And yours." They clasped hands.

"How is Arianna?" He couldn't wait a second longer to know, holding his breath for the answer.

Sophie and Thaddeus exchange worried glances. "She weren't dere."

"Mista Keldon, she never comes home," Maeve told him. "We thought she wuz with you."

He didn't know what to say. Where was she then? How would he ever find her? He looked toward the endless stretch of sea. She could be anywhere.

CHAPTER FIFTY

Arianna couldn't see her feet over her rounded belly and she waddled like a duck. She put her hand over her stomach. "Soon baby. I'll see you soon."

Vincent's family had been wonderful to her. Chantal and her husband Gerard had made her feel right at home. Gerard's mother had just arrived from France and had doted on her all week.

She was comfortable with her life, but she wasn't happy. She mourned for what she could have had with Keldon. She found herself reaching for him while she slept, only to awake and find his side of the bed empty.

Feeling restless, she stepped outside for some fresh air. The breeze billowed through her hair. She closed her eyes and hummed the song that was forever on her lips, the sweet melody of Keldon's. In an odd way, it comforted her.

"There you are."

Arianna stopped humming and turned to greet Chantal. Vincent's sister was a petite woman with lustrous long chestnut-brown hair and like her brother, she had amber colored eyes that twinkled with warmth.

"I have been looking all over for you," Chantal said. "I should have known you would be out here in the gardens. You were humming that melody of yours again."

"It soothes me. It makes me feel closer… to someone." She looked away, not wanting to meet Chantal's gaze.

"I suspect it is the baby's father. No? Perhaps one day you'll be reunited with him."

"I don't think so."

Chantal took her hand and gave it an affectionate squeeze. "You must have hope. Now give me a small smile."

Arianna tried, but she knew she fell short. "I thought I would take a stroll. Do you want to join me?" She rubbed her side feeling the baby kick her beneath the ribs.

"Oui, let's walk. How are you feeling? If you don't mind me saying, you look a bit peaked."

"I've been a little uncomfortable. I don't think the baby liked what I ate for breakfast. I have had an upset stomach ever since." Arianna cringed as a sharp pain sliced through her. "That was a wallop of a kick little one." She took a deep breath.

"Dear Arianna, how long have you had these little pains?" Chantal's brows knitted together.

"All afternoon and they seem to be getting stronger."

Chantal chuckled. "You don't have a sour stomach. You're going to have the baby. Come, we must get you back inside."

Chantal had been right. Arianna's water broke a few hours later, the labor hitting her hard. After fourteen hours, Arianna feared she wouldn't be strong enough to endure the final stages.

"She's feverish." She heard Chantal say as she dabbed her forehead with a cool rag.

Arianna drifted in and out of consciousness, caught between this world and a world she once lived in. She saw flashes of her life. They were like memories from a dream long forgotten. She went back to when she was a child with her mother and father teaching her to play the piano. Then she was with friends, Megan and Gregory... Then the fortuneteller at *Blue Run*, only the house looked ravished by a disaster. The fortuneteller told her she would go back in time. Her words came clearly to her, *"Trust the Scotsman. Trust him, for he will protect you. He may feel mistrust for you because of the other woman's black heart, but in time he will see you for whom you really are. He will love you. It will be his child you will bear."* The cryptic message had confused her before, but now she understood.

She heard the song she played so many times in her life. The sweet melody pacified her for a moment. Now she understood why she had always loved it. Why she had always known the song. It was a part of Keldon's life and hers, a bridge to bring them together and reunite their souls.

Then she remembered how she came to be here, in this *time*. She relived the rafter hurdling toward her. "I'm going to die." She heard someone scream or was it her own screams she heard? The terror she felt wouldn't leave and as Arianna saw the bright luminous threshold of death, the new life inside her made an entrance to the living.

CHAPTER FIFTY-ONE

Vincent and Bernadette celebrated their wedding on a beautiful day in May. Keldon couldn't be happier for his friends. In honor of their union, Keldon had the reception at *Willow Bend*, but he didn't have it in him to stay and enjoy the festivities. He smiled and chatted as he made his way to the front door. He needed to take a walk, clear his mind.

Bernadette leaned near Vincent to whisper in his ear. "Keldon needs you. Go talk to him."

"Are you sure?"

"Oui. You go to him," she said as she planted a kiss on his cheek.

"You are a treasure, my little bear." He returned her caress. "I will not be long."

Vincent found Keldon sitting at the foot of the willow just staring out toward the horizon. It reminded Vincent of the times he would find Arianna in the same spot. They were so well suited for one another. It was a shame they didn't see it themselves.

Keldon had heard Vincent's approach and looked up at him with a whisper of a smile before turning away. "Ye know how each part of the ship works together to make her sail? The wheel keeps her direction true. The ropes are there to secure her riggin', and the anchor to bring her to rest. Simple things really, but she would float adrift goin' nowhere without these things."

They stood there silently beside each other as the sun set below the horizon. The rich colors of orange and yellow were both bright and beautiful against the blue of the sky.

The next time Keldon spoke, it was so soft that Vincent struggled to hear him.

"I miss her. I'm like a ship without the wind to carry me." Keldon met his gaze.

His friend's eyes were vacant and spent by grief, making Vincent feel guilty. He had the decency to look away.

"I doonae know why I hadnae seen it sooner," Keldon said to him. "Arianna would never have left without tellin' someone where she was bound. I thought it would have been Maeve, but it wasnae. But who? It had to be someone close to her. Someone she would trust. I ask ye now as a friend, do ye know where she is?"

Before Vincent would divulge that information, he had to know if he was doing the right thing. "Will you accept the child she carries?"

"If she will take me back, I will claim the bairn as mine, as I should have done in the beginnin'."

Vincent sighed. He was breaking his promise to Arianna, but in his heart he knew it was for the best. "She's staying with Chantal and Gerard."

*****

Vincent and Bernadette left their wedding reception long before the guests were ready to call it a night. Miraculously, they were able to sneak out without anyone noticing them and headed back to the house they had created together.

Vincent couldn't explain why, but he actually felt a little nervous. Except for the few innocent caresses they had shared together, he hadn't been intimate with Bernadette. He wanted everything to be perfect. Through the long months, he had wooed her with flowers, courted her diligently and now they were finally married.

He opened the door to their home and he carried her over the threshold. He slowly put her down, letting her body cling to his. She put her hands around his neck and innocently looked up at him.

He could feel the power of her gaze, filling him with desire. To him, she was the moon, the stars and all things that made the universe whole. She was his very essence that would sustain him through life.

"This day is the happiest day of my life. I am married to a daring, handsome man."

Vincent smiled and leaned down touching his lips to hers. Then he deepened the kiss, tasting, savoring every moment. He lifted her into his arms once more and brought her to their room. He gently put her down, so that he could light the lamp on the table. He turned to look at her and saw her wring her hands then smooth her dress. She was nervous too.

"Do you want me to leave while you undress or I could…?"

"Stay," she finished for him. "I want you to stay."

He approached her. "May I help you with the your gown?" She nodded and turned to give him her back. Vincent's hands trembled and he closed and opened them again to loosen them up. He fumbled with the first button, but as each button revealed what lay beneath, he gained confidence. With the twelfth and final stay, he removed the beautiful satin gown, letting it fall to the floor. Bernadette then removed the corset and the other garments before she turned to face her husband, but she didn't look at him.

He tilted her chin so her gaze met his. "Don't be scared."

"I don't want to disappoint you."

"You doubt my love?"

She took a ragged breath, not realizing she held it. "You know I have been with others."

Vincent placed his finger on her lips. "Shush, it does not matter to me." He didn't want her to feel guilty, for all that was behind her now.

She removed his hand and shook her head. "It does matter."

She was trembling and he wanted to put her at ease. He had meant what he said. She was with him now and that was all that was important. He tried to pull her toward him, but she placed her hand firmly on his chest.

"I must say this." He stopped and waited for her to continue. "I let men use me before because I felt I had no other choice. I never gave myself to someone I loved. I'm not sure I know how."

"Ah, my little bear, come here." He opened his arms to her and this time she didn't hesitate. He held her close. "I love you, Bernadette." He kissed the top of her head. He would take everything slow with her, for he wanted her to know that not all men used women. She was like a newly found rose bud after the winter frost and he wanted to nurture her. He wanted her to blossom on her own accord.

His mouth found hers again, tasting her. His hand roamed freely over the span of her back. She moved her hands to undo his shirt, but she was shaking so badly she was unable to manage one button. He placed a restraining hand on hers. "If you are not ready, I will wait." He affectionately squeezed her hand. "I do not want you to fear me."

She placed her hands on either side of his face. "You are a kind man and I love you with all my heart. I trust you and I do not want to wait. I want to know how it feels to lie down with a man who loves me so much he's willing to deny himself."

"Oh, Bernadette." He groaned beneath his breath and captured her lips. Breathless they moved to the bed. He explored every curve with his caresses and she in turn did the same. Then he made her his wife.

Bernadette wrapped her legs around him and raised her hips to meet his every thrust. She never dreamed a man's hands could feel so warm, so gentle—loving. She was drawn to a height of passion she had never experienced before. She felt herself surrendering completely to his masterful seduction and gasped in sweet agony as she felt the explosion of passion only seconds before he responded in kind.

He moved to lie down beside her, bringing her with him so that he cradled her in his arms. He kissed the top of her head.

She sighed. "Will it always be so beautiful?"

"Maybe even better." He grinned.

"Um." A smile curved her lips as she thought about the possibility. She looked at him again. "I love you."

"I love you, too, with all my heart."

CHAPTER FIFTY-TWO

Keldon wanted to punch Vincent for keeping Arianna's whereabouts from him, but how could he hold a grudge? Vincent only protected Arianna from his stubborn pride. Besides, Bernadette would have seen to his death, if he had touched one hair of her husband's head.

Keldon looked out to the blackness of the night and took out his bagpipes. He played the song that reminded him so much of Arianna. He poured his heart out in every note he played. He could almost smell her sweet fragrance. He closed his eyes, relishing in the memory of her. To think she resided in New Orleans, not too far. "I'm comin' for ye on the 'morrow Arianna, to bring ye home where ye belong."

*****

As soon as he docked, Keldon rented a carriage and headed over to Chantal's home. He knocked at the door and an older woman answered. She spoke French and unfortunately very little English that Keldon could understand.

"I want to see Arianna Buchanan. She is my wife," Keldon shouted as if talking in a loud voice would force the older woman to understand his words.

Somewhere in the back part of the house, Keldon heard a baby cry.

"Pardon," the woman said as she hurried off.

Keldon entered the dwelling and waited for the woman to return. A few minutes later, she came back with the small bundle in her hands. "Arianna's bébé," she said.

"May I hold the baby?" He motioned to the child.

The woman nodded and handed him the small bundle. The child was all wrapped in a blanket and a bonnet was securely tied around its head.

Keldon's hands felt sweaty and too awkward to be holding such a small being. He was ready to give the child right back, but then his gaze took in the innocence of the soft, chubby face with pink pouty lips and a tiny upturned nose. Tears welled in his eyes as he stared at the child, *his* child. "So small." He looked at the woman, again. "Is the baby a lass... jeune fille... garcon... lad?"

"Aah … jeune fille... lass? Oui."

"I have a wee lass." Keldon touched her little hand that was curled into a fist. The baby stirred. She latched onto his finger, making Keldon chuckled. "Yer a strong lassie." He looked at the woman, again. "Arianna, the baby's mother, do ye know where she is?"

The woman seemed to understand what he wanted to know. She sadly shook her head. "She gone."

"Gone?" Keldon repeated.

Again, the woman sadly shook her head. "Oui."

Blood slid through his veins like cold needles, as the realization of what she told him sunk in. His eyes took in every delicate detail of the infant. Arianna had sacrificed her life to bring this small wonder into the world. His gaze locked onto the old woman again, wanting to know what had happened. Why was his daughter without a mother? "Tell me that ye are mistaken. Arianna dinnae die."

The old woman's eyebrows furrowed. "Arianna gone."

Keldon held the baby close to his chest as if he needed to protect her. The tiny little girl was all he had left of Arianna. He waited too long to let her know how much he loved her. How much he needed her. Now, she would never know. He felt his heart breaking into a million pieces. He wanted to scream at the top of his lungs at the injustice of it all, but he heard the little bundle in his arms whimper. He moved her away from his chest to look at her. Her eyebrows knitted together, her feet kicked and her hands started moving as she fought to release a little sound. This display would have made Keldon laugh, but instead he wanted to sob, too. "I know how yer feelin', my wee lassie." He cradled her close to him again, rocking her until she fell asleep.

Keldon never wanted to put her down. He would take care of her and love her. She was his daughter. *My daughter*, he thought to himself. He wasn't prepared for the wave of emotions that welled up inside of him. He was proud of the perfect miniature person he held. He would do right by her. He owed Arianna that much.

"I thank ye for carin' for my daughter," he told the old woman. He shook his head. "I'm sorry. I cannae make ye understand." He talked louder. "The wee lassie is my daughter." He pointed to the baby then to his chest. "I will take care of her now." This was the best he could do and he headed for the door. The old woman yelled for him to stop, running after him and trying to grab the baby. He pushed her aside. "I'm the baby's father," he told her again. "I willnae have someone else raise her." He put the baby in the carriage and rode away as the old woman chased after him, screaming for him to stop.

*****

Arianna and Chantal arrived back from shopping to find Gerard's mother in hysterics. Arianna understand some French. Chantal had been teaching her, but Mrs. Devereux was speaking so rapidly that she could only pick up a few words here and there. When Chantal's eyes grew wide, she realized something terrible had happened. She caught the word baby. She ran to the back room to find the cradle empty.

"Where is she? Where's my baby?" She confronted Mrs. Devereux.

Chantal broke the terrible news to her. "She says a tall dark-haired man came and took her."

"She let a stranger take her?" Arianna cried, as her world seemed to crumble down around her.

"She said the man asked for you by name."

"Oui, Oui." Mrs. Devereux nodded her head frantically.

The only tall dark-haired man Arianna knew was Keldon, but he didn't know she was staying here.

Then Mrs. Devereux remembered something else about the man and told Chantal.

Chantal translated. "She says the man had unusual green eyes."

"No." Arianna couldn't believe it. How did he find her? Surely Vincent would never break his promise to her.

"You know this person then?" Chantal asked hopefully.

"Yes, I do and how dare he?" Arianna balled her hands into a fist. "How dare he think he could just take her, when he didn't want to claim her in the first place?"

"This is the father. No?"

"He may have donated a vital part of himself to make that baby, but he by no means is a father!" Arianna stormed out of the house. She knew where the black-hearted scoundrel would be heading. She hoped Keldon's ship was still docked. If she had to, she would swim after him. He had taken everything from her. She wasn't going to let him take her child.

*****

Keldon boarded his ship with a gurgling baby in tow. His crewmen fell silent and stared at him, but no one questioned what he was doing with a baby.

He went directly down below to his cabin, laying the baby down on his bunk. He hadn't thought this through. He couldn't very well set sail without having supplies for the infant. He stared down at his daughter, who kicked her feet. "What do ye eat, lassie?" He would have to go back into town and ask someone what he needed. He placed pillows around his daughter so she wouldn't fall off the bunk. Then he headed back up top.

As soon as he poked his head out, he received a fist in his face. Stunned, he lost his balance and flew back down, landing on his arse.

"Oh my God, Keldon! Are you all right?" Arianna yelled down to him. She had arrived on the ship only moments ago and had been determined to do bodily harm to Keldon, but she didn't want to kill him—at least not yet. "Keldon answer me," she shouted again.

"Arianna? It cannae be."

Her anger returned at the sound of his voice. "You can better believe it's me. What did you think I would do? Did you really believe I would just let you take the baby away without a fight?"

It took a few seconds, but Keldon began to understand what had happened. The old woman wasn't telling him Arianna was dead. She was telling him she wasn't there. Arianna must have thought he kidnapped the baby. He jumped to his feet and started back up the steps. "Let me explain."

"Your actions were enough for me. Where is she? What have you done with her?" She took a step back as Keldon came out into the open. She had forgotten how tall and... How incredibly handsome he was. She was angry with herself for letting her emotions for him take over, but she couldn't help what she felt. She desperately wanted to hate him, but her traitorous heart wouldn't allow her luxury.

He took a step closer.

"You stay away from me!" she shouted.

He stopped in his tracks. "Arianna, please calm yerself."

"Calm myself? I will not! You're a snake... No you're worse than a snake... You're... you're pond scum... no you're ..."

Keldon had had enough of her insults and the men were beginning to snicker. He lunged forward and grabbed her, pulling her against him. She was about to protest further, so Keldon did the first thing that came to his mind to keep her quiet. He kissed her.

She struggled only for a moment then melted against him, putting her arms around his neck. When they came up for air, he saw the flicker of emotions cross her features and he felt her body tense. With one quick movement, she raised her hand to slap him, but he anticipated the reaction and caught her arm.

"Now, is that anyway to be treatin' yer husband."

"Husband! I'll have... Aah!" She screamed as he picked her up and headed for his quarters down below. "You put me down this instance. Do you hear me?"

"Aye, I hear ye just fine as does everyone in New Orleans." But he didn't slow his stride.

Arianna turned to the men on the ship. Recognizing Samuel, she looked to him for help. "Are you going to let him take me against my will?"

"We kin't interfere with de Captain's private matters." He turned his back to her.

"Wise man," Keldon said as he started down the stairs.

Having no other choice, Arianna folded her arms in front of her and waited until he put her down. "There's yer wee bairn." He placed her firmly on the floor and pointed to the bunk. Arianna raced over to check on her. She slept peacefully. Completely oblivious to anything that had happened.

Keldon stood back watching Arianna fuss over the child. She had changed since he last saw her. Her hair was long again and she was fuller in all the right places a woman should be. He felt the old familiar stirrings and he wanted to touch her, kiss every inch of her, but when she faced him, he saw that any hope of familiarity was definitely out of the question.

"So? Why did you do it? Why did you kidnap an innocent child?"

"I dinnae kidnap her. I thought ye were dead and I couldnae leave the baby with strangers. I did what I thought ye would have wanted me to do." He ran his hand through his hair in frustration. "The old woman kept tellin' me ye were gone and my French isnae what it should be. I dinnae understand her."

"You thought I was dead?" Arianna repeated.

"Aye, but I assure ye, I willnae make that mistake twice." His hand rubbed over his sore jaw.

Now, Arianna was confused. If he didn't come to take the baby away, why was he here?

Keldon must have read her mind for he approached her and took her hand. "Please, let me explain. This wasnae what I had planned."

His eyes pleaded and she knew she couldn't deny him. She nodded and he offered her a chair. He then knelt down beside her on one knee and took her hand.

"Dearest Arianna, I want ye back. It doesnae matter to me if the lass is mine. She willnae ever know differently. I will love her. From this day forward, if ye are willin', I will claim her as mine." He gently kissed her hand before he locked his gaze with hers. "Ye are my life and without ye my soul was dead. I doonae want to go through life without ye. If ye will have me back, I promise, ye willnae be sorry. I love who ye've become. I love ye, Arianna."

Her eyes misted over with tears. He loved her not Annabelle.

"Ye're cryin'." Keldon gently wiped the tears that slid down her cheek.

"I'm crying."

"Aye, but what does it mean?"

"It means, I love you, too." She threw her arms around him and he returned the embrace.

He didn't want to let her go, but she gently pushed him away. "I have something I must tell you."

"Aye."

"Sit down first." He did as she asked. He pulled the other chair close to hers. When he was situated, she told him. "The baby is yours."

"I told ye it doesnae matter."

"It does to me. I know the baby is yours because I've never been with any other man, but you. When I was delivering, I saw my life as it was before. Somehow, I did change places with your Annabelle and she took my place." Arianna could see the skepticism in his eyes, but she needed him to believe her. "I know this sounds crazy, but I know it's true. That's why I knew things before they were going to happen. I knew because from my time they *had* happened. I was not seeing the future. I was reciting the past."

At first, Keldon didn't respond. She seemed lucid but what she asked him to believe was ludicrous. Yet... there was things that made him think her story held some truth. She looked like Annabelle, but that was where the resemblance ended. She never once acted like the cold-hearted woman he had learned to despise. She had been different from the beginning, drawing him to her.

If she wanted to believe she somehow traded places, then so be it. As long as she was willing to stay with him, he didn't care who she thought she was. "I believe whatever ye believe."

Arianna knew he was just pacifying her. She couldn't blame him for his skepticism. One day, he would know. The truth always had a way of resurfacing. She may not have evidence to prove her identity, but she did have proof the child was his.

Arianna went over to the baby and picked her up. She then returned to Keldon, handing him the child. She removed the satin bonnet that was covering her small head, revealing the jet-black hair she possessed. "She's yours."

"Aye. That I already knew in my heart. She dinnae have to possess the color of my hair." He kissed the top of the baby's head. "What is the wee lassie's name?"

"Caresse. The name is French. It means beloved."

"Caresse Buchanan," he said thoughtfully. "A most fittin' name."

"Are you going to make us legal, Keldon Buchanan?" She asked with a glint of amusement in her eyes. "We aren't married."

"Aye, the divorce papers," he said remorsefully

"Yes. Well, you divorced Annabelle, but we were never married."

Keldon smiled. "We'll rectify that soon enough."

*****

Keldon persuaded the man of the cloth to perform the ritual that evening. Chantal, Gerard and Mrs. Devereux were present for the quiet ceremony. When the minister asked what their names were, Keldon said his then turned to Arianna questioningly. She answered so that there would be no confusion over her identity. "I am Arianna Ward."

Keldon nodded. "Aye, and I want to marry ye, Arianna Ward."

CHAPTER FIFTY-THREE

It had been four years since the Buchanan's made their home at *Willow Bend*, and Leighton McRae decided it was high time he paid them a visit.

He took the cobbled path that led to the house. In the distance, he spotted Keldon out front with a little girl. He could only assume this was Keldon's daughter. He smiled as he watched them play. Keldon picked the lass up and twirled her around. The child's laughter reached him, filling the air like the sound of tinkling bells.

Leighton hesitated, stopping in his tracks. Maybe he shouldn't intrude on their happiness, but then he decided he'd come this far, there could be no turning back now. Besides, Keldon had spotted him.

Keldon didn't raise a hand in welcome. Not exactly a good sign. He had every right to send him away, but Leighton still sauntered forward. When he finally reached him, they both stared at each other for what seemed like an eternity. Keldon surprisingly made the first move. He embraced Leighton, as old friends should. It made Leighton realize he should have never doubted their friendship.

"It has been far too long, my friend," Keldon replied.

"Aye. It was my own stubborn pride that kept me away."

Leighton's gaze wavered to Keldon's daughter, who in turn was staring up at him. The little girl had Keldon's thick, dark hair and the same cat-like green eyes that could look right through you. The resemblance was uncanny. "She's a bonny lassie, Keldon."

"Aye. That she is. I have a son also—Julian. He's upstairs with Maeve. No doubt tellin' her he isnae tired. He's two and half and a handful."

"A son and a daughter. Ye are blessed."

"Aye."

Leighton recognized the curious expression Keldon threw his way. His friend wondered why, after all these years, he came calling. Leighton didn't leave him in suspense. "I need to set things right with ye." Leighton cleared is throat, not sure how to begin. "I have misjudged Arianna cruelly. If ye have it in yer heart to let me do so, I want to make amends."

Keldon sighed. "Leighton, I have never said ye werenae welcome here."

"Aye, I know ye havenae, but I felt I deserved no less." He paused again and looked at the wee lass, remembering what he'd been told. "I saw an auld friend of ours."

"Aye, who might that be?"

"It was Doc Hathaway. He told me a bit of news that surprised me. He had asked me aboot ye and I told him of ye havin' a wee lass to call yer own. Do ye know what the man asks?"

Keldon shook his head.

"He says to me, when did Keldon remarry?"

Keldon lifted an eyebrow. "I doonae understand. Why would he ask ye that?"

"Weel, he had his reasons, but at the time I dinnae understand it myself. So I tell him ye dinnae remarry. I tell him ye are still married to the same woman. And he says to me that this is impossible because he knows that Annabelle Buchanan cannae bear ye any children."

"What do ye mean?"

"Just what I am sayin'. She cannae have children. Doc Hathaway explained to me that when Annabelle had done away with the bairn all those years ago, she was damaged.

Doc Hathaway had to take everythin'. She dinnae have the parts that would have enabled her to have another bairn. It seems this be a secret that Annabelle coerced him into keepin'."

Keldon stood there transfixed as the truth sunk in. From the beginning, Maeve claimed Annabelle was no longer with them and the story Arianna told him all those years ago had been true after all. By some twist of fate, Arianna traded places with Annabelle. He glanced at his daughter, whom he cherished. She innocently smiled up at him. Both of his children resembled him with their dark hair and green eyes, but they had their mother's smile. He turned to Leighton. "We should have known the truth all along."

"Aye, but we... I refused to see it," Leighton admitted.

"That is the past now. Come, my friend into my home and join me in a drink." Keldon scooped up his little girl, who giggled because he was tickling her. They headed back to the house and as they neared, they could hear Arianna playing the harpsichord and singing.

"That be the song, she sang all those years ago," Leighton stated. This time, he enjoyed the sweet voice the woman possessed. "It be the verra song ye play on yer bagpipes."

"Aye. It is the song and it seems to have a special bond for us. I just dinnae realize how much of a bond until I heard the words leave her lips. To me it is like the warm and wonderful feelin' of comin' home."

The moment they reached the room where Arianna was playing, Keldon put the squirming Caresse down. Arianna had just finished the last stanza and looked up. Her lovely arched brows rose in surprise at seeing Leighton standing there next to her husband, but she recovered quickly, offering a warm smile.

She rose from her seat to greet him. "Leighton, I am so glad you finally came to visit us. How have you been?"

"Lonely. I'm an auld man with nay family."

"You are wrong on both accounts," she said. She surprised Leighton further by giving him a welcoming hug. He gladly returned the embrace. When they parted, Leighton noticed there was someone hanging on his leg. He looked down and saw the little dark-haired girl smiling up at him.

Have you met our daughter, Caresse?" Arianna chuckled.

"Aye." He leaned down and picked her up. "She's a bonny lass, *Arianna*."

She regarded him quizzically. Leighton knew he had never acknowledged her as anyone, but Annabelle.

"Did you call me Arianna?"

"Aye, he did," Keldon answered. "He knows as I do, who ye really are."

"Why do I have the feeling I've walked in on the middle of a conversation? Just who am I?" Her lips curved.

Keldon pulled her to him, as he thought of the hauntingly sweet melody that still lingered in the air as though she had never stopped singing the song, the song that had somehow bridged the gap of time, and had brought her to him. "Ye are the song of my heart, Arianna Buchanan." He lovingly brushed his lips over hers. "That is who ye will always be."

The End

AUTHOR NOTE:

A FEW FACTS

Even though I have mentioned true figures, places and events, this story is fictional and the product of my imagination.

The War of 1812, General Jackson did protect the citizens of New Orleans from the British with the aid from the notorious handsome pirate, Jean Laffite. More than 2000 British were killed and 100 captured, while 8 Americans were killed and 13 wounded. The Louisiana and the Carolina were actual ships that aided in defending New Orleans.

General Sir Edward Pakenham, was the 37 year-old brother-in-law of the Duke of Wellington and a decorated general. His ill-fated death was true. His last orders were to continue the fight. Luckily, the man who replaced him wisely ended the slaughter. Veterans of the Peninsular Campaign in Spain helped with the British's campaign and most of a Scottish Highlander unit was lost on that fateful day. I tried to stay true to the facts of the battle, while intertwining it with the characters of the story.

Francis Scott Key wrote the song, "Star Spangled Banner". He never meant it to be anything more than a little ditty to be sung to pass the time away.

General Jackson captured Pensacola on November 7, 1814, giving us the opportunity of attaining Florida for the United States.

Human slavery is regrettable and unforgivable part of the American history. In the story, Maeve mentions slave badges. Charleston actually did issue these badges for the slaves to be hired out. The badges were made from thin copper sheets and were stamped. The most common occupation was servant and porter. The rare occupations were mechanics, carpenter and fisherman.

Paul Cuffee is another true figure in history. He aided the newly freed slaves to immigrate to Sierra Leone and established the Friendly Society of Sierra Leone, a trading organization.

The information about the Letter of Marque was from the Public Record Office in Richmond. I tried to stay as close to the originally written document meant for Captain Millin, an American privateer, Prince of Neufchatel during the War of 1812 for its authenticity. I of course needed to change the name of the captain, ship, amount of men and dates to fit the story.

Keldon's ship the Good Intent was a Schooner. They were usually altered to fit a pirate's specification. It had some luxury and comfort but it was light enough for high maneuverability, so if necessary it could make a quick escape.

I mentioned that the crew was careening the vessel they had confiscated. This was a chore that was done every three to four months to keep the ship in tip-top shape. Careening was necessary because the shipworm would bore into exposed wood below the waterline. Also another problem was the accumulation of barnacles, sea grass, algae, and muck. These things could reduce the speed of the ship. Speed to a pirate was sometimes the difference between life and death.

If you loved this Karen Michelle Nutt book, then you won't want to miss any of her other fabulous stories.

Following is a sneak peek of Storm Riders...

The hangman, a tall broad-shouldered man stood on the other side of Ace with his feet apart and his hands behind his back. The Deputy took his place near the steps.

Samantha studied Ace, her gaze sliding over him in admiration. Long, lean, and rather handsome even with a few days growth on his chin. He wore a brown cowboy hat, but his long hair peeked out. The color gleamed a rich dark brown as the sun beat down on the thick strands.

His eyes shifted in a subtle manner as if he were looking for someone.

"You have little faith," she whispered. She raised her hand, tapping her cowboy hat with a subtle gesture, but it caught his attention. For a split second, a look of surprised recognition flitted across his features. He didn't believe she'd show. She gave him a slight nod. He faced forward then with his shoulders back, standing tall before the crowd that chanted his death song.

The hangman lifted McTavish's hat to place the black cloth over his face, but Ace moved his head away. The hangman shrugged with indifference. Ace had the right to face his accusers. The hangman draped the rope around McTavish's neck, placing his hat firmly back down on his head. Then he tightened the rope around his neck. The reverend continued his sermon to save Ace's soul rather than words to comfort him.

Samantha tapped her earpiece. "Are you ready, Denny?"

"Aren't I always, luv?"

Her lips curved. "Let's show these eegits the meaning of a real show, shall we?"

"Your words are pure poetry to my ears, Sammy."

Denny could shoot a flea off a dog and she wasn't exaggerating. Denny was the best sharpshooter at the SR institute. She won her share of metals too, but horses were her specialty. She grew up on a ranch, spending more time on a horse than anywhere else. She would be able to outrun whoever tried to come after them.

She kept her eyes on the hangman's hand. The reverend closed his book and gave a nod. The hangman's hand pressed the lever and the prisoner dropped. At the same time a shot rang out, severing the rope before it could constrict around McTavish's neck and break it.

Her horse tensed, but she stroked his neck and leaned forward. "You're fine, boy. Stay with me."

People screamed and ducked. Deputy Goodman who stood at the foot of the stairs drew his gun, looking for the man responsible for the interruption.

He kept the patrons hopping with shots flying over their heads. Deputy Chester couldn't leave the scaffold, the way the bullets flew at his feet, making him dance a jig.

Bless you, Denny Randeli.

Samantha didn't waste time and rammed her feet into the horse's flank, sending them flying forward through the crowd of scrambling people. McTavish looked stunned, but he was already working to free his hands.

"Need some help, cowboy." She tipped back her hat and smiled. She pulled her knife out and he stumbled back. "Don't be stupid. Let me cut the ropes."

"Who are ye, lass?" His thick Scottish brogue laced his words.

"I'm the woman who's going to save your arse. Now turn around and let me cut you free."

He didn't hesitate now, whirling around and giving her his backside. A nice backside, too, but now wasn't the time to admire it. Keeping the horse steady, she leaned down and slashed the binds free from his hands. She shoved the knife back in its holder and offered her hand.

He turned to stare at her. In the bright of day, his eyes stood out like clear green gems with no other pigment clouding the color.

"Come on." She thrust out her gloved hand.

His grip was firm as he swung up behind her.

"Hold on," she told him. "Hiyah!" The horse bolted at the command and her sudden slam of her boot heel against its flank.

She maneuvered around the scrambling crowd with ease and jumped over obstacles in her way.

"St. Brigid in Heaven, you're an angel." McTavish clung to her, his hands around her waist—warm and large, the heat from him sent a strange feeling to the pit of her stomach.

She shook her head. It was the thrill of the escape, not how McTavish felt against her. She tried to convince herself with no avail.

"Do you have the package?" Denny's voice echoed in her ear, making her focus.

"Got him and we're on the right trail to lose anyone who follows. We'll stop at the first hideout and see if there's trouble. If it looks clear, we'll meet you back at the safe house tonight.

"Be safe," Denny told her.

"Back at you."

"Who are ye talkin' to, darlin'?" McTavish leaned his head next to hers, his breath whispering against her cheek.

"None of your concern, cowboy. Just keep holding on. We have a rough ride ahead of us if we want to cover our tracks."

She thought she heard him chuckle. "Oh, doonae fash yerself. I willnae let go."

OTHER STORIES BY KAREN MICHELLE NUTT

Time Travel:
Creighton Manor
Lost in the Mist of Time
At the Stroke of Midnight
Storm Riders (western, steampunk)
Heart of a Warrior
Echo of Time

Fallen Angels:
Eli: Warriors for the Light
(Fallen Angels, Book 1)
Lucca: Warriors for the Light (Book 2)
The Curse of Tempest Gate

Vampires and Shifters
The Gryphon and His Thief
Soul Taker
Moon Shifter
Destiny's Prerogative
Love's Eternal Embrace
Magic of the Loch
Autumn Moon

Paranormal Elements:
Wanted
Second Time Around,
"The Spirit of Love"
Mr. O'Grady's Magic Box
Black Donald's Coin
Shattered Illusions
A Twist of Time Anthology,
"Echo of Time"
Warriors: Tales of Honor, Courage, and Loyalty

Made in the USA
Las Vegas, NV
29 January 2024

ABOUT THE AUTHOR

Karen Michelle Nutt resides in California with her husband, three fascinating children, and houseful of demanding pets. Jack, her Chorkie, is her writing buddy and sits long hours with her at the computer.

When she's not time traveling, fighting outlaws, or otherworldly creatures, she creates pre-made book covers to order at Gillian's Book Covers, "Judge Your Book By Its Cover". You can also check out her published cover art designs at Western Trail Blazer and Rebecca J. Vickery Publishing.

Whether your reading fancy is paranormal, historical or time travel, all her stories capture the rich array of emotions that accompany the most fabulous human phenomena—falling in love.

Visit the author at: http://www.kmnbooks.com
Stop by her blog for Monday interviews, chats and contests at:

Website: http://kmnbooks.blogspot.com

Gillian's Book Covers
Judge Your Book By Its Cover
http://judgeyourbookbyitscover.blogspot.com/

Facebook:
https://www.facebook.com/authorkarenmichellenutt
Twitter: https://twitter.com/KMNbooks
Pinterest: http://pinterest.com/karenmnutt/
Amazon Author Page:
http://www.amazon.com/Karen-Michelle-Nutt/e/B002BLLBPE